She's meant to be the ultimate triumph in his twisted game of revenge. Will the mafia princess be the one to bring the monster to his knees?

TWISTED PRIDE

Cora Reilly

Cover design by Hang Le
Book design by Inkstain Design Studio

TWISTED PRIDE

PROLOGUE

SERAFINA

All my life I had been taught to be honorable, to do what was expected of me. Today I went against it all.

Dark and tall, Remo appeared in the doorway, come to claim his prize. His eyes roamed over my naked body, and mine did the same.

He was cruel and twisted. *Beyond redemption.*

Brutal attractiveness, forbidden pleasure, promised pain. I should have been disgusted by him, but I wasn't. Not by his body and not always by his nature.

I shut off the water in the shower, scared of what he wanted, completely terrified of what I wanted. This was his game of chess; he was the king and I was the trapped queen that the Outfit needed to protect. He moved me into position for his last move: the kill. Check.

He began unbuttoning his shirt then shrugged it off. He moved closer, stopping right before me. "You always watch me like something you want to touch but aren't allowed to. Who's holding you back, *Angel?*"

CHAPTER 1

SERAFINA

"I can't believe you're getting married in three days," Samuel said, his feet propped up beside mine on the coffee table. If Mom saw she would strangle us.

"Me either," I said quietly. At nineteen, I was already older than many other girls in our world when they entered the holy bond of matrimony, and I had been promised to Danilo for a long time. My fiancé was only twenty-one himself, so an earlier marriage wasn't very desirable. I certainly didn't mind. It had given me the time to finish school and stay home with Samuel for another year. He and I had never been separated for long, except for a few days when he had business to conduct for the Outfit.

Because of his father's sickness, Danilo was still busy taking over Indianapolis. A later wedding would have been even better for him, but I was a woman and supposed to marry before my twentieth birthday. I eyed the engagement ring on my finger. A prominent diamond in the center, we had to widen the band over the years as my fingers grew. In three days Danilo would put a second ring on me.

Mom came in with my sister, Sofia, who upon spotting us ran in our direction and wedged herself on the sofa between me and Samuel.

Samuel rolled his blue eyes but wrapped an arm around our little sister as she pressed up against him with big puppy dog eyes, tousling her brown mane. She had taken after Dad and hadn't inherited the blond hair of our mother like Samuel and I. "It's unfair that you're leaving right after Fina's wedding. I thought you would have more time for me."

I nudged her. "Hey." I wasn't really angry at her. I understood where she was coming from. Being eight years younger than us, she had always felt like a fifth wheel, since Samuel and I were twins.

Sofia gave me an embarrassed smile. "I'll miss you too."

"I'll miss you too, ladybug."

Mom cleared her throat, standing tall, her hands linked in front of her stomach. She was dressed in a fitted, elegant green dress. Her blue eyes lowered to our feet resting on the table. She tried to look stern, but the trembling of her mouth made it clear she was fighting a smile.

Samuel and I dropped our feet off the table at the same time.

"I thought I should warn you that Danilo just called. He's coming over because he just arrived in town and is supposed to meet your father and uncle."

Now I understood why Sofia, too, was dressed in a pretty summer dress. I didn't even know my father was expecting him. I was leaving for Indianapolis tomorrow.

I jerked to my feet. "When?"

"Ten minutes."

"Mom!" My eyes widened in horror. "How am I supposed to get ready with that much time?"

"You look fine," Samuel drawled, smirking, his short blond hair purposefully in a disarray. He could pull off the disheveled look, but I definitely couldn't.

I narrowed my eyes. "Oh shut up." I ran out of the room, almost bumping into Dad. He stepped back, looking down at me with a questioning smile.

"I need to get ready!"

I didn't have time to explain. He could ask Mom. I took the steps two at a time. The moment I stumbled into my bathroom and saw my reflection, I cringed. My God. My skin was flushed, and my hair curled wildly around my shoulders. My simple jeans and T-shirt didn't scream poised future wife either. Damn it.

I quickly washed my face then grabbed a flat iron. My hair was naturally curly, but I always straightened it when people other than my family were around. This time I had five minutes to do it. I stormed back into my bedroom, tore through my wardrobe. Choosing the right dress for such an occasion would have taken at least one hour. Now I had one minute, if I still wanted time to put on makeup. I grabbed a pink dress I ordered online a while ago but never wore and slipped it on. I was immediately reminded why I hadn't worn it before: it ended several inches above my knees, revealing more of my long legs than I usually displayed, especially when men were around. Danilo would be my husband in three days. It was only fair that he saw a bit more of what he was getting.

A nervous thrill took hold of my body, but I pushed it aside and quickly slipped on matching heels then hurried to my vanity. I didn't have enough time to put much effort into my makeup. My skin was quite flawless, so I decided against foundation and only put some blush and mascara on before rushing out of my room and down the corridor toward the stairs.

I slowed my steps considerably when I heard Danilo, Samuel, and Dad in the foyer below. It wouldn't be wise to appear as if I had rushed to get ready for any man, not even my fiancé.

They were shaking hands and exchanging pleasantries.

I had met Danilo a few times before. I'd been promised to him since I was fourteen and he sixteen, but this time felt more intimate. In only three days I would become his wife and share a bed with him. Danilo was very attractive and had much success with women, a ladies' man, but to me he had always been a perfect gentleman. He wore a white dress shirt and black pants, his dark hair immaculate.

I took the first step, placing my foot on the creaky stair on purpose, one long leg extended, my head held high.

All eyes turned to me. Danilo's gaze zeroed in on my exposed legs, then he quickly snapped his brown eyes up to meet my eyes, smiling. Dad and Samuel both looked briefly at my legs, but their reaction was less than thrilled. Dad was patient and loving with Mom and us kids, even Samuel, which made it easy to forget that he was Underboss of Minneapolis—and a feared one at that. I was quickly reminded just how scary he could be as he put his hand on Danilo's shoulder, wearing a hard expression on his face.

"I'd like to give you something in my office, Danilo," he said in a cold voice.

Danilo wasn't impressed by my father's mood change. He was going to be the youngest Underboss in the history of the Outfit, and he was practically already ruling over Indianapolis because his father was so sick. He gave a curt nod. "Of course," he said calmly, appearing so much older than his years. Hardened, grown-up. More man than I felt woman. Danilo gave me another smile then followed my father.

I descended the remaining steps, and Samuel barred my way. "Go change."

"Excuse me?"

He pointed at my legs. "You're showing too much leg."

I pointed at my arms and throat. "I'm also showing my neck and arms." I lifted one leg. "And I have nice legs."

Samuel stared down at my leg then up at my face with a frown. "Yeah, well, Danilo doesn't need to know that."

I snorted then quickly looked around, worried Danilo was close enough to overhear. "He will see more than my legs on our wedding night." Involuntary heat blasted my cheeks.

Samuel's expression darkened.

"Get out of my way," I said, trying to pass him.

Samuel mirrored my move. "Go change, Fina. Now," he ordered in a voice he probably reserved for business with other Made Men.

I couldn't believe his nerve. Did he think I would obey him only because he was a Made Man? That hadn't worked these last five years. I quickly reached for his stomach and pinched him hard, which wasn't easy considering Samuel was all muscle.

He jerked in surprise. I used his momentary distraction to slip past him then made a show of swaying my hips as I headed into the living area. Samuel caught up with me. "You have an impossible temper."

I smiled. "I have your temper."

"I'm a man. Women are supposed to be docile."

I rolled my eyes.

Samuel crossed his arms and leaned against the wall beside the window. "You always act like a well-behaved lady when others are around, but Danilo will get a nasty surprise once he realizes he didn't get a lady but a fury."

A flicker of worry flooded me. Samuel was right. Everyone outside my family knew me as the Ice Princess. Our family was notorious for being poised and controlled. The only people who really knew me were my parents, Sofia, and Samuel. Could I ever be myself around Danilo? Or would that put him off? Danilo was always controlled, which was probably why Uncle Dante and Dad had chosen him for my husband—and because he was the heir to one of the most important cities of the Outfit.

A knock sounded and I turned around to see Danilo step in.

His brown eyes met mine, and he gave me a small smile. Then his gaze moved on to Samuel leaning against the wall behind me. Danilo's expression tightened the slightest bit. I risked a look over my shoulder and found my brother glaring at my fiancé as if he wanted to crush him to dust. I tried to catch Samuel's gaze, but he was content killing Danilo with his eyes. I couldn't believe him.

"Samuel," I said in a forced, polite voice. "Why don't you give Danilo and me a moment?"

Samuel tore his gaze away from my fiancé and smiled. "I'm already giving you a moment."

"Alone."

Samuel shook his head once, his smile darkening, eyes returning to Danilo. "It's my responsibility to protect your honor."

Heat rose to my cheeks. If Danilo hadn't been in the room, I would have lunged at my brother and wrung his neck.

Danilo stepped up to me and kissed my hand, but his eyes were on my brother. Releasing my hand, he said, "I can assure you Serafina's honor is perfectly safe in my company. I will wait until our wedding night to claim my rights ... when she is no longer your responsibility." Danilo's voice had dipped in a threatening way. He had never hinted to sex before, and I knew it was to provoke my brother. Power plays between two alphas.

Samuel rocked forward, away from the wall, his hand going to his knife. I turned and stepped up to my twin, placing my hand against his chest. "Samuel," I said in a warning tone, digging my nails into his skin through the fabric of his shirt. "Danilo is my fiancé. Give us a moment."

Samuel lowered his gaze to my face, and for once his expression didn't soften. "No," he said firmly. "And you won't defy my command."

I often forgot what Samuel was. He was my twin, my best friend, my confidant first, but for five years he'd been a Made Man, a killer, and he wouldn't back down in front of another man, especially not someone he would have to meet as a fellow Underboss. If I pushed further, he would look weak, and he was supposed to take over as Underboss from Dad in a few years. Even though I hated doing it and had never done it before, I cast my eyes down as if I was submitting to him.

Danilo might be my fiancé, but Samuel would always be my blood, and I didn't want him to look weak in front of anyone. "You are right," I said obediently. "I'm sorry."

Samuel touched my shoulder and squeezed lightly. "Danilo," he said in a low voice. "My sister will leave now. I want a word alone with you."

My blood boiling, I gave Danilo an apologetic smile before I left. Once outside, my smile fell and I stormed through the foyer, needing to vent. Where was Dad? I turned the corner and collided with someone. "Careful," came a drawl I knew well, and two hands steadied me.

I looked up. "Uncle Dante," I said with a smile then flushed because I'd barreled into him like a five-year-old throwing a tantrum. I smoothed my dress, trying to look poised. After all, my uncle was *pure control*. He had to be as Boss of the Outfit.

Dante tilted his head with a small smile. "Is something the matter? You look upset."

My cheeks heated further. "Samuel embarrassed me in front of Danilo. He's alone with him now. Having a word. Can you please check on them before Samuel ruins everything?"

Dante chuckled but he nodded. "Your brother wants to protect you. Where are they?"

"Living room," I said.

He squeezed my shoulder before walking away. Anger was still simmering under my skin. I would make Samuel pay for it. I made my way upstairs and into his room. A few knives and weapons belonging in a museum decorated the walls, but apart from that it was practically furnished. In a week or two Samuel would move into his own apartment in Chicago and work directly under Dante for a couple of years before returning to Minneapolis and eventually taking over for Dad.

I sank down on his bed, waiting. With every second that passed, I became more nervous. I got up and paced the room. When I heard his steps, I stopped and hid behind the door, carefully slipping out of my heels. The door opened and Samuel stepped in. I jumped, trying to land on his back and wrap my arms around his neck like I'd often done in the past.

Samuel caught me, hoisted me over his shoulder despite my struggling, and threw me down on the bed. Then he actually held me down, tousling my hair and tickling me.

"Stop!" I screeched between laughter. "Sam, stop!"

He did stop but gave me a smug grin. "You can't win against me."

"I liked it better when you were a scrawny boy and not this killing machine," I muttered.

Something dark passed over Samuel's eyes, and I touched his chest and lightly shoved him, a distraction from whatever horrors he was remembering. "How badly did you embarrass me in front of Danilo?"

"I went over the details of your wedding night with him."

I stared at Samuel in horror. "You *didn't*."

"I did."

I sat up. "What did you say?"

"I told him he better treat you like a lady on your wedding night. No dominant shit or anything."

My cheeks blazed with heat, and I hit his shoulder hard.

He frowned, rubbing the spot. "What?"

"What!? You *embarrassed* me in front of Danilo. How could you talk about something like that with him? My wedding night isn't your business." My entire face was burning from embarrassment and anger. I couldn't believe him. He had always been protective of me, of course, but this took things too far.

Samuel grimaced. "Trust me, it wasn't easy for me. I don't like to think that my little sister is going to have sex."

I hit him again. "You are only three minutes older. And you have been having sex for years now. Do you even know how many women you've slept with?"

He shrugged. "I'm a man."

"Oh shut up," I muttered. "How am I ever going to face Danilo after what you did?"

"If it was up to me, you'd become a nun," Samuel said, and I lost it.

He had a way to drive me up the wall. I lunged at him again but like before it was futile. The last time I stood a chance fighting Samuel was more than five years ago. Samuel wrapped his arms around me from behind and held me in place.

"I think I'll carry you downstairs like this. Danilo is still talking to Dante. I'm sure he'll love to see his future wife this disheveled. Maybe he'll decide against marrying you if he sees you're not quite the obedient lady you want him to believe you are."

"You wouldn't dare!" I kicked my legs but Samuel carried me, lodged against his chest like I was a puppet.

Dad came in, his eyes moving from me pressed against Samuel to my twin gripping me tightly. He shook his head once. "I thought you'd stop the brawling once you got older."

Samuel released me and I stumbled to my feet. He smoothed his clothes, righting his gun and knife holsters. "She started it."

I gave him a look. Smoothing my hair and clothes, I cleared my throat. "He embarrassed me in front of Danilo, Dad."

"I told Danilo I'd rip his balls off if he didn't treat her right on their wedding night."

I scowled at my twin. He hadn't mentioned that detail to me.

Dad gave me a wistful smile, touching my cheek. "My little dove." Then he moved to Samuel and clapped his shoulder. "You did good."

I gave the two of them an incredulous look. Stifling my annoyance—and worse, my gratefulness for their protectiveness—I walked out of Samuel's bedroom into my own. I sat down on the bed, suddenly overcome with sadness. I was leaving my family, my home, for a city I didn't know, a husband I barely knew.

At the sound of an unfamiliar knock, I stood and walked toward my door, opening it.

Surprise washed over me when I saw Danilo's tall form. I opened my door wider but didn't ask him in. That would have been too forward. Instead, I stepped out into the corridor. "I can't ask you in."

Danilo gave me an understanding smile. "Of course not. In case you're worried, your uncle knows that I'm up here."

"Oh," I said, overwhelmed by his presence and the memory of what Samuel had done.

"I wanted to say goodbye. I'm leaving in a few minutes," he continued.

"I'm sorry," I said with as much dignity as my burning face allowed.

Danilo smiled with a small frown. "What for?"

"For what my brother did. He shouldn't have talked to you about …

11

about our wedding night."

Danilo chuckled and moved closer to me, his spicy scent wrapping around me. He took my hand and kissed it. My stomach fluttered. "He wants to protect you. That's honorable. I don't blame him. A woman like you should be treated like a lady, and I will treat you that way on our wedding night and on every night that follows."

He leaned forward and lightly kissed my cheek. His eyes made it clear that he wanted to do more than that. He stepped back, letting go of my hand. I swallowed.

"I'm looking forward to being married to you, Serafina."

"Me too," I said quietly.

With a last look at me, he turned around and left. My heart pounding in my chest, I returned to my room and plopped down on my bed. I wasn't in love with Danilo, but I could imagine falling for him. That was a good start and better than many other girls in my world got.

A few minutes later, someone knocked again. This time I recognized the unabashed pounding of a fist against wood. "Come in," I said.

I didn't have to look up to know who it was. I recognized Samuel's steps with my eyes closed. He sank down beside me. "Thank you for obeying me when Danilo was around," Samuel said quietly. He took my hand.

"You need to appear strong. I didn't want to make you look weak." I looked up at him, tears gathering in my eyes.

His expression tightened. "You hated it."

"Of course I did."

Samuel looked away, glaring. "I hate the thought that you will have to obey Danilo or anyone for that matter."

"I could do worse than Danilo. He's a gentleman when he's around me."

Samuel laughed darkly. "He is as good as the Underboss of Indianapolis,

Fina, and despite his age, he has his men under control. I've seen him in action. He is a Made Man like me and Dad. He expects obedience."

I regarded him curiously. "You never expected obedience from me."

"I wished for it," he muttered jokingly then turned serious again. "You are my sister, not my wife. That's different."

"Will you expect obedience from your wife?"

Samuel frowned. "I don't know. Maybe."

"How do you treat the women you are with?" I'd never met any of them. Made Men took outsiders into their beds before marriage, and those women weren't allowed into our homes.

Quickly and unexpectedly, Samuel's face seemed to close off. "It doesn't matter." He stood. "And it doesn't matter how Danilo is used to treating his whores. You are a mafia princess, my sister, and I swear by my honor that I will hunt him down if he doesn't treat you like a lady."

I smiled up at my twin. "My protector."

Samuel smiled back. "Always."

CHAPTER 2

REMO

"Are you ready? We've got a wedding to crash," I said, grinning. Excitement sizzled under my skin, a low fire that burned brighter with every second I got closer to my goal.

Fabiano sighed, checking his gun and shoving it back into his holster. "As ready I as I'll ever be for this insanity."

"Genius and insanity are often interchangeable. Both have fueled the greatest events in human history."

"I think you annoy me the most when you sound like Nino with your own brand of crazy," Fabiano said. "I can't believe I'm only a few miles from my father and can't rip him to shreds."

"You will get him. My plan will bring him to you eventually."

"I don't like the eventually part. I have a feeling this plan is about more than killing my father and punishing the Outfit."

I leaned back against the car seat. "And what would that be?"

Fabiano met my gaze. "About you getting your hands on Dante's niece for whatever insane reason."

My mouth pulled into a dark smile. "You know exactly why I want her."

Fabiano leaned back in his own seat, expression tightening. "I don't think even you know exactly why you want her. But I do know the girl will pay for something she wasn't responsible for."

"She's part of our world. Born and bred to be a mother to more Outfit bastards. Born and bred to obey like a mindless sheep. She was brought up to follow her shepherd without hesitation. He led her toward a pack of wolves. It's his mistake, but she will be torn apart."

Fabiano shook his head. "Fuck, Remo. You are a crazy fucker."

I wrapped my fingers tightly around his forearm, over his Camorra tattoo—the blade and the eye. "You are one of us. We bleed and we die together. We maim and kill together. Don't forget your oath."

"I won't," he said simply.

I released him. My eyes moved to the front of the hotel where Serafina's parents, Ines and Pietro Mione, had just walked out the door with a young dark-haired girl between them. Dressed in evening wear for the wedding of the year, Ines looked remarkably like her brother. Tall and blond and proud. So fucking proud and controlled.

"It won't be long now," I said, glancing down the street where the car with my two soldiers was waiting.

Fabiano put the keys in the ignition as we watched the Miones drive off. "Her twin will stay with her," he said. "And then there's the bodyguard."

My eyes sought out the middle-aged guy behind the wheel of a Bentley limousine parked in the driveway of the hotel. A fucking flower arrangement on the hood. White flowers. I wanted to squash them under my boots.

"They're making it too easy figuring out the car of the bride," I said with a laugh.

"Because they don't expect an attack. It's never been done before. Funerals and weddings are sacred."

"There have been bloody weddings before. They should know better."

"But those weddings became bloody because the guests got into fights with each other. I don't think anyone has ever attacked a wedding, especially the bride, on purpose. Honor forbids it."

I chuckled. "We are the Camorra. We have our own set of rules, our own idea of honor."

"I think they will realize that today," he said tightly.

My eyes scanned the front of the hotel. Somewhere behind its windows, Serafina was getting ready for her wedding. She'd be groomed to perfection, an apparition in white. I couldn't wait to get my hands on her, stain the perfectly white fabric blood-red.

SERAFINA

"You don't have to be scared, sweetheart," Mom said quietly so Sofia wouldn't hear her. My little sister was busy tugging at the pins keeping her hair in place on top of her head, grimacing.

"I'm not," I said quickly, which was a lie. It wasn't that I was overly scared of sleeping with Danilo, but I was nervous and worried about embarrassing myself. I didn't like to be bad at things, and I would be bad given I had no experience.

She gave me a knowing look. "It's okay to be nervous. But he's a decent man. Dante always talks in glowing terms about Danilo." Mom tried to sound casual but failed miserably. She stroked my hair like she used to do when I was little.

We both knew that there was a difference between being a decent man and a loyal soldier to the Outfit. Uncle Dante was probably basing his judgment of Danilo on the latter. Not that it mattered. Danilo had always been a gentleman, and he would be my husband in a few hours. It was my duty to submit to him, and I would do it.

My hairdresser took Mom's place and began pinning up my blond hair, arranging pearls and strings of white gold in it. Mom noticed Sofia fighting with her hairdo and quickly moved over to her. "Stop it, Sofia. You've already untangled a few strands."

Sofia dropped her hands with a resigned look. Then her blue eyes found mine. I smiled at her. Avoiding Mom's tugging hands, she came to my side and peered up at me. "I can't wait to be a bride."

"First, you will finish school," I teased her. She was only eleven and hadn't been promised to anyone yet. For her weddings were about looking pretty and the chivalrous knight she would marry. I envied her the ignorance.

"Done," the hairdresser announced and stepped back.

"Thank you," I said. She nodded and quickly slipped out, giving us a moment.

The dress was absolutely stunning. I couldn't stop admiring myself in the mirror, turning left and right. The pearls and silver embroidered threadwork caught the light beautifully, and the skirt was a dream consisting of several layers of the finest tulle. Mom shook her head, tears blurring her eyes.

"Don't cry, Mom," I warned her. "You'll ruin your makeup. And if you start crying, I will cry too and then my makeup will be ruined as well."

Mom nodded, blinking. "You are right, Fina." She dabbed her eyes with the corner of a tissue. Mom wasn't the emotional type. She was like her brother, my Uncle Dante. Sofia beamed up at me.

A knock sounded and Dad poked in his head. He froze and slowly stepped inside. He took me in without saying a word. I could see the emotion swimming in his eyes, but he would never show it openly. He came toward me and touched two fingers to my cheeks. "Dove, you're the most beautiful bride I've ever seen."

Mom raised her eyebrows in mock shock. Dad laughed and took her hand, kissing her knuckles. "You were, of course, a breathtaking bride, Ines."

"What about me?" Sofia asked. "Maybe I will be even more beautiful?"

Dad lifted a finger. "I will keep you as my little daughter forever. No marriage for you."

Sofia pouted and Dad shook his head. "We need to go to church now." He kissed my cheek then took Sofia's hand. The three of them walked out. Mom turned once more and gave me a proud smile.

Samuel appeared in the doorway, dressed in a black suit and blue tie. "You look dapper," I told him and felt a wave of wistfulness. He would be hundreds of miles from me once I moved into Danilo's villa in Indianapolis.

"And you look beautiful," he said quietly, his eyes taking me in head to toe.

He pushed off the doorframe and moved toward me, his hands in his pockets. "It'll be strange without you."

"I'll tell Sofia she needs to keep you on your toes."

"It won't be the same."

"You will marry in a few years. And soon you'll be even busier with mob business. You won't even notice I'm gone."

Samuel sighed then glanced down at his Rolex that Dad had given him for his initiation five years ago. "We need to go too. The ceremony is supposed to start in forty-five minutes. It'll take at least thirty minutes to reach the church."

The church was outside city limits. I wanted the celebration to take place in a renovated barn in the countryside, surrounded by forest, not in the city.

I nodded then checked my reflection once more before I took his outstretched hand. With linked arms we walked out of the suite and down into the hotel lobby. People kept glancing my way, and I had to admit I enjoyed their attention. The dress had cost a small fortune. It was only fair, since as many people as possible would see me in it. This wedding was the biggest social event in the Outfit in years.

Samuel opened the door of the black Bentley for me, and I slipped onto the backseat, trying to gather the skirt of my dress around me. Samuel closed the door and got in the front beside the driver, my bodyguard.

We pulled away and my stomach burst with butterflies. In less than one hour I'd be Danilo's wife. It still seemed impossible. Soon, the tall buildings gave way to the occasional field and trees.

Samuel shifted in the front seat, pulling his gun.

"What's wrong?" I asked.

We sped up. Samuel glanced over his shoulder but not at me. I turned as well and saw a car close behind us with two men. Samuel took his phone out and lifted it to his ear. Before he could say anything, another car came from the side and collided with our trunk. We spun around. I cried out, gripping the seat as the belt bit into my skin.

"Down!" Samuel shouted. I unbuckled and threw myself forward, my arms over my head. We collided with something else then came to a stop. What was going on?

Samuel shoved open the door and began firing. My bodyguard followed him. The windows burst, and I screamed as shards of glass rained down on my skin. A man cried out, and my head flew up. "Samuel?" I screamed.

"Run, Fina!"

I pushed through the gap between the front seats and found Samuel leaning against the side of the car, blood spilling out over the hand he pressed to his side. I struggled out of the door and sank to the ground beside him, touching him. "Sam?"

He gave me a strained smile. "I'll be fine. Run, Fina. They want you. Run."

"Who wants me?" I blinked at him, uncomprehending. He fired at our attackers again. "Run!"

I bolted to my feet. If they wanted me, they'd follow me if I ran and leave Samuel alone. "Call reinforcement."

I kicked off my heels and gripped my dress and began running as fast as I could. White petals from the destroyed flower arrangement stuck to my toes. Nobody shot at me. That meant they wanted me alive, and I knew that couldn't be a good thing. I turned to the right, where a forest spread out in front of me. It was my only chance to lose them. My breath came in short gasps. I was fit and a good runner, but the heavy fabric of my dress slowed me down. Twigs tugged at the dress, tearing it, making me stumble.

Heavier steps sounded behind me. I didn't dare look over my shoulder to see who was chasing me. The steps closed in on me. Oh God. This dress was making me too slow.

Had Samuel called reinforcement yet?

And then a worse thought banished my last. What if Samuel didn't make it? I turned to the right, deciding to run back to the car. Another set of steps joined the first. Two pursuers.

Fear pounded in my veins, but I didn't slow. A shadow appeared in the corner of my eye, and suddenly a tall shape came from my side. I screamed out a second before an arm slung around my waist. The force of it made me lose my balance, and I fell to the ground. A heavy body crushed mine. The air rushed out of my lungs and my vision turned black from the impact of landing hard on the forest floor.

I started kicking, thrashing, clawing and screamed at the top of my lungs.

But a few layers of tulle covered my face and made movement difficult. If Dad and Dante had arrived with reinforcement, they needed to hear me to be able to find me.

A hand clamped down on my mouth, and I bit down.

"Fuck!"

The hand pulled back and the voice was distantly familiar, but I couldn't place it in my panic. The tulle still obstructed my view. I made out two shapes above me. Tall. One dark, one blond.

"We need to hurry," someone snarled. I shivered at the stark brutality of the voice.

A heavy weight settled on my hips, and two strong hands gripped my wrists, shoving them down on the ground. I tried bucking away, but a hand came toward my face. I tried to bite again, but I didn't reach it. My range of motion was limited with my arms above my head. The tulle was removed from my face, and finally I could see my assailants. The man sitting on my hips had black hair and black eyes and a scar on his face. The look he gave me sent a wave of terror through my body.

I'd seen him before but wasn't sure where. My eyes darted to the other man holding my hands down, and I froze. I knew the blond man and those blue eyes. Fabiano Scuderi, the boy I'd played with when I was younger. The boy who had run off and joined the Camorra.

Finally, it clicked. My gaze darted back to the black-haired man. Remo Falcone, Capo of the Camorra. I jerked violently, a new wave of panic giving me strength. I arched up but Remo didn't budge.

"Calm down," Fabiano said. One of his hands bled from where I'd bitten him. Calm down? Calm down? The Camorra was trying to kidnap me!

Opening my mouth, I tried to scream again. This time Remo covered my mouth before I got the chance to hurt him. "Give her the tranquilizer," he ordered.

21

I shook my head frantically but something pricked the inside of my elbow and pierced my skin. My muscles became heavy, but I didn't black out completely. I was released and Remo Falcone slid his hands under me, straightening up with me in his arms. My limbs hung limply down at my sides, but my eyes remained open and on my captor. His dark eyes settled on me briefly before he started running. Trees and sky rushed by as I peered up.

"Fina!" I heard Samuel in the distance.

"Sam," I wheezed, barely a sound.

Then Dad. "Fina? Fina, where are you?"

More male voices rang out, coming to save me.

"Faster!" Fabiano shouted. "To the right!" Twigs snapped under foot. Remo breathed heavier, but his grip on me remained firm. We burst out of the forest and onto a street.

Suddenly, tires screeched and hope filled me, but it crashed when I was put inside a vehicle in the backseat, and Remo slipped in beside me.

"Drive!"

I stared up at the gray ceiling of the car, my breathing ragged.

"My, what a beautiful bride you are," Remo said. I raised my eyes and met his, wishing I hadn't because the twisted smile on his face burned through me like a thunderstorm of terror. Then I passed out.

REMO

Serafina passed out beside me. I regarded her closely. Now that she wasn't thrashing or screaming, I could admire her like a bride deserved. Dots of blood splattered her dress like rubies and marred the creamy skin of her neckline. Pure perfection.

"We seem to have shaken them off," Fabiano muttered.

My eyes were drawn to the back window, but nobody was following us for the moment. We had injured, not killed Serafina's two companions, so part of the forces would waste time tending to their injuries.

"She is a nice piece of ass," Simeone commented from behind the steering wheel.

I leaned forward. "And you will never look at her again unless you want me to rip your eyeballs out and shove them up your ass. One more fucking disrespectful word from you and your tongue will keep your eyeballs company, understood?"

Simeone gave a jerky nod.

Fabiano caught my gaze with a curious expression. I leaned back and returned my gaze to the woman curled up beside me on the seat. Her hair was pinned tightly to her head as if even that part of her needed to be tamed and under control, but one wayward strand had freed itself and curled wildly over her temple. I wrapped it around my finger. I couldn't wait to find out how tame Serafina really was.

I carried a limp Serafina into the motel room and set her down on one of the two beds. Reaching for a twig that had tangled itself in her hair, I removed it before undoing her updo, letting her hair spill out on the pillow. I straightened.

Fabiano sighed. "Cavallaro will seek retribution."

"He won't attack us as long as we have her. She's vulnerable and he knows he can't get her out of Vegas alive."

Fabiano nodded, his eyes moving to Serafina who lay limply on the bed, her face tilted to the side, her long elegant neck on display. My gaze lowered to the fine lace above the soft swell of her breast. A high-collared dress. Modest and elegant, nothing vulgar or overly sexy about Dante's niece, and yet she would have brought many men to their knees. She looked like a fucking angel with her blond hair and pale skin, and the white dress only emphasized that impression. The epitome of innocence and purity. I had to bite back a laugh.

"What are you thinking?" Fabiano asked warily as he followed my gaze toward the bride.

"That they couldn't have emphasized her innocence more if they'd tried." I moved closer, my gaze trailing over her narrow hips. "I prefer the blood stains on her dress."

"It was her wedding. Of course they would emphasize her purity. You know how it is. Girls in our circles are kept protected until they enter marriage. They must lose their innocence on their wedding night. Cavallaro and her fiancé will probably do anything to make sure she returns to them untouched. Danilo is Underboss. Her father is Underboss. Dante fucking Cavallaro is her uncle. No matter what you ask of them, they will deliver. If you ask them to hand over my father now, they will do it and we will be rid of her."

I shook my head. "I won't ask for anything yet. I won't make it that easy for them. They attacked Las Vegas. They tried killing my brothers, tried killing you and me. They brought war into my city, and I will bring war into their midst. I will destroy them from the inside. I will break them."

Fabiano frowned. "How?"

I regarded him. The hint of wariness in his voice was barely noticeable, but I knew him well. "By breaking someone they are supposed to protect. If there's one thing I know, then it's that even men like us rarely forgive themselves for letting people they are supposed to protect get hurt. Her family will go crazy with worry over her. Every day they're going to wonder what's happening to her. They're going to imagine how she's suffering. Her mother will blame her husband and brother. And they will blame themselves. Their guilt will spread like cancer among them. And I will fuel their worry. I will tear them apart."

Fabiano lowered his gaze to Serafina, who started stirring slightly. The rip in her wedding dress shifted, exposing her long bare leg. She was wearing a white lace garter. Fabiano reached for the skirt of her dress and covered her leg. I tilted my head at him.

"She's an innocent," he said neutrally.

"She won't return to them innocent," I said darkly.

Fabiano met my gaze. "Hurting her won't break the Outfit. They will come closer together to bring you down."

"We will see," I murmured. "Let's call Nino and see which route to choose next." Fabiano and I moved toward the desk and put the phone on loudspeaker.

We had just finished our call when Serafina moaned. We turned to her. She woke with a start, disoriented. She blinked slowly at the wall then up at the ceiling. Her movements were slow, sluggish. Her breathing picked up, and she looked down at her body, her hands feeling her ribs then lower, coming to rest on her abdomen—as if she thought we'd fucked her while she was passed out. I supposed it made sense. She would have been sore.

"If you keep touching yourself like that, I won't be responsible for my actions."

Her gaze darted to us, her body stiffening.

"We didn't touch you while you were unconscious," Fabiano told her.

Her eyes darted between him and me. It was obvious she wasn't sure if she could believe him.

"You would know if Fabiano or I had fucked you, trust me, Serafina."

She pressed her lips together, fear and disgust swirling in her blue eyes.

She began squirming and wiggling as if she was trying to get off the bed but couldn't control her body. Eventually she closed her eyes, her chest heaving, her fingers trembling against the blanket.

"She's still drugged," Fabiano said.

"I'll get her a coke. Maybe the caffeine will sober her up. I don't like her this weak and unresponsive. It's no challenge."

SERAFINA

I watched Remo leave the room and forced myself into a sitting position. "Fabiano," I whispered.

He came closer and knelt before me. "Fina," he said simply. Only my brother called me by that name, but Fabiano had always played with us when we were little and knew me by the nickname.

My mother hadn't raised me to beg, but I was desperate. I touched his hand. "Please help me. You were part of the Outfit. You can't allow this."

He pulled his hand away, his eyes hard. "I *am* part of the Camorra."

He stood and looked down at me without a hint of emotion.

"What will happen to me? What does your Capo want with me?" I asked hoarsely.

For a second his eyes softened, and that was the most terrifying answer he could have given me. "The Outfit attacked us on our own territory. Remo is out for retribution."

Icy terror clawed at my insides. "But I have nothing to do with your business."

"You don't, but Dante is your uncle and your father and fiancé are high-ranking Outfit members."

I looked down at my hands. My knuckles were chalk white from clutching the fabric of my dress. Then I noticed the red stains and quickly released the tulle. "So he's going to make them pay by hurting me?" My voice broke. I cleared my throat, trying hard and failing to hold on to my composure.

"Remo didn't divulge his plan to me," he said, but I didn't believe him for one second. "He might use you to bribe your uncle into handing over parts of his territory ... or his Consigliere."

Uncle Dante would never give up part of his territory, not even for family, no matter how much my mother begged him to, nor would he hand over one of his men, *his Consigliere*. He couldn't, not for one girl. I was lost.

My vision swam again and I slumped back down onto the mattress.

Through the fogginess I heard Remo's voice. "Change of plans. Let her sleep the drugs out of her system while we drive. We've spent too much time at this place. Nino called again. He suggests we head out now. He sent our helicopter to pick us up in Kansas. He heard from Grigory that Cavallaro has called upon every soldier to search for his niece and we are still on the fringes of his territory."

Dante was trying to save me. Dad and Danilo would be searching for me as well. And Samuel, my Samuel, would look for me. If we were still on Outfit territory not all hope was lost.

CHAPTER 3

SERAFINA

I woke in a car, curled into myself, half tangled in my dress. Fabiano was in the backseat beside me but didn't look at me. Instead, he was checking the rear window. Another man sat in the front behind the wheel and beside him was Remo.

I wasn't sure if they'd given me another tranquilizer or if my body had trouble fighting the effects of the first injection. I hadn't eaten all day and hardly had anything to drink. A low moan slipped past my lips.

Fabiano and Remo both looked down at me. Remo's dark eyes sent a shiver of fear down my spine, but Fabiano's gaze didn't offer any consolation either. I closed my eyes again, hating how vulnerable I felt.

I wasn't sure how long we'd been driving, but the next time I woke we were in a helicopter. I struggled into a sitting position. The strip with hotels and casinos spread out below, and my stomach constricted as the helicopter started its descent over Las Vegas. I didn't say a word to either Fabiano or Remo, and they didn't talk to me either. The tension was still palpable in the helicopter, but they had escaped from the Outfit and now I was in Las Vegas. In Camorra territory. At their mercy.

The moment we landed, Fabiano helped me out of the helicopter while Remo talked to someone on the phone. I needed to wash my face and clear my head so I could think straight again. I had been in my wedding dress for almost twenty-four hours. I felt sticky and sluggish and exhausted. And underneath it all a terror I had trouble containing throbbed inside of me.

I was pushed into another car, and eventually we pulled up in front of a shabby strip club called the Sugar Trap.

Fabiano gripped my arm again as Remo went ahead without a single glance at me.

"Fabi," I tried, but he tightened his hold. "I need to go to the bathroom and wash my face. I don't feel good."

He led me inside the deserted strip club toward the ladies' room and followed me inside to wait at the washbasins. Remo had ignored me mostly, but I had a feeling that would change soon.

I went to the toilet, hating that I knew Fabiano could hear me. There was nothing I could have used as a weapon, and even if there were, how would that help me surrounded by Camorrista? I dropped my skirt when I was done, breathing deeply, trying to hide my emotions.

"Serafina," came Fabiano's warning voice. "Don't make me get you out of there. You won't like it."

Straightening my shoulders, I came back out, feeling shaky from dehydration.

I bent over the washbasin and washed my face then drank a few gulps of water.

"You can have a coke from the bar," Fabiano said. Before I could say anything, he gripped me by the arm and dragged me out. My bare feet ached. I must have cut them on the forest ground. My eyes flitted around the room. It wasn't deserted anymore. As if drawn out by the commotion, several scantily clad women had gathered at the bar.

They avoided looking at me, and I realized I couldn't hope for their help. Not a single person in Las Vegas would probably risk helping me.

"Coke," Fabiano barked at a dark-skinned man behind the bar, who grabbed a bottle, opened it, and handed it to Fabiano. The man purposely wasn't looking at me.

Good Lord. Where had they taken me? What kind of hellhole was Las Vegas?

"Drink," Fabiano said, holding the bottle out for me. I took it and had a few long sips. The cold, sweet liquid seemed to revive my brain and body.

"Come." Fabiano led me through a door and along a bare-walled corridor toward another door. When he opened it and stepped inside with me, my stomach revolted.

Inside were two unknown men, both of them Falcones, I assumed. All of them were tall, with hard expressions and this air of unbridled cruelty that they were famous for. One of them had gray eyes and looked older than the other guy. I tried to remember their names, but then my eyes met Remo's and my mind turned blank.

The Camorra Capo had shed his shirt. There was a fresh wound on his left side that had been stitched up, but there was still blood around it. My pulse stuttered in my veins at the sight of his muscles and scars.

"Your twin almost got me there," Remo said with a dark laugh. "But not enough to stop me from capturing his beloved sister." He said beloved like it was something filthy, something worthless.

Fabiano released me and joined the other men, leaving me standing in the middle of the room like a piece of meat that needed inspecting. Dread settled in my bones because maybe that was exactly what I was to them. Meat.

Remo pointed at the gray-eyed man. "That's my brother Nino." Then he gestured at the younger man beside him. "And my brother Savio."

Remo stalked closer, every muscle in his upper body taut, as if he was a predator about to pounce. I stood my ground. I wouldn't give him an inch. I wouldn't give him anything. Not my fear and not a single tear. He couldn't force those from me. I didn't kid myself thinking that I could stop him from taking anything else.

"Serafina Cavallaro." My name was a caress on his lips as he slowly walked around me. He stopped close behind me so I couldn't see him.

I suppressed a shiver. "Not Cavallaro. That's my uncle's name, not mine."

Remo's breath fanned over my neck. "In every regard that matters, you are a Cavallaro."

I dug my nails into my palms. Nino's gray eyes followed the movement without a flicker of emotion on his face. Fabiano perched on the desk, looking at the man behind me but not me. Savio regarded me with a mix of curiosity and calculation.

I didn't say anything, only stared stubbornly ahead. Remo circled me and stopped in front of me. He was a tall man, and I wished for my heels. I wasn't exactly small, but barefoot only the top of my head reached his chin. I lifted my head slightly, trying to appear taller.

Remo's mouth twitched. "I hear you were supposed to marry your fiancé, Danilo Mancini, yesterday," he said with a twisted grin. "So I robbed you of your wedding night."

I remembered Mom's consoling words. That Danilo would be good to me. That I didn't have to be scared of him claiming his rights after our wedding. And Samuel's words that he'd hunt down Danilo if he didn't treat me like a lady.

As I stared up into the face of Remo Falcone, my worry of having sex with

Danilo seemed ridiculous. The Camorra wouldn't be good to me. The name of their Capo was spoken in hushed, terrified whispers even among women in the Outfit. And a terror unlike anything I'd ever encountered gripped me, but I forced it down. Pride was the only weapon I had, and I would hold on to it until the very end.

"I wonder if you let your fiancé have a taste before your wedding," Remo murmured, his voice a low vibrato full of threat, his dark eyes raking over me.

Indignation filled me. How dare he suggest something like that? "Of course not," I said coldly. "The first kiss of a honorable Outfit woman happens on her wedding day."

His grin widened, wolf-like, and I realized my mistake. He'd led me into a trap. My own pride a weapon he used against me.

REMO

She held her head high in spite her mistake. Her long blond hair trailed down her back. Cool blue eyes assessed me like I wasn't worth her attention. *Perfect.*

Highborn and about to take a deep fall.

"So proud and cold," I said, trailing a finger down her cheek and throat. "Just like good ol' Uncle Dante." She turned her face away with a disgusted expression.

I laughed. "Oh yes, that stupid Outfit pride. I can't wait to rid you of it."

"I'll take that pride to the grave with me," she said haughtily.

I leaned even closer, my body lightly pressing up against hers. "Killing you is the last thing on my mind, believe me." I let my eyes travel the length of her body. "There are far more entertaining things I can think of."

Terror flashed over her face, only briefly, then it was gone. But I saw it. So death didn't bother the girl, or so she thought, but the idea of being touched by me put a chink into that prideful exterior.

"So you have never kissed a man before," I mused, leaning in so close that our lips were almost touching.

She stood her ground, but a slight tremor went through her body. She pressed her lips together, refusing an answer.

"This will be fun."

"My family and fiancé will tear down Las Vegas if you hurt me."

"Oh, I hope they do, so I can bathe in their blood," I said. "But I doubt you'll be worth their trouble once I'm done with you. Or will your fiancé settle for the leftovers of another man?"

She finally took a step back.

My smile pulled wider. Her eyes darted to something behind me. To someone. I followed her gaze to Fabiano. His eyes met mine, his expression hard and unrelenting, but I knew him inside out. He'd known Serafina as a child, had played with her. There was a hint of strain in his eyes, but he wouldn't come to her aid, neither would Nino or Savio.

I turned back around to her. "Nobody will save you, so you better stop hoping for it."

She narrowed her eyes at me. "I decide what to hope for. You might rule over Las Vegas and over these men, but you don't rule over me, Remo Falcone."

Never before had someone spat out my name like that, and it sent a fucking thrill through me.

"Oh, Serafina," I said darkly. "That's where you're wrong, and I will prove it to you."

"And I will prove you wrong." Her blue eyes held mine, back in control, back to being her prideful self. But she had given me an opening earlier, had shown me a crack in her mask, and she couldn't undo it. I knew how to get under her skin.

"As much as I enjoy chitchatting with you, I need to remember the purpose of why you are here. And that's to pay back your uncle Dante."

A flash of fear in those proud eyes. I let my gaze travel the length of her, over her torn and bloody wedding dress.

"We need to send your uncle a message, a nice video of you," I murmured. I nodded toward Fabiano. "Take her into the basement. I'll join you in a few minutes." I wanted to see how he'd react.

Fabiano's jaw tensed but he gave a terse nod. He grabbed Serafina's wrist, and she tensed but didn't fight him, not like she would have undoubtedly fought me. He began to tug her along. She didn't beg him like I thought she would. Instead, she gave me another disgusted look. She thought she could defy me, thought she could hold on to her pride and anger. I would show her why I had become Capo of the Camorra.

"What are you going to do to her?" Savio asked, trying to sound unfazed, but he wasn't like Nino and me. He had some humanity left in him.

"What I said. Let her speak a message to her Uncle Dante . . . and record some additional material."

"So you're going to fuck her for the camera?" Savio asked.

I glanced at Nino, who watched me with narrowed eyes as if he, too, wasn't sure about my motives. I smiled. "Don't spoil my surprise. We'll all watch the video together once it's done."

I gave them a nod and headed downstairs. The moment I entered the corridor in the basement, Fabiano stepped out of the last door and closed it. His eyes settled on me. He met me halfway and gripped my arm. I raised my eyebrows.

"Serafina's virginity can be used as leverage against Dante and Danilo."

I narrowed my eyes at him. "Thank you for your input, Fabiano. I am

Capo. I've thought my plan through. Don't worry."

"Have you?" Fabiano muttered, and I brought us nose to nose.

"Careful. You've betrayed me for a woman once before. Do not make it a habit."

Fabiano shook his head. "Fuck. I won't betray you. I went to Indianapolis with you and kidnapped Serafina. I didn't hunt down my father like I wanted to. I put her in your fucking cell for you. I am loyal, Remo."

"Good," I said, stepping back. "Serafina is my captive, and I decide what happens to her, understood?"

"Understood," Fabiano said, gritting his teeth. "Can I go to Leona now?"

"Go. I'll have Simeone watch her cell tonight."

"He's a fucking pervert, Remo."

"He also knows I'll cut his dick off if he goes against my orders. Now go have fun with your girl while I take care of mine."

CHAPTER 4

SERAFINA

F abiano dragged me down a flight of stairs into a basement.

"Fabi," I said imploringly, tugging at his hold.

"Fabiano," he growled, not even looking at me as he pulled me through another narrow bare corridor. He seemed furious.

Before I could utter another word, he opened a heavy door and stepped inside a room with me. My eyes darted around. A cell.

My stomach lurched when I saw the toilet and shower in one corner, but even worse when I took in the stained mattress on the floor across from them. Red and yellow stains. Terror gripped me hard, and suddenly I realized what was supposed to happen here.

My eyes flew up to a camera in the corner to my right then back to Fabiano. He was Enforcer of the Camorra, and while my parents had tried to shelter me, Samuel had been more forthcoming with information. I knew what

Enforcers did, especially in Las Vegas.

Fabiano scanned my face and released me with a sigh. I stumbled back and almost lost my balance when my feet caught in my dress. "Will you …?" I pressed out.

Fabiano shook his head. "Remo will handle you himself."

I froze. "Fabiano," I tried again. "You can't allow that to happen. Don't let him hurt me. Please." The word tasted bitter in my mouth. Begging wasn't something I had been taught, but this wasn't a situation I had ever prepared for.

"Remo won't …" Fabiano trailed off and grimaced.

Pushing past my fear, I moved closer to Fabiano and gripped his arms. "If you are unwilling to help me, then at least tell me what I can do to stop Remo from hurting me. What does he want from me?"

Fabiano stepped back, so I had to release him. "Remo hates weakness. And in his eyes women are weak."

"So I'm at the mercy of a man who hates women."

"He hates weakness. But you are strong, Serafina." He turned and left, closing the heavy door and locking me in.

I whirled around, my eyes scanning the surroundings for something I could use against Remo, but there was nothing, and he wasn't a man who could be beaten in a fight. Strong? Was I strong? It didn't feel that way right now. Fear pounded in my chest, in every fiber of my body.

My eyes darted to the mattress once more. Yesterday Danilo was supposed to claim me on satin sheets in the holy bond of matrimony. Today Remo would break me on a dirty mattress like a common whore.

I braced myself against the rough stone wall, fighting my rising panic. All my life I had been raised to be proud and noble, honorable and well-behaved, and it didn't protect me.

The creak of the door made me tense, but I didn't turn to see who had entered. I knew who it was, could feel his cruel eyes on me.

I peered up at the camera once more. Everything that happened would be recorded and sent to my uncle, fiancé, and father. And worse … Samuel. I swallowed. They would see me at my worst. I wouldn't let it come to that. I'd hold my head high no matter what happened.

"Are you ignoring me?" Remo asked from close behind me, and a small shiver shot down my spine.

"Does that ever work?" I said, wishing my voice came out stronger, but it was already a fight forcing those four words out of my tight throat.

"No," Remo said. "I'm difficult to ignore."

Impossible to ignore.

"Turn around," Remo ordered.

I didn't move, focusing on the gray stone in front of me. It wasn't only an act of defiance. My legs refused to move. Fear kept me frozen, but Remo didn't need to know that.

His hot breath ghosted over my neck, and I closed my eyes, wedging my lower lip between my teeth to stifle a sound. "Open disobedience?" he asked in a low voice. His palms pressed down on my shoulder blades, and I almost crumpled under their weight, even though he didn't put much pressure behind the touch.

"On second thought," he said gently. "This position works well too."

The soft clink of a blade being unsheathed made me jump. Remo braced himself to both sides of me, a long dagger in one hand. His chest pressed up against my back. "I'll give you a choice, Serafina. You can either get out of your dress by yourself or I'll cut you out of it. What is it?"

I swallowed. I had expected another choice, one Vegas was famous for. A rush of relief filled me, but it was short-lived. I shifted my hand and covered the blade with my palm then curled my fingers around the cold steel.

"If you give me your knife, I'll cut myself out of my dress," I bit out.

Remo chuckled. A dark, joyless sound. "You want my knife?"

I nodded, and to my utter shock, Remo released the handle, and I held his dagger by the blade, the sharp edge cutting into my flesh. Remo stepped back, his warmth leaving my body. I stared at the deadly weapon in my hand. Slowly, drawing in a deep breath, I straightened and reached for the handle. I knew Remo hadn't given me a fair chance. He was playing with me, trying to break my spirit by showing me that even a knife didn't change the fact that I was at his mercy.

What he didn't know was that Samuel and I had spent all our lives fighting with each other, like siblings always do, but when he'd become a Made Man, he started working with me on my fighting skills because he knew how our world treated women. He had tried to make me strong, and I was. I knew how to handle a knife, how to defeat an opponent. But I had never won against Samuel, and he was always careful not to hurt me. Remo was stronger than Samuel, and he would hurt me, would enjoy it. I could not beat Remo in a fight, not even when I had a knife and he didn't.

Fabiano's words flashed through my mind. *Remo hates weakness.* Even if I couldn't beat Remo, I could show him I wasn't weak.

"Maybe I should take my knife back since you don't know what to do with it," Remo said, almost disappointed. He stepped closer.

In a fluid motion, I turned around and jabbed at Remo while my other hand pulled up my dress. Remo blocked my attack by hitting my wrist. My years of training with Samuel prevented me from dropping the knife despite the sharp pain in my wrist.

A smile crossed Remo's face, and I released my dress and rammed my fist into his abdomen while I slashed the knife at him once more. The blade grazed his arm and blood trickled down, but Remo didn't even wince. His smile got wider as he took a step back, completely unfazed.

I lunged at him but got caught in my long skirt. I barreled into Remo and tried to land another deadlier cut. We fell and Remo landed on his back with me on top of him. I straddled him and stabbed at his stomach, but he gripped my wrist with a twisted grin on his face. I tried to force the knife down, but Remo didn't budge. And then, suddenly, he showed me what it was like when he actually tried fighting back.

He bucked his hips, and before I could react, I landed on my back and Remo was on top of me. I struggled but he shoved my skirt up and knelt between my legs, moving closer until his pelvis thrust against me and I couldn't use my legs to push him away. His fingers curled around my wrists and he pressed them into the mattress above my head, the knife still in my grasp and utterly useless. He had me pinned under his strong body, completely at his mercy, both of my hands fastened to the ground.

His dark eyes held excitement and a flicker of admiration. For a moment, I felt proud, but then my situation dawned on me. I was on my back, on a dirty mattress, under Remo. He had me where he wanted me from the start.

Fear overpowered my determination, and my body stiffened, my eyes darting to the disgusting mattress under me. I sucked in a deep breath, trying to keep my panic at bay. Remo regarded me intently. "Let go of the knife," he murmured, and I did. I didn't even hesitate.

Be strong.

I swallowed hard, reminding myself of the camera. I'd take my pride to the grave with me. "Just get it over with, Remo," I said in disgust. "Rape me. I'm done playing your sick game. I'm not a chess piece."

Remo's dark eyes wandered over my face, my hair, my arms stretched out above my head. He leaned down, his cruel face coming closer. He stopped when our noses were almost brushing. His eyes weren't black; they were the darkest brown I'd ever seen. He held my gaze, and I held his. I wouldn't look away, no matter what he did. I wanted him to see me as I was. Not a weakness, not a pawn, but a human being.

"Not like this, Serafina," he said. His voice was low and dark, mesmerizing, but it was his gaze that held me captive. "Not like a whore on a stained mattress." He smiled, and it was worse than any glare or threat.

He brought his mouth down until his lips touched mine lightly, just barely, and yet a current shot through me. "I haven't started playing, and you aren't a mere chess piece. You are the queen." He took the knife and straightened, releasing me in the process. He stood slowly, drawing up to his full height and staring down at me.

"And what are you in this game of chess?" I whispered harshly, still lying on the mattress.

"I'm the king."

"You aren't unbeatable."

His eyes trailed over me until they returned to my face. "We'll see." He sheathed his knife. "Now get out of that dress. You won't need it anymore."

I sat up. "I won't undress in front of you."

Remo chuckled. "Oh this will be fun." He waited, and I returned his gaze steadily. "The knife it is, then," he said with a shrug.

"No," I said firmly, struggling to my feet. I glared at him and reached behind myself, pulling down the zipper with an audible hiss. Never taking my eyes off him, I pulled at the fabric until it finally fell to the ground, a fluffy halo around my feet.

"White and golden like an angel," Remo mused darkly as he took in every inch of me.

Even force of will couldn't stop my cheeks from blazing with heat, being exposed like this in front of a man for the first time. Left in nothing but my

41

white garter, white lace panties and a corset, goose bumps rippled across my skin at Remo's scrutiny.

He bridged the distance between us, and I held my breath. He stopped close to me, dark eyes tracing my face, and he raised his hand, causing me to stiffen. The corner of his mouth twitched. Then his thumb brushed over my cheekbone. I drew back, away from the touch, which made him smile again.

"Virgin bashfulness, how endearing," Remo said darkly, mocking me. "Don't worry, *Angel*, I won't tell anyone that I'm the first man who saw you like this."

I glared at him, fighting tears of embarrassment and fury as he bent down, reaching for the dress. "Step back." I quickly stepped out of the dress, and Remo straightened with the stained fabric wedged under his arm.

He regarded me. "You are a sight to behold. I bet Danilo would have had a boner from merely looking at you. I can only imagine what he feels now, knowing you are in my hands, knowing that he will never get what was promised."

I shook my head. "Whatever you take, it'll always be less than what he would have gotten, because I would have given myself to him willingly, body and soul, and there's nothing you can do about it. You will have to settle for the consolation prize, Remo Falcone."

Remo moved back slowly, a strange expression on his face. "You should take a shower, Serafina. I will have one of the whores bring you fresh clothes." He turned and disappeared with a soft click of the door.

The air left my lungs in a whoosh. I wrapped my arms around myself, trembling, trying to keep it together. It had taken considerable effort standing up to Remo, and now everything fell off me in waves of emotion. I stiffened when I remembered the camera, but then I decided it didn't matter. Remo knew I was terrified of him. My brave front wasn't fooling him.

REMO

Serafina was everything I'd hoped for and so much more. A queen in my game of chess, indeed. Noble and proud like a queen and arrogant and spoiled like one too. She made me want to break her. Break those white wings. An angel in appearance but one with clipped wings, happy to be grounded, happy to never roam the sky. Content to become the beautiful tamed bird in Danilo's gilded cage.

I emptied my scotch and hit the bar. Jerry refilled my glass. The whores had gathered at the other end of the bar as far away from me as possible. As usual.

"She's so beautiful," the whore who had brought Serafina clothes said to the others.

She was. Serafina was a masterpiece, almost too beautiful. Her golden hair and unblemished skin against the dirty mattress had felt like sacrilege, even to me, and I had committed almost every sin conceivable.

I drank another scotch, considering returning to the basement, to Serafina. *Whatever you take, it'll always be less than what he would have gotten. You will have to settle for the consolation prize.*

Her words were an insistent pounding in the back of my head. And fuck, I knew she was right. Taking from Serafina what I wanted wouldn't feel like a victory. There was no challenge in doing so. She was weaker and at my mercy. I could have her in every way by the morning and be done with it, but it would feel like a fucking defeat. It wasn't what I wanted. Far from it. I had never settled for a consolation prize. I didn't want less than what she would have given to Danilo. I wanted more. I wanted everything from her.

I slammed the glass down on the counter and turned to the nearest whore. "In my office. Now."

She nodded and rushed off. I followed her, already painfully hard. Fucking hard since I'd seen Serafina in her underwear. Fucking desperate to bury myself in her pussy and rip her innocence from her. I always got what I wanted. I didn't wait for anything. But if I wanted the ultimate triumph, I would have to try my hand at patience, and it would be the biggest challenge of my life.

The whore perched on my desk but got up when I entered. I unzipped my pants and shoved down my briefs. She knew her cue. We'd fucked before. I often chose her. She got down on her knees as I tangled my hand in her red hair and started fucking her mouth. She took all of me as I thrust into her, hitting the back of her throat, making her gag, but for once it did nothing to sate the burning hunger in my veins. I scowled down at her face, trying to imagine it was Serafina, but the whore regarded me with that fucking submissiveness, that disgusting reverence. No pride, no honor. They all got a choice and chose the easy way, never the hard painful one. They would never understand that nothing could be gained without pain. Weak. Disgusting.

I tightened my hold on her hair, causing her to wince, as I came down her throat. Stepping back, my dripping cock slid out of her mouth. She peered up at me, licking her lips like I had given her a fucking gift. My fingers itched to reach for my knife and slash her throat, relieve her of her pitiful existence.

She lowered her gaze.

"Get up," I snarled, losing my patience. She scrambled to her feet. "Desk."

She turned around and bent over the desk, sticking her ass out, then reached behind herself and pushed her skirt up, revealing her naked ass. She parted her legs and braced herself against the desk. No pride. No honor.

I stepped up behind her, pumping my cock, but I was already getting hard again. I reached for a condom, ripped it open with my teeth, and rolled it down my dick. Spitting down in my hand, I lubed my sheathed dick then pressed up against her asshole and began pushing into her. The whore's knuckles turned white from her grip on the desk. When I was buried up to my balls in her ass, I leaned forward until my chest was flush with her back, and for the first time she tensed. I never got this close to her. I brought my mouth close to her ear as my fingers clamped down on her hips.

"Tell me, Eden," I whispered harshly. She held her breath hearing me say her name. I never had before. They thought I didn't know their names, but I knew every fucker I owned, soldier and whore. "Have you ever considered telling me to go fuck myself?"

"Of course not, Ma . . ."

"What did you want to call me? Master?" I slammed into her once, making her gasp. "Tell me, Eden, am I your fucking master?"

She hesitated. She didn't even know how to answer that fucking question, and it made me furious. "I'm not your fucking master," I growled.

"Yes," she agreed quickly.

I turned her face so she had to stare into my eyes. "Do you have a sliver of honor in that used up body of yours?" I asked gently.

She blinked.

My mouth pulled into a snarl. "No. Not one fucking ounce." I gripped her neck and started thrusting into her. She winced and it made me raving mad. Still slamming into her, I muttered in her ear, "Do you ever wonder where Dinara is?"

She tensed under me, but I didn't let up. "Have you thought of her at all?"

She let out a sob. She had no right to cry, no fucking right, because she wasn't crying for her daughter but only for herself. A fucking disgrace of a mother. "Do you ever wonder if I do to your little girl what I do to you now?"

She didn't say anything. I straightened and kept fucking her until I finally came. I stepped back, thrust the condom down on the ground, and cleaned myself with a towel that I kept handy before I pulled up my briefs and pants.

She turned, mascara smudged under her eyes, and I tossed the towel at her. "Clean yourself. And dispose of the fucking condom. It's dripping my cum all over the floor." She picked up the towel from the floor and wiped the floor first then cleaned herself. Dirty whore.

"Get out of my sight before I kill you," I said.

She rushed past me, opened the door, and almost bumped into Savio, who stepped back with a disgusted expression. He cocked an eyebrow as he stepped in. "You're still fucking that bitch? Why don't you just kill her like she deserves?"

"She doesn't deserve death. It would be too kind to kill her." And I gave Grigory my word that the bitch would suffer.

Savio nodded. "Maybe. But I thought you'd be up virgin pussy, not this used up piece of trash."

"I'm not in the mood for virgin pussy."

Savio looked curious. "I imagine it'll be really tight and kind of hot knowing you're the first to be in there."

"Never been with a fucking virgin, so I can't fucking tell you. Is there a reason why you're here disturbing my post-fuck-fury?

"What's the difference between that and your pre-fuck-fury? Or your general mood for that matter?"

"You're a fucking smart ass like Nino."

Savio sauntered in and leaned his hip against the desk. "I thought I'd tell you Simeone went into the basement with a tray of food for your girl and didn't come back up yet."

I shoved past Savio, so fucking furious I had trouble not killing every single person in the fucking bar. I raced down the stairs when I heard Simeone's cackling and spotted him in the doorway to Serafina's cell, not inside of it. I slowed, knowing there was no rush. He wasn't that stupid. Stupid enough, but not so stupid to try touching something that was mine.

"Get out, you disgusting pervert," I heard Serafina's voice.

"Shut up, whore. You aren't in Chicago. Here you are nothing. I can't wait to bury my cock in your cunt once Remo is done breaking you in."

"I won't shower in front of you. Get out!"

"Then I will call Remo and tell him to punish you."

Oh … so he would call me? Interesting. I stalked closer, not making a sound. Simeone's back twitched like he was busy jerking off, which was probably the case.

My mouth pulled into a snarl, but I held back my anger.

More silence followed and I approached without making a sound. Simeone's profile appeared in my view, leaning in the doorway with his hand clutching his ugly dick as he rubbed it furiously. I stopped a few steps from him, and there was Serafina in the shower, her back turned to him.

Simeone was practically salivating on the ground and jerking off, watching Serafina shower. She was a sight to behold, no argument. Her skin was pale like marble. Her ass two white orbs I wanted to sink my teeth into. There wasn't a blemish on her body, not a single imperfection, so unlike my own. She had been protected all her life, kept safe from the dangers of this world, and here she was at my mercy.

"Turn around. I want to see your tits and cunt," Simeone ordered, his hand moving faster on his cock.

Simeone was so wrapped up in watching her and wanking off, he didn't notice me. "If you don't turn around, I'll call Remo."

"I won't turn around, you pig!" she hissed. "Then get Remo. I don't care!"

"You little whore! I will turn you around myself."

Simeone made a move as if to push off the doorway, when Serafina turned around, one arm wrapped protectively over her breasts, the other hand shielding her pussy. The water pouring down her face almost hid her tears. She gave Simeone the most disgusted look I'd ever seen, her head held high ... and then she spotted me.

"See, that wasn't so difficult, was it?" Simeone rasped.

My lip curled. I pulled the knife from my holster, slid my fingers through the knuckle holder, relishing in the feel of the cold metal against my skin. She watched unmoving as I stepped up to Simeone. Her perfect proud lips wouldn't utter a warning.

I wrapped my arm around his throat in a crushing grip and pressed my knife against his lower abdomen. He cried out in surprise and let go of his cock. "You were going to call me?" I asked.

His terror-widened eyes blinked up at me as his face turned red from the pressure of my grip. I loosened my hold so he could speak.

"Remo, I made sure she wasn't messing around. It's not how it looks."

"Hmm. Did you know that no man has ever seen what you just saw?"

He shook his head frantically. I lifted my gaze to Serafina, who was watching with a frozen expression.

"You see, now you have seen something that I had no intention of sharing," I explained in a pleasant voice. I slid the knife into his abdomen, only a couple of inches. He cried out, flailing in my grip. I held him fast, my eyes never leaving Serafina. Blood trickled down over my hand. His filthy blood.

Serafina dropped her arms to her side. I didn't think she noticed. She stared at me in open horror. For once her prideful mask had slipped and revealed her true nature: a softhearted, breakable woman. And I took in the sight of her firm breasts and the golden curls at the apex of her thighs, perfectly trimmed into a triangle. For her wedding night. What a pity that poor Danilo would never get to see it. She was mine for the taking.

"Remo," Simeone spluttered. "I won't tell anyone what I saw. Please, I beg you."

"I believe you," I said mildly. "But you will *remember.*" I drove the knife deeper into his flesh, moving slow, letting him savor every inch of the blade. "Did you imagine how it would be to sink your filthy cock into her pussy?"

He gurgled.

The knife was buried to the hilt in his abdomen. "Did you imagine to bury yourself to the hilt inside her?" His eyes were bulging, his breathing labored.

I twisted the knife and he screamed again. Then I pulled it back out as slowly as it had gone in. His legs gave way, and I let him drop to the ground. He clutched his wound, crying like a coward. It would be another ten or fifteen minutes before he died. He'd wish it were less. "Remember what I told you about your eyeballs and tongue? Your cock will join them."

I brought the knife down on his cock, and Serafina whirled around with a gasp.

SERAFINA

My hands were splayed out against the white tiles of the shower. I couldn't breathe. Terror clogged my throat. Nothing in my upbringing had prepared me for this. Nothing could have. I was falling apart fast. Faster than I'd ever thought possible.

Pride and honor were the pillars of our world, the pillars of my upbringing. I needed to cling to them. He could take everything from me, but not that. Never that.

Simeone was screaming and I pressed my palms against my ears, trying to shut him out—to no avail.

Ice Princess no more.

My eyes were blurry from tears and water. But the image of Remo sinking his knife into a man with that twisted smile on his face was etched into my mind. How was I supposed to stay prideful? How was I supposed to hold my head high and not let him see my fear? Nothing had ever scared me more than Remo Falcone.

Monsters aren't real, my mother had told me a long time ago when I was afraid to sleep in the dark and kept crawling into Samuel's bed. I hadn't believed her back then, and that was before meeting Remo.

The screaming stopped.

I shuddered and lowered my hands slowly. Something red caught my eyes. I looked down at the shower floor where red water was pooling around my feet. I blinked. And then it clicked. Floor-level shower. Remo bringing down the knife on the man's ... My feet looked even paler against the red. My vision shifted and something broke apart in me. I was standing in someone's blood.

I heard myself screaming and tried to get out of the blood but the ground was slippery. I twisted around, holding onto the shower walls. And then I saw the rest of the cell. The entire floor was covered in blood, and amidst it all stood Remo, tall and dark, knife still gleaming in his hand. His chest and arms were smeared with blood. Red. Red. Red. Everywhere.

I was still screaming and screaming until I couldn't scream anymore because there was no air left in my lungs. And I could not breathe.

Remo sheathed his knife and stalked toward me.

I flailed, trying to get away from him, from the blood, from the sight of the dead man behind Remo.

My feet slipped on the floor, and I was falling. My knees sank into the blood, my hands followed.

Remo pulled me up, my body pressed against his, and the smell of blood filled my nose. I clutched at his shoulders for balance. And then I pulled one

50

hand back and it came away red. And one glance down. Red. My skin. Red. Everything red.

My eyes found Remo's blood covered body. Red. Red. Red.

I started struggling against his hold. I fought with all I had. "Please," I gasped out. Remo lifted me in his arms, and I had no fight left in me. He carried me barefoot through the cell, stepping over the dead man. When had he got rid of his shoes?

A hysteric laugh bubbled up my throat, but it turned into a sob. This was too much.

Remo walked into another cell and set me down on the floor of the shower. I sank down, curling up on my side, unable to remain in a sitting position. My chest was heaving, but I wasn't breathing. Through my foggy vision, I watched Remo getting out of his bloody clothes and coming toward me. Naked. I didn't register more than that.

I closed my eyes.

He moved his arms under my knees and back and lifted me once more. Then cold water splashed down on me, and I sucked in a deep breath, my eyes shooting open. Remo shifted with me in his arms, leaning forward, his forehead pressed against the tiles as he looked down at me. His body shielded me from the cold water raining down on us, and his dark eyes held mine.

"It takes a while before the water gets warm down here," he said calmly.

So calm. My eyes searched his face. Eerily calm. No sign that he had just killed a man in a barbaric way. I shuddered, my teeth chattering. Even when the water turned warm, my teeth kept clanking together, and they didn't stop even when Remo stepped back out of the shower with me still in his arms.

Remo walked out of the cell and carried me through the corridor. Panic tore at my chest.

"Fuck," someone said. A man.

"Get me a fucking blanket, Savio," Remo growled.

He tightened his hold as he carried me upstairs. I closed my eyes, too shaken to put up a fight. Something soft and warm covered me, and then I was put down on warm leather.

"You can't drive through the city naked. And there's still blood on your body."

"You can drive," Remo said, and then his body eased in beside me.

"Where the fuck are we taking her?"

"Home."

"Nino won't like that one fucking bit. You know how protective he is of Kiara."

"I don't give a fuck. Now shut up and drive."

I focused on breathing, focused on remembering what made me happy. Samuel. Mom. Dad. Sofia.

I wasn't sure how much time had passed. The minutes seemed to blur together, when Remo picked me up again and eventually put me down on something soft. My eyes peeled open, heavy-lidded and burning from crying.

The first thing I registered was the bed I was lying on. Soft satin sheets, blood-red. A majestic canopy bed made from black wood, the posts twisting as if two branches had wound around another to form each. Heavy blood-red drapes hung from the canopy, blocking the bright sunlight streaming into the bedroom. I put my trembling hand flat against the smooth sheet, white against red, like in the shower. I shuddered and started hyperventilating again.

Remo appeared beside the bed and sank down, causing the mattress to dip under his weight. He was naked except for a knife holster, which was strapped to his chest. Muscles and scars and barely restrained strength.

I averted my eyes, my teeth beginning to chatter again. Remo reached over me. "Don't," I said weakly. Then firmer, "Don't touch me."

Remo's dark eyes held mine with intent. He bent low until his face filled my vision. "After what you saw me do today, you still defy me? Don't you think submitting to me will make things less painful for you?" His voice was soft, low, almost curious.

"Yes," I whispered, and something shifted in his eyes ... was that disappointment? "But I'd rather take pain than submit to your will, Remo."

He smiled darkly and reached over me again. Before I could react, he pulled a blanket over my body, covering my nakedness. My eyes widened.

"How can you know what you prefer if you've never experienced either? Neither pain..." he brushed his lips lightly across my mouth, not a kiss but a threat "...nor pleasure."

A shiver traveled down my spine. My throat was dry, my limbs heavy.

"I want to show you both, *Angel*." He paused, his dark eyes burning into me. "But I fear you'd rather kill yourself than give yourself to me." He pulled his knife out and put it down beside me. "You should end your life, take the easy way out, because nobody will come to save you, and I won't stop until I've broken you, body and soul."

I believed him. How could I not with the intense determination and coldness in his dark eyes? I reached for the knife then pushed into a sitting position and pressed the blade against Remo's throat. He didn't flinch, only regarded me with unsettling eyes.

"I won't ever kill myself. I won't do that to my family. But you will never break me. I won't let you."

Remo tilted his head, again with a hint of curiosity. "If you want to kill me, do it now because you won't get another chance, *Angel*." My hand holding the knife shook. Remo didn't take his eyes off me as he shifted closer to me, climbing up on one knee then the other until he leaned over me. I pressed harder and blood welled to the surface. My eyes focused on the red coating the blade against Remo's skin.

Remo moved over me and drove the knife harder into his flesh. I yielded, fixated on the blood trickling down his throat, on its smell, its bright color.

Remo lowered himself on top of me, the knife between our throats, his body covering mine with only the blanket between us. He regarded me, dark eyes peeling away layer over layer of protective walls that I tried to put up.

Hysteria swirled in my chest, the memories of the basement clawing at the fringes of my mind. Remo curled his hand around mine and the handle then slowly pried my hands off it and took the knife from me. He dropped it to the bed beside us.

I could feel every inch of his strong, muscled body against mine, but my eyes couldn't focus on anything but the blood on his skin, dripping from the cut I had inflicted. He pressed two fingers to my throat, feeling my erratic pulse. "Still in the grasp of panic, hmm?"

I swallowed. He pulled away and stood. Then he bent over me. "You are safe in your weakest moments, *Angel*. I don't enjoy breaking the weak. I will break you when you are strong."

He grabbed the knife and turned around, presenting his back to me. My eyes traced the tattoo of the kneeling fallen angel. Was that how Remo saw himself? A fallen angel with broken wings? A dark angel risen from Hell?

And what was I?

Before he left the room, he glanced over his shoulder at me. "Don't try to run, *Angel*. There are more men like Simeone waiting to get their hands on you. I'd hate having to send them after you and hurt you."

As if anyone could hurt me worse than Remo would.

I forced a smile. "We both know you're lying. You won't let anyone hurt me."

Remo cocked one dark eyebrow. "I won't?"

"You won't because you want to be the one to break me, to make me scream."

Remo's mouth pulled into a smile that raised the little hairs on my skin.

A smile that would haunt me forever.

"Oh, I will make you scream, *Angel*. That I swear."

Suppressing a shudder, I dug my nails into my palms and forced more words from my tight throat. "Don't waste your time. Kill me now."

"We all have to let part of ourselves die to rise up stronger. Now sleep tight. I'll return later for a proper video message for your family."

"Why did you even save me from Simeone? Why not let him start the torture you have in mind for me? Why bring me here to your mansion?"

Remo regarded me as if he, too, was wondering the same thing, and his silence told me that my guess had been right; this was indeed the Falcone mansion. It surprised me that he would risk bringing me into his family's home.

"Like you said, I will be the one to make you scream and no one else." He closed the door.

I shut my eyes and pulled the covers tighter around myself.

A power play. A twisted game of chess.

I wasn't going to be a pawn or a queen, and Remo wouldn't be the king.

CHAPTER 5

REMO

grabbed sweatpants to put on before I headed downstairs into our gaming room, where Savio, Nino, and Adamo were sitting. Since Kiara had joined our family, my days of walking through the house naked when I pleased were fucking over. My brothers regarded me as if I was a bomb about to detonate.

I flashed them a smile.

Adamo shook his head but didn't say anything. He didn't try to hide his aversion toward me or his reluctance about becoming a Camorrista.

Nino rose slowly. "You shouldn't have brought her here."

I grabbed the pizza menu. "Savio, order pizza for us and an extra one for Serafina."

Nino came around the sofa. My eyes flickered over the tension in his limbs. "Remo, take her somewhere else."

"No," I said. "She will stay here, under this roof, where I can keep a fucking eye on her."

My brother stopped in front of me, a deep frown pulling his brows together. That was the equivalent of an angry outburst from him. "This situation might cause another one of Kiara's episodes."

"Kiara is your wife, not mine. Make sure she doesn't see anything that she isn't supposed to see. Where is she anyway?"

"In our wing. The moment Savio told me you were bringing Serafina, I told her to stay there."

"See? No problem." I moved past him toward the bar and grabbed a beer. Nino followed as Savio ordered pizza in the background.

"It is a huge problem. Your captive is upstairs, free to roam the place as she sees fit. She could walk around the house and cross Kiara."

"I doubt Serafina will do that right now. She's too shaken and probably taking a beauty sleep as we speak. She can't escape from the premises, and one of you will have to guard her to make sure she doesn't do something stupid."

Nino assessed me. "I really hope you know what you're doing. This is supposed to bring the Outfit down. Don't forget that, Remo."

My mouth pulled wide. "It will crush them. They will bleed out slowly, painfully, without ever feeling my blade. This will destroy them."

Nino gave a nod because even if emotions were still hard to grasp for him, he knew the effect mind games had in a war.

"You disgust me," Adamo muttered.

"Four days," I reminded him.

He stood, jutting his chin out. "What if I say no?"

Savio shoved him. "You'd be a fucking disgrace, a traitor. What would you do? Where would you go?"

Adamo shoved him back. "I don't give a fuck. Anything is better than becoming like you."

I stalked toward him. He lifted his chin. "You say this because from the day of your birth you've been protected. You've never been subjected to true cruelty. You are a Falcone, Adamo, and one day you will be proud to be one."

"I wish I wasn't a Falcone. I wish you weren't my brother."

"Adamo," Nino warned, looking at my face.

"Fuck you!" Adamo shouted and ran off upstairs.

"He'll come around, eventually," Nino drawled.

"How much time until the pizza arrives?" I asked Savio.

He exchanged a look with Nino before replying, "Twenty minutes."

"Time for a phone call," I said, nodding at Nino, who hesitated briefly but then took out his mobile and scrolled through it.

Nino handed me the phone with the number I didn't recognize. "That's Dante's number if he hasn't changed it from our last call years ago."

"Good. Get some of Kiara's clothes. A white nightgown if she has one."

Nino frowned deeply but walked past me and disappeared into his wing.

"How are you going to keep her in check? Make sure she doesn't try to run or kill herself?"

"She's been sheltered all her life. She's far from home, far from the men who've protected her. Freedom scares her more than captivity."

Savio laughed. "You sound awfully sure of it."

I grinned. Nino returned, looking as close to pissed as he ever did. He held the clothes out to me. Among them a silvery satin nightgown. Perfect. "Kiara suspects something's the matter."

I took the clothes, not bothering to comment, and walked past him toward my wing where I barged into Serafina's room without knocking. My eyes wandered from the empty bed toward the wall behind it, where Serafina tried opening the window, which she couldn't do without the necessary keys.

She whirled around, the blood-red sheets wrapped around her body, her blond hair a wild mane slithering down her shoulders. Her skin glowed so innocently white against the red of the covers. I wanted to run my tongue over it to see if it would taste as pure as she looked.

Not cowering in the bed as I'd expected but trying to escape. This little birdy seemed desperate to escape my cage, only to flutter right into Danilo's. Her eyes and face held remnants of her earlier panic, but she tilted her chin upward and narrowed her eyes at me. Determined to play with the big boys.

I strolled into the room. Her shoulders pulled back, an act of defiance, but her hand flew up to press the sheet against her body, her fingers splayed out against the red, visibly shaking. My eyes never leaving her, I set the clothes down on the bed, catching the hint of her sweet scent. I'd caught it earlier, as if she'd been massaged with vanilla oil in preparation for her wedding night. My nostrils flared. "Trying to escape my cage, little bird?"

She tossed me a haughty look. "You're awfully fond of creatures with wings."

"I enjoy breaking them."

Her lip curled, and still she managed to be perfectly beautiful. I could guess the images that ran through her mind, of me torturing tiny animals. That was for cowards, for men not capable of facing a worthy opponent. "I'm not that kind of psychopath."

"What kind are you, then?"

I smiled. "You won't be able to open the window. Don't waste your energy trying to escape."

"Did you have the locks installed specifically for me, or do you make a habit of locking women in your bedroom so you can rape and torture them for your personal entertainment?"

I stalked toward her, backed her against the windowsill then braced myself against the glass, glaring down at her. "No," I said. "My father had them installed for my mother."

Disgust flashed across Serafina's face. "You Falcones are all monsters."

I leaned down, breathing in her scent. "My father was a monster. I'm worse."

Her pulse thudded in her veins. I could see her fear throbbing against the unblemished skin of her throat. I stepped back then nodded toward the clothes. "For you. Tomorrow morning you will wear the silver nightgown."

Serafina walked toward the bed sideways to keep an eye on me then scowled at the heap on her bed.

I raised the phone to my ear and pressed the call button. After the second ring, Dante's cold voice sounded. "Cavallaro."

"Dante, good to hear your voice."

Serafina's head jerked toward me, and she sank down on the bed, her prideful mask cracking as her fingers curled into a fist, gripping the sheet.

Silence rang on the other end, and I smiled. I wished I could see Cavallaro's expression as he was being faced with the consequences of his actions, and the realization that his niece would pay for his sins.

"Remo."

I heard male voices in the background and a hysteric female one. Serafina's mother. "I would like a word with you, Capo to Capo. From one man who had his territory breached to another. Two men of honor."

"I'm a man of honor, Remo. I don't know what you are, but honorable isn't it."

"Let's agree to disagree on that."

"Is Serafina alive?" he asked quietly.

I trailed my eyes over the glaring woman, clutching the red blankets around her naked body.

I heard a furious voice in the background. "I will break every fucking bone in your body!"

"Is that her twin?"

Pain flashed across her face, and she swallowed.

"Is she alive?" Dante repeated, his voice shaking with anger.

"What do you think?"

"She is, because alive she is worth more than dead."

"Indeed. I don't have to tell you that I will kill her in the most painful way I can think of if a single Outfit soldier breaches my territory to save her, and I can be very creative when it comes to inflicting pain."

Even from a distance I could see her blood pounding furiously in her veins as she stared down at her fist.

"I want to speak to her."

"Not yet."

"Remo, you crossed a line, and you will pay for it."

"Oh, I'm sure you think so."

"What do you want?"

"It's not time for that kind of conversation yet, Dante. I don't think you are quite ready for it. Tomorrow morning we will have another date. Set up a camera. I want you, her brother, father, and fiancé in a room in front of that camera. Nino will give you instructions how to set everything up. I will set up a camera myself so we can see and hear each other."

Serafina's eyes met mine.

"Remo—" Dante's voice held a warning, but I lowered the phone from my ear and ended the call.

Serafina stared at me, wide eyed. I moved closer, and she stiffened but otherwise didn't show her fear, despite the exhaustion on her face. "Tomorrow we will start playing, *Angel.*"

I left, wanting her to ponder my words. Nino waited in the corridor as I closed the door. I raised my eyebrows in passing. "Pizza's arrived?"

Nino followed close behind me then grabbed my shoulder. "What kind of video do you have in mind for tomorrow?"

I regarded him, trying to gauge his mood, but even now it was still difficult. "I'll give her a choice."

Nino shook his head once, almost disapproving. "This woman is innocent. She's not a debtor. Not a whore who steals money. She hasn't done anything."

"Kiara changed you."

"Not in this regard. We've never preyed on the innocent, Remo. We've never laid a hand on someone who didn't deserve it, and this woman, this girl … she did nothing to deserve that choice."

I held his gaze. "You know me better than anyone else," I murmured. "And yet here we stand."

Nino tilted his head, gray eyes narrowing. "You're playing a dangerous game. You don't know your opponent well enough to be sure of her choice."

"She will choose what they all do, Nino. She's a woman. She's been coddled all her life. She will take the easy way. I want to hear her say it in front of that fucking camera, want Dante hear his niece offer her fucking body to me, want them all to hear it, and she will."

Downstairs, I grabbed one of the pizza boxes before I returned to the guest bedroom in my wing. This time, Serafina sat on the bed and didn't look up when I entered. She held the silver nightgown in her hands. "What if I refuse to wear it?"

"You can wear your nightgown for the show or be naked. Your blood will look just as enticing against your white skin as it would against the nightgown."

A small shiver rippled through her body, and she let the piece of clothing flutter to the ground at her bare feet.

I walked closer. "Here. You haven't eaten in more than a day." I set the pizza box down on the nightstand.

She eyed it suspiciously. I waited for her to shove it away, to try punishing me by starving herself, like my mother had always tried with our father. It hadn't worked with him, and it wouldn't work with me.

"I hope it's poisoned," she muttered then reached for a slice and took a big bite. She chewed then raised her eyes to mine. She swallowed almost defiantly. "Are you going to watch me eat?"

Maybe breaking her wings wouldn't be as easy as I'd thought.

Early the next morning Fabiano came over. I was doing kicks against the punching bag in our game room, needing to release my pent up energy.

He leaned against the doorframe, assessing me for a couple of heartbeats.

"Say what you've got to say," I growled and landed a hard kick.

"Jerry called me into the Sugar Trap a couple of hours ago so I could deal with the mess you created. I found Simeone with his cock stuffed into his mouth. I'm not sure I want to know what happened."

I narrowed my eyes. "If you didn't want to know, you wouldn't be here."

He pushed away from the doorframe and moved toward me. "Did he touch her?"

I stopped my kicks. "He didn't. He thought he could watch Serafina showering."

Fabiano evaluated my face. "Where is she?"

"In bed."

His eyebrows rose. "In your bed?"

I didn't say anything, but I met his eyes straight on.

He sighed. "So, you ..." He searched for the right word then gave up. "I thought you wanted to use her virginity as leverage against Cavallaro and her fiancé?"

I tried to gauge Fabiano's feelings, but he was too good at masking them. If he put that kind of effort into hiding his feelings, he would only disapprove of me taking Serafina with force.

I stalked toward him. "Do you harbor feelings for her?"

He grimaced. "Really? I have Leona. I'm not interested in Fina."

"But you don't like the idea of me hurting her?"

"You are Capo. You do with her whatever you want, but no, I don't like the idea of you punishing her for something the Outfit did."

I respected Fabiano for his honesty. Most men were too cowardly to tell me the truth to my face. "Then you should leave now because I have a call set up with Dante and her family in two hours, and Serafina will play the leading role."

He looked away, a muscle in his cheek twitching. "I should return to Leona."

"You do that. Go to your girl. And I will go to mine."

"She isn't yours, Remo. She didn't choose you. That's a big difference," Fabiano said before he turned and left. I returned to the punching bag and kicked it harder than before.

SERAFINA

Even the next morning, the pizza lay heavily in my stomach, but at least now my stomach was churning for another reason than terror. I considered eating another piece for breakfast. I needed all the energy I could get if I wanted to figure out a way to beat Remo at his own game because no matter how sheltered I was, I knew Remo wouldn't have set up a video call with my family if he didn't know he had something to show them that would hurt them.

I barely slept through the night. Remo hadn't locked my door after he left, but I didn't try venturing outside, fearing it was a trap. I was still too shaken to plan my flight in a way that would guarantee its success.

I slid the satin nightgown over my head, even if I didn't want to give Remo even that small victory, but I'd have to pick my battles if I wanted to survive.

Steps in front of the door made me stiffen, and I got up from the bed, preferring to stand when facing Remo, but it wasn't the scary Capo who entered. Savio Falcone stood in the doorway, his brown eyes taking in the length of me. I wrapped my arms around my chest before I could think better of it.

"Come," he ordered with a nod toward the open door.

I walked toward him, and he made a move to grab my arm. "Don't you dare touch me," I hissed.

His eyebrows shot up, and he smiled arrogantly. "Then move your pretty ass. And take my advice, don't ever talk to Remo like that or you'll find yourself wishing you had never been born."

I sent him a scathing look as I followed him through the house, taking in my surroundings. It was a spacious, twisted place that quickly left me confused. I could feel Savio's eyes on me occasionally, more curious than sexual, but still his presence made me nervous. He was tall and muscled and too confident.

Eventually he led me down a steep staircase into a basement.

"Of course you Falcones have your own underground torture chamber," I muttered, but even I could hear the undercurrent of panic in my voice.

A desolate, abandoned smell hung in the air. Thankfully no excrements or blood.

Savio didn't say anything, but he motioned for me to enter a room on the right. Remo was already inside. "Here she is. I'm meeting Diego. Tell me how it went," Savio said with a laugh.

"You'll get to see the recording," Remo said, his dark eyes locked on mine. "Stand over there," he ordered, pointing at a spot in the center of the room. I followed his command, my brain whirring. The room was empty. No mattress, no chair, nothing except for a table with a camera that was pointed at me.

Remo walked around me, scanning my outfit. The silvery satin nightgown clung to my body, and as my nipples puckered in the cold basement, Remo's eyes were drawn to them. I shivered.

Nino came in as well, and my terror increased as I watched him re-adjust the camera and put a big screen on the table in the corner. He turned the screen so it was facing our way. "Remo," he said, and his brother went over to him. Nino frowned, but Remo touched his shoulder then looked at me. My nails found their way into the soft flesh of my palm.

The screen flashed to life, and on it I saw my family and Danilo, and my legs almost buckled.

Samuel jerked, his eyes so full of despair it tore at me, and Dad had dark circles under his eyes. Dante and Danilo were better at controlling their emotions, but they, too, didn't look their usual composed selves.

"I'm so glad you could make it," Remo said in a British accent, all posh and sophisticated. Wrong. A man like him shrouded in an air of violence and cruelty was anything but an English gentleman.

Remo smiled cruelly at them then turned to me, and his dark eyes flashed with excitement. "Serafina, in Las Vegas women get a choice ..." His voice had returned to its normal, low, threatening vibrato.

"Don't you dare!" Samuel shouted, lunging toward the camera as if it was Remo. Dante gripped his arm to stop him, but even my uncle appeared at the edge of control.

Remo ignored them, except for a twitch of his lip. He pulled out the knife he'd used to slaughter Simeone and showed it to me. "They can pay for their

Twisted Pride

sins with pain or pleasure."

I shuddered. "You have no right to judge other people's sins," I whispered harshly. Remo slowly walked behind me, too close, his breath hot against my neck. My eyes landed on the screen and met Samuel's desperate gaze. He looked on the verge of breaking. I needed to be strong for them, for him and Dad, and even Dante and Danilo. For the Outfit.

"What do you choose, Serafina? Will you surrender to torture or pay with your body?"

I held Samuel's gaze. I'd take my pride to the grave with me. Women were built to give birth. These men could brave pain and so could I.

Remo stepped back into my view. "If you don't choose, I will make the choice for you." His eyes and face said he knew my choice, was sure of it, because I was a woman, weak and insignificant.

I smiled arrogantly. "I will choose the bite of cold steel over the touch of your unworthy hands any day, Remo Falcone."

His eyes flashed with surprise, respect . . . and terrifying excitement. "I will enjoy your screams."

"Remo, this is enough," Dante ordered.

Remo only stared at me, murmuring, "We have only just begun." Without a warning he gripped me, whirled me around, and jerked me against his body—his chest, *every inch of him* pressing against my back and ass. His hand cupped my chin, tilting my head up so I was forced to look at him. He wanted to see my eyes, my expression, my fear and terror when he made me scream.

I returned his gaze with all the hatred and disgust I could summon. I hoped I'd be strong enough to deprive him of my screams, prayed for it. "Where would you like to feel my blade?"

He held the gleaming steel right before my eyes, letting me see the sharp edge of it. I had seen that both Remo's and Nino's Camorra tattoos covered

67

scars on their forearms. Maybe it meant something, maybe not. I had nothing to lose at this point.

"Or did you change your mind about your choice? Will you pay with your body after all?"

I didn't trust my voice because terror clogged my throat, and Remo could see it. I gripped his wrist and guided the knife to my arm until the cool blade touched the soft skin of my forearm, close to my veins.

Something flickered in Remo's eyes and triumph filled me, because for some reason this spot got to him. I kept my hand on his as the blade rested against my sensitive skin.

Remo pressed and I tensed at the slight burn, but he wasn't really cutting yet—as if he couldn't bring himself to do it. I couldn't believe it was because he had reservations about hurting me; this was the cruelest man in the west after all. And it definitely wasn't because he couldn't bear to destroy my unblemished skin. I was sure he'd love to be the first to leave a mark. There was something else holding him back, something dark and powerful. I pushed against his hand, pushed it down on my arm, and the blade cut my skin, but Remo resisted.

I searched his dark eyes, wondering what went on in their depths, terrified of ever finding out. Remo's eyes hardened, turned harsh, brutal, and finally he pressed the blade down and it cut through my skin. Sharp pain burned through me, and I shook under the force of it, my hand still on top of his as he drew the knife across my skin, but not stopping him. For some reason his eyes reflected my pain as if he could feel it more profoundly than I did.

Remo released my chin, his arm snaking around my waist to keep me upright, but I kept my head tilted up, my eyes burning into his. I bit down on my lower lip as a scream clawed up my throat. Copper filled my mouth. Then it spilled over my lip, down my chin.

Remo stopped the blade, something in his eyes keeping me frozen.

"Enough!" Dad roared. "Stop it. Stop it now!"

Remo's brows drew together as our gazes remained locked. He released my waist and stepped back. My legs buckled, and I fell to the ground, my knees colliding with the hard floor. I barely registered the pain. I sat back on my haunches as I cradled my arm in my lap. The cut wasn't as deep as I thought, but blood soaked my silver satin gown, and the blood from my lip quickly joined it. I looked up to see Remo turning off the camera then the screen. Samuel's desperate face disappeared from view.

Nino stood against the wall, his eyes on my wrist and an unsettling expression on his face. Remo had his back turned to me, facing his brother, but his shoulders were heaving.

I forced my body to stand, despite the shaking of my legs, and let my bleeding arm hang in front of me on display.

Nino tore his gaze away and stared at Remo. I wasn't sure what passed between them, not sure I ever wanted to find out.

Remo slowly turned his head, his cruel eyes meeting mine, dark pools of rage leaving me breathless. For once he didn't smirk or smile, didn't look superior or furious. He looked almost confused in his own terrifying, otherworldly way.

And I swore to myself that no matter the price, no matter what it would cost me, one day I would be the one to bring Remo Falcone to his knees, the one to break the cruelest man I knew.

CHAPTER 6

REMO

Nino's expression was strained, but he wasn't about to lose his shit again. He was staring into my eyes, no longer at Serafina. He swallowed then the cold mask took hold of his face and he straightened. My eyes fell to the scars on his wrist covered by our tattoo, then to similar scars on my skin, not as straight, not as focused. I almost touched the fucking scar over my eyebrow like I'd done in the weeks after...

"You will have to stitch her up yourself. You played this game and lost. You underestimated your opponent," he drawled then left, leaving me standing there, fucking furious and fucking ecstatic.

I turned around slowly. Serafina was swaying but trying to stand tall. Her chin was covered in blood from the wound in her lip, from biting down on it to stop a scream. She didn't give me a single one. My gaze dipped lower. Her nightgown was stained with the blood still trickling from the cut in her arm, which she cradled against her chest.

She was supposed to choose differently like all the other women always did. Instead, she'd caught me off guard, had taken the painful road, had forced my fucking hand. She hadn't given me the triumph of offering her body to me on a silver platter in front of Dante fucking Cavallaro and her fiancé. Nino was right. I'd underestimated my opponent because I compared her to the women I'd dealt with so far, but Serafina was nothing like them. Proud and noble. I wouldn't underestimate her again.

And I would get that fucking scream. I would get more than that.

My eyes were drawn to her arm. Why had she chosen that spot? When I looked back up, Serafina met my gaze with one of triumph. She knew she had won.

I stalked toward her, anger simmering under my skin. She tensed, swayed again but didn't fall. I took her arm and inspected the wound. It wasn't deep. I hadn't put enough pressure behind the blade to cut deep. I hadn't wanted to cut her at all, which was a new experience. Seeing the blood on her perfect skin didn't give me the deep satisfaction it usually did.

"How did it feel to hurt me? Does it excite you?" she asked fiercely.

I leaned close, cupping her chin. She held her breath as I trailed my tongue over her lower lip, tasting her blood. I smiled darkly. "Not nearly as much as this."

She jerked back and stumbled, but I caught her, because this wasn't the fall she would take.

"We need to treat your wound."

She didn't protest and followed me silently back upstairs to the first floor, and my grip on her arm held her steady. I led her into my bedroom then my bathroom, where I kept the only medical kit in my wing. Nino was the one who usually handled this kind of shit. She leaned against the sink. "You should sit down," I told her.

"I prefer to stand."

I let go of her and she clutched the edge of the sink to steady herself. I bent down to retrieve the medical kit, but my eyes were drawn to the high slit in her nightgown revealing a long, slender leg. She shifted so her front faced me. I smirked up at her, but her skin was pale and a fine sheen covered her face. I grabbed the medical kit and straightened, regarding her more closely to judge whether she was going to pass out or not. She narrowed her eyes at me and straightened her shoulders with obvious effort.

The corner of my mouth twitched. I took out tissue adhesive. The wound wasn't deep enough to require stitches. I couldn't remember the last time a cut from me didn't lead to stitches—or a funeral.

I took out disinfectant spray, and she stiffened but didn't make a sound when the stinging spray hit her wound, but she did bite down on her lower lip again.

"If you keep doing that, the result will be twice as painful."

She sent me a scathing look but released her bottom lip.

I began to put the adhesive on her wound, feeling a strange aversion to seeing the cut I had inflicted. I couldn't quite define the feeling; it was foreign to me.

"So is this how it's going to be? You cutting me open and stitching me back together?" she seethed.

"I'm not stitching you up. I'm gluing you together."

She didn't say anything, but I could feel her eyes on me. She tapped my forearm with my Camorra tattoo, brushing the crisscrossing scars there. "I wonder who inflicted those cuts," she mused.

I froze and my head shot up. She held my gaze with the same look of triumph I had seen in the basement.

"I wonder who stitched you up afterward? Did you and Nino cut each other in some twisted brotherly ceremony and stitch each other up when you were done? You have the same cuts. Maybe I should ask him."

I pushed her against the sink with my body, my hands clamping down on the marble counter as I shook with rage … and other emotions I would never allow.

Serafina looked at me, despite the fear taking over her perfect features.

"Never mention those scars again. And you won't talk to Nino about this, not a single word, understood?" I growled.

She pressed her lips together, not saying a word. A droplet of blood squeezed past her lips and trickled down on her chin.

Exhaling, I stepped back, grabbed a washcloth and soaked it with warm water. I grabbed her chin but she reached for my wrist.

"Hold still," I ordered, and she dropped her hand and let me clean her chin. Then I took a closer look at her lip. Her teeth had only nicked the upper layer of skin. "You are lucky. This will heal on its own." I was so close to her, her scent hit me again.

Her voice snapped me out of it. "How long will you keep me here?"

"Who says I'm ever letting you go?" I asked in a low voice before I drew back and led her out of my room.

After returning Serafina to the guest room, which I locked this time, I was about to start doing my daily training, kicking the punching bag, when Kiara stormed into the game room. Nino was close behind her and tried stopping her, but she tore away from his grip and stalked toward me, looking furious.

I turned to her, raising my eyebrows. She didn't stop until she was right in front of me and shoved me hard, her eyes brimming with tears. I caught her wrists because she looked like she would slap me next, and that was something we both didn't want to happen.

A second later, a steely grip closed around my forearm. "Release her now," Nino ordered.

I met his gaze, not liking his tone one bit. His grip tightened further. A warning. A threat. We had never really fought against each other, for good reason, and I would lay my fucking life down before I would allow it to happen. But Kiara could be the reason why Nino might risk it.

Savio rose slowly and even Adamo put down his controller.

I let go of her wrists, and Nino unfastened his hold on my arm. He tilted his head in acknowledgment, a silent thank-you.

"What are you doing to that girl?" Kiara asked forcefully.

I narrowed my eyes. "I can't see how that's any of your business."

"It is my business if you are forcing yourself on a woman," she hissed, but her voice shook.

"I'm Capo. I rule over this city. I decide what happens to the people in my territory."

I turned to face the punching bag, but Kiara squeezed in front of it. Fury burned through me, but I shoved it down my throat despite the fucking bitter taste. She was Nino's. She was a fucking Falcone. I grabbed her by the waist and set her to the side like a fucking doll before I faced the punching bag once more. She had frozen under my touch as usual. Unfortunately, that lasted only one fucking second.

She stepped in front of me again.

"Kiara," Nino said in warning, but she glared at him.

"No! Nobody protected me. I won't stand by when the same happens to someone else."

"Get out of my way," I said in a low voice, feeling my own anger rising.

"Or what?" she whispered harshly.

"I said get out of my way, Kiara."

She took a step toward me, bringing us almost chest to chest. "And I said no. It's a mountain I'm willing to die on. I don't care about your vendetta with the Outfit or what happened in your past. An innocent woman won't suffer for it."

I couldn't believe she mentioned our fucking past. Nino should have never told her about it!

Nino moved closer, watching me, not Kiara. Fucking dread flickered in his eyes—something I still had to get used to because my brother had always been emotionless until he met Kiara.

I tried stepping past his wife, but she grabbed my wrist. My gaze darted to her thin fingers then back up to her face. Nino shifted slightly, muscles tensing. I gave him a wry smile. Was he thinking about attacking me? His expression stayed cautious. I met his gaze and twisted my free hand so he saw my tattoo and the crisscrossing scars beneath it. He should know that no matter how infuriating his wife was, I'd never hurt her. His brows drew together, and he relaxed with a small nod.

Kiara tightened her hold. "You protected me from my uncle when he wanted to humiliate me by dancing with me on my wedding. You helped Nino kill him—"

I interrupted her, growing tired of her emotionality. "You can calm down. I want Serafina to come to my bed willingly and not by force. So you can fucking release me now."

She regarded me closely. "She won't. Why should she? You kidnapped her."

"And you were forced into an unwanted marriage to my brother. What's the difference?"

She removed her fingers from my wrist. Nino wrapped his arm around her shoulder. "It's not the same," she whispered.

"The only difference is that in your case your family decided who got you, while Serafina's family had no say in the matter. Neither of you had a real choice."

She shook her head and peered up at Nino with so much fucking love I knew I could never hurt a single hair on her body. She returned her gaze to mine. "Let me talk to her," she said, not asking but *ordering*.

"Is that a fucking order, Kiara?" I asked in a threatening voice. Maybe she needed reminding that I was her Capo.

Nino squeezed her shoulder, but she held my gaze then stepped forward out of his grip and closer to me. "No," she said softly, looking at me with those big brown eyes as if that would warm my heart. "I am asking you for permission as your sister-in-law and as a Falcone."

"Fuck," I snarled and glared at Nino. "Couldn't you have chosen an airheaded wife? She's as good at manipulation as you are."

Nino's mouth twitched and he looked proud. Fucking proud.

"I'm not sure why I put up with all of you," I muttered.

"Does that mean I'm allowed to talk to her?" Kiara asked hopefully.

"Yes. But I should warn you ... Serafina isn't as docile as you are. If I were you, I'd watch my back. She might end up attacking you to save herself."

"I'll take my chances," she said then turned on her heel and headed straight for my wing. Nino followed her because he was obviously concerned for her safety.

I released a harsh breath and kicked the punching bag with so much force the hook ripped out of the ceiling and the bag crashed to the ground.

Savio chuckled as he came up to me. "At first, I really loathed the idea of having Kiara under our roof, but I enjoy her presence more every day."

"Why don't you call someone to fix this fucking bag instead of grating on my nerves."

Savio grinned. "Will do, Capo. I know someone you can release your pent-up energy on. I was supposed to train with Adamo. Why don't you take over? The kid needs a good ass kicking."

"Why don't I just hang you from a hook and use you as a punching bag instead?"

Savio laughed and sauntered off.

Staring at the mess on the floor for another moment, I turned around to Adamo, who had his arms crossed over his chest and was glaring. "Come on, kiddo. Train with me."

Adamo and I had never trained together unless you counted the mock fights I'd entertained him with when he was a small kid and didn't hate my guts yet.

For a moment, he looked like he was going to refuse, but then he pushed up to his feet. He trudged after me in that annoying way he'd adopted recently, just to drive me up the walls. I grabbed my keys then tossed them toward Adamo. "Catch."

He did, frowning.

"You're going to drive us there."

"Really?" he asked and for once wasn't glaring at me.

"Really. Now move. I don't have all day."

Adamo hurried past me, not trudging, and I followed after him, shaking my head and smiling. Nothing got that kid as excited as driving cars or rather racing them.

When I arrived in the driveway, he was already behind the wheel of my new neon green Lamborghini Aventador, grinning like the cat that got the fucking cream. The moment my ass hit the passenger seat, he revved the engine and we shot down the driveway.

"There's a gate at the end. You remember that, right?" I muttered, buckling up.

Adamo hit the button and the gates slid open, and we raced through them with about an inch between the side mirrors and the unrelenting steel.

I shook my head but Adamo didn't slow down. We weaved through traffic, and honks followed us everywhere. A police car shot out of a side alley and started chasing us with sirens howling and lights flashing.

"Oh man," Adamo whined, hitting the breaks and pulling over.

The officer got out, hand on his gun, and strolled toward us while his colleague stayed back, his gun at his side. That was the problem with a new car.

Adamo let the window down, and the officer looked at him. "Get out of the car."

I leaned forward, my forearm with my tattoo propped up against the dashboard and smiled darkly at the man. "Unfortunately, Officer, we have somewhere we need to be."

The police officer registered my tattoo then my face and took a step back. "This is a misunderstanding. Safe travels."

I nodded and sank back against the seat. "Drive."

Adamo looked at me with a hint of admiration in his eyes. Then he pulled away from the curb in a slower pace but still too fast. His mood soured the moment we got out of the car in front of the abandoned casino that served as our gym.

I waited for Adamo in the cage, but he took his sweet ass time getting ready. When he finally shuffled toward me, I really wished he were someone else because I wanted to viciously destroy my opponent. Adamo climbed in and closed the door before he faced me.

He had grown these last few months. He was still much scrawnier than Nino and me, and even Savio, but he was filling out nicely despite his reluctance to fight. His arms hung limply at his side as he watched me with apprehension.

"Come on, kiddo. Show me what you got."

"Don't call me kiddo," he grumbled.

I smiled challengingly. "Make me. So far nothing I've seen has hinted at you being more than a sulking kid."

He curled his hands to fists, eyes narrowing.

Better.

"At least I don't enjoy hurting girls."

So that was what had his panties in a bunch. "You don't enjoy doing anything else with them either," I taunted, trying to finally get him to act on his anger. I couldn't give any less fucks if Adamo was a virgin or not. I didn't understand it one bit, but he could fuck whomever, whenever, however he wanted.

"I like girls."

"Not their pussies, obviously."

He flushed bright red. We still had a lot of work to do.

"Have you kissed a girl at least?" I took a step closer to him.

He looked away and my smile widened. "Who was it? A girl from school? Or a whore after all?"

His eyes flashed with anger, and he charged at me. His kick was surprisingly well placed, but I blocked it with both of my forearms then punched Adamo's side hard—not nearly as hard as I wanted, though. He gasped but still sent several punches my way.

We found a good rhythm, and I could see Adamo getting into it, as if this was one of his annoying video games. I had to admit I enjoyed the sparring. It wasn't more than that, though, because if I had really fought Adamo, the kid would have been on the ground. Eventually, we leaned against the cage, sipping water and dripping sweat.

"I didn't think you'd hold back. I thought you wanted to kick my ass because I'm a fucking disappointment in your eyes."

I lowered the bottle. "What makes you think I held back?"

He snorted. "You are the strongest fighter I know. I wouldn't stand a chance against you."

"Not yet. Maybe one day. And you aren't a disappointment."

He shook his head. "I'll never be like you and Nino or even Savio."

"I don't want you to be like any of us. I only want you to be a Falcone and be proud of it."

Adamo stared at me with a frown then looked down at his bottle. "Can we do another round?"

"Sure," I said, even if I was eager to return to Serafina.

"Don't hold back as much this time," Adamo said.

My lips pulled wide, and I set the bottle down. I should have fought with Adamo before.

SERAFINA

I lay on the bed, staring up at the ceiling, worrying about my family, especially Samuel. He was so protective of me, what if he did something stupid like attack and get himself killed? I wanted to be saved but if something happened to Sam, I wouldn't survive. I'd rather suffer pain and endure Remo's presence than see my brother get hurt.

A heavy weight settled in my stomach when I remembered the look in his eyes when Remo had put the knife against my skin. That look had hurt so much more than the shallow cut. But the cut had given me an important piece of information about Remo. He had a weakness, and it had something to do with those scars and his brothers.

Steps sounded in front of my door and someone knocked. I sat up, surprised. Nobody had bothered to knock.

The lock sounded and the door swung open as I stood, and a young woman with dark hair and dark eyes, wearing a red summer dress, stepped in. She was shorter than me, and must be the source of the clothes Remo had brought me to wear; it explained why the maxi dress I was wearing ended mid-calf.

I had never met her, but I knew who she was. Not a single person in our world didn't know her.

"Kiara Vitiello," I said. The poor Famiglia woman who was thrown to the Falcone wolves to be devoured. Everyone had heard of that union. It had been the gossip of the year among Outfit women. I had only felt pity for the girl, but she didn't appear as if she needed or wanted it.

"Kiara Falcone now, but yes, that's me." She looked over her shoulder with a small frown, and I followed her gaze, finding Nino Falcone standing behind her.

"You don't have to stay. Serafina and I are going to talk. She poses no danger to me."

He was worried I'd attack his wife? Maybe using her as a human safety shield would have gotten me out of the mansion, but I wasn't that brave. If I failed, I knew what that would mean because the look in Nino's eyes sent an icy shiver down my spine.

"I will stay," he said firmly, looking straight at me as he walked in, closed the door, and leaned against the wall. "And if you make a move toward my wife, the consequences will be very unpleasant."

Kiara's cheeks turned red. She gave me an apologetic smile before stepping close to him, touching his chest. I didn't hear what she was saying, but Nino's expression remained stoic. He shook his head once, and she sighed.

She came toward me. I eyed her warily. Not only had she been a Vitiello, but she was now a Falcone. Neither were names that set me at ease.

"I'm sorry. He's very protective," she said with a small smile.

I gave Nino the once-over. "That's obvious."

His expression remained a cold mask. Remo would have given me his twisted smile or that scary signature look, and I had to admit I preferred it to Nino's unreadable face, because I had no doubt that he was just as brutal and messed up as his brother but even harder to read.

Kiara extended her hand. "Call me Kiara."

I hesitated then took it. "Serafina."

Her eyes fell to my arm. "I'm sorry."

"That's not your apology to hand out," I told her as I returned to the bed and sank down.

"I fear it's the only one you're going to get," she said with a hint of disapproval. At least she seemed appalled by her crazy brother-in-law hurting me.

"I don't want Remo's apology. I want him lying at my feet in his own blood."

I sent Nino a smile, gauging his reaction, but his expression didn't change. He might as well have been carved from ice. If he couldn't be taunted into carelessness, my chances of getting past him were nil. If I ever tried an escape attempt, I would have to make sure he wasn't close by.

Kiara's eyes widened a tad as she perched on the edge of my bed, smoothing out her dress. "I think you will have to join the end of the queue. The world is full of people who want the same."

Oh, I liked her. Stifling a smile, I asked, "Are you one of them?"

She pursed her lips. "No, I'm not."

"He's the one hurting you then," I said with a nod toward her emotionless husband, only now something dangerous flickered in his eyes. He definitely wasn't indifferent to his wife.

Kiara glanced at Nino, and the smile tugging at her lips surprised me. "Nino would never hurt me. He is my husband."

She sounded honest and more ... she sounded in love. I'd heard the rumors of what had happened to her and what the Falcones had done to her uncle. Maybe she was just grateful.

"Why are you here?" I asked eventually.

"I thought you'd like female company."

"I'd like to return to my family, to my home. I'd like Remo to stop his twisted games. That's what I'd like," I whispered harshly, feeling bad for snapping at her but not being able to help myself.

She nodded. "I know."

"I doubt you've come to offer your help. You are loyal to the Falcones."

Again, her eyes moved to Nino. "I am. They are my family."

I looked away, thinking of my own family, of Samuel, and my heart clenched tightly. She startled me when she leaned closer, and Nino, too, tensed and straightened. Despite my apparent apprehension, she brought her mouth close to my ear and whispered, "These men are cruel and brutal, but it's not all there is to them. I think you can get under Remo's skin. I wish it for both of you." She pulled away and straightened. "I'll see what I can do so you are allowed to spend your days outside of this room. We could sit in the garden. There's no reason why your captivity should be more unpleasant than absolutely necessary."

I stared at Kiara. She surprised me, but if she really thought anyone could get under Remo Falcone's skin, then life in Vegas had twisted her brain.

CHAPTER 7

SERAFINA

There wasn't a clock anywhere in the room, but it must have been early afternoon by now. Except for the cold pizza and the tap water, I hadn't had anything to eat or drink. Maybe this was another part of Remo's game.

Glancing out of the window, I tried to find the end of the premises, but from my vantage point the gardens surrounding the Falcone mansion appeared endless.

What was Samuel doing now? I closed my eyes. He would blame himself for what happened. I knew him. He had always seen himself as my protector. I wished I could hear his voice, could tell him that it wasn't his fault. And Mom and Dad ...

I hoped they had at least found a way to keep the truth from Sofia. She was too young, too innocent to be burdened with the cruelness of our world.

The sound of knocking followed by the lock being turned made me face the door. I winced at the dull pain in my forearm. A teenage boy in fight shorts and a T-shirt stepped into my room. He had slightly longer curly brown hair and was lean but muscled.

"Hey," he said hesitantly, brown eyes kind. "Remo sent me to get you."

I didn't move from my spot at the window. "What are you, his servant?"

The boy smiled an unguarded, honest smile. A smile few could afford in our circles. "I'm his youngest brother, but that's as good as the same in Remo's eyes."

His kindness confused me. It didn't seem fake. My eyes flitted down to his forearm, free of the markings of the Camorra, the knife and the eye. "You haven't been inducted yet."

The smile dropped. "I will be in two days."

"But you don't want to," I said curiously.

Caution replaced the open friendliness. "We shouldn't keep Remo waiting."

He opened the door wider and gestured for me to walk through. I wondered what he would do if I refused to follow him. He was taller than me and definitely stronger, but I got the impression he would have a hard time laying a hand on me. If he'd been my only opponent, I might have taken my chances, but Remo was downstairs.

Finally, I moved toward him and followed him through the long winding hallway.

"I'm Adamo, by the way," he said.

I glanced up at him. "Serafina."

"I know."

"I suppose you Falcone brothers were all in on the kidnapping," I muttered.

His brows drew together, but he remained silent. There was a hint of . . . embarrassment and disapproval on his face.

After a few minutes, we arrived in the lower part of the mansion, in some sort of entertainment hub with a bar, sofas, TV, and a boxing ring. A punching bag lay amidst rubble, and Remo was glaring down at it as if it had personally insulted him. He, too, was in fight trunks and nothing else.

The memory of how he'd held me under the shower, of how I'd been pressed up to him completely naked resurfaced. I hadn't registered much at the time, and even in the immediate aftermath, but now my gaze trailed over the display of hard muscles, the many scars that spoke of his violent past and present. Every inch of Remo screamed danger. His height, his muscles, his scars, but worse: his eyes.

They found me and as always it was a struggle to meet them. Around Remo you felt like the omega in a pack of wolves. Your eyes wanted to avoid his out of a deeply buried *primal* impulse because Remo *was* the alpha. There was no mistaking it.

Adamo left my side and went over to the sofa, where he plopped down and picked up a controller. A gun lay on the coffee table in front of him.

Remo stalked closer. "Adamo," he clipped, indicating the gun. Damn it.

Adamo grasped it and shoved it under his leg.

"I wouldn't even know how to use it," I lied.

Remo smiled darkly. "You are a good liar." His skin glistened with a fine sheen of sweat as if he hadn't bothered showering after a workout.

"Why did you call me down? Do you have another torture session planned for me?"

Remo glanced down at my wound, his expression hardening—all sharp cheekbones and tight jaw. "There's food in the kitchen for you and something to drink, unless you prefer hard liquor, then this is where you'll get it." He nodded toward the bar to my left where an array of bottles, most of them less than half full, awaited consumption. Scotch, bourbon, whiskey, gin ...

I definitely wouldn't get intoxicated while I was being held captive by the Camorra. "I'm free to walk around the house?" I asked.

Remo smirked. "I don't think we've reached that level of trust yet."

"We won't reach any level of trust, Remo."

Steps echoed out in the hall behind me, and I turned halfway but not enough to lose sight of Remo. I preferred keeping him in my line of vision. As if he knew exactly what I was doing, one corner of his mouth twitched upward.

Savio walked in with that arrogant swagger. "Got someone to fix the punching bag."

Remo tore his gaze from me. "And it took you four hours?"

"Took care of some other business while I was at it," Savio said with a shrug.

Remo shook his head with obvious disapproval. "One day I'm going to seriously lose my shit on you."

Savio didn't look concerned, and I doubted it was because he was as emotionless as Nino. Savio knew he had nothing to fear from his older brother. The realization surprised me, and I filed it away for later use.

"Now that you're here, keep an eye on our guest while she's eating in the kitchen. I'll take a shower then take over her watch."

My mouth curled. "I'm not your guest. I'm a captive."

"Semantics," Remo said.

Maybe in his twisted mind.

"I could have watched her too," Adamo grumbled from his spot on the sofa.

Savio and Remo exchanged a look. Either they worried their younger brother would help me or they worried he wouldn't be able to stop me from escaping. Interesting.

Remo narrowed his eyes at me then strode past me, his arm brushing mine, causing me to draw back.

"Come," Savio ordered. My eyes lingered on Adamo, who was scowling at Remo's retreating back. Maybe the Falcones had a weak link in their midst.

Tearing my gaze away, I followed Savio to the back of the ground floor and through a door, which opened to a huge kitchen.

He pointed toward a pot on the stove. I approached it and lifted the lid, finding a creamy orange-colored soup. "What is it?"

"How would I know?" Savio drawled, sinking down on a chair at the kitchen table. "Probably something without meat. Kiara is vegetarian."

I frowned, trying to decipher the emotion in his voice. I thought I detected a hint of protectiveness when he said her name. Turning on the stove, I took a whiff. "Pumpkin soup," I said.

Savio shrugged. "I'm having a bowl as well."

I stared at the arrogant bastard. Did he think I'd fix him lunch? "Why don't you haul your lazy ass off the chair and get your own bowl?"

He *did* haul his ass off the chair and advanced on me. He braced himself against the stove on either side of my waist, cornering me. "I'm not Remo," he said quietly, "but I'm a Falcone, and I love bloodshed. You better watch your tongue."

I didn't say anything. Savio was scary in his own way. The soup started bubbling behind my back, and Savio finally withdrew, turning around. I opened a drawer to look for a ladle when a plan took form. Remo was upstairs, showering. I hadn't seen Nino anywhere, only Adamo was in the living room, and potentially a workman, who, knowing Vegas, wouldn't come to my help. It was the best opportunity I've had so far.

I gripped the heavy pot by its handles and swung back to gain momentum, but before I could release my hold, Savio whirled around. I catapulted the pot with the boiling soup at him. In an impressive show of reflexes, he lunged to the side, avoiding the pot and most of its contents. Splatters of yellow soup covered him from head to toe. I took my chance and tried to rush past him. His hand shot out, clamping down on my wrist, and he shoved me away with an infuriating air of arrogance. Spinning myself around, my hipbones collided with the edge of the table. I fell forward, my elbows hitting the hardwood, my butt jutting out in an undignified way.

"I like your ass from that vantage point," Savio commented.

"As long as you like it from a distance," Remo warned.

I whirled around.

Standing in the open door, Remo took in the mess on the floor and on his brother. "What the fuck happened here?"

Savio grimaced at his shirt then scowled at me. "That bitch tried to boil me alive."

I straightened, trying to hide my fear of what my punishment would be for the attack, but then Remo laughed, a low rumble that raised goose bumps on my skin.

"I'm glad you find it funny," Savio muttered. "I'm done. Next time you're busy, do me a favor and ask Nino to watch her." He stalked out without another glance.

"Clean that up," Remo ordered with a nod toward the floor, the amusement gone from his voice.

I remained where I was.

Remo walked around the lake of orange on the floor and stopped right in front of me, forcing me to tilt my head back. He cupped my chin. "Let me give you a piece of advice, Angel. Choose your battles wisely," he murmured threateningly. "And now you will clean the floor. I don't give a fuck if your highborn hands aren't supposed to get dirty."

I lowered my eyes from the harshness of his gaze but tried to mask it as me drawing back from his touch. "Where's a mop?"

Remo turned and headed for the door. "I'll be back in exactly two minutes and you won't move a fucking inch, understood?"

I pressed my lips together, a small act of defiance—if it could even be considered that—because Remo knew I'd obey. Very few people would have dared to defy Remo in that moment. I hoped one day to be among them.

REMO

I headed for the utility cupboard. Savio leaned against the bar, nursing a drink and his bruised ego. "Next time you should pay more attention."

He glared. "I think from the two of us, you have more reason to worry. She's yours, not mine. Wait till she tries to boil your dick."

"I can control Serafina. Don't worry." I took a mop and a bucket out of the closet before I returned into the kitchen. Serafina stood at exactly the same spot, frowning down at the floor.

She kept surprising me. The photos I'd seen of her on the internet and the accompanying articles had suggested she was an ice princess. Cold, prideful, fragile. As easy to crush as fresh snow, but Serafina was like eternal ice. Breaking her with force was difficult, not impossible, because I knew how to break, but that would have been the wrong approach. Even eternal ice yielded to heat.

I handed her the bucket and the mop, which she both took without protest. She avoided my eyes as she set out to fill the bucket with water and put it down on the ground. It became apparent pretty quickly that Serafina had never wielded a mop in her life. She used too much water, flooding the floor.

Leaning against the counter, I watched her in silence. She should have taken a rag, gotten down on her knees, and cleaned the floor properly, but I knew her pride would stop her from kneeling in my presence. Proud and strong and painstakingly beautiful, even sweaty and covered with soup.

The floor was still smeared with soup when she finally gave up. "The mop's not working properly."

"It's not the mop's fault. Trust me."

"I wasn't raised to clean floors," she snapped, wayward strands of hair clinging to her cheeks and forehead.

"No, you were raised to warm a man's bed and spread your legs for him."

Her eyes widened, anger twisting her perfect features. "I was raised to take care of a family, to be a good mother and wife."

"You can't cook, can't clean, and probably have never changed a diaper in your life. Being a good mother doesn't seem to be in your future."

She shoved the mop away so it clattered to the floor and moved closer then jerked to a halt halfway. "What do you know about being a good mother? Or a decent human being?"

My chest constricted briefly, but I pushed through it. "I know how to change a diaper for one, and I provided my brothers with protection when they needed it. That's more than you can say for yourself."

She frowned. "When did you change a diaper?"

"When Adamo was an infant, I was already ten," I said. It was more than I had wanted to reveal in the first place. My past wasn't Serafina's business. "Now come. I doubt you can do better than this. The cleaning staff is coming in the morning anyway."

"You let me clean this even though you have people for it?"

"Your pride will be your downfall," I said.

"And your fury will be yours."

"Then we'll fall together. Isn't that the beginning of every tragic love story?" My mouth twisted at the word. What a waste of energy. Our mother had loved our father. She'd hated him too, but her love had stopped her from doing what was necessary. She'd let our father beat and rape her, had let him beat us because it meant he wouldn't lay a hand on her. She never stood up to him. She cowered and worse ... turned his anger toward us to protect herself. Her one act of fucking defiance was to punish our father by killing his sons. She tried to pay him back by killing her own flesh and blood because she was too fucking weak to retaliate in any other way. In a house full of weapons, she couldn't find the courage to ram a blade into our father's back like she should have done the first time he laid a hand on her. She chose the easy way.

"We won't have a love story. Not a tragic one, not a sad one, and definitely not a happy one. You can have my hatred," Serafina said fiercely.

"I'll take it," I murmured. "Hatred is so much stronger than love."

Nino joined me on the terrace in the evening. "Savio told me what happened."

"She's strong-willed."

"She's trouble," he corrected. "Keeping her under this roof poses a considerable risk."

I gave him a wry smile. "Don't tell me you are scared of a girl."

Nino's expression didn't change. "Fortunately, fear isn't among the emotions I've unlocked."

"Then keep it that way," I said. Fear was as useless as love—and even more crippling.

"I'm concerned about Adamo. His initiation is in two days. Keeping Serafina as a captive in the mansion might increase his reluctance to take the oath."

I turned to him. "You think he'll refuse the tattoo?"

Nino sighed. "I don't know. He's slipping away. I can't get him to talk to me anymore. Kiara is the only one he spends time with."

"Adamo is rebelling, but he's still a Falcone. Should I push him more?"

Nino shook his head. "I think that would make him pull away further. We have to hope that he comes around eventually."

"The initiation is in front of our underbosses and captains. If he refuses . . ." I trailed off.

Nino nodded because he understood. Adamo refusing the tattoo would be shameful, a betrayal. There was only one punishment for refusing the tattoo: death.

"I suppose it wouldn't be the first time we'd have to kill a considerable number of Camorrista," I said.

"These men are loyal. It would be unfortunate to dispose of them, and we'd be faced with too many opponents at once."

"It won't come to that."

Nino nodded again and stood quietly beside me. "Have you given Serafina something for the pain?"

"Pain?" I echoed.

"Her wound might sting."

"It's a shallow cut. It can't possibly cause her more than slight discomfort."

Nino shook his head. "That's what I thought when I treated Kiara's wound, but she was surprisingly sensitive to pain. And Serafina won't be any different. Maybe worse. It's probably the first cut she's suffered, probably the first act of violence at all, Remo. She'll feel pain more profoundly than you and I do."

I considered his words and realized he was probably right. From what I'd gathered, Serafina had probably never even been hit by her parents. The first act of violence . . . I didn't dwell on those thoughts. "Do we have anything for pain?"

"I have Tylenol in my room. I can bring it to her after dinner. Kiara is cooking her cheese lasagna again."

"No, I will give it to her when I bring her a slice of the lasagna."

"Okay," Nino murmured, regarding me carefully.

"What?" I snarled, his silent judgment grating on my nerves.

"Originally the plan was to keep Serafina in the Sugar Trap."

"Originally I didn't know what kind of woman she was. And she is safer here. I don't want anyone to get their hands on her. It would ruin my plans."

"I'll get the Tylenol," Nino said, turning around and leaving me standing there.

I went inside and made my way into the kitchen, which smelled of herbs and something spicier. Kiara glanced up from the chopping board. She was slicing tomatoes and throwing them in a bowl with lettuce.

"No one's eating salad around here," I told her as I strode toward her. The tensing of her body was barely noticeable anymore.

"I'm eating it, and Nino will too, and maybe Serafina prefers to stay healthy as well," Kiara said. I stopped beside her and glanced into the oven where a big pan was bubbling over with cheese.

"Serafina has more pressing problems."

Kiara's eyes shot up, and I gripped her hand before she could chop her fingers off. "Nino needs to show you how to hold a knife properly," I demanded then released her.

She put down the knife. "When will you send her back?"

I stared down at her.

She pushed a strand behind her ear, looking away. Kiara was still quick to submit. "You *will* send her back, right?"

Nino came in with the Tylenol, glancing between his wife and me. He frowned but didn't comment.

"When's the lasagna done?" I asked.

"It should be ready now." She gripped the handle, and I stepped back so she could open the oven. She nodded. "Perfect."

Nino took oven mitts and gently pushed his wife to the side. "Let me."

He set the bubbling pan onto the stove, and Kiara smiled at him, touching his arm. "Thank you."

His expression softened, and I still couldn't wrap my mind around it. My brother loved—or whatever he was capable of—Kiara. Taking the Tylenol from his pocket, he handed it to me. "Give me a piece of lasagna for Serafina."

Kiara pursed her lips but did as she was told. "Why can't she have dinner with us?"

"She's a captive," Savio muttered as he came in. He was still pissed because of the soup incident.

"She can be a captive and eat dinner with us, don't you think?" She looked up to Nino for help. He touched her waist and a look passed between them I couldn't read.

Sick of their silent exchanges, I left with the lasagna and the Tylenol. When I stepped into the bedroom, Serafina was sitting on the windowsill, her arms wrapped around her legs. I wondered what kind of clothes she'd worn in Minneapolis. I couldn't imagine she'd opted for floor-length dresses like Kiara. Serafina didn't turn my way when I stepped in, not even when I crossed the room and set the plate down on her nightstand.

"Tell Kiara I'm sorry I wasted her soup."

"Are you sorry?" I asked as I stopped in front of her. Her blue eyes were still firmly focused on the window.

"I'm sorry for wasting it, not for throwing it at your brother. I'm sorry I missed, though. You can tell him that."

I stifled a smile and regarded her closely, her elegantly curved mouth, her immaculate skin. My eyes lowered to her forearm. She held her arm at an awkward angle so it wasn't pressed up against her leg. I held out the Tylenol. "For the pain."

Her gaze fell to my palm. Then she looked up. I could tell she considered refusing, but again she surprised me by taking the pills, her fingertips brushing the scars on my palm. Her blond brows furrowed.

"Those are burn marks, aren't they?"

I withdrew my hand and curled it into a fist at my side. "Eat. I have plans for you tomorrow." I turned on my heel before I walked out and locked her door.

CHAPTER 8

SERAFINA

The next morning I took a quick shower, holding my arm out of the stall so it wouldn't get wet. The painkillers had helped with the sting. I hadn't expected that kind of consideration from Remo, and I suspected he had ulterior motives for the gesture, but it had given me another piece of the puzzle. The scars on his palms held a special meaning. I had a feeling they were connected to the scars his tattoo covered.

The sound of the lock startled me, and I quickly put another one of Kiara's long summer dresses on before I stepped out of the bathroom, my hair still damp and barefoot.

Remo stood with his arms crossed in front of the window, tall and dark and brooding like the love interest in romance movies. He turned and scanned my body. It was unsettling how physical his gaze felt on my skin.

"I'm taking you outside for a walk in the gardens."

I raised my eyebrows. "Why?"

"Would you prefer to spend your captivity holed up in here?"

"No, but I'm wary of your motives."

Remo smiled darkly. "I want to keep you sound of mind and body. It would be a shame if these four walls broke you before I can."

I glared at him, glad he couldn't hear my thundering pulse.

"Now come," he ordered with a nod toward the door, his eyes lingering on my body.

I followed after him and almost bumped into him when he paused in the hallway, glancing down at my feet. "Won't you put on shoes?"

"I would if I had any that fit me. Kiara is a six and I'm a seven and a half."

Remo regarded me a moment before touching my lower back, and I lurched forward in surprise. He indicated I walk ahead, the corners of his mouth tipping up, those dark eyes assessing me.

My body tingled from his touch, and my heart throbbed in my chest. Remo's closeness terrified me, and he could tell. I made sure to keep my distance, but Remo trailed after me, his gaze burning my neck, his tall frame a shadow over my back.

I managed to relax when we stepped outside into the bright sunshine. Remo led me through the sprawling gardens that had different pools, shooting targets set up, and perfectly manicured greenery. The warm grass felt wondrous under my bare feet, but I didn't let it distract me from my main objective: scouting my surroundings.

Remo was oddly quiet, which was unsettling because it meant something was going on behind those dark cruel eyes.

"You can try to run, but you can't escape," Remo said firmly when I scanned the property boundary. The high walls around the premises were topped with barbed wire, and when we walked close enough I could hear the hum of electricity.

"Are you looking for a weakness in our safety measures?" he asked with a hint of dark amusement. "You won't find any."

"Everything, *everyone*, has a weakness. It's only a matter of finding it," I said quietly, stopping.

Remo stepped in front of me, his dark eyes triumphant as they slowly traced the length of me. "And you are Dante's weakness, Serafina."

"I'm only his niece. Dante has condemned so many men to death in his life, do you really think he cares about the life of one girl?"

Remo cupped the back of my head, holding me in place as he brought our faces closer. I let him, softened in his hold, knowing it wasn't the reaction he wanted. His dark eyes searched mine, and I had to fight not to look away.

"I wonder if you really believe it or if you hope I believe it," he said in a low voice.

"It's the truth."

His lips widened in a harsh smile. "The truth is that you are a woman, something precious, something they must protect. It's engrained in them, burned into them irrevocably from the day of their birth. Their honor dictates they keep you safe, and every second you are in my hands, they are failing you, failing themselves. With every second that passes the shame of their failure eats away at their honor. As Made Men we live on honor and pride. They are the pillars of our world, of our fucking self, and I'm going to tear them down pillar by pillar until every fucking member of the Outfit is crushed beneath the weight of their fucking guilt."

My breath had lodged itself in my throat, and I could do nothing but stare at the man in front of me. Maybe he'd underestimated me, but I—and I feared even the Outfit—had underestimated Remo Falcone as well. His actions spoke of barely restrained violence and led you to believe that he lacked any sliver of control, that he could be driven into rash acts. But Remo was dangerously intelligent. A ruthless man with the power and wit to get his revenge.

"Maybe they will feel guilty, but they won't waver. They won't risk any part of the Outfit for me. Not for the soundness of my body, not for my life, and least of all for my innocence, Remo. So take either or all. You won't weaken Dante or the Outfit."

Remo's thumb stroked the side of my throat. I wasn't sure if he did it on purpose or without noticing, and it wasn't the touch but the look in his eyes that made me shiver.

"They will protect your innocence at any cost because it's the only pure thing in their fucking lives. They think your innocence could wash away their sins, but they breathe sin. We all do. One hundred virgins can't wash the sin from our veins. Definitely not from mine."

""Not even an angel?" I murmured, tilting my head up, peering at him through my lashes. My pulse throbbed in my veins, aware of the risk I was taking. But I was forced into Remo's game, willing or not, and I could either be a pawn or a player.

Something in Remo's dark eyes shifted, something hungry and lethal unfurling. He leaned closer, his breath hot against my lips. "You are playing a dangerous game, *Angel.*"

I smiled. "So are you."

His lips pressed against mine. I hadn't expected it. Almost kisses, like threats ghosting over my skin, had been his tactic ... until now. This wasn't a ghost touch. It was substantial, and yet it felt like the promise of a kiss, a threat of what lay ahead. Stunned by Remo's action, I held his gaze. Finally, I ripped away and raised my palm to slap him, but he caught my wrist. He jerked me closer once more.

"That's the kiss Danilo would have given you in church, and maybe even later on your wedding night. Polite. Controlled. Reverent." His voice dipped low. "That's not a kiss."

Anger surged through me. "You—"

Remo's mouth crashed down on mine, fingers bruising my hip as his other hand cradled my wrist between our bodies. His lips conquered mine, his tongue tasting the seam of my mouth, sucking at my tender lower lip, demanding entrance. Heat flushed through me, and my lips parted slightly. Barely. A flicker of submission and Remo plunged his tongue into my mouth, tasting me, consuming me. His taste was intoxicating, his body's heat overpowering. His thumb pressed into my wrist, his palm sliding from my hip to my lower back. Small sparks of electricity followed in his touch's wake.

My head swimming, I was unable to pull back, unable to move at all. Finally, Remo let me free. I sucked in a desperate breath, lightheaded, confused, my body tingling from head to toe.

Remo exhaled. "That, *Angel*, was a kiss. It's the only kind of kiss you'll ever get from me, and it's the kiss you'll use to measure every kiss that follows."

I stumbled away from Remo, shaking. "What have you done?" I stammered. I pressed shaking fingers to my lips, horror striking down on me like lightning. That was supposed to be Danilo's privilege. My first kiss.

Remo had taken it.

No.

I had given it away.

Remo shook his head, glowering. "I cut you with my blade and you didn't shed a single tear, but a kiss makes you cry?"

I turned away, trying to get a grip on my emotions. All my life I had been raised to be the perfect wife, to gift myself to my husband. And just like that I'd allowed Remo to plunder part of my gift. For a moment, I felt like bawling. Then I felt Remo's warmth against my back, not touching but lingering between us.

"Are you scared of Danilo's wrath if he finds out his angel hides a few black feathers beneath the glowing white of her plumage?"

I glanced over my shoulder at his striking face. "You don't know anything about Danilo or me."

"I know your weakness, and I know his."

I faced him once more. "You, too, have a weakness, and one day your enemies are going to use it against you with the same cruelty you bestow upon them."

"Maybe," he growled. "Maybe they'll rise after I've burned down their pride, but not everyone is built to rise from the ashes."

I scoffed. "You sound like a martyr. What do you know about burning?"

Remo didn't say anything, only looked at me with cruel intention, the same expression I'd seen when he'd cut me.

My eyes darted down to the wound on my arm, and Remo's gaze followed. Brick after brick, I was tearing down a wall Remo had no intention of lowering.

Remo grabbed my arm and led me back toward the mansion. I didn't say anything, didn't even look his way. I knew when to retreat, knew when to give in, because this battle had only just begun.

The second I was alone in my room, I headed into the bathroom and splashed cold water on my face to clear my head. Looking up, I cringed at the state of my lips. Red and swollen.

I could still feel Remo's touch, could still taste him. How could I have let that happen? I should have pushed him away, but I didn't. Remo had stopped. Not only had I allowed him to steal my first kiss, I'd enjoyed it in a twisted, all-consuming way.

I walked back into the bedroom and dropped down on the bed, staring up at the dark canopy. Something about Remo overwhelmed me. He had a way of drawing me in. I lifted my arm to stare at my wound. It still felt tender but seemed to be healing. I was glad for its presence; it had not only allowed me a glimpse behind Remo's cruel mask, it also served as a reminder of what he was: a monster. One kiss didn't change that. I couldn't let his manipulation get to me. Remo was Capo. He knew how to make people act how he wanted them to act.

I covered my face with my palms, taking deep, calming breaths. I wished I could talk to Samuel, see his face, be in his arms. Without him, I felt lost. He'd figure something out. My stomach constricted thinking of my brother. If Samuel knew I had allowed Remo to kiss me, hadn't raised even a finger against him to fight him off, what would my brother think of me then? And what about Danilo? He was my fiancé. That kiss had been promised to him.

Samuel remained at the forefront of my mind. He was the person I really cared about. And my family. God, my family. I wished they'd never find out about the kiss, but I had a feeling Remo would tell them all about it.

REMO

A fucking kiss when I wanted so much more. But kissing Serafina had been like the first hit off a crack pipe. It got you addicted from the very first taste. I wanted to kiss her again, wanted to steal every piece of her innocence.

The sound of steps made me look up. Nino was headed my way and sank down on the sofa across from me. He assessed me in that analyzing way he always had.

"What happened?"

"Got a taste of Serafina."

Nino nodded, his eyes narrowing in thought. "You kissed her?"

"Yes, but it won't be the last taste I get of her."

"How did she react?"

"She didn't fight it if that's what you're asking," I said quietly.

He frowned. "I didn't come to talk to you about Serafina. It's obviously a topic you won't allow me to reason with you."

"What do you want to talk to me about, then?"

"I think we should have a conversation with Adamo. Tomorrow is his day, so I want to make sure he's on the same page as we are."

I nodded. "It's probably for the best. Where is he?"

Since he wasn't playing his games, he could only be upstairs sulking or wanking off. Probably the latter considering he didn't get any action. "I got something to sweeten the deal for him," I said.

Nino raised his eyebrows. "Don't tell me you got him a car?"

I grinned. "He's turning fourteen so why not? I'm tired of him crashing my cars. Maybe he'll treat his own possessions with more care."

"The legal driving age is fifteen in Nevada."

"And drugs and homicides are against the law. What's your point?"

"He'll get himself killed in one of our races," Nino drawled. "Are you going to discuss the drug issue with him?"

"I will. Why don't you get him? We'll take him on a test drive and have a word with him."

"Who's going to watch over Kiara and Serafina? Savio went off to meet with Diego again."

"I'll call Fabiano while you find our little brother."

Nino got up and disappeared, and I speed dialed Fabiano. "Remo, what do you need? I'm busy with that asshole Mason."

"Make it quick. I need you here to watch Serafina and Kiara while Nino and I have a talk with Adamo."

"About tomorrow, I assume," Fabiano said. I could hear a man crying in the background.

"Yeah. Be here as quick as possible."

"Fifteen minutes." Fabiano hung up.

Upstairs I could hear a commotion. Adamo was stomping and Nino was speaking to him in a calm drawl.

I stood and moved into the entrance hall, grabbing the keys to Adamo's first car. Nino appeared on the stairs, a disapproving look on his face. Adamo followed close behind him with a scowl on his own baby face. Nino stopped beside me, and I could see that he wasn't impressed by Adamo's antics, which was why he'd gone upstairs and I hadn't. Losing my shit on him today wouldn't help matters.

Adamo came to a halt on the last step with his arms crossed over his chest. "What do you want? I'm busy."

"Calm," Nino murmured to me. After training together, I'd thought Adamo and I had come to a sort of truce. Apparently he'd changed his mind again.

I grabbed the front of his shirt and jerked him closer. I cut him some slack because he was a kid, but my patience had its limits. "Why don't you wipe that sulk off your face, kiddo, or I'll give you a reason for it."

He jutted his chin out. "Do it. Then I'll have another reason to refuse the tattoo tomorrow."

"Adamo," Nino warned.

My fingers tightened and I stared into his eyes long and hard. "Do you think you can survive on your own?"

"I have friends," he muttered.

"Friends who keep you around because you give them weed and crack for free. They don't give a fuck about you. If you can't provide them with free drugs, they'll drop you," I growled.

Adamo blanched. "Who told you?"

"Do you think I didn't notice that someone's been stealing our shit for months now? Fabiano has been keeping a fucking eye on you."

"The punishment for stealing from the Camorra is death," he said challengingly.

"It is," I said. "But not for you."

The entrance door was unlocked, and Fabiano entered, shirtsleeves rolled up, forearms tinged pink. Blood was difficult to wash off.

Adamo's eyes widened. "What did you do?"

Fabiano nodded at Nino and me in greeting.

"Fabiano talked to one of your friends, that useless piece of shit Mason."

"You killed him?" Adamo asked horrified. Fabiano raised one eyebrow at me.

I shook my head. It wasn't time to divulge information yet. Adamo could do the talking.

"Don't hurt Harper," Adamo whispered.

I frowned at the tone of his voice. "That girl in your junkie group?"

Fabiano grimaced. "She was with Mason when I went after him, sucking his cock."

"You're lying!" Adamo jerked out of my grip and lunged at Fabiano, trying to land an uppercut. Fabiano blocked him and shoved him to the ground, but Adamo pushed up to his feet and went for it again. I didn't intervene. Adamo needed to realize that his actions had consequences, and it gave me the time to stomach the fucking truth that my brother had fallen for a useless bitch who probably whispered sweet nothings in his ear in exchange for drugs.

Fabiano grasped Adamo's arm and thrust him face-first into the wall.

"Stop this shit," he warned, "or I'm going to defend myself for real."

He released Adamo, who turned at once, head flushed and eyes full of dread. "What did you do to Harper?"

Fabiano glanced at me. Nino shook his head at me, obviously worried I was going to lose my shit.

"Don't tell me the little slut gave you head in return for drugs, Adamo. You should know better." We had so many fucking whores who could suck cocks, why did he have to find a girl who used him?

Adamo glared. "Harper and I are in love. You wouldn't understand."

"She sucked another man's dick. How does that mean 'I love you?'" I snarled.

"She wouldn't! You're trying to ruin things for me."

Fabiano sighed. "I'm not lying. Mason had his cock shoved up to his balls inside her mouth."

"Shut up," Adamo said fiercely.

"I told you it's difficult to find what you're looking for," Nino told our brother. "People will always try to gain something from being with you."

Adamo shook his head, a stubborn gleam in his eyes. "What did you do to her?"

I nodded at Fabiano.

"Nothing. I sent her away before I beat some sense into your friend."

"He's alive."

"Broke a few of his bones, but alive, yes," Fabiano said.

I should have had him killed. If I had known the exact details, I would have given the kill order.

Adamo looked relieved. "You kept them alive so I'll take the tattoo tomorrow, right?"

"That wasn't the plan," I said. "I thought you'd want to be a Falcone."

Adamo looked away. "You never spare anyone without good reason."

"Get a drug test, Nino," I ordered.

Nino disappeared into his wing.

"I'm clean," Adamo blurted but his voice shook.

I turned my back to him, my fingers curling to fists. Why did Adamo have to make this so fucking hard? I wasn't sure how to deal with his shit, especially the drugs. He needed to realize that he was treading a dangerous path.

"I told the truth," Fabiano said to Adamo.

"Maybe Mason forced her. You don't know anything," Adamo muttered.

Nino returned and motioned for Adamo to follow him into the guest bathroom so he could pee on the test strip. When they emerged and I saw Nino's expression, I lost it. I grabbed Adamo by the collar and threw him to the ground.

"What did I tell you about taking drugs? Do you want to end up like all the lost losers roaming our streets? What the fuck is wrong with you?"

Adamo shrugged. "My friends and I only take it now and then to relax."

I breathed harshly. Adamo lay completely still beneath me. I took a deep breath, stifling the fury burning through me, then got to my feet. "You won't ever take anything again or I will kill every single of your so-called friends. Rich parents or not. And now you will take your new car for a test drive to Harper's home and tell her you won't give her free drugs anymore. If she wants drugs, she can come to me and pay the regular price. Understood?"

Adamo blinked up at me. "Understood," he said slowly, sitting up. "My new car?"

I thrust the keys to the ground beside him. "Bought you that Ford Mustang Limgene in red and black that you've had as your screen saver for months now."

Adamo took the keys. "For my birthday?"

"For your birthday and your initiation. Now talk to Harper and take Nino with you," I said then walked into the living room, straight toward the punching bag. I began kicking and punching, but my rage didn't lessen.

Fabiano joined me after a moment. "I suppose I don't need to watch the girls anymore?"

I didn't say anything. I didn't want to think about Serafina now because if I started thinking about her, I might end up ruining my own fucking plan.

Fabiano stepped in my line of vision. "That girl led him on."

"I know," I growled and sent the bag flying. The hook groaned but stayed anchored in the ceiling. "How about a sparring match?"

"You don't look like you want to spar. You look like you want to destroy someone," Fabiano commented, but he began unbuttoning his shirt. I tugged at my own T-shirt and dragged it over my head then shoved down my pants and swung myself into the boxing ring, wearing only my briefs.

Fabiano did the same and stood across from me. I motioned him forward, and he went into attack mode at once.

We hit and kicked hard and fast. Fabiano's punches spoke of suppressed anger, and my own were fueled with fury. I shoved him into the ropes, but he caught himself. "Is this because of Serafina?" I taunted.

"No," he shot back. "I always enjoy kicking your ass, Remo."

He lunged at me again.

"What's going on here?" Kiara asked from the entranceway.

We ignored her.

"If nobody bothers to give me an answer, I'll head upstairs and talk to Serafina."

"You won't," I ordered, and Fabiano landed a hard punch in my side.

Snarling, I did a sidekick and got his shoulder. "Kiara!" I held up my palm toward Fabiano to pause the match.

She froze. "I thought she could have dinner with us. I have mac and cheese in the oven."

"You won't go anywhere near her without someone to watch your back, understood?"

She nodded eventually. Then her eyes moved on to Fabiano. "Why don't you call Leona. I made enough food so you can join us."

"That's a good idea," I said then jumped out of the ring. It was obvious that I wouldn't get rid of my anger today.

"Will you bring Serafina down, then?"

"No," I said tersely.

"Why not?" Kiara asked, and I stalked toward her. She didn't back off as I stopped right in front of her.

"Because I don't fucking trust myself around her today, okay?"

Kiara nodded, a deep worry line forming between her brows. "Okay."

"I can bring her food up later," Fabiano suggested.

I slanted him a hard look. "Yeah, why not?" My voice rang with warning.

He held my gaze for a long time until he grabbed his phone from the pocket of his pants off the ground and brought it to his ear. I put my clothes back on, not giving a shit that I was sweaty. Kiara trailed after me as I sank down on the sofa. She didn't know what was good for her. Now that she wasn't completely terrified by my presence anymore, she was starting to annoy the fuck out of me.

"Is it because of Adamo?"

"What?"

"Your sour mood."

I smiled darkly. "You haven't seen me in a sour mood yet, and if I can help it, you won't."

She pursed her lips. "He's conflicted. He doesn't want to disappoint you, but he also doesn't want to kill and torture in your name."

I didn't say anything, only returned her gaze until she looked away. She

109

had more trouble holding my eyes than Serafina did.

"He's killed before."

"And he feels guilty for it."

I braced myself on my thighs. "Nobody forced his hand back then. He could have hidden like all the other spectators of the fight. He could have run. He could have shot the asshole's leg or arm, but Adamo shot him in the head. Maybe Adamo doesn't want to be a killer, but he is. It's in our nature, Kiara. He can fight it as long as he wants, but eventually the darkness seeps through. It's what it is."

"Maybe," she agreed.

"Fabiano was a good boy once. Goldilocks with remorse and a squeaky clean white shirt, but now he's my Enforcer."

Fabiano snorted. "I was never good and definitely not goldilocks."

"I should get dinner ready. Can you help me with the mustard jar in the kitchen? I can't open it," Kiara said.

I nodded toward Fabiano. "He can help you."

Kiara shifted nervously, her eyes sliding to Fabiano then back to me. My eyebrows shot up. I got to my feet.

Fabiano gave a small shrug. "Leona will be here in five minutes."

I followed Kiara into the kitchen and took the mustard jar she held out to me. "I didn't think I'd live to see the day that someone was less scared of me than of Fabiano or anyone else for that matter."

Kiara flushed. "I know I'm safe with you," she said quietly.

Fuck, she was. I held out the open jar. "Here."

"Thank you."

"You're safe around Fabiano as well," I told her.

"I know," she said. "But it takes a bit longer for the message to get through to my brain."

"You should be wary of a brain that makes you love my brother and trust me, Kiara," I muttered.

She laughed. "It's not my brain, it's my heart."

I narrowed my eyes then turned on my heel and walked out, not in the mood for emotional nonsense.

CHAPTER 9

SERAFINA

I wasn't sure if it was Remo's plan to break me by letting me stew with my own thoughts all day. I had nothing to do except relive this afternoon's kiss, torn between guilt and a flicker of terrifying excitement, because that kiss had been unlike anything I'd ever felt before. And every time that realization hit me, my guilt doubled. I knew I wasn't supposed to enjoy it—not only because Danilo was the man I was supposed to be kissing, but also because Remo was the last man I was allowed to kiss.

Whenever Samuel had returned from a night out with friends while I was stuck at home, I'd be overwhelmed by a wave of longing and jealousy. I wanted to be free to party with him, but that would have been my ruin—even if Samuel had been at my side to protect my honor. I couldn't be seen in a club, dancing the night away. We'd had a few secret house parties, which had been exhilarating even if Samuel had been glued to my side every second so none of his friends got near me. Not that any of them would have dared. They were all Made Men or on their way to becoming one. My father was Underboss. My uncle was the boss of the Outfit. My fiancé as good as the underboss of Indianapolis and my brother a Made Man. No guy ever looked at me twice, at least not the guys allowed near me. I could have been naked and thrown myself at these guys and they wouldn't have batted an eye … from fear of losing it—and their life.

And I had been okay with it, had accepted it because we were bound by the rules of our world. It wasn't as if I wanted to sleep around like Samuel, even if the few stories he'd shared with me in the beginning when he was overexcited about losing his virginity had made me curious.

The lock clicked and I quickly sat up, bracing myself. I wouldn't allow Remo to catch me by surprise again.

My eyes widened when Fabiano stepped inside, carrying a plate. I stood. Why was he here? Would he help me after all?

Fabiano regarded my face then shook his head as if he could read my mind. "I'm bringing you dinner."

He came in but left the door ajar, and I wondered why he did it. I doubted it was so I could run. Was he worried of being alone in a room with me?

"Here," he held out the plate with steaming mac and cheese to me.

I glared. "Do you remember how you, Samuel and I played together? Do you remember how you and him pretended to be my protectors? Do you remember that?" For a moment we did nothing but stare at each other, but he didn't allow me to glimpse behind his emotionless mask.

With a sigh, he walked past me and put the plate down on my nightstand. "You should eat," he said firmly.

I whirled around to face him. "Why? So I stay healthy just so Remo can break me?"

113

Fabiano glanced down at my arm and grabbed it, inspecting the wound closely. "That's Remo's doing?"

"Who else enjoys slicing up people?"

Fabiano's mouth switched into a wry smile. "Pretty much every man in the mob, Fina."

He touched the wound lightly. "It's not deep."

"I'm sorry that my wound doesn't fulfill your high standards. Next time maybe you should cut me."

Fabiano shook his head. "Remo cuts deep. Hits hard. Kills brutally. He doesn't do half-assed cuts like this."

I tugged my arm free. "So what? Maybe he wants to save the bloody fun for later."

Fabiano's blue eyes searched my face with a small frown. "Maybe."

For some reason, his scrutiny annoyed me. "When people said you were a traitor who ran off with his tail between his legs, I didn't want to believe them, but now I see they were right."

Fabiano leaned down, and the look was one I hadn't seen on his face before, one that reminded me that he was now Enforcer. "I didn't run. I'm loyal."

I huffed.

He took a step closer, and I backed off. "I am. My fucking father sent one of his men out to kill me. That man couldn't go through with it and dropped me off in Bratva territory so they could finish the job for him. Without Remo, they would have succeeded. I'm alive because of my Capo, because of those four Falcone brothers who stood together when the world was against them and against me."

I blinked, utterly shocked by his words. "Your father tried to kill you? Why didn't you tell Dante?"

He glared. "I'm not a fucking snitch. And the Cavallaros have stuck with my bastard of a father for too long. I don't give a fuck if your grandpa thinks highly of him. My father is a disgrace."

"My grandfather is very sick. He probably won't live much longer."

"Good," Fabiano said fiercely.

I swallowed. "Even if my grandfather doesn't hold a protective hand over your father anymore, Dante won't give him to the Camorra. He'll deal with him."

Fabiano smiled sadly. "Dante will hand my father over. Trust me." He took a step back. "I only wished you weren't the one who's going to make it happen."

I touched Fabiano's arm. "I know you can't help me escape, but at least let me talk to Samuel, Fabi. I miss him so terribly."

"That's not his decision," Remo said in a low voice as he stalked into the room. Fabiano gave a terse nod, exchanging a look with his Capo that I couldn't read. Then he walked out without another look at me.

"Trying to talk my Enforcer into betraying me?"

"Unfortunately, everyone I've met so far is loyal to you." It was true and they couldn't even blame it on fear. Despite his reputation, the people close to Remo seemed to tolerate him, maybe even liked him. Remo left the door open as well, and he kept a few arm lengths between us. Something about him was off, and it set my alarm bells off.

"Let me talk to my brother," I said. I couldn't bring myself to say please.

Remo tilted his head, his expression assessing. "What about Danilo? Don't you want a chat with your fiancé? After all, he'd be your husband by now if it weren't for me."

"Samuel. I want to talk to Samuel."

His eyes narrowed briefly before they traveled the length of me. "What do I get in return for allowing you to talk to him?"

"I'm not a whore," I snapped. "I won't give you *that* in return for a call."

Remo approached slowly, like a predator. "You will give it to me for free?"

"Hell will freeze over before that happens."

He backed me into the wall. The violent vibe he gave off was even stronger than usual, and it was starting to make me nervous. I wasn't sure what had him on edge like that, but I knew to be wary.

"Isn't your brother worth a kiss?" he taunted.

"My brother wouldn't want me to give away a kiss for him."

"You already gave away your first kiss, Angel. What do a few more matter?" His dark eyes raked over my face until they lingered on my lips.

I scowled. "One kiss and you'll let me talk to my brother? Tomorrow?"

"One kiss," he agreed with a dark smile.

I pushed to my tiptoes, gripped his neck to pull him further down, and smashed my lips against his for a second before drawing back. "There you go. One kiss."

Remo shook his head, his face still close to mine. "That wasn't a kiss."

"You didn't stipulate the details of the kiss. I kissed you. Now fulfill your part of the bargain."

Remo cupped my face, caging me in with his body. "I showed you what I consider a kiss. I won't settle for less."

I glowered, but trying to stare Remo down was a ridiculous notion.

"Not brave enough?" he murmured.

I shivered at the low vibrato of his voice. Gripping his shirt, I tugged him down violently. Our mouth clashed but Remo held himself still, waiting for me to make the next move, daring me to do it. With a burst of indignation, my tongue nudged his lips and despite the heat rising into my cheeks, I held his dark gaze. My moment of control was ripped from me the second Remo deepened the kiss. He took the lead, demanded with his mouth and tongue for me to surrender. I had trouble keeping up. His scent and heat sucked me in, made my body spring to life in the most terrifying way possible.

Remo's hand touched my waist and then it moved up, closer to my breast. My reaction was instinctual, instilled by defense training with Samuel; I jerked my knee up. Remo's reaction was quick, his hand shooting down, but the momentum still made my knee graze his groin. He growled and I stilled, frozen with fear because of the look in his eyes. He breathed harshly, his gaze burning me with its intensity. Yet a flicker of relief filled me because I doubted I'd have found the strength to end the kiss.

"You shouldn't touch someone without their explicit permission or they might try to defend themselves," I said, because obviously I didn't know when to shut up.

"I don't ask permission for anything," Remo said sharply.

Despite my hands trembling, I pressed my palms against Remo's chest and pushed. He didn't budge, cocking one dark eyebrow. I held his gaze, and he took a deliberate step back, finally letting me free. My eyes darted down to his hands, curled to white-knuckled fists at his side then back up to his face. I shivered at the harshness of his expression and without thinking about it, I looked away and walked toward the window, bringing space between us.

He followed and his breath fanned over my ear as he leaned down. "I'd better leave now. Tonight isn't a good time to be around you. Goodnight, Angel."

His fingers brushed my hair away, and he pressed a kiss to the side of my neck, the tender spot between my shoulder and throat, making me jump in surprise. I clapped a hand over the spot, stunned by the tingling.

The door closed with a soft click then the lock turned. I shuddered out a breath and braced myself against the windowsill. Would Remo allow me to talk to Sam now? I should have asked, but I had been too overwhelmed by Remo's presence.

This game was getting dangerous in more than one sense. The only question was who would lose control of it first?

REMO

I stayed in front of Serafina's door, fingers clutching the handle in a death grip. I had half a mind to walk back in and see how much else I could coerce from Serafina with her brother, but I resisted the urge. Taking a deep breath, I leaned my forehead against the wood. That was how Nino found me.

I saw his legs out of the corner of my eye, and even without looking up, I could imagine the analyzing expression he was giving me. "How did things go with Adamo and Harper?"

I straightened and as predicted, Nino was regarding me with that quiet scrutiny that drove me up the wall. "Dante called. He wants another word with you. He seems to be losing his patience," he said.

"He won't risk an attack, not if it means I could kill Serafina."

Nino inclined his head. "Still ... we should start making demands."

"Maybe you're right. Think of some ridiculous demand he won't possibly agree to; I'm not done playing yet. Ask him for Indianapolis or Minneapolis. I don't care."

A muscle in Nino's jaw tightened, a clear sign of his annoyance with me. "Alright. I'll send him a message."

"Tell him that I'm allowing Serafina a video chat with her brother tomorrow. He better be ready at eight a.m."

"You're cutting it close. Adamo's initiation starts at eleven."

"Enough time," I said then frowned. "You didn't tell me what happened with Harper."

"As expected, she used Adamo to supply her with drugs. The moment he told her he couldn't give her anything, she dropped him and admitted to fucking around with that other guy. Adamo is crushed. He takes these things too personal."

"Is he angry?"

"Angry at Mason, not at the girl."

I smiled. "That's enough. We still need someone Adamo can deal with tomorrow. Tell Fabiano I want him to bring Mason to the initiation."

Nino looked thoughtful. "Maybe it'll work. Jealousy and a broken heart are good motivators for brutal acts."

"Where is he?"

"Outside, smoking. I allowed him one cigarette."

"I'll go talk to him."

"I'm not sure he's the best dialogue partner at the moment."

"Nor am I."

"That's the problem," Nino said with a twisted smile.

"Go fuck your wife and stop pissing me off."

"You haven't been to the Sugar Trap since you brought Serafina here."

I sighed. "Maybe I'm not in the mood for whore pussy. I'm taking a few celibate days."

"You haven't done that since you started fucking."

"Stop analyzing everything, Nino," I growled and stalked off before I punched him.

I found Adamo on a lounge chair beside the pool, scowling into the dark, the cigarette dangling from his mouth giving his face an eerie glow. He didn't look up when I sank down beside him.

He took a deep drag of his cigarette, and it took every ounce of my almost non-existent control to not rip the fucking thing out of his mouth.

"I hate it," he muttered.

"Hate what?"

"Hate that with our last name people always want something from us."

"You shouldn't have tried to make friends by giving them drugs," I said. "We're not Santa Claus. We're selling the shit, not handing it out for free, and we never fucking take the shit ourselves."

"When will people ever like me for myself and not for what I can give them? They only see my name. That's all they care about."

"You've got people who care about you," I said roughly.

Adamo glanced at me.

"You've cost me millions so far with the cars you crashed and the drugs you let disappear. What would I do to anyone who stole something from me?"

"You'd torture and kill them," Adamo said quietly.

"I would and have." I paused. "But here you are, safe and sound, and you know you will remain that way until the day I take my last fucking breath."

Adamo lowered his head.

"Tomorrow you're going to swear loyalty to the Camorra. You will take the oath and the tattoo," I ordered.

"I don't give a fuck about the Camorra," Adamo whispered, and my anger rose, but then he spoke up again. "But I will swear loyalty to you because even if I hate what you, Nino, and Savio do, you are my family."

I straightened up then looked down at my brother for another moment. "Don't waste your energy on another thought of that girl. She's worthless. There are many more girls out there. She used you. Maybe now you'll start using them as well."

Adamo frowned. "I can't help how I feel." He swallowed audibly. "She's been fucking him the entire time."

"So what? You fucked her. He fucked her. You move on."

"I didn't," he said quietly. "We didn't get that far."

"Please tell me she at least gave you head," I muttered.

Embarrassment flashed across Adamo's face. I sank back down.

"Can I ask you a question?" he said quietly.

I had a feeling this was turning into the sex talk I'd avoided with Savio by throwing him a freebie with two whores; he gladly accepted.

"How long does it take to get control?"

"Control?" I echoed. I didn't bother controlling myself during sex, but I had a feeling Adamo didn't mean that kind of control.

Adamo tossed his cigarette to the ground. "To hold back, you know? I kind of ... you know ..."

"Shot your cum the second she put her mouth on you," I provided.

Adamo grimaced and looked away. "Yeah."

I chuckled.

Adamo scowled. "Don't make fun of me."

"I'm not," I said. "You've never been with a girl, so it's pretty normal."

"Did it happen to you too?"

"No, but I fucked out of anger. That gave me better control."

"I bet Mason and Harper had a good laugh behind my back," he said miserably, then added in a low voice, "I want to kill him. Mason."

"I know."

Adamo's eyes widened. "You're going to make me kill him tomorrow."

"You will have to kill someone in front of our soldiers. It's either him or someone you don't hate. Mason is a dead man either way. He can die by your hand or Fabiano's."

I regarded my brother. He was biting his lip, staring down at the pool. "I'll do it." I touched his shoulder, and for once he didn't try to shake me off.

CHAPTER 10

SERAFINA

I was still in bed when the lock turned and didn't have time to sit up before Remo stepped inside the room.

Feeling vulnerable lying in the bed, I pushed into a sitting position. Remo regarded me with an intent expression. I was only in a chemise and shorts and was acutely aware of how little the fabric covered. Swallowing my nerves, I got out of bed, not wanting to show weakness. Remo's eyes followed my every move, lingering on my breasts. My body betrayed me as my nipples hardened in the cool air.

"I'm fairly sure God designed your body to drive men into insanity," Remo said darkly.

Stifling the excited thrill Remo's words sent through me, I retorted, "You believe in God?"

"No. I don't. But looking at you, I could turn into a believer."

I huffed. "There's a cozy warm place in Hell reserved just for you."

"I've burned before."

I slanted him a look. He'd said the same words before, and I wondered what exactly he meant by it.

"You have a video call with your brother in five minutes, so you better hurry."

I didn't have a bathrobe to pull over my clothes, so I reached for a dress but Remo shook his head. "Stay as you are." He grabbed my arm then paused, dark eyes roaming over me.

"I thought we were in a hurry?"

"You are. I'm not. I don't give a fuck if you talk to your brother or not." Despite his words, he led me out of the room, through the hallway and downstairs.

"Again in your torture chamber?" I asked, shivering violently when my bare feet hit the first stone step leading down into the basement. I wasn't sure how the floor could be that cold when outside the sun was blazing.

I cried out when Remo lifted me in his arms. "Don't want you to catch a cold. That would be a shame. I'll have to ask Kiara to shop for clothes that fit you."

I was frozen in his hold. "You can send me back to Minneapolis. I have enough clothes there."

"I think Danilo wants you in Indianapolis, Angel, or have you forgotten?"

I realized I had. My wedding seemed so very far away, and it was the last thing on my mind.

Remo chuckled joylessly. His stupid manipulations were getting to me. How was he doing it?

I didn't answer his question because he knew. My traitorous body mourned the loss of his warmth when he set me down on my feet in the cell where he'd recorded the last message to my family. I wrapped my arms around myself, suddenly overwhelmed by the memories. My gaze flitted to my wound. With the Tylenol I barely noticed its existence and it was scabbing over. It wasn't the pain or the cut that bothered me. It was the memory of Samuel's and Dad's expressions when they'd seen me in Remo's hands. They were suffering more than I did, and that was the worst thing about all this.

Remo stepped up to me, his body a warm presence at my back, and he took my wrist, lifting it so he could inspect my wound. His thumb lightly traced my skin. He leaned in. "I won't cut you again, Angel. Don't be afraid."

That wasn't what I was scared of most. "You won't?" I asked curiously, tilting my head so I could evaluate his face. Why would Remo say something like that?

Remo cuts deep. Hits hard. Kills brutally.

Remo dropped my wrist, something in his expression shifting, his guard slipping in place. "Time for your call with Samuel."

He went to the screen on the table and turned it on followed by the loudspeakers. I moved closer when Samuel's face appeared. My heart clenched violently at the sight. His hair was a mess, his expression haunted, and dark circles spread under his eyes. He probably hadn't slept at all since my kidnapping.

Guilt crashed over me for not being as bad off as they all imagined. I could tell Samuel was struggling to keep his expression controlled. He wouldn't show weakness in front of his enemy.

"Sam," I said quietly, my voice shaking.

"Fina," he got out. His eyes scanned me and the skimpy outfit I was in. He swallowed, a muscle in his jaw flexing. "How are you?"

"I'm okay," I said. His brows drew together in disbelief.

"How much longer she stays that way depends on your Capo's willingness to answer my demands," Remo added.

What demands?

Samuel began shaking. I touched my palm to my chest, letting him know that he was in my heart. He mirrored the gesture then his eyes hardened as they settled on my forearm. "How bad is it?"

"Not bad," I said.

I could see he didn't believe me. He thought I was trying to protect him. I could feel Remo's eyes on us the entire time, but I tried to ignore him.

"How are Mom and Dad doing?"

Samuel's expression was cautious. He couldn't tell me everything with Remo close by. "They are worried about you."

"How's Sofia doing?" I whispered, fighting back the tears.

Samuel's eyes flitted to Remo, and I stiffened in turn. I shouldn't have mentioned my sister in front of him.

Remo made an impatient sound. "I don't kidnap children, don't worry."

"You only kidnap innocent women," Samuel snarled.

Remo pressed up behind me, and Samuel's expression switched from fury to dread. "Who says she's still innocent?"

Samuel jerked. Remo gripped my hip in warning, but I didn't care.

"It's not like that," I said fiercely.

Samuel's eyes found mine, searching, and a flicker of relief showed on his face.

Remo grasped my chin, turned my head, and gave me a harsh kiss. I froze in shock, not able to believe he was doing this in front of my brother.

He released me abruptly. "How innocent she returns to you depends on your cooperation. Tell your uncle that, Samuel."

I twisted out of Remo's hold and looked at Samuel, my cheeks heating up in embarrassment.

"Take me in her stead. I'll exchange myself for her."

"No!" I shouted desperately, but Samuel wasn't looking at me. I whirled around on Remo, wide eyed. A cruel smile played on his face. I caught his gaze. "No," I said forcefully. His eyes lingered on my lips then dipped lower before they locked on mine once more and relief coursed through me. Remo wouldn't exchange me for my twin. He wouldn't release me. Not before he got what he wanted. I wasn't sure what that was, but I had a horrible feeling it wasn't something my uncle could give him.

"Serafina is worth too much, I'm afraid. Time to say goodbye."

I turned back to my twin. "I love you, Sam," I whispered. Words I'd never said to him when other people were around because emotions didn't belong in public, but I didn't care anymore. Let Remo see how much I loved my family.

A haunted look passed Samuel's face, and he surprised me by rasping, "And I love you, Fina. I'll save you." For him to say those words in front of another man, his enemy, he must be even more worried for my life than I thought.

The tears spilled over then. Remo walked past me and switched the screen off. I didn't hold them back. I let the tears flow freely, not caring if Remo saw them. Remo watched me with narrowed eyes. Maybe my emotions annoyed him. I couldn't care less.

"I thought Danilo was the man who owned your heart, but now I see I was wrong."

I wiped at my eyes. "He's my twin. I've never been without him. I would walk through fire for him."

Remo nodded slowly. "I believe you."

REMO

Nino, Adamo, Savio, and I drove to the initiation together. My thoughts kept straying to Serafina. I'd locked her in the bedroom again, and Fabiano would keep an eye on her and Kiara while we were gone. I would have preferred to have him at the initiation as well, but someone needed to protect Kiara and make sure Serafina didn't do something stupid. I doubted she'd find a way out of the bedroom, but if anyone could do it, then it was her.

Nino was driving and Savio and Adamo sat in the back. It reminded me of the past, the months we'd spent on the run from the Russians, part of the Camorra, and the other mob families. We'd been on the road almost constantly, never staying anywhere for long, and still our pursuers almost got us a couple of times.

Nino slanted a look at me as if he, too, was remembering those days.

We pulled up in front of one of our casinos on the outskirts of Vegas, where the initiation would take place. The parking lot was crowded with limousines. My soldiers were already there. I got out first, not waiting for the bellhop to open my door, and stalked inside the casino with my brothers on my heels. The place had been closed since yesterday for the occasion. Inside familiar faces greeted me. Some of my men were nursing drinks at the bar. Others were engaged in conversation with each other. None of them were playing poker or roulette, even though the croupiers were there just in case. They knew it was a test. An alcoholic shouldn't run a bar. And my underbosses and captains better not gamble or do drugs. Lower soldiers had more leeway.

Eleven Underbosses and their Consiglieres were invited for the initiation. Most of them were barely older than me. When I'd taken over power, I removed most of the old Underbosses and chose their young ambitious heirs or bastards. Similar to me and my relationship with my father, only a few of them had been sad to see their fathers gone. Only three cities fell under the rule of older Underbosses, who were loyal to the bone.

I shook their hands before we gathered in the center of the room. I put a hand on Adamo's shoulder. He stood tall, for once his expression not betraying his emotions, but I could feel his tension under my palm. "Today we've come here to initiate my brother Adamo."

The men nodded a greeting at him. They had all dressed in suits for the occasion, and my brothers and I had followed the tradition of dressing up. "As with every initiate, blood has to be paid."

Nino dragged a struggling Mason toward us. Fabiano had locked him in the utility closet. Adamo tensed under my hand, and I squeezed his shoulder lightly.

Nino threw the asshole to the ground. He wasn't in school anymore. A drop out, who'd managed to gather a posse of well-off, much younger kids around himself and introduced them to drugs. His father had been a Made Man before I disposed of him in my claim for power, but the son was even more useless than the father.

His mouth was covered by tape, and his eyes were wide with terror. I handed Adamo one of my guns. As an initiate, he wasn't allowed to bring his own guns. Adamo pointed the barrel at Mason's head. I was close enough to see the slight tremor of his hands. I squeezed his shoulder again, encouragement as much as a reminder not to show weakness, and then he pulled the trigger.

Mason slumped forward dead. Adamo shuddered under my hand and slowly lowered the gun, his expression hard, but in his eyes I could see the hint of conflict. It would get easier with time. The men nodded their heads in approval, and Adamo met my gaze.

"It's time to get the tattoo."

Nino came forward with the tattoo equipment, and Savio carried a chair over. Adamo sat down, rolled up his sleeve, and held out his forearm.

"I think it's time for some entertainment while we wait for Nino to finish the tattoo."

I clapped my hands, and one of the bartenders opened another door. A row of our most beautiful whores streamed into the room, half naked. Most of my men took me up on my offer, but a few chose drinks over female entertainment. I stepped over to my brothers. Nino was still outlining the knife. He was quick and accurate. I wouldn't want anyone else do our tattoos. Even Savio stayed beside Adamo, but his eyes strayed through the room to look for a whore for later. Adamo's jaw was clenched as he watched Nino ink him. The kill bothered him more than it had Savio, Nino, or myself, but like all of us, he would get over it eventually.

"Do you want a drink, Adamo?" Savio asked.

Adamo looked up in surprise. "Sure."

"Whiskey, neat?"

Adamo gave a nod then winced when Nino started filling in the pupil of the eye. Savio came back with four glasses on a tray and handed one to each of us. I raised my glass. "Us against the world."

"Us against the world."

We downed the whiskey, and Adamo started coughing, not used to hard liquor. Nino lifted the needle with a frown. "I'll mess this up if you keep moving." He set his empty glass down and waited for Adamo to calm himself before he continued.

When the tattoo was done, Nino stood and I called my men over. The whores remained in the back. They knew they weren't welcome. Adamo stared down at his inked arm. I held out the arm with my tattoo. Adamo closed his fingers over it, and I closed mine over his, causing him to hiss with pain. "Will you be my eye?"

"I will."

"Will you be my knife?"

"I will."

"Will you bleed and die for our cause?"

"I will," Adamo said firmly.

"Today you give me your life. It's mine to decide over till death sets you free. Welcome to the Camorra, Adamo."

I released him and stepped back. Nino clapped his shoulder, and Savio did the same. Then my soldiers welcomed my brother into our world. Nobody paid any attention to the corpse lying in its own blood on the ground. The cleaners would remove it later.

Alcohol flowed more freely. Savio and Adamo sat together at the bar. A rare sight. Soon, two whores approached them, one latching on to Savio, the other pressed up to Adamo.

Adamo shook his head and after a moment, Savio disappeared with the two whores through the door behind the bar.

Nino joined me where I leaned against a roulette table. I'd exchanged a few words with each of my Underbosses. Most of them would return to their cities very soon, worried Dante might attack after all.

"I'm surprised you're not fucking a whore."

My eyes strayed to the gathered women, but none of them got my attention. "I've fucked all of them before. It's getting boring."

Nino raised his eyebrows but didn't comment. "We should go to Adamo."

I nodded but we both stopped when one of the whores, C.J., sat down beside him at the bar and they began talking.

"Maybe she can talk him into losing his virginity," I muttered.

Nino shrugged. "She's a decent woman. He could do worse for his first time."

I gave him a look. "Can you cut the compassionate bullshit?"

He smirked. "It's got nothing to do with compassion. C.J. is a good, a logical choice for Adamo. She's skilled and will try to please him. Plus, she will pretend he's a good fuck. Pure logic."

"You enjoy pissing me off with your logic."

"It's quite satisfying, yes."

I shook my head at my brother. "One of these day, you, Savio, and Adamo will be my death."

"The only thing that will kill you is your lack of control."

My thoughts drifted back to Serafina, the sight of her in the skimpy nightclothes, the way her nipples had puckered in the cold. Fuck control. Fuck patience. I'd never wanted anything as much as Serafina, and yet I couldn't have her.

Nino shook his head. "Exchange the girl for Scuderi before you're in too deep."

"I'll exchange her the moment she lets me deep inside her."

"Telling you 'I told you so' one day will be as satisfying as annoying you with my logic."

"It's my game, Nino. I'm the best player on the field. I will win."

"There won't be any winners, Remo."

CHAPTER 11

SERAFINA

It was around lunchtime when someone knocked. I hadn't seen Remo since he'd brought me back to my room after my call with Samuel yesterday. Savio brought me breakfast in the morning without a word. He was probably still pissed.

Kiara opened the door with a shy smile and two bags in her hands. "I bought clothes for you. I hope they fit."

She stepped in followed by Nino. I hopped off the windowsill. My limbs were starting to feel sluggish from lack of use. I'd worked out almost daily before my kidnapping, and now all I did was sit around.

"I assume that means my stay won't be ending anytime soon," I said bitterly.

Kiara sighed. "I don't know."

My eyes moved over to Nino, who looked his usual stoic self, not that I had expected an answer from him.

Kiara held the bags out to me. "I got you sandals and a pair of sneakers. A few pairs of shorts, tops, and dresses. And underwear. I really hope I got the right size."

I took everything from her and went into the bathroom to change. The clothes fit, even if they weren't my usual style. I left the bathroom wearing shorts and a top as well as the sandals.

"And?" Kiara asked hopefully.

"It all fits."

"Why don't you join me in the gardens? It's beautiful outside, and I'm sure you can't stand these walls anymore."

I frowned. "I can't stand this city, but I'd love to join you." My eyes darted to her husband whose expression had tightened at her suggestion. "If he allows it."

Nino gave a quick nod, but it was obvious that he didn't approve.

I followed Kiara outside while Nino walked behind us to keep an eye on me.

"Let me get the salad I prepared so we can have lunch," Kiara said when we arrived on the ground floor. I made a move to follow her into the kitchen but Nino grabbed my wrist, stopping me. "You'll stay here."

I wrenched my wrist out of his grip, narrowing my eyes at him. "Don't touch me."

Nino didn't as much as twitch. "If you think about trying something, don't. I don't want to hurt you, but if you hurt Kiara, I'll make it very painful for you."

"It's not her I want to hurt. She can't help being married to you."

"Indeed," Nino agreed.

Kiara returned with what looked like a Cesar's salad, her gaze flitting between her husband and me. "Everything okay?"

"Yes," I said, because even if I hated the Falcones, Nino's protectiveness was something I could respect.

Soon we were seated around the garden table, eating salad. My eyes began wandering the premises once more, but I knew there was no easy way to escape. To my surprise, Nino gave us more space. He settled on a chair in the shadows with a laptop he'd grabbed on the way out.

"I can't imagine how horrified you must have been when you were told Nino Falcone was going to be your husband," I said.

Kiara chewed slowly then swallowed. "It's was a shock at first. The Camorra doesn't have the best reputation."

I huffed. "They are monsters."

"The monsters in my family hurt me. I haven't experienced any kind of humiliation or pain in Las Vegas," she said firmly.

"Still. I was already nervous on my wedding day. I can't imagine how it must have been for you."

Kiara shrugged. "What about your fiancé? What kind of man is he?"

"He's Underboss of Indianapolis."

"That doesn't answer my question ... or maybe it does."

"I didn't know him very well," I said when Remo stepped outside. "But I have every intention of getting to know Danilo better once I'm finally married to him."

Remo gave me a hard look. "I'm sure he'll be a delight."

I narrowed my eyes. "He is."

"I'm taking Serafina for a walk around the property," he said to Kiara. She nodded and he turned to me. "Come on."

Despite my annoyance at his commanding tone, I stood, glad to move my legs. Remo's eyes scanned me from head to toe as he led me past the pool. "Kiara got you clothes."

"I need to workout," I said, ignoring his comment. "I can't sit around all day. I'm going crazy. Unless that's what you want, you need to let me run on a treadmill."

Remo shook his head. "No need for a treadmill. I run every morning at seven. You can join me."

I allowed myself a quick scan of his body. Of course he worked out. His body was all muscle. I knew he and his brothers were into cage fighting and running was a good way to improve your stamina. "That sounds reasonable."

Remo's mouth twitched. "I'm glad you think so."

"What did you demand of my uncle for my freedom?" I asked him after a while.

"Minneapolis."

I jerked to a stop. "That's ridiculous. My uncle won't give you any part of his territory. Even my father wouldn't give up his city to save me."

Remo's smile darkened. "I think your father would gladly give me his city if it were up to him."

I swallowed. I didn't want to think of my family. Not when Remo was watching me closely. I'd cried enough in front of him yesterday. "You know Dante won't meet your demands."

Remo nodded.

"Then why make them?"

"This is a game of chess, Angel, like you said. I need to bring my pieces in position before I strike."

Remo sounded so awfully sure of himself, it made me worry that maybe he'd really win in the end.

I turned away from him and continued walking. "I'm surprised Luca Vitiello agreed to your plan. I used to think the Famiglia was honorable, but apparently they are stooping as low as the Camorra now."

Remo touched my shoulder and pulled me to a stop. "Tell me, Serafina, what's the difference between an arranged marriage with Danilo and being my captive?"

I stared at him incredulously, but before I could deliver a reply, he spoke again.

"You didn't choose Danilo. You will be given to him like an unwilling captive and the ring around your finger will be your shackle, the marriage your cage." His dark eyes held triumph as if I couldn't possibly argue my defense. My eyes darted to the ring around my finger. Its sight didn't hold the same pride and excitement it used to.

"You will have to surrender to his body, whether you desire him or not, and your body and soul are at his mercy. Tell me again, how is your arranged marriage different to being my captive?"

Remo leaned down, holding my gaze the entire time, and I didn't step back. His lips grazed my chin, then my cheek, and finally my mouth. "Your 'no' means nothing in a marriage. Do you call that freedom?"

Pressing my lips together, I glared at him, too proud to admit his words made sense. Remo had a way to twist things the way he wanted them until you believed they were the truth.

"Did you ever fantasize about Danilo? Do you desire him?"

I glared. "That's none of your business."

Remo shook his head as he stroked my throat, then my collarbone with his rough fingertips. "You didn't. Your mind said yes to him, and you hoped your body would follow." His fingers on my skin made thinking straight difficult, but I didn't want to give him the satisfaction of pulling back. "I wonder how long it'll take for your mind to say yes to me because your body has been screaming yes from the very first moment."

I ripped away from him. "You are insane. Neither my body nor my mind say yes to any part of you, Remo. I think being the undisputed ruler of Las Vegas has made you a megalomaniac."

Remo's dark eyes sent another shiver down my spine, and I stalked off, running as much from his terrifying expression as the weight of the truth. Despite my hate for the Camorra's Capo, his kisses and closeness wreaked havoc within me.

I suspected it was due to my captivity, a form of Stockholm Syndrome. I made sure to keep my distance as Remo led me back to my room, and he didn't try to touch me again. Before he locked me in, I asked, "What do you really want, Remo?"

He regarded me with unsettling intensity. "You know what I want."

"Body and soul," I muttered.

One corner of his mouth lifted. "Body and soul."

He closed the door and I was left with the whirlwind of thoughts in my head. I needed to figure out a way to get away. Maybe my family was already planning some insane hostage rescue. Samuel surely was. If not openly then definitely in his head. There was no way anyone would survive an attack on Camorra territory. And I didn't kid myself into thinking that Remo would release me any time soon. He was making demands, but he didn't want them to be fulfilled. Yet.

REMO

As promised, I picked Serafina up at seven so she could run with me. Usually I preferred to do my morning run alone, but I couldn't resist her presence.

Serafina had put on shorts, a T-shirt, and sneakers.

She followed me quietly through the house but stopped when I led her toward the driveway. "Where are we going?"

"We're going running, like I said. Did you think I do my laps in the garden?"

I opened the door to my Bugatti SUV for her, and she got in without another word. I got behind the wheel and pulled down the driveway, feeling her eyes on me. I enjoyed her confusion.

I took us to a trail in a nearby canyon where I'd run before. Soon it would be too warm, but this early in the morning the temperature was perfect for running. Serafina followed me out of the car and looked around the gravel parking lot. We were the only people around. Her eyes were assessing and attentive. She'd try something, and I had to admit I couldn't wait for it.

We jogged beside each other for a while before she spoke up. "Aren't you worried I'll run?"

"I caught you once before."

"I was stuck in my wedding dress, so I was too slow."

"I'll always catch you, Angel."

After thirty minutes, we stopped for a drinking break. I could tell that Serafina was scouting the terrain. Taking a deep gulp of water, I watched as she got down on her haunches and laced up her sneakers again. When she straightened, I knew from the tension in her limbs that she was about to do something. She threw sand at my face and actually managed to get some of it into my eyes. Through blurry vision, I saw her dashing off. Chuckling, despite my burning eyes, I took chase. I'd dealt with worse.

Serafina was quicker than last time, and she didn't stay on the trail, which was a huge risk on her part. If she got lost around here, she'd die of dehydration before she found her way back to civilization. I picked up my own pace. Serafina jumped to avoid rocks and practically flew over the ground. It was a beautiful sight. So much more beautiful than having her locked in a room.

Eventually, I caught up with her. Her legs were much shorter, and she was less muscular. When I was close enough, I slung my arm around her waist like last time. We both lost our balance from the impact and fell. I landed on my back with Serafina on top of me. She rammed her knee into my stomach and kicked to get out my hold. Before she could do real damage, I rolled over and pressed her into the ground with my weight, her wrists pushed up above her head.

"Gotcha," I murmured, panting, dripping sweat.

Serafina's chest heaved, her eyes indignant and furious. "You enjoy the chase."

"Actually, I don't," I said in a low voice, bringing our lips closer. "But with you I do."

"You knew I'd run," she muttered.

"Of course. You are meant to be free. Which makes me wonder why you allow someone like Danilo to cage you."

She wriggled under me. "Let me go."

"I'm enjoying being on top of you and between your lithe legs." I rocked my pelvis slightly.

She stiffened. "Don't."

I licked a droplet of sweat off her throat before I pushed off her and stood. Serafina ignored my outstretched hand and stumbled to her feet. Her hair had fallen out of her ponytail, and she was covered in dirt and sweat.

"I prefer you like this."

She frowned. "Dirty?"

"Untamed. Seeing you in that white atrocity can't compare. Too perfect, too groomed, too fake. I bet Danilo would have loved it, though."

She didn't say anything, and I knew part of my words got through to her. My eyes were drawn to her forearm, which she was rubbing absentmindedly. A small part of the cut had opened again and was bleeding.

A flicker of guilt caught me off guard. It wasn't an emotion I entertained very often. I took her arm and inspected the wound. Dirt had gotten in it. "We need to clean that to prevent infection."

Her blue eyes searched my face, but I had trouble reading the expression on hers. I led her back to the car. It was getting hotter and after the chase, we both needed a shower. I took a fresh bottle of water from the trunk and poured it over Serafina's wound, cleaning it carefully with my fingertips. She winced occasionally but didn't say anything. "The silent treatment isn't your usual style," I commented.

"You don't know me."

I smirked. "I know you better than most people. Better than Danilo."

She didn't contradict me.

"Hate can set you free," I said.

"So can love," she said. "But I doubt you'd understand."

Serafina was silent on the way back to the mansion, her gaze distant as she peered out of the side window.

I returned her to her room, knowing she had a lot to think about before I headed into my own room for a shower. When I came down into the game room later, Savio was lounging on the sofa, typing on his phone. Upon spotting me, he set it down and grinned.

"Nino isn't happy that you took the bitch running."

I sank down beside my brother. "It offends his logic."

Savio laughed. "But honestly, Remo, he has a point. That girl is unpredictable."

"That makes her all the more fun," I said.

Savio gave me a curious look. "You're enjoying this more than I thought. And you haven't even fucked her … or have you?"

"No, I haven't. Serafina is a surprising challenge."

"Too much work for my taste," Savio said with a shrug. "I prefer girls who shut up when I tell them to, who suck my dick when I want it. Less hassle."

"Eventually, you've had it all. You've fucked in every position possible, have done all the kinky shit you can think of. It becomes more difficult to get the thrill from the beginning."

He leaned forward on his knees. "You're not thinking of keeping her …
are you?"

"No."

I called Dante in the afternoon. He picked up after the second ring, his voice
cold and hard but with an underlying tension that gave me a thrill.

"Dante, I wanted to ask when you were going to fulfill my demand."

"I won't, just as you intended. I don't have time for your games, Remo.
This is between us, between you and me. Why don't we meet in person, Capo
to Capo, and settle this like men."

"You want to duel me? How archaic of you, Dante. You didn't strike me
as the primitive type."

"I'll gladly convince you of the contrary."

I almost agreed because the idea of shoving my knife over and over into
the cold fish was too fucking enticing. Fighting Dante would have been a
highlight. Since cutting Luca into bite-sized pieces was out of the question for
now, Dante was the opponent I longed for. There was only one thing I wanted
more than killing Dante: having Serafina in every way possible and destroy the
Outfit through her.

"We will have to postpone our duel to a later point, Dante. For now, I
have demands I want you to fulfill if you want to have your niece returned to
her family in one piece."

"I won't negotiate with you, Remo. You won't get an inch of my territory.
Now say what you really want. We both know what it is."

I doubted he knew what I really wanted. Maybe only Nino did. "And what do I want?"

"You want my Consigliere. Fabiano is your Enforcer and I assume the deal you struck with Vitiello entailed your promise to deliver Scuderi so you can all have him dismembered together."

"I doubt Luca will be part of Scuderi's disembodiment. He'd rather chop you into pieces, Dante."

"Vitiello isn't the ally you think he is. His Famiglia is prone to betrayal. It's unwise of you to make me your enemy."

"Dante, we've been enemies from the moment I claimed power. And the moment your fucking soldiers breached my territory, it got personal. I don't need Luca as an ally as long as I know his hatred for you trumps his hatred for me."

"One day his and your rashness will be your downfall."

"Very likely," I growled. "But until that happens, your conscience will have to live with Serafina's gradual downfall."

I hung up. With every day that Serafina was in my hands, my position got stronger.

CHAPTER 12

SERAFINA

The next few days after my attempt at running away, I fell into a strange routine. Remo picked me up for a run in the morning. Sometimes I wondered if he wanted me to risk escaping again because the chase gave him a thrill, but I didn't waste my energy on it. Remo was too strong and fast. I had to beat him with wit. Unfortunately, he was as intelligent as he was cruel. He could twist my words faster than I thought possible, and I occasionally caught myself enjoying our strange debates.

I didn't have to hold back when I was around Remo. I didn't try to present my best side to him like I had done with Danilo because I didn't care about his approval. I was myself, unfiltered, careless, and strangely enough Remo seemed to get a sick kick out of it. The Capo was a mystery to me. He hadn't tried to torture me or force himself on me like I'd expected, and I couldn't help but be wary because Remo's motives were cruel.

"Once I set you free, you'll return to Danilo like a well-trained carrier pigeon." Remo said as we jogged along the canyon trail one day.

"Your bird analogies are starting to get old," I muttered. I was glad Remo didn't know Dad called me dove. He'd only use it to his advantage.

"But they are so very fitting, Angel."

I slanted a look at him. He had a strange smile on his face. His shirt clung to his body with sweat and showed the outline of his muscles and his gun holsters. "What are you in your ornithology scheme? The vulture waiting for the poor pigeon to drop out of the sky so you can tear into her?"

Remo let out a deep chuckle, which sent a shocking shiver down my spine. I sped up, trying to force my body into submission. "I don't think you'll ever fall from the sky. I'll have to snatch you out of the air like an eagle."

I snorted, not caring if it was an undignified sound. "You are insane."

He fell silent, easily following my faster pace. Remo was fit to the point of admiration, I had to give him that.

After we returned to the car, we shared a bottle of water. "Why are you doing this?"

He cocked one eyebrow. "Giving you water?"

"Treating me decently."

He smiled darkly. "Why do you sound almost disappointed?"

Part of me was because I knew the man in front of me was ruthless and cruel to the very core. More monster than man. The weaker part was relieved and didn't want to question his motives. "When will the torture begin?"

Remo propped his arm up against the roof of the car and stared down at me. "Who says the torture hasn't already begun? Just because I'm not torturing you doesn't mean I'm not torturing others through you."

I flinched. My family. They were suffering because they imagined the horrors I was going through, horrors that weren't taking place—yet.

"You are a monster," I bit out.

Remo leaned even closer, radiating heat and power, the scent of fresh sweat and his own forbidden aroma wrapping around me. I returned his gaze. Dark eyes. Monster eyes, but God help me, they always kept me frozen with their intensity.

"You know, Angel, I think you enjoy my monstrosity more than you want to admit."

I didn't have a chance for a comeback. Remo's lips crushed mine, his tongue sliding in, and my body reacted with a wave of heat. I clutched his shoulders, meeting his tongue with the same fervor.

Then realization struck me. I tried to shove him away, but Remo didn't budge. He wrapped his arms around me, molding our bodies together. Breathtaking, terrifying, intoxicating.

I bit down on his lower lip, but Remo didn't pull back. He growled into my mouth and tightened his hold, his kiss turning even harder. The taste of his blood swirled in my mouth, and I pulled away in equal disgust and sick fascination. Remo's mouth was covered with blood. He truly looked the monster then. A dark smile curled his lips, and I opened the door and got into the car, trying to catch my breath, trying to escape his overwhelming presence. I caught sight of my reflection in the rearview mirror and cringed. My lips, too, were red with Remo's blood. In that moment, I didn't look any less a monster than he did.

The moment Remo picked me up the next morning, I knew it wasn't for a run. For one, he was too early, and second he was only in his briefs. I tore my gaze away from his body.

"We need to record additional motivation for your uncle," Remo explained. "Come."

I perched on the bed, not moving an inch. Another recording?

When I didn't follow his command, Remo raised his eyebrows. "Come," he said with more force, and it took considerable effort to remain motionless. I stubbornly returned his gaze.

He stalked toward me and bent over me. "Maybe I'm being too lenient with you," he murmured, fingers nudging my chin up.

I smiled then gasped when Remo jerked me to my feet and threw me over his shoulder. His big warm hand rested on my butt as he carried me, and for a few moments I stilled in shock. More because of my body's reaction to the feel of Remo's palm than to my head hanging down over his shoulder. I started wiggling and Remo's squeezed my butt cheek in warning.

I rammed my elbow into his side, but apart from a sharp exhale, Remo didn't falter. "Let me down," I wheezed, horrified by the way my center tightened at the feel of Remo's hand on my backside. If he found out, I'd die on the spot.

Remo didn't set me down, however, until we were back in the cell. My head swam for a moment, but when my vision cleared I noticed the shackles hanging from a chain at the wall. Remo nudged me forward. "Arms up," he ordered.

"What?" I gasped out.

He didn't wait for me to comply. He grabbed my wrists and secured me. Confusion then terror shot through me. Maybe he was finally sick of torturing others when he had me to have fun with.

Remo leaned down and I shivered. His dark eyes roamed my face, and he gave a shake of his head. "Calm down. We need to give your family a show. I'll give that perfect throat a hickey for a few convincing photos, nothing else. Don't get your panties in a bunch over nothing, Angel."

"You want to make my family believe I'm shackled up in a cell?"

"Among other things," he murmured. His hands reached for the hem of my chemise and tugged hard. The fabric came apart until only the seam of the neckline held it together. My nipples hardened and Remo watched silently then released a harsh breath.

I swallowed. "These photos are fake. I'm not dangling from chains all day, and you're not ripping my clothes off," I muttered.

He smiled down at me. "Would you prefer if I didn't have to fake them, Angel?"

I swallowed again, goose bumps rising on my skin.

"I didn't think so," he said in a slightly rougher voice then carefully brushed my hair away from my throat. I held my breath when his lips were almost at my skin. "You smell so fucking sweet. Owning you one day will be the sweetest triumph of my life."

"You'll never own me."

Remo pressed his lips to my skin. Then his tongue darted out, licking along my pulse point. He sucked and nibbled on my throat, his fingers cupping my head, tilting it to the side. My eyes fluttered shut. The sensations were foreign and mesmerizing. Remo's mouth on my throat seemed to send shockwaves through my body, creating sensations I'd never experienced before. His warm body pressed into me, his scent flooding my nose.

I was motionless, stunned, confused by my body's reaction. How could my throat be such a sensitive spot of my body? How could it fill me with so much forbidden desire?

He pulled back but didn't straighten immediately, his face still close to my throat as he exhaled. When he finally stood, his dark eyes sent a new ripple through my body. His fingertips brushed over my tender throat, and my lips parted in a small exhale. Our eyes locked and one corner of his mouth lifted.

"Did you like that?"

"Of course not," I snapped.

"I thought you were a good liar."

My cheeks heated and I glared but didn't say anything because I wasn't sure if my next lie would be any more convincing.

"It's okay, Angel," Remo said in a low voice. "There are worse things than enjoying pleasure."

I wanted to lash out at him, but he wasn't even the main reason for my anger. I was furious at myself, enraged by my body for its reactions.

"I'm Danilo's," I said firmly.

Remo narrowed his eyes. "Are you reminding me or yourself?"

"I'm promised to him. I want him, not you."

"You can have an Underboss, someone who's learned to do another man's biding, or the Capo, a man who has men follow his command."

"I can have a monster or a man."

"Do you really think Danilo isn't a monster?

"He isn't a monster like you."

Remo nodded. "He's a lesser monster. Who'd want to settle for less?"

"You don't even want me, Remo. All you want is to hold my fate over my family's head. Stop toying around."

He stepped back, turned around, and picked up his phone. "Look broken for a moment."

I glared.

"That's not the look we're going for." He waited. Then his jaw tightened, and he came toward me again, holding my chin. "I said it before, choose your battles wisely. I'm not a patient man nor a decent one."

He retreated and finally satisfied with my expression, he took a few photos. Guilt left a bitter taste in my mouth, but I wasn't sure how long it would take for my family to free me, if they succeeded at all, and I had to think of self-preservation even if I hated myself for it.

He unshackled me and I rubbed my wrists then touched my tender throat. Remo watched me. "I like seeing my mark on you."

I didn't say anything.

Later, I spent a long time staring at my reflection in the bathroom mirror. Remo had left his marks like he'd said. They were red and purple, and made me feel a wave of shame because of how my body had reacted. I wasn't sure what was wrong with me.

A knock drew me out of my reverie. Dragging myself away from the mirror, I went into the bedroom, where I found the youngest Falcone. He looked somewhat lost in the middle of my room.

"I have a few books and ice cream for you. It's one of the hottest days of the summer. I thought you could use cooling off," he said, holding up four books and a bowl filled with ice cream.

His gaze moved to my throat, and his brows drew together. He walked past me and put everything down on my nightstand before he shoved his hands into his pockets, looking awkward. My eyes lingered on the fresh tattoo on his forearm.

"You are a Made Man now."

He glanced down then nodded slowly. "I'm a Falcone."

I went over to the nightstand to take a look at everything.

"It's chocolate chip. It's all we got. Savio's got a sweet tooth. The rest of us not so much."

"So you gave me Savio's ice cream? He'll love that after the soup I threw at him."

Adamo burst out laughing. "I wish I could have been there. He's so full of himself. I bet his expression was hilarious." He sobered then cleared his throat.

I smiled. "He was shocked."

It was difficult to believe that Adamo was related to Remo. There was a slight resemblance, but Adamo's hair was curly and not as dark, and his eyes were a warmer brown. But the biggest difference was their personality. I picked up the bowl and pushed a spoonful of the sugary treat into my mouth before sinking down onto the bed.

Adamo came a bit closer and leaned against one of the posts. "I wasn't sure what kind of books you like, so I brought a memoir, a thriller, a romance, and a fantasy book. We don't have many new books. I don't think I'm allowed to give you my kindle. You could use it for other stuff."

I smiled. "It's okay." Despite my intention to hate on every Falcone, it was difficult not to like Adamo. "I think I'll pass on the thriller, though. I've had plenty of thrill in my life recently."

"I know," Adamo said quietly. He indicated my throat. "What happened there?"

Heat shot into my cheeks, and I allowed myself another taste of the ice cream to gather my thoughts.

Adamo watched me closely. "Did he hurt you?"

I considered lying, making up a brutal story to drive a wedge between the brothers, but for some reason I couldn't do it. "No. He's hurting my family by making them believe he's hurting me."

Relief flashed across Adamo's face, and for a second it annoyed me, but then I thought of Samuel and understood.

"You'll be united with them soon," he said.

I swallowed and nodded. Adamo touched my shoulder lightly then drew back. "Sorry I should have asked before touching you."

I shook my head. "How did you end up being so polite and kind when you are related to Remo? Were you raised by different parents?"

"Remo and Nino were raised by our parents, but Savio and I were mostly raised by Remo and Nino."

I stared. "They raised you?"

He nodded then rubbed the back of his head as if he realized he shouldn't have told me. "I should go."

I tried to imagine Remo raising a child. It blew my mind, especially since they all must have been on the run at the time.

Night had fallen and I was reading in bed, when suddenly the lights went out. I blinked into the unexpected darkness and climbed out of bed, putting the book down on the nightstand.

Following the trail of silvery moonlight, I glanced out of the window. The lights in the garden and every other window of the mansion that I could see were out as well. In the distance I could make out lights from other houses.

My pulse picked up. What was happening? My eyes searched the shadows of the perimeter, and then I saw two figures running across the lawn toward the house.

The Outfit. It had to be.

They had come to save me.

Euphoria pulsed through me, followed by fear. This was Remo's territory. The Falcones knew every inch of their property and the Outfit didn't. What if Samuel was among the attackers?

I clung to the windowsill, immobilized by terror at the thought. Dante and Dad would have never allowed my brother to come here. He was the heir to Minneapolis. He was too important for such a risky endeavor.

Maybe the dark gave the Outfit an advantage. Maybe it caught Remo and his brothers by surprise. Who knew how many of them were even in the mansion?

The lock of my room turned, and I faced the door. This was my chance to run. The Outfit didn't know where in the house I was being kept. They probably expected to find me in the basement. I needed to find them first. It would take too long for them to search every part of the mansion.

A tall figure stepped into the room. It was difficult to make out much, and it didn't matter who had entered. I attacked without hesitation, storming toward my opponent, hoping to ram my elbow into his stomach. Unfortunately, backlit by moonlight I was an easy target. My opponent sidestepped me then grabbed my shoulder and thrust me forward. I collided with the wall and a firm chest pressed against my back.

"No soup today?" Savio taunted, but his voice was filled with tension. I tried shoving away from the wall, but Savio didn't budge. "Do I have to knock you out or will you stop the fucking struggling?"

I jerked my head back, hoping to hit his nose, but he was taller than I remembered, and the back of my head collided with his chin.

"Fuck," he snarled. He lodged his arms around my chest and waist like Samuel had done in jest not too long ago, and despite my thrashing, he carried me through the room and shoved me into the bathroom. "I won't carry you into our panic room like that. Fuck it."

I whirled around to face him.

"Don't fucking move," he growled.

"The Outfit will kick your asses. I bet you shit your pants when the lights went out," I hissed.

Savio chuckled. "It was Nino who turned off the lights. We know every inch of this fucking house by heart. We don't need lights. By the way, our surveillance camera showed a guy with blond hair. I wonder who will kill him. Remo or Nino?"

I froze. Samuel?

Savio closed the bathroom door. I rushed forward and hammered my fists against the wood. "Let me out! Let me out!"

"Scream all you want," Savio said. "Maybe it attracts an Outfit fucker so I can have some fun as well."

I pressed my palms against the door and slowly sank down onto my knees. Savio had to be lying. Samuel wasn't here. If Remo or Nino got him in their hands ...

CHAPTER 13

REMO

My brothers and I were watching the cage fight of Savio's next opponent. Kiara had already fallen asleep against Nino as usual. I doubted she ever watched more than a few seconds of a fight. Violence just wasn't in her nature.

"I can't wait to fight him," Savio said when his next opponent drop-kicked the other fighter into the cage. Not bad.

My phone lit up and so did the phones of my brothers. For a moment neither of us moved. I reached for it. An alarm had been raised. What the fuck? I opened the alert. Someone or something had touched the electric barbed wire at the top of the walls.

Nino was faster. He held up his phone with the live recording of the affected area. Four men had put a ladder over the fence, laid a wooden board over the electric wires, and climbed over the wall.

I stood, drawing my gun and a knife. Nino shook Kiara awake then turned to Adamo. "Take Kiara into the panic room. Shoot for the kill, no questions asked."

"What's the matter?" Kiara whispered. Nino shook his head, kissed her, then pushed her toward Adamo, who grabbed her hand and tugged her along, his own gun pulled.

"I'm going to turn off the lights on the premises," Nino said. "We can ambush them more easily that way."

I nodded. "Savio, go get Serafina. I want her in the panic room as well."

Savio frowned. "I want to kick Outfit asses."

"Savio," I snarled. I couldn't fucking believe the Outfit really dared to attack our mansion. It wasn't Dante's style. Way too risky.

With a glare, Savio ran up the stairs. Nino entered the code into his phone that was connected to our central control system and blackness fell upon us. It took my eyes a few seconds to adapt. Moonlight streamed in through the windows, and soon my brother and our surroundings became more than abstract shapes. I stepped up to Nino.

"They're heading toward the north wing," he said. The cameras had night vision, so we had no trouble following the attackers' progress. A blond head was among them, and I had a feeling I knew who it was. Samuel had come to save his twin, probably without his Capo's orders. If they were here on Dante's plan, they would have retreated the second the lights went out. That they still continued with it meant someone who didn't care about his life was the leader.

"Come on," I said. Nino and I crept into the garden, past the pool, in the direction where the attackers were headed. "Samuel is mine," I said quietly.

Nino didn't say anything, only shut down his phone so the glow of the screen wouldn't give us away. We reached the corner of the north wing and both crouched down. I peered around and found two men, one of them blond, working on the terrace door to Savio's domain while the other two scanned the area, guns pointed ahead. They had turned over the table and were half hidden behind it. It was massive wood. Maybe it would hold back the bullets.

"Two alive, Samuel and another," I ordered. Nino gave a terse nod. He'd give me a lecture later. He was pissed that we were being attacked because I'd brought Serafina here, that I'd put his wife in danger.

Nino and I raised our guns and began firing. Whoever our opponents were, they weren't the best shots. The first went down almost immediately. The two at the terrace door dropped behind the table and began firing as well. Eventually we ran out of bullets. The fun was about to begin. Nino pulled his knife. Clutching my own knife, I ran toward the remaining three attackers. Two went for me, one for Nino.

Samuel slashed his knife at me, and I blocked it with my own. The other Outfit fucker jabbed toward my stomach. I dodged that attack as well and rammed my blade into his thigh. He went down with a cry, but I grabbed him by the collar and jerked him up to block Samuel's next attack. His knife went straight into his companion's stomach. Before Samuel could attack again, Nino grabbed him from behind, one arm locked around his throat, the other over his arm with the knife. I dropped the Outfit bastard and jumped forward, hitting Samuel's wrist and breaking it so he would drop the knife.

He grunted but didn't drop the knife. He struggled like a madman, and Nino lost his balance. Fuck.

They both landed on the ground, Samuel on top of Nino. Grabbing my gun, I lunged at Samuel, grasped him by the throat, and hit his temple with the butt of the gun. With a groan, he went slack. Nino shoved him off himself. I touched Samuel's throat to make sure he was alive.

"Did you keep your opponent alive?" I asked Nino, panting.

"Of course. I knew it was unlikely that you'd not kill at least one of them."

I chuckled. Nino stepped up to me. "If we torture him slowly, send pieces of him to his parents and Dante, the Outfit will do our biding. I can't imagine they'll risk losing both Serafina and Samuel."

"I don't think he acted on Dante's orders."

"Probably not. But Dante won't abandon his nephew because he tried saving his twin."

I nodded. "Take the other survivor into a cell and wake him. Find out everything he knows. I'll send Savio to join you or else he won't stop bitching."

"What about Samuel?"

"I'll take him to another cell. Then I'll have a word with Serafina."

"Are we going to deal with him together?"

I regarded the blond man on the ground. "Yes. If he's anything like Serafina, he'll be fun to break."

SERAFINA

The lights came back on. My eyes burned from the onslaught of brightness. I was still kneeling on the bathroom floor when Remo's voice rang out.

"Go into the basement and help Nino torture the Outfit asshole."

I could feel the color draining from my face. I'd heard the shooting, had prayed that the Outfit would win ...

I forced myself to stand when the lock turned.

Remo came in covered in blood, and I started trembling, terrified my greatest horrors had come true.

For a couple of heartbeats, Remo regarded me. "Your brother tried to save you."

Terror gripped me like a vise. I could not breathe. I didn't want to believe it. "You're lying," I gasped out, voice broken and hollow.

A dark smile curled his lips. "He's a brave one."

I rushed toward Remo, clutched his bloody shirt.

Remo's dark eyes held mine. The predatory gleam in them made my heart thud even faster.

"No," I said again. "Samuel isn't here. He wouldn't risk it. Dante wouldn't allow it."

"I think your twin would gladly put his life down for you, Angel. I doubt he came on your uncle's orders. That means no reinforcement."

I swallowed. Oh Samuel. My protector. How could you be so stupid?

If Samuel was dead, I couldn't go on living, not with the knowledge that he'd died to save me. Tears burned a hot trail down my cheeks. "If you ... if you ..." I couldn't even say it. "Then kill me now."

"He's not dead yet," Remo murmured, dark eyes scanning my face. "We'll see how long he lasts, though."

Samuel wasn't dead. Not yet.

My eyes widened. "Let me see him."

Remo touched my throat, coming closer. "Why? So you can say goodbye?"

I bit my lip. "To see the truth."

Remo smiled. "I'm not lying." He grabbed my wrist and dragged me out of my room. He led me down into the basement, and holding me by the arm so I couldn't storm inside, he opened one of the cells. Inside lay Samuel, covered in blood and not moving except for the shallow rise and fall of his chest. His blond hair was matted with blood. My chest constricted so tightly I was sure to pass out any second.

"What did you do?"

"Not much yet," he said as he closed the door. "Hit him over the head. Once he wakes, Nino and I will tend to him." I knew what that meant.

A terrifying, agonized scream echoed through the basement. I flinched violently.

"That's Nino's doing. He's talking to the other survivor."

Soon those would be Samuel's cries. Soon he'd be submitted to the horrors he'd wanted to save me from. Horrors I'd been spared. Bile traveled up my throat.

My twin would suffer and die for me.

I grasped Remo's arm, my eyes begging with him, even though I knew he didn't have a heart I could soften. "Please don't. Torture me instead."

Remo smiled darkly, cupping my face. "I don't want to torture you. And I told you I won't ever cut you again, Angel."

Of course. I knew what he wanted, what he'd wanted from the start, and today he'd get it. Swallowing my pride because it wasn't worth Samuel's life, I lowered myself to my knees right in front of Remo. I tilted my face up, tears stinging in my eyes. "I'm on my knees. I'm begging you to spare him. Whatever you want, it's yours, Remo. Take it. Take everything."

His dark eyes flashed with an emotion I couldn't read. "You didn't beg for your own life. You didn't offer me your body to avoid pain, but you do for your brother?"

"I do. I'd do anything for him," I whispered. "I'm offering you everything. You can have it all. I'm giving it to you freely, willingly, if you spare my brother."

Remo grasped my arm and hoisted me to my feet. Without another word, he dragged me upstairs and into his bedroom. He released me and closed the door. His breathing was harsh.

My fingers shook as I reached for my dress and pulled it over my head. Remo's eyes scorched my skin as I reached for my bra and unhooked it, letting it drop to the floor. With a hard swallow, I pushed my panties down my hips until they joined my bra on the floor.

"It's yours," I said quietly. All I could think about was Samuel down in that basement, lying in his own blood and the torture that awaited him at the hands of Remo and Nino. I had heard the rumors of what they'd done to Kiara's uncle.

Not taking his eyes off my face, Remo advanced on me. His hands touched my waist and I trembled. "So strong," Remo murmured. "So very difficult to break."

"You won. You broke me. I begged you. I'm offering you my body. Please spare Samuel."

His eyes traveled the length of my body before they locked on mine once more. "You aren't broken, Angel. Sacrificing yourself for someone you love isn't weakness."

"Spare my brother, Remo." With shaking hands I reached for his belt, but he stopped me. And my world fell apart because if he didn't take me up on my offer, what else could I give him in return for my brother's life? What else did he want?

Remo leaned down to my ear. "Such a tantalizing offer." He exhaled. "You'd hate me fiercely."

"I would," I whispered.

"You would. So you don't hate me fiercely yet?"

I shuddered. I couldn't bear his mind games, not now, not when Samuel's life depended on it.

Remo kissed the spot below my ear. "I *will* spare your brother, Angel," he said in a low voice, and I froze because I couldn't believe it. "I will send him back to the Outfit with a message. It needs to be loud and clear so they understand I won't have my territory breached."

I nodded mutely. I'd agree to anything to save my brother. I didn't understand any of this.

"You will come down with me into the cell beside Samuel's. I will have a talk with him." I stiffened in Remo's hold. "*Just a talk* and tell him that his actions have consequences, and then I'll return to your cell and you're going to scream and beg as if I'm hurting you. You will make him believe it. Then I will release him so he can return home with the remains of the other Outfit soldier and the knowledge that you will suffer brutally for every single one of their mistakes."

I gave a nod. Samuel would hate himself for it. He would suffer worse than before, but it was better than the alternative. I needed to save him no matter the cost. I could tell him the truth once I was back home.

"Good," Remo said quietly. He gathered my clothes from the ground, his eyes level with my center for a moment before he straightened. "Now get dressed."

I didn't understand why he hadn't taken me when it was obvious how much he wanted me. He could have had me in every way he wanted. I wouldn't have fought him. He could have sent the warning message by recording Samuel's torture and my screams and sending the video to my family. He didn't have to keep Samuel alive to deliver it.

What else could he want?

REMO

Serafina had offered herself to me, but she'd done it out of despair, out of love for her brother. Not because she wanted to.

She loved her brother fiercely, wanted to protect him at any cost, like I would my brothers. I could respect that. I'd never admired a woman on her knees more than I did Serafina. She followed me quietly through the mansion. I could have asked anything of her, but that wasn't how I wanted things to go. Far from it.

I opened the door to the cell beside Samuel's, and Serafina stepped in.

The door to the third cell swung open, and Nino stepped out, covered in blood, his brows drawing together when he spotted Serafina. I closed the door and faced him.

"What's going on?" he asked. His eyes scanned my face. "*Remo.*"

I smirked. "Change of plans."

He moved closer. "We're not letting him go."

"We will."

Savio joined us in the hallway, clothes drenched in blood as well. He didn't say anything, only regarded us carefully.

Nino shook his head. "You're losing yourself in your game."

"I'm not. I know exactly what I'm doing, Nino. Torturing and killing Samuel won't make the same impact as my plan does. He'd become a martyr. His death would forge Dante and his family closer together. They would unite in their loss. But shame and guilt will rip them apart."

"So this isn't about Serafina?"

"Of course it is. She's the center of my game."

Nino shook his head again. "We promised Fabiano his father, and I want this game over. I want her out of our mansion. Speed up the process."

"Some things take time."

"Your game has been evolving a lot since we kidnapped her. Are you sure it's because you think it necessary or is it because she's making you?"

"She's not making me do anything. You know me. I can't be coerced to do anything."

"I'm going to Kiara. Adamo took her back to our wing. I don't have the necessary patience for you tonight." Nino stalked off.

Savio raised his eyebrows.

"What did the Outfit bastard say?" I muttered.

"He was one of the younger soldiers. Made Men from Samuel's group.

Apparently, the blond asshole has already quite the loyal following in the Minneapolis Outfit."

"I assume Dante and Pietro Mione didn't know?"

"They didn't."

"You can leave. I'll handle this alone."

Savio hesitated. "Are you really sure your plan is going to work? Nino is the logical genius."

"He doesn't take emotions into consideration. Emotional warfare is far more effective in this case than open violence."

"Not as much fun if you ask me."

I shook my head. "Oh, it's fun for me, trust me."

Savio snorted. "I'll go take a shower. You have whatever kind of fun you prefer."

He sauntered off and I stepped into Samuel's cell. His wrists and ankles were tied together, but his eyes were open in his bloody face and full of hatred. "You fucking bastard," he rasped.

I smiled. "I'd be careful with the insults if I were you."

"Fuck you," Samuel spat. "As if anything I say matters. You're going to torture me to death anyway."

I knelt beside him. "I don't think that's the right punishment for you, *Sam.*"

Fear replaced the hatred in his eyes. He arched up. "Don't! Don't you dare touch her."

I straightened. "Someone will have to suffer for this. And I know you will suffer twice as much if I hurt your twin."

"No! Torture me. Kill me."

"Unfortunately, that's not an option. You will return to the Outfit with the memory of your sister's screams."

Samuel froze. "No," he gasped out.

I turned.

"Remo!" he roared, but I closed the cell door.

I stepped into Serafina's cell. She was pale and still so painstakingly proud and beautiful, I allowed myself a moment to admire her.

She tilted her head toward me, her blue eyes burning with emotion. "Samuel will be safe?"

"By my honor."

Her lips curled, but she didn't say anything.

"I hope you can be convincing. I want your best screams."

Her eyes narrowed briefly, giving me a fucking kick as usual. It was so much better than her desperate surrender.

She closed her eyes, chest heaving, elegant throat flexing.

I needed to own this woman. Body and soul and everything else she could offer. I fucking burned with the desire to possess her in every way possible.

Finally, Serafina screamed, and it was so fucking real that my body reacted to the sound, but not in a way it usually did, not with excitement and the thrill of the hunt. There was something close to revulsion filling my body, hearing her agonized cries and imagining they were real.

My hands curled to fists, my muscles tensing because a deeply buried instinct wanted me to protect her from whatever caused those screams. Unfortunately for her, nothing could protect her from me.

I couldn't fucking take it anymore. I stalked toward her, gripped her arm. "Enough," I growled, breathing harshly.

Serafina's eyes snapped open. They searched my face, and a second too late I realized she got deeper than anyone was allowed. "Enough," I repeated, my voice shaking with rage and confusion.

"Enough?" she whispered so softly. The sound was like a fucking caress.

Maybe I should end it now. Do what Nino said, end this fucking game.

Get rid of Serafina and Samuel both.

I cupped her head and pressed my forehead to hers. She trembled, overwhelmed.

"Maybe I should kill you."

"Maybe," she breathed. "But you won't."

I should have contradicted her, but she was right and she knew it.

"You promised."

I pulled back from her. "And I will keep my promise. I'll release your brother now. I'll have one of my men fly him and the corpses to Kansas City. How he gets back to Outfit territory from there is his own problem."

She nodded.

"Come," I ordered.

I didn't touch her as I led her back to her bedroom. She moved toward the window and perched on the windowsill, pulling her legs against her chest. I stopped with my fingers against the light switch then lowered them, leaving the room in the dark.

Serafina twisted her head, staring at me. She was backlit by the silver moonlight as she perched in the window frame. She'd never looked more like an angel than in this fucking moment, and I realized I was on a precarious path.

Her whispered words broke the silence. "I wonder whose game is more dangerous, yours or mine, Remo?"

CHAPTER 14

SERAFINA

Over the next couple of days, Remo kept his distance. We didn't go on runs, and Kiara or one of his brothers brought me food.

The look in his eyes when I'd screamed in the basement, it was difficult to describe, but I knew for some reason it had bothered him.

Nino had informed me this morning that Samuel was back in Minneapolis. I believed him. Remo had promised and despite my difficult feelings toward the Capo, I knew he'd keep this promise. I also knew that Samuel and my family were suffering every day I was here.

Nino treated me even colder than before—if that was even possible. I had a feeling things between Remo and him were strained because of Samuel. Nino probably would have killed my brother. It was the obvious solution, the one Dante would have chosen. But Remo ... he was unpredictable. Cruel. Fierce.

I didn't understand him.

If he'd tortured and killed Samuel, I would have hated him with brutal abandon, would have done anything I could to kill him. But he hadn't. I was scared about his motives, but more than that ... I was scared because a twisted part of me was grateful. I wasn't sure exactly why, but Remo had done this because of me.

It was way past midnight when I heard my door open. I couldn't sleep, my mind whirring with thoughts.

Lying on my side, I watched the tall figure step in. I knew it was Remo from the way he moved, from his tall frame, the shock of his black hair. "You're awake," he said in a low voice.

"Did you want to watch me sleep?"

He moved closer. His face lay in shadows, and my pulse picked up. He sank down on the edge of the bed, and I rolled onto my back.

"No," he said in a strange tone. "I prefer you awake."

He leaned over me, one of his arms braced beside my hip.

"What do you want?" I muttered.

"I want you gone."

My eyes widened. "Then let me go."

"I fear it's not that easy." He bent lower and then his palm touched my belly and slowly slid down. I held my breath, becoming still in a mix of shock and anticipation. He cupped me through the covers and my clothes. The touch was light, almost questioning, and I was completely frozen. My center tingled and that, more than Remo's touch, sent a fierce stab of fear through me. I wanted him to touch me without a barrier between us, wanted to get a taste of something utterly forbidden, something I wasn't allowed to want.

Neither of us said anything. I knew what paralyzed me, but what restrained Remo?

He exhaled slowly and stood. Without another word, he disappeared.

Good Lord, what was happening? With him. With me. With the both of us.

That middle of the night visit seemed to have done something to Remo because he returned to our previous routine of taking me on runs and walks through the gardens. I wasn't sure if I should be relieved or worried. I'd almost missed our daily arguments because he took me seriously and was strangely excited about my comebacks. He didn't want me to be the restrained lady. Far from it. Remo thrived on chaos and conflict. His presence left me breathless and overwhelmed.

I slanted Remo a look as he walked beside me in silence. His expression was harsh, his dark eyes forbidding. I stopped and after a moment he did too. He narrowed his eyes.

"Why did you really let Samuel go? I want the truth."

Remo glared down at me. "I think you're forgetting what you are. I don't owe you the truth. I don't even owe you these fucking strolls through the gardens. You are my captive, Serafina."

Serafina? "What about 'Angel?'" I retorted.

Remo gripped my upper arms. "Careful. I think handling you with kid gloves gave you the wrong idea."

"I think I have exactly the right idea."

Remo's fingers tightened. I lifted my hands and pressed them to his chest. The muscles flexed under my touch. Remo lowered his gaze to my hands then slowly looked back up. The expression on his face burned a fierce trail through my body. Fury and desire.

Remo jerked me against him, knocking the air out of me. One hand gripped my neck, and his mouth pressed against my ear. "I don't remember you pushing me away when I touched your pussy a few nights ago, *Angel*," he growled.

Shame washed over me from the memory, but worse, so much worse ... longing.

"Every fucking day you want me a little more. I can see it in your eyes, can see the struggle in them. You aren't allowed to have me like I'm not allowed to have you."

"You are Remo Falcone. You are Capo. You rule over the West. Who could stop you from having me?" I murmured. My God. What was wrong with me?

His fingers shifted on my neck, loosening, and he pulled back to meet my gaze, and I wished he hadn't because the fierceness in his eyes was like the first breath of air after holding your breath for too long.

"The only force on this earth that can stop me is *you*. You're the only one I'd allow to do so," he said in a dark voice. He kissed me, a slide of his lips over mine. "How much longer will you?"

I wanted to deepen the kiss. My fingers trembled against Remo's chest. I wanted to look away from his dark eyes and at the same time I wanted to drown in their power. I wanted so many things when he was around. Things I'd always be forbidden to want.

A man of unparalleled cruelty. My captor. My enemy.

I stumbled back, wheezing.

"Do you want to run again?" The dark amusement in his voice wasn't as convincing as it usually was. He sounded strained.

I didn't want to run, and that was the problem because I should want to run from the desire. I took another step back.

Remo smiled darkly. "I don't think I've ever seen you as scared of me as you are now."

Terrified. I was completely terrified. I turned and ran back to the mansion.

On the terrace I collided with Kiara, and we had to grip each other to keep our balance. My eyes met Nino's—he was standing behind her as always—and for a moment I was sure he'd attack me, but Kiara pulled away from me.

"Hey, are you alright?" she asked, touching my arm, looking concerned.

I nodded jerkily.

"You sure? Did Remo do something?"

Did he? Or did I? The lines were getting blurry. Remo was right. Every day I was here things got more complicated. Captivity broke me, only not in the way I thought it would.

Nino's gaze moved past us. I knew whom he was seeking.

"No," I whispered in reply to her question.

Kiara frowned. "Come on. Let's go inside."

"Kiara," Nino warned.

"No," she said firmly. "This is getting ridiculous. Serafina won't hurt me."

She took my hand and led me inside where she pushed me down on the sofa. Remo and Nino remained outside. I could hear the low rumble of their voices. It sounded as if they were in an argument.

Kiara handed me a glass of water then sat down beside me. "Is it because of your brother? Nino said they allowed him to return to the Outfit. That's good, isn't it?"

I nodded. It was. My brother. My family. The Outfit. My fiancé. I owed all of them loyalty. I owed them resistance and a fight.

"Serafina?" Kiara touched my thigh.

I met her compassionate gaze and touched her hand. "I'm losing myself."

Her eyes widened then flitted to the French windows. "You know, I was completely terrified of Remo in the beginning. But I saw sides of him that made me realize he's more than brutality and cruelty."

"Remo is the cruelest man I know. He is beyond redemption."

She smiled sadly. "Maybe he just needs someone who will show him the path to redemption."

I laughed harshly. "I hope you don't think that's going to be me. The only path I'll show him is the road to Hell. I hate him."

Kiara squeezed my thigh but didn't say anything. I was relieved when Nino took me up to my room, not Remo.

I traced the line of the healed cut on my forearm, wishing it were still fresh, wishing Remo would hurt me again. More than that, I wished I didn't need that kind of reminder because Remo Falcone was beyond redemption. I shouldn't need reminding.

The next day Remo and I did our longest run so far despite the exceptionally hot late August sun. We both needed to relieve pent up energy it seemed. We hardly spoke. I tried to keep my mind blank, tried not to think of my family who was suffering because Remo refused to make a new demand. Guilt became harder to bear every day. The guilt over not suffering the way I should be.

My eyes registered a shadow above our heads. A large black and white bird of prey with a red head. "Look," I panted. "There's your spirit animal. A vulture."

Remo stopped and laughed. A real laugh. Not dark, taunting, or cruel. "Good to know you find me that repulsive."

I wished. He took a bottle of water from the small running backpack and handed it to me. God, how I wished I found Remo's body repulsive. I took a sip of water then handed him the bottle back.

"When are you going to ask my uncle for Rocco Scuderi?" I asked to distract myself and him.

Remo's expression hardened, his eyes returning to the sky. "Vultures wait for their prey to drop dead. I think the Outfit's almost there."

"You can't win this game. The moment you return me, the Outfit will rise and strike back. An endless spiral of violence will start."

"Why would you say that, Angel? Don't you want to be returned? Danilo is waiting eagerly to wed and bed you."

I followed the large bird's flight, wondering how it would feel to be free like that. A marriage to Danilo seemed so unreal in that moment, so far away, when I had already been less than forty minutes away from being married to him. That girl in the beautiful white wedding dress, she felt like more of a stranger every day. My eyes were drawn to my hand, but the ring wasn't there. For the first time since my engagement to Danilo, I'd forgotten to put the ring on in the morning.

"One month," Remo reminded me as he led me through the garden.

It took me a moment to understand what he meant. "Since you captured me," I said quietly.

One month. Sometimes it felt so much longer, sometimes like only yesterday. I had never thought I'd survive a single day in the hands of the Camorra, in Remo Falcone's hands, and now I'd survived so many more. Remo was more patient than I'd thought. I was fairly sure my family and the Outfit was at a point by now that they'd hand Scuderi over, even if my grandfather disapproved. He was an old man close to death.

I stared down at my bare feet in the grass. As a child I'd loved to run around barefoot, but eventually I had stopped because I was told it was undignified. Ice Princess. I'd enjoyed being her in public, even if she wasn't a reflection of my true self. It was who I was supposed to be as Dante's niece, as Danilo's wife.

Controlled. Dignified. Graceful.

I caught Remo watching me. No control. Unbridled emotion. Furious passion.

One month.

I averted my eyes. Remo led me closer to the mansion.

"I want to know what's going on in your head," Remo said.

I was glad he couldn't. "Maybe I'll tell you if you tell me what's going on in yours."

Remo stopped. "Right now I'm imagining how it would feel to bury my face between your legs, Angel."

I froze. Remo obviously enjoyed my shock if his smirk was an indication. I didn't get a chance to retort because a low moan sounded above us. My eyes darted to the open window, my brows pulling together. Remo moved behind my back, standing very close and leaning forward slightly so his face was beside mine. He nodded up to the window. "That's Nino and Kiara's bedroom."

A woman moaned again, an abandoned, uncontrolled sound full of pleasure.

I took a step back but bumped into Remo, who didn't budge. "That's the sound a woman makes when a man is eating her out."

"You are disgusting," I gritted out, trying to get away, but Remo's arms wrapped around me from behind, keeping me in place.

"Please," Kiara gasped out. "Please, more."

"Do you want to know why I know Nino is currently licking pussy? It's because you don't hear him. His face is buried in it."

Kiara's moans turned louder, desperate, and then she cried out.

I wanted to be disgusted, but my body reacted hearing these sounds. Heat gathered between my legs.

"Have you ever made this sound, Angel?" he murmured. "No, you haven't. But don't you wonder how it would feel to be overwhelmed with so much pleasure to force these kinds of moans from your lips?"

I stopped struggling, but Remo didn't loosen his hold on me. His firm chest, warm and strong, still pressed up against my back. "A tongue between your thighs, licking, sucking. Don't you want to know how that would feel?"

I pressed my lips together, but I could do nothing about the trickle of wetness between my thighs. Above us new moans rang out. Kiara, followed by deeper, more restrained grunts.

"You are a grown woman, and yet you've never come so hard you lost yourself. You've never had a man buried between your thighs, eating you out." Remo's mouth brushed my ear. Then his tongue slid along the outer rim until it reached my earlobe. He circled it then drew it between his lips and sucked lightly, and I felt it all the way between my legs. He released my earlobe and exhaled. Something hard dug into my lower back. I should have drawn back in disgust, but I was utterly frozen.

"Are you wet, Serafina? Wet for me?" Remo rasped in my ear, and a small shiver passed through my traitorous body upon hearing his voice.

"I won't ever bow to your will, Remo," I whispered harshly.

"Who says I want you to bow, Angel? I want you to give me yourself freely because you want to, because you choose to. Have you ever chosen anything only because you wanted to? Without heeding the consequences? Without regard to what's expected of you? All your life you've bowed to your parents' will, your uncle's will, the Outfit's will, and once I'll release you, you'll bow to Danilo's will."

I hated Remo, hated him for making sense, hated him for getting under my skin. And I hated myself for letting him.

"One day you will realize that you were never freer than in your time with me. Whatever you do, no one from the Outfit must know, and even if they find out, they won't blame you, Angel."

I closed my eyes, trying to ignore how good Remo's body felt against mine, trying to block the moans growing in crescendo, but my throbbing center was difficult to forget. Remo's arms around me shifted until his thumb brushed the underside of my breast. I stilled but didn't push him away, didn't utter a word of protest. His mouth found my throat, nibbling, licking, biting, and his hand slipped under my shirt. Rough fingertips slid over my skin, higher and higher until they reached my nipple through the lace of my bra.

My lips parted from the sensation.

"Won't you tell me to stop?" Remo murmured in my ear before his tongue led a wet trail down my throat. His free hand cupped my cheek and twisted my face around so he could assault my mouth with an all-consuming kiss. His tongue licked every crevice of my mouth, tasting, consuming, owning my lips.

"You better tell me to stop, Angel, because if I don't stop now, I fear I won't stop at all."

I barely listened to his words, too caught up in the sensation his fingers on my nipple created, too overwhelmed by the moans ringing out above us. Remo released my face and nipple, gripped my hips in a bruising hold, and got down on his knees. Glancing over my shoulder, shock washed over me to see the Capo kneeling before me.

He pushed up my skirt and bit into my ass cheek then slid his tongue over the spot. His palm cupped my other cheek, hard, kneading possessively before he slid up and wedged his fingers under the strap of my thong. He tugged hard and the drenched fabric jerked against my center and clit. I gasped in surprise and pleasure.

Remo chuckled against my ass cheek then circled his tongue over the soft skin while his fingers kept tugging at my thong. How could this feel so good, so overpoweringly perfect? How could the sensation of fabric rubbing against my sensitive flesh bring me down like that?

Remo tugged harder and I arched, biting down on my lip to keep the sounds in. He sucked the skin of my ass cheek into his mouth as he gave my thong a few hard tugs. Waves of heat and tingling spread from my center to every nerve ending in my body. I was getting closer to something impossible, wondrous, mind-blowing. Something I'd never felt, not even close. Then Remo dropped his hand and released my skin from his mouth. I had to hold back a sound of protest. Gripping my hips, Remo turned me around. I stared down at him. He knelt before me, his eyes dark and possessive, a dangerous smile playing around his lips.

Even kneeling at my feet, Remo oozed dominance, control, power. Looking down at him I still felt like the one he brought to her knees.

I narrowed my eyes, wanting to step away from him. Away from his violence and darkness that seemed to draw me in like an undercurrent.

As if he could feel my resistance, Remo tightened his hold on my hips and leaned forward, pressing a soft kiss to my white panties, right over my throbbing nub. My hand flew forward, gripping his muscular shoulders to steady myself. His eyes pierced me to the core with their intensity as he leaned his rough cheek against my thigh, his mouth close to my center. "I can smell your arousal, Angel," he said in a raw voice that traveled through my body like a jolt of electricity.

As I watched, he smirked, parted his mouth, stuck his tongue out, and traced the small valley where my panties clung to my folds. I began to tremble.

"Will you let me pull down your panties and taste your pussy?"

I didn't say anything. Not yes, but worse. Worse ... I didn't say no. Because I didn't want to. I wanted Remo, had never wanted anything more.

REMO

Serafina stared down at me with hatred, but she didn't fight when I hooked my fingers in the waistband of her thong. I waited a couple of heartbeats, relishing in her silence, bathing in her surrender. I pulled down her panties. She shuddered but lifted her feet so she could step out of her panties. I pushed her skirt up. "Hold it up, Angel."

Her elegant fingers curled around the hem of her skirt, and she pressed it up against her flat stomach.

I was at eye level with her pussy. The trimmed hair above her clit glistened with her juice, and her lips were swollen with arousal. I leaned forward, breathing in her heady scent. Before I'd kidnapped Serafina, I'd entertained different scenarios of how I would conquer her, break her, but this hadn't been among them. I had to admit I enjoyed it tremendously.

I ran my rough palms up her smooth thighs. She trembled, but not from fear, and fuck ... with Serafina I preferred any emotion but fear.

My thumbs stroked her soft folds and parted them, revealing her small nub. She released a shaky breath, face half terrified, half expectant. "My mouth being the first to taste your pussy, I'll be very thorough, Angel."

I leaned forward and licked her clit lightly. She bit down on her lip, stifling a sound. She closed her eyes, her cheeks blazing. I pulled back a couple of inches. "Yes, don't watch, my little angel. Maybe you'll manage to pretend I'm someone else."

Her eyes flew open, furious, and she returned my gaze. She wouldn't look away again.

I dove in with small, gentle licks, testing how she'd react. A flood of her juice was my reward. I'd never been with a virgin or someone inexperienced, and I hadn't gone down on a woman in ages, much less ever been gentle with one. This was a new experience but one I found myself enjoying. My cock throbbed every time my tongue delved between her lips, from her opening up to her clit. I tasted every part of her sweet pussy, traced the smooth inside of her lips, her opening, knowing my cock would soon claim that part of her.

Serafina shook, her legs starting to give in.

"Hold on to the wall," I ordered, and she complied without protest, leaning forward, her forearms braced against the rough façade, golden hair curtaining her face as she glared down at me while I ate her pussy. My teeth grazed her clit lightly, and she jerked, a small moan slipping out.

I brushed the inside of her knee and pushed. She parted for me until she stood with her legs in a V over me. I tilted my head up, my hands curling over her hips and firmly pulled her down on my mouth and sucked each fold lightly before I closed my lips around her clit. She started rocking against my face almost desperately, and I complied with her silent demand by practically burying myself in her pussy, lapping at her, diving into her tightness, sucking. Then her lips parted, her brows pulling together in shock and astonishment, and she tensed.

My eyes drank in the expression on her face, the wild abandon of passion on her perfect features, the shock, the resignation, the delight. Possessiveness wasn't one of my character traits, because I owned everything that mattered, but seeing Serafina in the throes of her orgasm and knowing I was the first man to give it to her, I felt fucking possessive. She was mine, body and soul, and would be until I decided to set her free.

I smirked against her as her pussy throbbed. After another long lick, I leaned my head back against the rough stone and licked my lips. Realization filled Serafina's eyes, and her face twisted with horror and shame.

I smiled darkly. She shook her head, stepping back, tugging at her skirt until it covered her pussy again.

I stayed on the ground, my cock throbbing in my pants, my chin coated with her juices, and my body swelled with sweet triumph. "Run, *Angel*. Run from what you've done," I murmured with a dark smile, and Serafina did. She whirled around, blond hair whipping through the air, and stormed away.

No one knew better than I did that you couldn't run from what you've done.

I pushed to my feet, wiped my chin with the back of my hand, and set out to find my angel. She'd received pleasure; now it was time she gave something back.

I wanted nothing less than every last part of her. Her innocence, her heart, her soul, her body. Her purity and her darkness.

I would take everything.

CHAPTER 15

SERAFINA

'd never experienced this acute sense of shame before. I didn't stop running until I reached the bedroom and shut the door, but even then I continued into the bathroom, snatching at my clothes, needing them gone. I dropped them on the floor, everything except for my thong, which was still with Remo.

What had I done?

I turned on the shower and slipped under the spray of warm water, rubbing myself clean, rubbing between my legs, but the warm, wet, throbbing sensation remained. It wouldn't go away. I slumped against the wall. I had let Remo put his mouth on me, his tongue inside me, and I had enjoyed it.

My body hummed with the remnants of pleasure, a distant memory my body was eager to refresh. I'd never experienced sensations like that. But worse, Remo's words had been proven true. I'd never felt freer than in that moment with Remo between my legs, showing me pleasure. It had felt amazing, freeing, and utterly wrong. All my life I had been taught to be honorable, to do what was expected of me, and today I'd gone against it all.

Dark and tall, Remo appeared in the doorway, come to claim his prize. His eyes roamed over my naked body, and mine did the same.

He was cruel and twisted. *Beyond redemption.*

Brutal attractiveness, forbidden pleasure, promised pain. I should have been disgusted by him, but I wasn't. Not by his body and not always by his nature.

I shut off the water, scared of what he wanted, completely terrified of what I wanted. This was his game of chess; he was the king and I was the trapped queen that the Outfit needed to protect. He moved me into position for his last move: the kill. Check.

He began unbuttoning his shirt then shrugged it off. He moved closer, stopping right before me. "You always watch me like something you want to touch but aren't allowed to. Who's holding you back, *Angel?*"

"Nothing's holding me back. I don't want to," I muttered with false bravado, the lie ringing loud and clear.

"Is that so?" Remo asked quietly. He reached for my hand, and I let him. Let him put my palm against his strong chest, let him slide it lower, over the hard lines of muscles, over the rough scars. He placed my palm over his belt then released me. "Don't you want to be free of society's shackles for once? To do something forbidden?"

What I wanted more than anything was his twisted smile gone. I gripped his belt and tugged him toward me, angrily, desperately, because I was falling, already lost, content to lose myself. His lips crashed down on mine, tongue domineering my mouth, hands rough against my ass. He jerked me up and against him so his erection pressed against my center.

I gasped, which he swallowed with his lips.

My fingers hooked in his waistband, scared and curious. Remo caught my gaze, his full of hunger and harshness. He ripped his mouth away from mine, backing me into the wall. "Be brave, Angel."

I curled my fingers in his belt and held his gaze as I opened the buckle. The clink was the sound of my last wall crumbling. Gripping his zipper, I pulled it slowly down, terrified and aroused. Then I paused.

Remo bent low, his mouth brushing my ear. "I'm not a patient man. You are playing with fire."

Forcing down my nerves, I turned my face, bringing my own lips to his ear. "Oh, Remo, I will be your first angel. Patience is a virtue, and you will be rewarded for it." I kissed his ear then trailed my tongue over the rim.

He exhaled and pulled back so he could look at my face, and the look in his eyes, it almost made my knees buckle. For a second, I had him. I held the reins on the cruelest, most powerful man in the west, and it was thrilling. But Remo wouldn't be Remo, wouldn't be Capo, if he didn't know how to take his power back.

He grabbed his pants and pulled them down together with his boxers. His erection sprang free, and Remo braced himself against the wall with his hands on either side of my head.

I stared down at him and sank back against the wall. He was long and thick and impossibly hard. I tore my gaze away, only to be hit with Remo's penetrating stare.

My cheeks blazed with heat, and Remo smiled as he leaned forward, trailing his tongue over my heated cheekbone. "Tell me, Angel, what will be my reward for my patience?"

I stood on my tiptoes, curling my fingers over Remo's neck, pulling myself up and against him. His hardness rubbed against my naked stomach, and he groaned a low, dangerous sound. "Something forbidden. Something you aren't meant to be gifted."

Remo's body became taut, eager, and he tipped my head back, his lips brushing mine. "Something you promised to someone else?"

My throat tightened, but Remo kissed me hard, not allowing me to dwell on it. He hooked one of my legs up over his hip, opening me up. His fingers brushed my center, and then two fingers breached my opening. Pain shot through me. I ripped myself from his mouth, tensing, a choked sound bursting from my throat.

Remo stilled, his fingers deep inside of me. He pulled back, a hint of surprise on his face, then it was gone. He regarded me intently, almost curiously. My chest heaved as I tried to grow used to the stretched sensation of having his fingers in me. Remo touched his forehead to mine. "I think you were right, Angel, my reward will be worth it."

Anger flooded me. "Did you enjoy hurting me?" I whispered.

Remo kissed my lips. "This isn't me hurting you. This is me trying not to hurt you. You will know when I want to hurt you." He pulled his fingers out then slid them back in. My muscles clung to him, and I exhaled. He held my gaze as he established a slow rhythm. I leaned my head back against the wall, never averting my eyes.

Remo's dark eyes dragged me deeper and deeper down into their abyss. Pleasure slowly replaced the feeling of being stretched. I began rocking my hips, causing Remo's erection to rub over my belly. His breathing deepened, but he kept up pumping his fingers into me at a slow pace, watching me, his other hand clinging to my outer thigh. A deep throbbing spread from my center, and I gasped, and not from pain this time. Remo's thumb flicked over my nub, and I splintered from the inside out, into thousands of particles filled with sensation.

Remo watched me hungrily, almost reverently, and I smiled, not even sure why. I was still reeling from my high when Remo pulled his fingers out and grabbed my other thigh, lifting me up, my back against the wall, my body trapped between it and his chest. And I knew what he wanted. My hands flew up to his chest, resisting. When his erection brushed my inner thigh, I gasped out, "No!"

Remo's dark eyes flew up to mine, angry, incredulous ... but he did pause. "Not like this," I said quietly. "Not against a wall." This would happen on my terms, not his.

The anger lessened. "You are right," he said darkly. He hoisted me higher so my legs wrapped around his middle, and my center pressed up against his six-pack. Then he walked with me out of the bathroom and into the bedroom. "I will fuck you on the bed, Angel. I put white sheets on for the occasion. What a pity it would have been if I didn't stain them with your blood."

Shock and indignation shot through me because I realized my sheets had been white for a few days now, but then Remo kissed me. I dug my nails into his shoulders angrily and battled his tongue.

We tugged and kissed and suddenly we were on the bed. Remo knelt between my legs, shoving them further apart, his mouth harsh against my throat, and I became still, soft, scared. This was it.

Remo stilled above me and raised his head. Our eyes met. I don't know what he saw in mine, but he cupped my cheek, startling me. His kisses became light, gentle, almost caring. So wrong. That wasn't Remo. That was a lie. "Shh, Angel. I'll be gentle."

His fingers stroked my breasts, my side, oh so gently, and his mouth ... his mouth dusted me with loving kisses. Even though I knew them to be false, knew I was supposed to shove him away, to put up a fight, I kissed him back. Lost, lost, lost.

Remo molded our bodies together, shifting, and then I felt a light pressure against my opening.

I gasped and tensed. Remo watched my face, full of intent, and his eyes ... they quieted my hesitation, my fear, any protest I might have come up with.

He slid into me slowly, inch by inch, never taking more than my body could give, but still he seemed to tear me apart. A slow conquest but a conquest nevertheless. I'd expected brutality and cruelty. I wished for it. But this gentle Remo, he terrified me the most. He didn't let me escape, not even the only way I could. He wanted to consume me with his eyes. He sunk all the way into me, and then he paused as I shivered under the force of the intrusion. His dark eyes said what I'd known all along.

He possessed me. He *owned* me.

I was the queen.

He was the king.

Checkmate.

REMO

This was the ultimate victory over the Outfit. They didn't know it yet, but they would soon. Serafina trembled under me, her marble cheeks flushed, lips parted. She was in pain, and somehow it didn't please me because I had tried not to hurt her. I gave pain willingly, deliberately, freely. Not by accident.

I held myself still, content in the feeling of her tight walls squeezing my cock mercilessly. I was fucking ecstatic feeling the slickness around me and knowing it was her virgin blood. The sweetest reward for my patience I could imagine.

My eyes roamed Serafina's perfect features, and her blue eyes met mine, searching, wondering. I pulled out of her slowly, recognizing the signs of pain in her expression, then pushed back in even slower.

I rocked my hips slowly, keeping my movements as controlled as possible. Her face twisted with pain and pleasure, and I angled my hips to increase the latter. She gasped, surprised. I kept up the slow rhythm. Patience wasn't my forte, but I knew this prize would be worth it too.

She gasped again. Her pale blue eyes rose to mine, questioning and confused and scared. Scared of my consideration, of my gentleness. She hadn't expected it from me, had accepted her fate. She had braced herself for me fucking her like an animal. She had expected agony and bruises, humiliation and cruel words. She had prepared herself for it, had promised herself to fight me.

This was something she hadn't prepared for, something she couldn't fight because she was too desperate for it. She was proud and noble, but she was still only a sheltered woman. Showing her kindness was like giving her water in a time of drought.

It was something new to me. I fucked hard. Women were pleasure and money. Bargain and burden. They weren't allowed to be more than that.

She moaned, her marble-like cheeks flushing. She was getting closer. I lowered my mouth to her lips, slid my tongue in, tasting that unblemished sweetness.

My fingers slid up her side, over her slender ribs to the swell of her breast. She gasped again. I brushed her nipple with my thumb, the touch feather soft because that was how she liked it, as inexperienced as she was. She'd soon enough see that pain and pleasure worked well together. I reached between us and slid two fingers over her clit. She shuddered and I repeated the motion and thrust my hips faster, forcing one astonished gasp after another from her lips.

I lifted her leg up over my back, changing the angle and sliding a bit deeper into her.

She cried out and threw her head back, baring that elegant neck. Pain and pleasure. I couldn't take my eyes off her face as she gasped and whimpered and moaned. Her gaze sought mine again. She hardly ever looked away. She was the first woman who dared to hold my gaze while I fucked her, the first woman I allowed to do so. My fingers slid over her clit as I sunk into her in deep controlled strokes over and over again.

I wanted my prize, wanted to force it from her quivering body, wanted her complete surrender.

Her tight walls clamped around my cock as she came under me. I closed my lips over the perfect skin at her throat and bit down, wanting to leave my mark. My angel. She tensed and shuddered even harder.

I leaned down. "And you thought I wouldn't own you, Angel," I said softly then kissed her ear.

She glared up at me, shame and hate mingling on her perfect features. Her cold, proud eyes blazed with emotions I had summoned.

"Now that we got this out the way, why don't I fuck you like I wanted to from the start?" I said in a low voice. Serafina was a chess piece.

There was a flash of fear, but I didn't give her time to consider my words. She was slick around my cock. I slid all the way out of her and thrust back into her in one hard push. She gasped from pain this time. I hummed my approval. I soon found a pace that was fast enough to be painful but not so overwhelming that she'd not feel the dark promise of pleasure behind it.

She closed her eyes. "No," I snarled, giving her a far less restrained thrust, showing her that I was still holding back. She looked at me with hate and disgust. I claimed her mouth, growing even harder under the intensity of her emotions. Hate was good.

I sucked her nipple into my mouth, and she tensed. Oh yes. Fucking Serafina was better than my imagination had promised. "I can't wait to send these sheets to Danilo and your family," I rasped against her wet skin.

She clawed at my back, and I groaned, my cock twitching.

She fought against the pleasure, clung to the pain, even preferring it. I reached between us, found her nub, and flicked my finger over it. She squeezed harder around my cock, causing my eyes to close under the blinding pleasure. "If you stop fighting the pleasure, it'll be less painful, Angel," I murmured against her pink nipple before I sucked it back into my mouth. I hit deeper than before, still not as hard and deep as I wanted, but Serafina whimpered.

I lifted my head. She bit her lip, holding back the sound. "Surrender to the pleasure. It'll be worth it."

She hit me with a hateful gaze but didn't pull back when I kissed her mouth and slipped my tongue inside. She'd rather suffer through the pain than stop fighting the pleasure. Proud and strong. Determined not to give me another one of her sweet releases. I claimed her mouth, hard and fast, like my cock did her tight center.

I decided to allow her that small victory. I'd already won the prize and the war. I let loose, submitted to the pressure in my balls. I thrust into her one last time then shot my cum into her with a violent shudder.

I stared into her eyes as I claimed her body. She was mine. I couldn't wait for Cavallaro and her fiancé to find out.

CHAPTER 16

SERAFINA

Remo pulled out of me, and I winced, sucking in a sharp breath. I rolled over to my side, away from him, but the shame stayed with me. Remo brushed my hair away and kissed my neck then lightly bit down, and I shivered. "You are mine now, Angel. I own you. Even if I ever let you go, I'll still own you. You will always remember this day and deep down you will always know that you are mine and mine alone."

I closed my eyes, trying to hold back tears, fighting them, holding on to my composure with sheer force of will. The sheets rustled as Remo got out of bed, and I didn't look over my shoulder to see what he was doing. I heard the water running in the bathroom.

He returned moments later and ran his fingers down my spine then back up before he grabbed my shoulder and rolled me onto my back. My eyes found his. He parted my legs, his eyes taking in my thighs covered in my blood.

Not taking his eyes off my face, he knelt between my legs. I tensed, confused but too stunned and overwhelmed to act. With a dark smile, he leaned forward and ran his tongue over my thigh, licking up the blood. I was frozen. He traced a finger up my leg and circled my opening with it. I stiffened. I was sore but Remo slid his finger inside of me very slowly. His dark eyes held mine and after a moment, he gently pulled his finger back out, now slick with my blood. A horrible suspicion wormed its way into my head, and he proved it right. Remo put his blood-coated finger in his mouth with a twisted smile. "The taste of blood never disgusted me, and your virgin blood is sweeter than anything else."

My nose wrinkled in disgust, and shame warmed my cheeks.

Remo assessed me calmly as he released his finger from his mouth. He stroked my inner thighs as he lowered himself to his stomach between my legs.

"What are you doing?" I asked.

Remo pressed a kiss to my center. "Claiming my missing prize."

My hand shot out, wanting to shove him away, but he caught my wrist and pressed it to my thigh.

His mouth gently moved over me, followed by his tongue. He was so gentle, my body responded despite my soreness. He held my gaze as he traced his tongue along my slit over and over again. Then he closed his lips over my clit and began sucking softly.

I moaned, unable to hold it in. Remo smiled against my flesh. I stopped fighting it and sank into the mattress, my legs parting further. Remo kept up the soft touch of his tongue and mouth but pulled back slightly. "There you go. Let me make you forget the pain."

And he did. There was still an undercurrent of a dull ache, but somehow it heightened every spike of pleasure Remo's tongue brought me.

"Look at me," Remo ordered, his lips brushing against my folds. I met his gaze and started trembling as my core tightened. Pain and pleasure mingled as Remo's tongue worked my nub. My lips parted and I cried out, unable to contain it. Remo's eyes flashed with triumph, and he pressed closer to my center, devouring me. I thrashed under him, gasping. It was painful and mind-bendingly pleasurable. I was torn apart and put back together, miss-matched and wrong but back together.

I slumped against the bed, resigned, exhausted, my body throbbing with pain and the remnants of my orgasm. Remo stayed between my legs, but his tongue had slowed. His fingers pulled me apart, and he lapped at my opening. I moaned as it caused another aftershock. Everything about this was wrong and filthy. With a last kiss to my clit, Remo climbed over me and claimed my mouth. The taste of blood and my own juices made me shudder.

Remo pulled back. "Pain and pleasure," he rasped. "What do you prefer, Angel?"

Shame crashed down on me hard and fast. "I hate you."

Remo smiled darkly and pushed off me. "There is a washcloth on the nightstand." His erection and upper thighs were smeared with my blood, but he didn't bother covering himself as he walked out of the room, leaving me alone.

The door clicked shut.

I sat up, wincing again. My eyes were drawn to the sheets, and I closed my eyes again. This was supposed to happen on my wedding night. It was supposed to be Danilo's privilege, and I had given it away because that was exactly what it was: giving not taking. I got up and moved slowly toward the bathroom. The soreness wasn't even the worst part. Not even close. That was the shame, the guilt over what I let happen.

I stepped into the shower and turned it on. The water was hot, on the verge of being painful but it felt good. I leaned back against the wall and slowly sank down. Pulling my legs up against my chest, I cried because Remo was right: what I'd done today, I'd never forget. Even if I returned to the Outfit, how could I face my family again? How could I face Danilo, my fiancé, the man I had promised myself to?

I wasn't sure how long I sat like this when Remo stepped into the bathroom. I didn't look up, only saw his legs in my peripheral vision. He moved closer and then the water stopped. He crouched before me. I still didn't look up. My throat and nose were clogged from crying and I started to shiver without the warmth of the water.

"Look at me," Remo ordered. "Look at me, Serafina."

When I refused to do as he asked, he reached for my chin and nudged it up until my gaze met his. His dark eyes searched my face. I couldn't read the emotions in his eyes. "If it helps, try telling yourself I raped you," he whispered in a low voice. "Maybe you will start believing it."

Nothing had ever cut deeper than Remo's words. He didn't need a knife to make me bleed. I glared at him, wanting to hate him with every part of my being, but a tiny, horrible part of me didn't, and it was that part of me I despised more than I could ever hate Remo.

REMO

After claiming Serafina, I left her in the bed. I needed time to gather my fucking thoughts. I went to my bedroom and put on briefs but didn't bother cleaning my thighs or face. It was late in the evening, so Kiara should still be in her bedroom with Nino.

I could still taste Serafina, sweet and metallic.

The sweetest triumph of my life.

Fuck. This woman ...

I fixed myself a drink, a bourbon, then leaned against the bar, swirling the liquid in the glass, fucking averse to washing away her taste. The memory still burned bright.

This was the moment I'd worked toward, had been patient for. For once in my life I'd been patient.

Your reward will be worth it.

I will be your first angel.

Serafina was so much more than I'd hoped for. She was magnificently gorgeous, ruinously breathtaking. Even lesser men would kill to have someone as regal as her in their bed only once. I almost got a fucking boner thinking about how Danilo would feel seeing the sheets with Serafina's virgin blood on them, how acutely he'd feel the loss of something he had desired from afar for years, something that had almost been in his reach only to be painfully ripped from him. It was enough to drive even the most controlled man into a rampage.

And her father and brother ... for them it would be a painting of their greatest failure.

"That smile on your face creeps me the fuck out," Savio muttered as he came in, smelling of perfume and sex.

"Thinking of my next message for Dante," I said, setting the glass down without taking a single sip. I couldn't bear the idea of getting rid of Serafina's taste just yet.

Savio's eyes flitted down to my upper thighs coated in Serafina's blood then up to my face.

He crossed his arms. "Either you mauled a kitten and rubbed your face and groin all over the spoils or you had a disturbing meeting with virgin pussy."

Something dark and possessive burned my chest hearing him talk like that about Serafina. I shoved it down. "Not a virgin anymore."

Savio regarded me curiously then shook his head with a disbelieving laugh.

"You really got her to come willingly into your bed. Fuck, Remo, you must have twisted that girl's mind."

I grinned. "And tomorrow I'll bathe in my triumph and send Dante the sheets."

Savio laughed, came toward me, and downed the drink I'd poured for myself. "To your twisted mind and all the twisted shit it comes up with. You wanted to break her and you broke her."

I left him standing there, not in the mood to talk about Serafina anymore. My body yearned for her, for more. For everything. When I entered the bedroom, I found the bed empty, except for the stained sheets. I followed the sound of running water into the bathroom.

Serafina was huddled in the shower and the sight caused an unpleasant twinge in my chest. I turned off the water then knelt before her. "Look at me," I said. "Look at me, Serafina."

Her blue eyes held anguish and guilt when I forced her face up.

"If it helps, try telling yourself I raped you," I murmured. "Maybe you will start believing it."

Hatred flared in her eyes, and for once it didn't give me a thrill.

I got up, frustrated by my body's reaction. I stalked back into the bedroom and stripped the bed of its sheets, not wanting them ruined. Serafina would probably try to burn them to destroy any proof of what we'd done, but she couldn't burn the memory. I threw them into the hallway before I returned to Serafina. She stood now, her fingers clutching the edge of the shower stall, her other hand pressed against her stomach. She took a step, wincing.

I moved closer and her eyes darted down to my bloody thighs. She grimaced. "Why don't you clean up?"

"Because I want to remember."

"And I want to forget," she bit out.

"You need to own up to your actions, Angel. You can't run from them," I said, stopping in front of her.

Hatred swirled in her blue eyes, but not all of it was directed at me. "Leave."

I narrowed my eyes.

"Leave!" she rasped.

"The Tylenol will help with your soreness." I turned and walked toward the door.

"I don't want the pain gone. I deserve it," she muttered. I paused in the doorway and tossed a glance over my shoulder, but Serafina wasn't looking at me. She was glaring at the floor.

I left the bathroom, took new sheets from the wardrobe and threw them on the bed before I headed out and locked the bedroom door. Stuffing the discarded sheets under my arm, I hesitated. I couldn't pinpoint exactly what, but something didn't sit well with me. Ignoring the sensation, I went downstairs.

Nino crossed my path as I headed into the game room. He, too, was only in his briefs. His eyes flitted down to the stained sheets then lower to my thighs before he raised his eyebrows. "I don't suppose it's menstrual blood."

"It isn't. It's Dante's downfall."

Nino trailed after me in that annoying, brooding way he had when he disapproved of something I did. "Not only his downfall."

I moved on into the office. Our father's office. It was one of the few rooms we'd left mostly as it was, but neither of us worked out of it. I narrowed my eyes at him. "Are you referring to Serafina?"

"She will be ruined in her family's eyes, in her circles. Some might even consider her actions betrayal. She is a woman and Dante won't kill her for it, but she will be shunned ... if she's allowed to return to her home at all. I assume you intend to send her back now that you got what you wanted."

Something in his voice set me off. "I haven't gotten everything I wanted

---

from her yet. Not even close. And she will stay until she gives me every little thing I desire."

Nino stepped in front of me. "Is this even still about revenge?"

"It has never been only about revenge. It's about obliterating the Outfit from within, not mere revenge." I sidestepped him and went in search for something I could wrap the sheets in. Finally, I found a box and stuffed them inside.

"Don't lose yourself in a game you don't have full control over, Remo."

The worry in his voice made me look up. I touched his shoulder. "When have I ever been in control? Losing control is my favorite pastime."

Nino's mouth twitched. "As if I don't know it." His expression turned serious again. "In these last few weeks you've spent a lot of time with Serafina. We need you, Remo. The Camorra can't risk an endless conflict with the Outfit. Go in for the kill."

"These sheets are the point of my knife. Are you going to help me with that note to Dante and her family?"

Nino sighed. "If it puts an end to this, then yes."

I rummaged around for a fancy piece of stationery in the old wood desk then took out a pen.

"Now let's figure out the best words to crush them. I thought we could start with a reference to the bloody sheets tradition of the Famiglia for an additional kick."

Nino shook his head. "I'm glad you are my brother and not my enemy."

CHAPTER 17

SERAFINA

I hovered beside the bed, unable to move. The white sheets were gone, sheets covered in my blood. Remo had taken them, and I knew why.

I closed my eyes for a moment. He would send them to my family. They would find out what had happened. What would they think?

Would they hate me? Banish me?

This wasn't rape. I could not defend my actions. There was no force, no torture, no violence. Samuel had risked his life for me. Men had died because of me, and I had betrayed them all.

I turned away from the bed, unable to bear its presence, and headed toward the window. I climbed on the windowsill, wincing at the sharp twinge between my legs. A painful reminder I didn't need. Every moment of what I'd done was burned into my memory, blazing fiercely when I closed my eyes.

I slept with Remo Falcone.

Capo of the Camorra.

My enemy.

Not Danilo. Not my fiancé. My eyes found my engagement ring discarded on the nightstand. I hadn't worn it today, and now I could never wear it again without feeling like a fraud. I swallowed. He would see the sheets as well. I had given away what had been promised to him for five years. What was worse was I had wanted to give it away.

I could still feel Remo's body on mine, the way he moved in me.

It was ... wondrous. Freeing. Intoxicating.

Sin.

Betrayal.

My ruin.

What I did couldn't be undone. A kiss could be denied. A touch could be concealed. This? This had left scars. There was tangible proof, and Remo would flaunt it in my family's faces.

You have to own up to your actions, Angel.

I knew I needed to, but I wasn't sure if I could.

REMO

The next morning I found Serafina perched in her usual spot on the windowsill. The sheets weren't rumpled. She must have slept leaning against the window or not at all.

"You sent out the sheets," Serafina said quietly, not looking my way. Of course, she knew. She was not only beautiful, she was stunningly intelligent. A lethal combination.

"I did. Express delivery. They should arrive at your family's home tomorrow morning or maybe even tonight."

She didn't turn, didn't react. Only looked out of the window. Her hair was brushed over her other shoulder, her slender neck bared to my view. My teeth marks marred her unblemished skin. Her shoulders gave a small twitch. Then she stiffened her spine. "What did you tell them? I assume you sent them a note with your gift." There was the slightest waver in her tone, a chink in her cool voice.

I stalked closer. "What would you have wanted the note to say?"

She peered over her shoulder at me, a beautifully hateful expression perfectly frozen on her face.

"Who knew hatred could be this beautiful?" I said as my fingertips slid over the soft bumps of her spine through her thin satin robe.

She jumped up, whirled around, and slapped my hand away. "Don't touch me."

I pressed her into the wall, one hand curled around her wrists as I shoved them into the wall above her head. "Yesterday you let me touch you, let me eat your pussy, let me fuck you. You gave me yourself, willingly, desperately, *wantonly.*"

The last word broke through her mask. "You would have forced me eventually."

My eyes locked on hers, my grip on her wrists tightening. "I thought you were brave, Angel. I thought you wouldn't choose the easy way, but now I see you can't even stand down the truth of what you did."

She didn't look away.

"Now tell me again, why did you give yourself to me yesterday? And be brave. Was it because you feared I'd take your gift without asking or because you wanted to be the one who decided to whom you wanted to gift it to?"

She swallowed hard. "I wanted to gift it to Danilo. It was his privilege."

"Did you really? Or did you feel obligated to gift it to him because someone promised that gift to him without your consent."

"Don't you dare talk about consent."

I moved closer. "Why did you give it to me?"

Her eyes flashed and tears sprang into her eyes. "Because I wanted to!" She snapped her lips shut and finally looked away. A tear slid down her perfect cheek, and she took a shuddering breath. "They won't forgive me for it. They will hate me fiercely, but never as much as I hate myself, never enough."

I leaned down and grazed my nose over her pulse point, my hand cupping her face.

"Do it," she whispered, begged, and I drew back, looking into the blue pools of despair.

"Do what?" I nuzzled the soft spot behind her ear.

"Hurt me."

My mouth brushed her chin and higher over her lips.

"Hurt me." She said it harsher this time. I gripped her waist and turned her around, pressing her into the wall, her wrists still above her head, my body caging her. I was already painfully hard. The hand that wasn't holding her wrists moved under her satin robe, and I found her bare beneath. I exhaled against her neck then bit down lightly, causing her to shudder. My fingers moved to her flat belly then lower to the trimmed curls until I dipped between her folds. "Hurt me, Remo!"

"I will, Angel. Patience is a virtue. Don't you remember?" My fingers slid deeper.

She wasn't wet like she'd been yesterday, just barely aroused, mostly broken and desperate to exchange one form of pain for another. I unbuckled my belt and took out my cock before easing it between her beautiful firm ass cheeks. Her breath caught but I dipped lower to her pussy. She was tense as a fist against my tip, sore, braced for the pain.

I didn't push in. Instead my fingers started playing with her pussy, light, teasing, coaxing touches. Nothing like what she wanted.

"Why can't you just hurt me?" she whispered, tilting her face sideways and upward.

Yes, why? My hands always gave pain readily.

I held her in place, arms raised above her head, her front pressed to the wall, my cock wedged between her thighs, and watched her cry. I claimed her mouth for a kiss, tasting her tears as my fingers stroked between her pussy lips. Soon I could feel her surrender. My fingers slipped through her wetness, and her pussy loosened against my tip. Using my foot I shifted her legs further apart then looked into her teary blue eyes as I eased into her. She winced and I kissed her mouth again, slow and languid, until I was sheathed in her up to my balls, my cock buried deep inside her.

"Now *your* patience will be rewarded, Angel."

She smiled joylessly against my mouth, and I pulled all the way out of her then slammed back in. She gasped, her body coiling tight, trapped between my chest and the wall. Her pussy clenched mercilessly around me. I stroked her clit as I drove into her again. My body longed to go even harder, and so did she, but I held back not wanting to do any lasting damage.

Fuck.

What the fuck was Serafina doing to me?

Her eyes held mine as if she could find salvation there, but we were both damned, and I was dragging her closer to damnation every day.

My balls slapped against her with every thrust, and I was losing control, not just of my fucking dick but also of everything else. Serafina was still tight and her moans hesitant, pain stronger than pleasure. Claiming her mouth for a kiss, I abandoned control and came with a violent shudder.

She shivered in my hold as my cock twitched inside her. I pressed my forehead to hers, staying inside for a few moments. Her warm breath fanned over my lips, and finally I pulled out of her. Her whimper made me kiss her shoulder blade. Then I lifted her into my arms.

I carried her over to her bed and laid her down then pressed up to her back, and she let me. She was quiet. I ran my fingertips over her smooth arm. Her sweet scent mingled with mine and the muskiness of sex. The perfect mixture.

"And do you feel better? Did the pain help?" I murmured against her shoulder blade as I kissed it again. I wasn't sure why I felt the urge to kiss her like that, but I simply could not stop.

"No," she said quietly.

"I could have told you that."

"You know all about pain and its effects, don't you?"

"I don't think one person can ever know everything about pain. Everyone feels pain differently, reacts differently. It's a curious thing."

Serafina's body loosened further in my embrace. "I think I prefer pain. It doesn't make me feel as guilty as pleasure does."

I buried my nose in her hair. "You have no reason to feel guilty."

She didn't say anything and eventually her breathing evened out. I lifted my head carefully and found her asleep. Her pale lashes fluttered, her face peaceful. I'd never understood the appeal of watching someone sleep, had always found it dull, lacking. I had been so fucking wrong.

I kept stroking her arm then kissed her skin again. Fuck. How was I going to give her back?

I rested my head back on the pillow. I wasn't tired despite the long night I'd had, but I couldn't bring myself to get up with Serafina in my arms.

Closing my eyes, I allowed myself to relax. I had fallen into a light slumber when Serafina stirred, jerking me awake. She stiffened in my hold.

"It's strange when your nightmares are less horrendous than reality," she whispered.

"I've lived it, Angel. It makes you stronger."

"I wished you had taken me on the first day, back in that basement on that dirty mattress like the whore that I am."

The words ripped from her throat as if every syllable was pure agony.

I tensed, turning her around to me, feeling so fucking angry. For an instant, Serafina shrank back from the force of my fury, but then she met my gaze. She lay unmoving on her side, eyes full of anguish.

"You aren't a whore. Is your fucking virginity all that matters to your family?"

"It's not just that I'm not a virgin anymore," she whispered. "It's to whom I lost it to. They won't understand. They won't forgive. They will hate me for what I've done."

"Shouldn't they be relieved that you didn't suffer through pain and humiliation? You succumbed to pleasure. So what? All of them have sinned worse than that, even your brother, particularly your fiancé. What right do they have to judge you?"

She blinked slowly. Then she surprised me by leaning forward and kissing me. A soft kiss. A soft nothing that felt like fucking everything. My brows drew together, trying to gauge her mood.

"I'm lost, Remo."

I cradled her head and kissed her again before I rasped, "My note said that I ripped your innocence from you, that you fought me like a spitfire and that I enjoyed every second of breaking you."

She held her breath, searching my eyes. "You made it sound like you raped me." She swallowed. "Why did you lie? Was it because it would hurt my family worse?"

I smiled darkly. "I fear your family would have been more crushed if they knew you gave yourself to me freely."

"They'd hate me."

"Now you can decide what you tell them when I return you to them."

"You will?" she asked quietly.

I drew back and sat up then turned my back to her. "You were never meant to be a captive forever."

Her fingertips traced my tattoo. "Now that you got what you wanted from me, you'll ask for Scuderi." There was a strange note to her voice, but I didn't turn around to see her face because then she would have seen mine as well.

"Do you think they'll still want me now that I'm ruined?"

Serafina was many things, but ruined wasn't one of them, and anyone who declared her as such was a fucking fool. "Your family loves you. They will do anything to save you, even now. Especially now."

I rose to my feet and left without another look at her.

It was nearing midnight when my phone rang. I turned away from the screen where Savio and Adamo were playing a racing game. Nino and Kiara had already retired to their room to fuck. Without looking at the screen, I knew who it was. I picked up.

"Dante?"

My brothers slanted me curious looks. "I got your message," Dante gritted out. I could practically feel his fury. It wasn't as exhilarating as I'd expected.

"I know you don't follow the Famiglia's bloody sheets tradition, but I thought it was a nice touch."

Adamo grimaced and his car crashed into the wall. Savio had stopped playing altogether.

There was silence on the other end. "There are rules in our world. We don't attack children and women."

"Funny that you say that. When your soldiers attacked my territory, they fired at my thirteen-year-old brother. You broke those fucking rules first, so stop the bullshit."

Adamo's eyes widened, and he glanced down at his tattoo.

"You know as well as I do that I didn't give the order to kill your brother, and he's alive and well."

"If he weren't, we wouldn't be having this conversation, Dante. I would have killed every fucking person you care about, and we both know there are so many to choose from."

"You have people you don't want to lose either, Remo. Don't forget that."

Savio and Adamo watched me, and it took considerable effort to keep my fury at bay. "I thought the sheets might have made you see reason, but I see that you want Serafina to suffer a bit more."

I hung up. After a couple of heartbeats, my phone rang again, but I ignored it.

"I take it Dante isn't willing to cooperate yet," Savio said with a grin.

Adamo shook his head, pushed to his feet, and stormed upstairs.

Savio rolled his eyes. "For a few days he's been almost tolerable. I suppose that's over now."

I stood, switched the phone to silent mode, and shoved it into my pocket. "I'll have a word with him."

"Good luck," Savio muttered.

I didn't bother knocking before I stepped into Adamo's room. My eyes scanned the floor, which was littered with dirty clothes and pizza boxes. I walked toward the window and flung it open to get rid of the horrid stench.

"Why don't you clean your room?"

Adamo hunched over in front of the computer at his desk. "It's my room and I don't mind. I didn't invite you to come in."

205

I walked up to him and tapped against his tattoo. "You'd do well to show me respect."

"As my older brother or my Capo?" Adamo muttered, jutting his chin out.

"Both."

"For what you did to Serafina, you don't deserve my respect."

"What did I do?"

He frowned. "You forced her?"

I brought our faces closer. "Did I?"

"You didn't?"

"Are we going to keep exchanging questions? Because it's getting annoying."

"But you slept with her," Adamo said in confusion.

"I did," I said. "But she wanted it."

"Why?"

I laughed. "Ask her."

"Do you think she's in love with you?"

My muscles tautened. "Of course not. " Love was a delirious game for fools, and Serafina was many things but not a fool.

"I like her." Adamo regarded me almost hopefully. I wondered when our world would rid him of the last shreds of his innocence.

"Adamo," I said sharply. "I kidnapped her so she could serve the purpose of getting revenge on the Outfit. She won't stay so don't get attached." He shrugged. Sighing, I touched his head then left.

Oh, Serafina.

I headed toward my wing, but instead of continuing to my room, I stopped in front of Serafina's door. I knew Dante would agree to give me Scuderi any day now. I unlocked the door and entered. Serafina was curled up on her side, reading a book. She put it down when I closed the door and walked toward her.

She frowned. "Just because I slept with you once—"

"Twice," I corrected.

"Just because I've slept with you *twice* doesn't mean I'll sleep with you whenever you feel like it."

I sank down beside her. "Is that so?" I trailed my fingertips over her exposed arm. Goose bumps rose on her skin.

"I'm too sore. I think last time was too much," she admitted, her cheeks turning pink.

My fingers halted on her collarbone. "Do you need to see a doctor?"

"It's not that bad." She narrowed her eyes a tad. "Are you concerned for me?"

Ignoring her question, I said, "I didn't come for sex anyway."

"What did you come for, then?"

If only I knew. I removed my gun and knife holster and dropped it to the floor beside the bed before I stretched out next to her and propped my head up on my hand.

"Don't tell me you've come to cuddle," she said.

My mouth twitched. "I've never cuddled with a woman."

"You did today."

I considered that. I'd held her in bed after sex, had watched her sleep in my arms. "I was only there to make sure you didn't drown in self-pity."

"Sure," she muttered. "You said you never cuddled with a woman. Do you make a habit of cuddling with men, then?"

I chuckled and slid my hand into her hair. She leaned into the touch ever so slightly. I wasn't sure she noticed. "I don't anymore." At the questioning lift of her eyebrow, I continued. "I used to cuddle with Adamo and Savio when they were really small."

Her nose wrinkled. "Sorry. I can't see it. Considering how exhausting small kids can be, I'm surprised you didn't end up killing them."

My fingers twitched but I restrained my anger. "They are my brothers, my flesh and blood. I'd die before I ever hurt them." I fell silent.

Serafina was quiet too. "I don't understand you, Remo Falcone."

"You aren't supposed to."

"I'm perceptive. Before you know it, you'll reveal more to me than you want."

I feared she was right. A chess piece. A means to an end. That was all Serafina could ever be. Nothing more.

My smile turned cruel. "Serafina, I know losing your virginity to me makes you think we share a special bond. But two fucks don't make you anything special to me. I've fucked so many women. One pussy is like any other. I took something from you, and now you want to justify it with fucking emotional bullshit."

She stiffened but then gave me a cunning smile of her own. Her fingers curled over my neck, and she pressed her forehead against mine like I had done before. "You took something from me, true, but you're not the only one doing the taking. Maybe you don't see it yet, but with every bit you take from me, you're giving me a bit of yourself in return, Remo, and you will never get it back."

I harshly claimed her mouth and rolled on top of her, pressing her into the mattress with my weight. "Don't," I snarled into her ear. "Don't think you know me, Angel. You know nothing. You think you've seen my darkness, but the things you haven't seen are so pitch black no fucking light on this earth can penetrate them."

"Who's not brave now?" she whispered.

I shook with anger. I wanted to fuck my rage out of my system. Wanted to hurt. Wanted to break something. I moved down her body and shoved her nightgown up then ripped her thong down her legs.

"I told you I'm sore," she said softly.

Fuck, why did she have to sound so vulnerable in that moment? What the fuck was she doing to me? I pushed her legs apart. She didn't stop me despite the tension in her limbs. Taking a deep breath, I lowered myself to my stomach, resting between her thighs.

Her body softened immediately when she realized I wasn't going to hurt her. I jerked her toward my mouth, and she winced. I softened my lips against her folds, and soon she was writhing and moaning, her legs falling open, trusting, and fuck, it was better than any rage fucking had ever been. I took my time, enjoying the way she allowed herself to surrender to pleasure. My fingertips traced the soft flesh of her inner thigh, the relaxed muscles there. No sign of tension or fear.

She came with a beautiful cry, her body arching up, giving me a prime view of her gorgeous nipples. I trailed kisses up her body until I reached her lips. "You're all about giving and taking. I gave you my mouth. How about you giving me yours now?"

"You can have my hand, no more," she said firmly.

"I want to come down your throat, not in your hand."

She held my gaze. "You can have my hand or nothing."

"The last time a woman gave me a hand job, I was fourteen. After that I came in a mouth, pussy, or ass."

"I'm not like them, Remo."

No, she wasn't. Serafina was everything. Cunning and strong. Loyal and fierce. She could have been Capo if women were allowed that place in our world.

I rolled on to my back and crossed my arms behind my head. Serafina sat up. She tried to mask her inexperience, but her nerves shone through when she fumbled with my belt. I didn't help her. My cock was already painfully hard when she pulled it out of my briefs. Her touch was too soft as she stroked me, but I enjoyed watching her. Soon she found the right pressure and tempo, and I reached down between her legs and drew small figure eights along her clit and folds. When Serafina began shaking with the force of her orgasm, and her hand tightened around my dick, my own release overwhelmed me, and I came like a fucking teenager all over my stomach.

I used her thong to clean my stomach despite her frown. Then I pulled her down against me. She was stiff but eventually she put her head down on my shoulder.

"That wasn't so bad," I drawled. "But if you want to bring me to my knees, you'll have to use your mouth."

She huffed. "I'll figure out another way to bring you to your knees, Remo."

If anyone could, then it would be her.

CHAPTER 18

SERAFINA

I woke with someone pressed up against my back, a warm breath fanning over my shoulder.

I didn't pull away, only stared at my hand, which rested atop his on the bed. The skin on my ring finger was lighter from wearing my engagement ring for five years, and now it lay on my nightstand abandoned. And how could I ever wear it again? How could I ever face my fiancé again after everything I had done? Everything I still wanted to do.

Deep down I knew I didn't want to marry Danilo anymore, but it was my duty, even now. I ran my fingertips over Remo's hand, and he woke with a current of tension radiating through his body. I assumed he wasn't a man used to sharing a bed with someone.

He exhaled and relaxed but didn't say anything. I turned his hand over until his palm was up then traced the burn scars there, wondering how they'd come to be. My touch followed the scars up to his wrists, where crisscross scars fought for dominance with his burn marks. Remo's breathing changed, became cautious, dangerous.

"Will you ever tell me how you got those?"

He bit the nape of my neck. "Why should I?"

Yes, why should he spill his guts to me? I turned around in his hold. His expression was forbidding, but his eyes held a hint of something even darker. "You're right," I whispered, holding his gaze. "I'm only your captive. The queen in your game of chess. Something meaningless, easy to forget the moment you give me back." Even as I spoke the words, I couldn't imagine Remo really letting me go, not with the way he looked at me, and I wasn't sure if the realization terrified or relieved me. Because how could I return to the Outfit?

"Oh, Angel, forgetting you will be impossible."

And I smiled. God help me, I smiled.

Remo shook his head slowly. "This is madness."

"It is." It was and worse ... betrayal. Dad. Mom. Sofia. Sam. Guilt gripped me in its choking hold. I swallowed. "My family ..." I didn't say more.

Remo's face hardened and he untangled himself from me and stood. My eyes took him in, the harshness of his expression, those cruel eyes, the scars and muscles.

Remo was the enemy. He was trying to destroy the people I loved by using me as his weapon. I couldn't forget that. He put on his clothes and gun holster. Then he nodded grimly. "That's the look you're supposed to give me, Angel. Hold on to your hatred if you can."

"Can you?"

He didn't say anything, only smiled darkly. He turned around and left. The fallen angel tattooed to his back seemed to mock me because every day I felt a bit more like an angel falling.

Kiara picked me up around lunchtime. I could tell from the way she was looking at me that she knew I'd slept with Remo. Nino had probably told her, and Remo had told him and probably everyone else. I hadn't dared to ask him if the sheets had arrived yet. The mere idea that my family and fiancé saw them drove bile up my throat.

We settled on the sofa. She'd ordered vegetarian Sushi, which was set up on the table in front of us. I didn't see Nino anywhere, but I knew he was close and would storm in at the slightest sound of distress from Kiara.

We ate in silence for a while, but eventually Kiara couldn't contain her concern anymore. She touched my shoulder, her eyes flitting to the bite marks on my throat. "Are you okay?"

I set down the sticks and met her gaze. "I'm a captive in these walls, and I betrayed my family. I let Remo dishonor me. I'm ruined. So what do you think?"

She pursed her lips. "You're only ruined if you allow others to make you feel that way."

"You don't understand." I snapped my lips shut, shame washing over me because everyone knew the stories about her. "I'm sorry."

Kiara shook her head, a flicker of pain in her eyes but she straightened her shoulders with a smile. "I felt ruined for years ... until I didn't anymore, and then I was free."

"If my family and fiancé find out Remo didn't force me, they won't forgive me."

"Do you want to return to your fiancé?"

"Do you think I want to stay with Remo?" I muttered. "He kidnapped me. He keeps me locked in a room. He is my enemy. Sex won't change that."

Kiara regarded me closely. "Maybe there's a chance for peace between the

Outfit and the Camorra. You could be that chance. Something good can be born from an act of brutality."

"But there won't be. My dad, my uncle, my fiancé, my *brother* won't ever agree to any kind of peace. They are proud men, Kiara. You know how Made Men are. Remo took me from them, stole my ... stole my innocence."

"It's either stolen or given."

I looked away. "They won't see it that way. He ripped something from them, took something they considered their possession. He insulted my family, my fiancé. They won't forget or forgive. They'll retaliate. They'll avenge me with brutal intent."

"Do you want to be avenged?"

"Remo kidnapped me. He took everything from me."

"Everything?" Kiara said curiously.

"Everything that used to matter." I took my chopsticks again and continued eating, hoping Kiara got the hint that I didn't want to talk anymore.

Remo came to my bedroom again that night. I had expected him and didn't say anything as he dropped his gun holster on the ground then lay down beside me. I only regarded him, trying to understand him, myself, us. But I saw the same confusion in his eyes that I felt every time he was close.

We were both caught in an undercurrent, dragging us down into its unforgiving depth, unable to swim to the surface on our own. The only people who could save us only wanted to save one of us and see the other drown, but we were entangled. One of us would have to let go first to reach the surface.

And just like the night before, Remo's mouth forced me into submission, lips and tongue and teeth, harsh one moment, gentle the next. He didn't try to sleep with me, and for some reason it made things worse because I didn't want him to hold back. I wanted him to take without consideration, without mercy. Because when he was something more than the monster I knew him to be, he took something I was even less willing to give.

He pressed against my back, breathing harshly, his erection a demanding presence pushing into me.

"When will you set me free?" I asked.

"Soon," Remo murmured but didn't elaborate. For some reason I heard the echo of the word "never."

Never. Never. Never.

And it didn't scare me as much as it should.

I considered asking about the sheets. Dante must have contacted Remo by now. But I was too scared, didn't want to know their reaction. Remo's lips brushed my shoulder blade.

"You always do that."

Tension shot through his body as if I'd caught him committing a horrendous crime. "I think Danilo ruined your uncle's plan to keep it cool."

I stiffened as well. "What?"

Remo's hold tightened, not allowing me to turn around. "Dante tried to pretend the sheets didn't have the desired effect, but this afternoon Danilo called me, and he wasn't as controlled as the cold fish wanted me to believe."

I sucked in a shaky breath. "You talked to Danilo?"

"He was furious, murderous. He told me he'd cut my balls and dick off and feed them to me." Remo paused and I tensed further. "And I told him that he could try but that it wouldn't change the fact that I was the first man inside you."

I wrenched myself out of his embrace, whirled around on him, kneeling on the bed.

Remo smiled darkly. My eyes caught the holster on the floor. I lunged, ripped the gun from the holster, released the safety, and pointed it at Remo's head.

He rolled on his back, arms stretched out in surrender. There was no fear, no apprehension in his eyes.

I straightened on my knees beside him. "If you think I can't go through with pulling the trigger, Remo, you are wrong. I'm not the girl from before who couldn't cut your throat."

Remo held my gaze. "I don't doubt you can kill me, Angel."

"Then why aren't you scared?" I asked fiercely.

"Because," he murmured, gripping my hips. I tightened my hold on the gun, but I allowed him to keep his hands on my skin. "I'm not scared of death or pain."

Without lowering the gun, I straddled his stomach, and my core clenched at the feel of his muscles.

Remo's eyes flashed with desire. I leaned forward, resting the barrel against his forehead. "If I kill you now, I'm free."

"There are still my brothers and hundreds of loyal men who will hunt you down," Remo said, his thumbs stroking my belly in a distracting way. I had already been wet from Remo's earlier ministrations, but a new wave of arousal pooled between my legs now.

"But I'd still be free of you and that's all I care about."

Remo smiled darkly again. He lifted one arm and I tightened my finger on the trigger. "You can't be free of me. Because I'm in there." He touched my temple lightly, though it was another spot he should have touched because it was his presence in another place that scared me far more. "You will always remember that I'm the one you gifted yourself to for the very first time."

I gave him the cruel smile he used on me whenever I got too close. "The memory will fade. Two times don't matter after a while. I'll sleep with Danilo for the rest of my life, and I'll forget that there ever was a man before him."

Remo jerked into a sitting position, his eyes flashing with fury. The gun dug into his forehead, but he didn't care. His grip on my hip tightened, and his other hand cupped my head. "Oh, Angel, trust me when I say you'll remember me for the rest of your existence."

I lifted up and positioned myself over Remo's erection. I touched my palm to his cheek, causing his eyes to flash with an emotion that scared him and me equally. I released the trigger but didn't drop the gun. I lowered myself on Remo's length slowly, despite the fierce twinge. My head fell back when he was buried all the way inside me.

"Devastating."

I lowered my head, locking gazes with Remo.

"Devastatingly beautiful," he murmured. I lowered the gun and pressed it to his chest.

"There's nothing in there for you to shoot."

I engaged the safety, wrapped my arms around his neck, and rocked my hips, the gun dangling loosely in my hand. Pain and pleasure shot through me. Remo groaned. I moved faster, lifting and falling. Remo held me tightly, his eyes dark and possessive as he let me be in control.

Remo's teeth scraped my throat, leaving marks, and my nails raked over his back, leaving my own marks in turn. It was painful but I rode him hard and fast, relishing in the burning sensation. Remo sucked my nipple into his mouth, and his thumb rubbed my clit. Pleasure spiked fiercely, mingling with the pain in a delicious dance.

Both were spiraling higher and higher, and I knew one of them would eventually shatter me, and I longed for it. Needed it. Remo flicked my nub and pleasure overpowered all else. I cried out, dropping the gun as I desperately held on to Remo's shoulders, my nails digging in. Remo held my gaze with fierceness and hunger, and I felt alive and free and weightless.

I was still shuddering from the force of my orgasm when Remo flipped us around, locking my knees under his arms, parting me wide and thrusting into me in one hard push, going so much deeper than before. I arched up, lips parting in a choked sound, half moan, half whimper. Remo didn't pause. He slammed into me, hard and fast, shoving me into the mattress over and over again, ripping every last shred of innocence from me. The gun lay beside us on the bed.

Remo had been right. A bullet to his head wouldn't free me of him. At this point, I wasn't sure if anything could.

REMO

Sitting on the sofa in the game room, I stared down at my phone. Two missed calls from Dante. The last from yesterday. Three days since my entertaining call with Danilo. I couldn't bring myself to talk to Dante, knowing I had him right where I wanted him.

"It's time to end this. Dante called me today. He'll exchange Scuderi for Serafina."

"I'm Capo. I decide when and how to set her free."

Nino leaned forward, arms braced on his thighs. "Remo, if you have feelings for her—"

I cut him off. "I'm not like you. One woman won't turn me into an emotional mess."

He narrowed his eyes but his expression remained calm. "Then send her back. Fabiano is getting impatient and so am I. There's nothing else to gain from this. Dante won't give us more than Scuderi. You already made them believe you tortured and raped Serafina. They are on their knees, but Dante is Capo. He won't give up more than his Consigliere."

"Next time he calls, I'll take his call," I said with a shrug.

Nino assessed me. "I told you there would be no winners in this game."

"We are the winners."

He shook his head but didn't say anything.

I stood and went over to the boxing bag. Kicking and punching it didn't help with my fucking inner turmoil, and Nino's judgmental presence didn't help either.

I kicked the bag once more then stalked upstairs and burst into Serafina's bedroom. She was reading on the windowsill. By now, Adamo must have brought her half of our library. She put the book down and stood. In the last few days, a gradual power shift had started and I couldn't allow it.

Serafina moved closer, scanning my face cautiously. She stopped in front of me. Instead of dealing out harshness like I'd intended to, my eyes took in her soft lips, lips I couldn't get enough of, lips that drove me insane with desire.

"You have a very strange look on your face."

"I can't think about anything else than having you on your knees in front of me with those perfect lips around my cock." It was a half-truth, the only truth she'd ever get.

"I was on my knees once," she hissed.

I shook my head. "That doesn't count. You can be on your knees and still be in control."

"I won't kneel."

"That's a shame considering there's no better way to bring a man to his knees than to kneel in front of him while you suck his cock. Didn't you want to bring me to my knees?"

She pushed me back and I sank down on the edge of the bed. I pulled her between my legs so her knees pressed up against my erection. I slipped my palm between her closed thighs and rubbed her through the fabric of her panties. "I wake with a fucking boner every morning, dreaming about your lips and your tongue, Angel. How it would feel to fuck your sweet mouth."

She was burned into my fucking mind, not just the feel of her body …

Her brows drew together, but her mouth opened as her breathing deepened. Using my thumb, I grazed her clit while my other finger slid along her slit. Her panties soon stuck to her folds with her juices. "I eat your pussy almost every day. Don't you ever wonder how it would be to return the favor? To control me with your mouth?"

Her eyes flashed and she moaned when I pressed my hand harder against her center. Slowly, I withdrew my hand and smiled darkly. I gripped her hips and pressed down, not enough to make her knees buckle but to show her what I wanted. She resisted so I loosened the pressure and finally she lowered herself to her knees, head held high. My cock hardened further at the sight of Serafina before me. I unbuckled my belt and unzipped my pants before I took my cock out. I began stroking myself, swirling my thumb over my slick tip.

Serafina watched with parted lips but narrowed her eyes when she noticed my smirk. After another swirl of my thumb, gathering my pre-cum, I brushed her lips and pushed into her mouth. Her tongue tasted me hesitantly, and my fucking dick twitched. Serafina noticed, of course, and smiled in triumph.

I pulled my finger out and placed my hand over her neck, but I didn't push her toward my waiting cock, knowing she'd resist again if I tried to coax her into doing what I wanted.

Finally, she reached out, curling those elegant fingers around the base of my cock. She squeezed experimentally, and I stifled a groan. And then Serafina leaned forward and slid my tip into her mouth. She licked the tip then sucked, unpracticed moves that drove me insane with desire. I began thrusting into her mouth, driving my cock deeper into her, but not all the way in, still holding back when I'd never held back for a woman in my entire life.

My balls clenched every time she hollowed her cheeks, and the sight would have brought me to my knees if I weren't already sitting. Kneeling before me, challenge and triumph in her blue eyes, Serafina owned me. Body ... and whatever black soul was left.

My phone rang and I tightened my hold on her neck when I took the call. "Dante, what a pleasure," I got out.

Serafina tried pulling back, her eyes going wide, but my hand on her neck kept her in place as I thrust into her mouth. She glared and scraped her teeth over my dick, which made my eyes roll back and my cock twitch. I smirked. She'd have to bite down much harder for me to release her. Pain only turned me on more.

"I'm not calling to exchange pleasantries," Dante said coldly.

I turned the loud speaker on and loosened my hold on her neck. Serafina jerked back, but I grabbed her arm and hoisted her up. Then I pulled her onto my lap, her back against my chest, one of my arms wrapped around her chest. My feet shoved her legs apart and kept them spread eagle. Serafina scowled but couldn't say anything. I brushed two fingers over her folds, finding her fucking dripping with arousal. I grinned and shame flashed across her face. "That's a pity," I said to Dante.

I slid two fingers into her and began fucking her while my other hand cupped her breast.

"We should come to a solution," Dante said. I could hear the barely restrained fury in his voice.

"I'm sure we will," I said as I slid my fingers in and out of Serafina's pussy and swirled my thumb over her clit. "You know I want Scuderi. I want you to hand him to me in person."

Serafina's muscles clenched around my fingers as I fucked her slowly. She twisted her head back and bit into the side of my neck. My hold loosened, and she wrenched free of my grip and stormed into the bathroom, slamming the door shut.

"In two days. In my city. I want you to bring him all the way to Vegas. You get Serafina. I get Scuderi. I want her fiancé there as well. I'd like to meet him in person."

Dante was silent. "We will be there."

"Nino will send you the details. I'm looking forward to meeting you." I hung up, but the triumph I felt lasted only a moment. My eyes found the door behind which Serafina was hiding.

Two more days.

Then I'd set her free.

It would be up to her if she flew straight into Danilo's cage …

My chest constricted but I pushed past the sensation. Serafina was never meant to be mine.

I stood, and tearing my gaze away from the door, I left.

CHAPTER 19

SERAFINA

"Wear this," Remo ordered, throwing my wedding dress down on the bed. I stared at the white layers of tulle, at the blood stains and the tears. I hadn't seen it in almost two months. It didn't feel like something I'd ever owned. Nothing I was meant to wear ever again.

"Why?" I asked.

Remo turned toward me, his dark eyes hard. "Because I told you to do it, Serafina."

Not *Angel*. Serafina. What was going on? I narrowed my eyes. "Why?"

He moved closer, glaring down at me. "Do as I say."

"Or what?" I said harshly. "What could you possibly do to me? You have taken everything from me that mattered. There's nothing left for you to take, to break."

Remo's mouth turned cruel. "If you really think that's true, then you are weaker than I thought."

I swallowed hard, but I didn't put on the dress. We both knew I was so much stronger than he'd ever imagined. Maybe that was why he kept doing this, pushing me away.

Remo reached for his knife and pulled it out with a bone-chilling clink of the blade against the sheath. Goose bumps rose on my skin, but I stood my ground because if I knew one thing it was that Remo wouldn't hurt me. Not anymore, not ever again.

Whatever twisted bond had formed between us, it prevented him from causing me pain.

Gripping the neckline of my nightgown, he sliced through the fabric with a sharp slash of the knife. The shreds pooled at my feet, leaving me in only my panties.

His dark eyes roamed over my body, the knife still clutched in his hand, and my core tightened with need. He gripped my hip and wrenched me toward him, his lips crushing down on mine. I gasped as his tongue conquered my mouth, teeth clanking. He backed me up against the bed until I fell back. He slashed through my panties with his knife, and the closeness of the blade caused a shiver to pass down my spine. Remo towered over me and freed his erection, his eyes furious and hungry and terrifying.

Holding his gaze, I opened my legs for him because I was lost, had been lost from the moment Remo had laid eyes on me, and as I looked up at him, I knew without a doubt that he, too, was lost.

The corners of his mouth lifted as he lowered his gaze to my center. He got down on his knees, pushing my legs even further apart. Remo buried his face in my lap. I arched up, my nails digging into the crisp sheets, my gaze finding my torn wedding dress. Remo's mouth claimed me relentlessly, with tongue and lips, bites and licks. There was no escaping. He wouldn't let me.

He made me surrender, not with force, not with violence … He dove in, swirling until I was a slave to the sensations he created. My orgasm crashed over me like an avalanche, but my eyes remained locked on the stained white fabric of my dress—a sign for my honor, my purity.

Both lost.

Both taken … No. *Given.*

Remo's mouth traveled up my stomach, licking and nibbling, tongue flicking my nipple. He bit down lightly then soothed the spot with an open-mouthed kiss. His body covered mine, his palms pressed into the bed beside my head, the knife still clutched in his grasp. For a moment our eyes locked, and I hated him, hated myself, hated us both, because hate became harder to hold on to each day that I spent with him.

We both needed our hate, and yet it was slipping through our fingers like sand. There was no way to contain it. Lost. His dark eyes reflected my inner turmoil. Losing ourselves to each other.

My gaze returned to my dress when Remo thrust into me in one all-consuming merciless stroke. His mouth pressed up to my ear as he slammed into me angrily. "When I saw you in that dress, I knew I needed to be the one to rip your innocence from you. I knew I needed to be the one to make you bleed. Who knew you'd make me bleed in return?"

I shuddered, my throat tightening even as my body throbbed with traitorous pleasure. Finally I tore my gaze from the dress to glare up at Remo—my captor, my nemesis, my ruin … and yet, despite what he'd taken from me, hatred wasn't the only thing my weak, idiotic heart felt. But that was a truth I would take to my grave.

"I hate you," I whispered as if saying the words aloud would make them true.

Remo's eyes bore into mine, filled with emotions, his mouth twisting in a dark smile because he *knew.* He moved closer, tongue sliding along the seam of my lips. "Nothing tastes sweeter than your lips, even when they're spewing lies, Angel."

His next thrust hit deep, and I could not hold back. Blinding pleasure rushed through my body. My lips parted but I swallowed my cry. I wouldn't give it to Remo. Not today. He bit down on my throat, and the force of my orgasm doubled. The moan clawed itself out of my throat. He couldn't even allow me that small victory. His own face twisted with strain as he kept thrusting, shoulders flexing. He kissed my mouth softly then my ear, and I knew he would deliver words meant to break, words worse than any torture could ever be. I'd known it from the moment I'd seen his cold face this morning.

"You wanted to know why I need you to put on your wedding dress," he rasped as his thrusts became less controlled.

My chest tightened with dread.

Remo kissed my ear again. "You see, I arranged a meeting with Dante for tonight, and I promised to give you back. Danilo will be there as well, and I thought he'd appreciate finally seeing you in your wedding dress. Even if I stole what you promised to him."

Shock and fury crashed down on me, and I slapped Remo hard. He gripped my wrist and pressed it into the mattress over my head as he thrust into me again, eyes staking claim on me over and over again, taking more with every thrust. But he couldn't lock me out anymore, because I, too, had laid claim to a part of him.

His body tightened, coiling tight with pleasure, and as always, my own traitorous body submitted to him again. I cried out. Remo linked our fingers, pressing them deeper into the mattress as his mouth found mine for a kiss full of anger and dominance. When he finally stilled on top of me, my eyes moved up to my dress.

"You are mine, Angel. Body and soul," he rasped. And God help me, he spoke the truth.

When I put the dress back on, it felt like a sacrilege wearing something so pure and white. Goose bumps rippled across my skin when the heavy fabric settled around my legs. I stared down at the layers of tulle, the blood stains and tears. Had I really chosen this dress? Had I ever felt comfortable wearing it?

Remo regarded me with a hard expression. "I still remember the first time I saw you in it."

I didn't say anything.

Remo reached for my engagement ring on the nightstand, and the little hairs on my neck rose. He stopped right in front of me and took my hand then slid the ring on with a twisted smile. "This marks you as Danilo's, doesn't it?"

I stared at him fiercely, unyieldingly because he knew the mark he had left went deeper than an expensive ring. Something in Remo's eyes shifted, a flicker in his harsh mask, yet he still held my hand. He released me abruptly and stepped back. "Danilo will be delighted to get you back."

"I'm not the girl I used to be."

Remo's gaze hit me like a sledgehammer, but he didn't say anything, even though I wanted ... needed him to.

Up until the very end, I was convinced Remo would keep me. I kept denying the truth until I was faced with the result of my sins: the exhausted faces of my family and fiancé.

They waited in the abandoned parking lot. Dad, Dante, Danilo. Samuel wasn't there, and I knew it was because he would have lost it. Behind them on the ground lay a tied up man, probably Fabiano's father. His back was turned to me so I couldn't be sure.

Their eyes were drawn upward toward one of the buildings, and when Remo pulled me out of the car, I found the reason why. Nino was perched on the roof as a sniper. Fabiano got out of the car as well, his own gun drawn.

Remo led me a few steps away from the car. Then he stopped. "You were very ill-advised attacking our territory, Dante," he said pleasantly, his grip on my hip tight as he held me against his body. My eyes lingered on the ground because my guilt sat so heavily on my shoulders I couldn't find the courage to meet the gazes of the men who'd come to save me. The white fabric of my dress seemed to mock me, and I focused on the bloodstains.

Bracing myself, I finally raised my head and wished I hadn't.

Nothing had ever hurt worse than the look on Dad's face. He took in my bloody dress, the bruises on my throat where Remo had marked me over and over again. Remo had made his claiming of me as apparent as possible, flaunted it in front of everyone, and it had the desired effect. Uncle Dante, my fiancé Danilo, and my father regarded me as if they had been gutted. Remo's ultimate triumph.

I wanted to scream at them that I hadn't suffered the way they thought I had, wished they would hate me, but I wasn't brave enough for the truth.

"Next time you consider fucking with us, look at your niece, Dante, and remember how you failed her."

Dante's face was stone, but there was a flicker of something dark in his eyes.

I couldn't meet their eyes. Burning shame sliced through me at what I had let Remo do, at what I had done. What I had wanted to do, what I still wanted to do.

Remo leaned closer, his lips brushing my ear. "I own you, Angel. Remember that. You gave me a part of yourself and you'll never get it back. It's mine no matter what happens next."

Dante, Danilo, and my father looked on the verge of attacking, their body's tense, expressions twisted with hatred and fury. They wanted to protect me when I no longer wanted saving, couldn't be saved because I was irrevocably lost.

I turned my head slightly, meeting Remo's cold gaze. "I'm not the only one who lost something," I whispered. "You gave me part of your cruel black heart, Remo, and one day you will realize it."

Something flashed in Remo's eyes. Those cruel eyes that haunted his victims' nightmares ... how long would they haunt me? Especially all the times they hadn't looked upon me with cruelty or hatred but with a far more terrifying emotion.

Then he tore his gaze away from me to stare at my uncle. All I could think was that he hadn't denied my words. I had Remo's cruel black heart and maybe that was the most painful realization of all.

"Hand over Scuderi," he said.

Dante gripped the rope that coiled tightly around a struggling Scuderi and dragged him toward us. I'd known my uncle all my life, but I'd never seen that look on his face. Utter fury and regret. He thrust Scuderi to the ground halfway toward us. "Release my niece, *now*," he ordered.

Remo chuckled. This was a trick. This had to be a trick. Remo had said it himself: I was his. He owned me. Body and soul. He wouldn't let me go. The worst was that deep down I hoped he wouldn't—and not just because I didn't want to live among the family I'd betrayed so horribly, but also because the idea that he could give me up so easily tore at me.

His dark eyes locked on mine, possessive and triumphant, and he leaned down. For a heart stopping moment I was sure he'd kiss me right in front of everyone, but his lips lightly grazed my cheek before they stopped at my ear. "I never thought you'd give me this look on the day I released you— as if giving you freedom is the worst betrayal of all. You shouldn't want someone to cage you in. You should long for freedom." He exhaled, his hot breath against my skin making me shiver. "Goodbye, Serafina."

Remo released me then shoved me away from him. I stumbled forward, away from him, my heart thundering in my chest. Strong hands grabbed me and quickly ushered me away from Remo. I walked toward my family, my fiancé—freedom—but it didn't feel anything like being free.

Dante was beside me and Danilo stepped toward me, *reached for me*, and I flinched, feeling unworthy of his touch after I'd betrayed him, betrayed the Outfit with Remo. Dante and my father both tensed, and Danilo lowered his arm and stepped back from me with a look full of utter hatred toward Remo. But Remo's expression was the worst because when I met his gaze I knew what it said.

I own you.

I half fell into my father's arms, and he hugged me tightly, whispering words of consolation that I didn't catch, pulling me away toward their car. My eyes weren't on him.

Fabiano loaded his father into the back of the car before he got in. With another glance at me, Remo followed and drove away. *Drove away.*

And again I shivered because part of me, the part that terrified me most, missed Remo.

I own you.

He did.

Dad got into the back of the car with me, still hugging me to his chest and stroking my hair, and a new wave of guilt overcame me. Dante got behind the wheel, and Danilo sat beside him. My fiancé glanced at me through the rearview mirror, and I ducked my head, my cheeks flaming with shame.

"You are safe now, Fina. Nothing will ever happen to you again. I'm sorry, dove. I'm so sorry," Dad whispered against my hair, and I realized he was crying. My father. A Made Man since his teenage days. Underboss of Minneapolis. He was crying into my hair, right in front of his Capo and my fiancé, and I fell apart. I clutched his jacket and cried, ugly cried, for the first time since I could remember, and my father hugged me even tighter.

"I'm sorry," I gasped out, broken words full of despair. Words weren't enough to convey the extent of my sins. Of my betrayal.

"No," he growled. "No, Fina, no." He shook, his grip painful.

"Remo ... he ... I."

Dad cupped my head. "It's over. It's over now, Fina. I swear, one day I'll hunt him down. I will kill him for what he did to you ... for ... for hurting you."

I swallowed. He thought Remo had raped me. They all did, and I couldn't tell him the truth, was too cowardly to tell him. Closing my eyes, I rested my cheek against his chest. Dad held me tightly, rocking me like a little girl, like he could restore my innocence by doing so.

Would the truth set him free? Set them all free or would it break them worse? I wasn't sure of anything anymore.

REMO

Fabiano kept tossing glances at his father resting on the backrest of the car, looking fucking eager to tear into the man.

"Your plan really worked. You crushed the fucking Outfit," Fabiano said, turning to me. I stared at the road. The triumph I'd been working toward, destroying the Outfit from within, I held it in my hands. I'd seen it on the faces of my enemies. I knew they'd keep suffering.

Fabiano shifted in his seat. "Remo, you realize we won, right? We got my father. Your insane plan worked."

"Yeah, my plan worked …"

"Then why—" Fabiano's eyes widened.

My grip on the steering wheel tightened.

"We can try kidnapping her again. It worked once, who's to say it won't work again," he said almost incredulously.

"No," I said harshly. "Serafina doesn't belong in captivity."

Fabiano shook his head. "They will marry her off to Danilo. Even if you spoiled the goods, she's still Cavallaro's niece, and Danilo would be foolish to refuse a marriage because she isn't a virgin anymore."

I wanted to kill someone, wanted to spill blood. "She won't marry him."

"Remo—"

"Not another word, Fabiano, or I swear you won't get a chance to rip your father to shreds because I will and then maybe do the same to you."

He sank back into the seat with a frown. "Should I call Nino?"

"We'll see him in five fucking minutes," I growled. "Now shut the fuck up."

We met at the Sugar Trap. Fabiano dragged his father down into the basement while I sat down at the bar. Jerry put a bottle of brandy and a glass down in front of me without a word.

Nino joined me after a couple of minutes. "Matteo and Romero's plane arrived thirty minutes ago. They'll be here soon."

"Good. A sign of goodwill for Luca."

"He still isn't happy about the kidnapping. But now that we gave Serafina back and give his brother and Captain a chance to partake in the torture, he'll probably come back around. We don't need a conflict with the Famiglia. The Outfit will start attacking viciously soon enough."

"Set up a cage fight for me. Two opponents. Death match. Tomorrow. The day after at the latest."

Nino grasped my shoulder. "Remo. We can't have you play with your life now. We need you strong."

I stood and gave him a twisted smile. "If you want me strong, give me someone to kill. I want blood. I want to maim and kill. And I'm not risking my life. I will fucking obliterate every fucking person who enters the fucking cage as my opponent."

"It won't make you miss her any less."

I lunged at him in blinding rage. For the first time in my fucking life, I attacked my brother. Nino blocked my fist and took a step back, and I jerked to a halt, stopping myself after realizing what I was doing. My chest heaved as I stared into my brother's cautious gray eyes.

Jerry had run off and a moment later Fabiano stormed inside but froze when he saw me and Nino facing each other, standing almost chest to chest.

"Fuck," I rasped, taking a step back. I held out my arm, tattoo on display, my palm up. A silent apology, the only one I was capable of. Fabiano turned back around, leaving us alone. Nino linked our arms, my hand on his tattoo, on his scars, and his palm on mine.

"You walked through fire for me, Remo," he said quietly, imploringly, "but you should know, I'd do the same for you. I wouldn't have asked you to send her back if I'd known ... And I'll walk straight into Outfit territory for you and get her back if that's what you want."

"That's not what I want."

"She won't return to you of her own free will."

"Then so be it. Now find someone I can kill and set up the fucking death match."

Nino squeezed my arm then released me.

"I think for the first time in my life I envy you your lack of emotions."

CHAPTER 20

REMO

"If they don't arrive soon, I'll start without them. I don't give a fuck if it offends Luca fucking Vitiello or not," Fabiano growled as he stood over his father, who lay on his side on the ground, mouth taped, arms and legs bound together. He stared up at his son with terror-widened eyes.

"They'll be here any second," I muttered.

I could tell Fabiano was barely listening. He was too focused on his father. He'd waited a long time for this moment. Fuck, I got it. I'd do anything for a chance to torture my father to death. I still remembered the fucking day I found out my traitorous half-brother had killed the asshole, something I'd dreamed of since I understood our father wasn't the invincible god he made himself out to be. That he could, in fact, be killed. Since I was a fucking kid, I'd dreamed of erasing our father from our lives ...

If there were a Hell, I'd walk straight down into it to make a deal with the Devil so he'd give me the chance to kill the man just once. Maybe twice.

"Not the scrawny boy you can torture for your own amusement anymore, am I?" Fabiano murmured as he crouched in front of the other man. I prided myself on my scary smile, but Fabiano's expression surpassed everything. He'd enjoy today.

The door creaked open, and Fabiano straightened. Nino came in, followed by Matteo and Romero. I had been surprised when Luca had told me he'd send them but not come himself. I supposed he had less reason to tear into Scuderi than the others. He had been gifted Aria because Scuderi sold his daughters off like cattle, and anyone could admit Aria was a very nice gift. An image of another woman with blond hair and blue eyes entered my mind, uninvited. I shoved it down.

I'd set her free.

"Nothing better than bonding over shared torture," Matteo said with a grin as he sauntered into the cell in the basement of the Sugar Trap. That asshole always looked as if he'd walked straight out of a photo shoot for a fashion magazine. One day I'd fuck up his pretty face. Romero gave me and Fabiano a curt nod before his eyes, too, fell on Scuderi.

I pushed off the wall and extended my hand to Matteo, who took it after a moment.

"I still can't stand your fucking face, Remo," he said with a smirk. "But for this I might hesitate a millisecond before cutting your throat once we're back to being enemies."

"That millisecond will be the moment I'll cut your head off, Matteo," I said with a twisted smile of my own.

He released my hand. "May the craziest fucker win."

My smile widened and I caught Nino's gaze across the room. We both knew who that would be because when it came to crazy fuckery I was the undisputed master.

I turned to Romero, who didn't display the careless attitude of Vitiello. He obviously was wary about being in a basement in Vegas. I didn't have the slightest intention to attack either of them today. War with the Famiglia would have to wait until the Outfit was crushed and its territory split between us.

He briefly shook my hand. "Your methods are dishonorable," he said tersely.

"You disapprove of them and yet here you are ... benefiting from them."

Romero pulled his hand away, his brown eyes returning to Scuderi and his expression filling with hate.

I went over to Scuderi and smiled down at him. His eyes flickered with terror. "I must say you've gathered many enemies over time, and we've all come together to tear you apart."

I reached down and ripped the tape from his face then straightened and returned to my spot at the wall. Maybe his agonized screams would drown out the voice of regret in my head.

Serafina walking away in that fucking white dress and that last look she gave me. Fuck it all.

Fabiano circled his father. "Father, I've been waiting for this chance for a very long time, and I have every intention of making it last for as long as possible. Lucky for me, Nino is a master at prolonging torture. With a little luck we can keep you alive for two or three days. That way we can all get the fun we deserve."

Scuderi tried to push himself into a sitting position but failed. His expression became pleading. If he thought that would warm Fabiano's heart, he didn't understand what Fabiano did on a daily basis as my Enforcer. "I'm your father, Fabi. You already lost your mother. Do you want to lose me as well?"

Fabiano lunged, smashing his fist into the man's face. Bones crunched. I watched from my spot against the wall. This wasn't my moment. Despite my need to maim and kill, I'd hold back. Matteo, Fabiano, and Romero had more reason to spill Scuderi's blood.

"Shut up," Fabiano snarled.

Matteo had begun twisting a Karambit knife in his fingers, an eager gleam in his eyes I knew all too well.

"I've got small kids who need me," Scuderi tried in a hoarse voice.

Fabiano lifted him by the collar and jerked him up against the wall, getting in his face. "They'll be better off without you. My sisters and I would have that's for sure."

Nino put a chair down in the center of the room, and Matteo helped Fabiano drag Scuderi over to it. They tied him up despite his struggling.

His beady eyes found me. "Remo, you are Capo. I could be of use to you. I know everything about the Outfit and Dante. If you let me live, I'll tell you everything."

Fabiano scoffed as he pulled his knife from the holster around his chest.

I smiled cruelly at the disgusting bastard before me. "You will reveal everything I want to know. I know you're in very capable hands that will coerce every truth out of you."

"Oh we will," Matteo said with his fucking shark grin. He stepped up to Fabiano, and they exchanged a look. Then Matteo leaned over Scuderi and brought the knife down on his chest. "Gianna sends her regards. I told her I'd let you suffer, and I will."

Matteo left a long cut across Scuderi's chest, making the bastard scream like a fucking coward.

Romero moved up to Scuderi after that. He wasn't holding a knife in his hand. He smashed his fist into Scuderi side twice then into his stomach. Some men preferred to dish out pain with their fists, others with a cold blade. I enjoyed either, depending on my mood and what my opponent feared more.

"You gave Lily to a fucking old bastard so you could get a child bride for yourself. You're a disgrace of a father." He punched the man again.

Fabiano took over. "I hope you will spend your last hours considering that not a fucking soul on this planet will be sorry you're gone. If you find time for sane thoughts between the agony." He inflicted a long cut on the man's arm. The sight of the red rivulets trailing enticingly over bare skin made my body hum with excitement. Fuck, I wanted to spill blood, dish out agony. I wanted to fucking destroy someone.

Nino leaned beside me. It wasn't time for him to help yet, and his attention was on me, not the scene in the center of the cell.

"Stop the assessment," I said in a low voice.

Nino narrowed his eyes slightly but complied and finally turned toward the torture. Matteo, Romero, and Fabiano took turns beating and cutting Scuderi until his screams and begging filled the cell.

After a few hours, Fabiano, covered in blood and sweat, indicated for Nino to get involved. My brother rolled up his sleeves and after another lingering glance at me, he moved toward the medical kit that would ensure Scuderi didn't die too soon.

Romero leaned against the wall. Matteo and Fabiano had taken turns torturing Scuderi over the last hour, and I had a feeling they'd be the ones to deal with him in the remaining hours of his life. My own body hummed with the need to destroy, the need to give pain and feel pain, to fill the fucking void in my chest.

My body screamed for sleep, but except for a few toilet breaks, I stayed in the cell while Fabiano dealt with his bastard of a father. It wouldn't be much longer.

Fabiano's shoulders heaved as he stared down at his father. The man was breathing shallowly.

Fabiano turned to me, blood splatters dotting his face. His naked chest was completely coated with it. Our eyes met. "Remo…will you…?" His voice was hoarse.

I pushed away from the wall and walked up to him, not sure what he was asking of me. Fabiano clutched the bloody knife in a death grip, the look in his eyes reminding me of the boy I'd found in Bratva territory many years ago— a boy desperate for death because his father had taken everything from him.

Nino motioned for Matteo and Romero to leave, and with a last look at me, he closed the door. Fabiano swallowed before he held out his forearm with the Camorra tattoo. "You gave me a home. A purpose. You treated me like a brother…" He glanced down at his father. "Like family. I know you wanted nothing more than to kill your father and had that taken from you. I know it's not the same, but…will you help me kill my father?"

I linked arms with Fabiano, clutching his forearm tightly. "We aren't blood but we are brothers, Fabiano. I'll walk through fire for you." I stared down at the fucker who'd wanted his own son dead then back up to Fabiano. "And there's nothing I'd rather do than kill him with you. It's an honor."

Fabiano nodded, then got down on his knees beside his father. I did the same. Fabiano raised the knife above his father's chest then looked at me. I closed my fingers over his and together we jabbed the blade down, right into Scuderi's fucking heart.

Fabiano's shoulders sagged and he released a harsh breath as if the man's death finally set him free. I wondered if anything would ever do the same for Nino and me?

SERAFINA

Outside of Las Vegas we traded in the car for the private jet belonging to the Outfit. I huddled in my seat, my cheek pressed to the window, watching the city grow smaller in the distance. Dad sat across from me, looking and not looking at me, caught somewhere between utter relief and hopeless despair.

I knew what a pitiful sight I was. Bloody and torn dress. Bite marks all over my throat. Dante was talking quietly on the phone, but he, too, slanted the occasional look at me. The only one who hadn't looked at me after I flinched from his touch was Danilo. He leaned forward, forearms braced on his knees, staring blankly at the floor.

Guilt and a flicker of sadness washed over me. For him. For us. For what could have been and never would.

I swallowed and looked away. I met Dad's gaze. He forced a small smile and reached for me as if to touch my legs over the tulle of my dress, but then he hesitated as if he was worried about my reaction. I snatched his hand and squeezed. His eyes were still glassy and haunted. *I'm a sinner, Dad. Don't cry for me.*

He lifted his other hand with the phone. "Do you want to call Samuel? I sent him a message that we got you."

I nodded fiercely, my throat clogging. Dad's eyes darted to my throat once more, and the hint of something cruel and harsh flared in them. Something he had never showed at home. He gave me his phone, and I hit speed dial with shaking fingers.

"Yes?"

For a second, hearing Samuel's voice immobilized me. "Sam," I croaked.

There was silence. "Fina?"

The word was a broken exclamation that splintered me apart. Tears trailed down my cheeks, and I could feel all eyes on me. I closed my own. "I'm sorry."

Samuel sucked in a sharp breath. "Don't ... don't apologize. Not ever again, Fina."

I couldn't promise that. One day I'd have to deliver the apology that would make Sam hate me. A higher voice rang out in the background. "It's okay, Mom," Samuel soothed. "I'll give her to you." He addressed me again. "I'll give you Mom now. I can't wait to hold you in my arms, Fina."

I sniffled. "Me too."

"Fina," Mom said softly, trying but failing at sounding composed and not like she was sobbing.

So many broken hearts. So much pain and despair.

Remo Falcone was indeed the cruelest man I knew, and I had to be the coldest bitch on this planet, because even still my stupid heart thudded faster when I thought of him.

"I'll be home soon," I whispered.

"Yes ... yes," Mom agreed. We hung up eventually because it got to be too much, the silence of suppressed crying and the distance we couldn't bridge.

"Where are we going?" I hadn't asked before because I'd just assumed we'd go back to Minneapolis ... but I was as good as Danilo's wife. Would they take me to Indianapolis? Or maybe to Chicago because Dante needed to question me about every little detail of my captivity?

Dad leaned forward and cupped my cheek. "Home, Fina. Home."

I nodded. My eyes found Danilo, who was watching me. Our gazes locked briefly, but then guilt forced me to look away. I'd have to face him eventually. I wasn't sure what to tell him.

The rest of the plane ride passed in utter silence. I knew they all had so many questions to ask but held back for my sake, and I was glad because I still wasn't sure what to say to any of them.

With every second that passed, my skin crawled more and more trapped in my wedding dress. It felt so utterly wrong, like being wrapped in lies and deceit.

Mom and Samuel waited in front of our house when we pulled up with the car. I didn't see Sofia anywhere, probably to protect her from the sight, and I was glad. She didn't need to see me like this.

I trembled when Dad helped me out of the car, his fingers tight around my forearm as if he worried I might faint. Dante and Danilo stayed back as we walked toward the house. Samuel staggered toward me. My twin. My confidante. My partner in crime.

He froze when his eyes registered my state, the marks on my throat, and his expression became one I'd seen the first time shortly after he'd become a Made Man five years ago. Cold, cruel, out for blood. He caught himself, bridged the remaining distance between us, and hugged me to his body, lifting me off the ground in a crushing embrace. I buried my face in the crook of his neck, shivering.

"I thought I'd never see you again," he rasped.

I wasn't the person he knew. She was gone. If he knew what I'd become, if they all knew, they'd hate me. And rightfully so.

Can you un-lose yourself?

I clung to Samuel for a long time, just breathing in his comforting scent, relishing in the feel of him. Eventually, he set me down and my eyes fell on Mom, who stood behind Samuel, her hand covering her mouth, tears running down her face. Dad had wrapped his arm around her, steadying her. Their anguish cut me deeply.

They thought Remo had raped me. I looked like I had been raped with my ripped and bloody dress. Mom rushed forward and embraced me so tightly I could barely breathe and she sobbed into my hair, and my heart ... it just broke hearing it. And not for the first time, I wished Remo had done what everyone thought so I could cry rightfully with my mother and with all of them.

I should have told her the truth, but the words didn't pass my lips. Soon. Dad and Samuel joined us, and I sighed, because right then I allowed myself a moment of contentment being united with them. Samuel wrapped his arm around my shoulders as he led me inside our home.

"Where's Sofia?" I asked.

"She's with Valentina and the kids in a safe house close by. They'll come over soon," Dante explained from behind me.

I nodded.

"I need to shower," I said and regretted my words when I saw the look my family exchanged. I quickly moved away and headed upstairs into my room, starting to tear at my dress, but the thing clung to me. Angry, desperate tears gathered in my eyes.

"Sam!" I called, and in a blink he was there. "Can you ... can you help me with the dress?"

He nodded and pushed my hair to the side to reach the zipper. He froze, releasing a shuddering breath. I knew what he saw: the bite mark on the nape of my neck. He leaned forward, burying his face in my hair. I allowed him a moment to gather himself even as my own heart broke and broke and broke. "I will kill him."

A threat. A promise. Not my salvation as he hoped it could be.

He pulled down the zipper. I stumbled into the bathroom, not looking at him, and closed the door. The warm water didn't wash away my shame and guilt. How could I remain among the people I had betrayed? How could I look into their faces knowing they had suffered more than I had?

I closed my eyes. They were happy to have me back. I had to focus on that. But why, why wasn't I happy? I stepped out of the shower, dried myself, then wrapped a towel around my body. I stepped back out to grab clothes.

Samuel perched on the edge of my bed, his expression tight. His eyes flitted to my throat then to my thighs. My gaze followed his and I saw the hand-shaped bruises on my inner thighs where Remo had held me in place when he'd buried his face in my lap.

I felt the color drain from my face, grabbed some clothes, and returned to the bathroom. Shaking, I quickly dressed in a soft dress and tights. With a deep breath, I emerged and approached Samuel hesitantly. He was staring down at his hand on the bed, tightly curled into a fist.

I sat beside him, curling my legs under my body. Samuel raised his eyes and the look in them was like a wrecking ball of guilt. His gaze darted to my throat again, to Remo's marks, and utter despair filled his face.

"Oh, Fina," he said in a broken murmur. "I won't ever forgive myself. I failed you. I should have protected you. These last two months I almost went crazy. I can't stop thinking that I had to sit back while you went through hell. That I'm the reason why you suffered worse." He swallowed. "When Remo sent us those sheets ..." His voice broke.

I threw myself at Samuel, wrapping my arms around his neck and burying my nose against his neck. "Don't. Please don't blame yourself. You did nothing wrong."

I did. I wronged you all.

His arms came around me, and he shuddered. "You were supposed to be protected, to be safe from the horrors of our life. I never wanted you to find out how cruel the mafia could be. No one will ever touch you again, Fina. I won't leave your side. And one day Dad and I will get our hands on Remo, and then we'll show him that we can be as cruel and merciless as the Camorra. He will be begging for mercy."

"It's over," I whispered. "It's over, Sam. Let's not talk about it ever again.

Please." I knew Remo better than he did, and nothing they could do would make Remo beg for mercy.

He nodded against me, and we stayed like that for a while. "When I heard your screams in the basement, I thought I'd go insane," he said darkly.

I pressed my face into the crook of his neck, not able to look at him when I delivered the truth. "Remo didn't torture me. He wanted you to believe he did. He wanted me to make you believe you hurt me so you'd suffer. I ... I ... only wanted to save you."

Samuel cupped my head and pulled back, his eyes softer than before. "It was my job to save you and I couldn't. Even if those screams weren't real, I can see what he did to you ..." Samuel swallowed, his eyes lowering to the bite marks once more. "You were meant to be treated like a princess, cared for and cherished ... not ... not ..." He shook his head and buried his face in his palms. "I can't get the image of those sheets out of my head, can't forget Mom's sobs or the way she fell to her knees in front of Dante and begged him to save you, or how Danilo destroyed Dad's entire office. I can't forget Dad crying. He's never cried, Fina. Dad and I have done and seen so much, but we both fucking cried like fucking babies that day. I swear by my honor, by everything I love, that I won't rest until I've rammed my fucking knife into Remo Falcone."

I kissed the top of his head and held him because despite being the one who had been kidnapped, Remo hadn't broken me, and I realized it had never been his intention. He'd done worse.

"Sam," I said, gathering my courage because I needed to save him, needed to save them all with the truth even if it ruined me. "I didn't suffer like you all think. Remo didn't rape me, he didn't torture me."

Samuel pulled back and I braced myself for the inevitable, for the disgust and hatred, resigned myself to it, but his eyes held pity and sadness.

He stroked my throat then touched the faded cut on my forearm.

Something dark swirled in the depth of his blue eyes when they locked on mine. "You were innocent. You've never been alone with a man and then you were at the mercy of a monster like Remo Falcone. You had nothing to protect yourself. You did what you had to, to survive. The brain is a powerful tool. It can survive the cruelest horrors by creating alternative realities."

I shook my head. He didn't understand. "Sam," I tried again. "I wasn't raped."

Sam swallowed and kissed my forehead as if I was a small kid. "You'll realize it eventually, Fina. Once you've healed, once the brainwashing ceases, you'll see the truth. I'll be there for you when that happens. I won't ever leave your side again."

And I realized then that he'd never believe the truth because he couldn't. The sister he knew and loved wouldn't have slept with Remo, and if I wanted to return to him, to my family, I needed to become her again.

I wasn't sure if she was still inside of me somewhere or if Remo had ripped her from me, just like he did my innocence, and kept her for himself.

CHAPTER 21

SERAFINA

After covering the bite marks with concealer, I left my room with Samuel at my side. Mom was in the dining room, setting plates up for dinner. Usually the maids did it, but I got the impression she needed to keep busy. She'd lost weight. She had always been tall and thin, but now she was willowy.

Samuel's words flashed through my mind, that she'd fallen to her knees and begged Dante to save me. My mother was a proud woman. I don't think she'd ever begged for anything in her life nor knelt. But kneeling for the ones we loved … that was something she and I would always do. I walked over to her. She smiled but her eyes held questions and fears.

"Can I help you?"

Her eyes flitted down to my throat. "No, Fina. Just rest."

I didn't feel like resting. "Where are the others?"

"Your father and uncle are talking to Danilo in the office. Sofia will be here soon. She'll be so happy to see you again."

I smiled but my thoughts strayed to Danilo. My fiancé. My gaze fell to the engagement ring around my finger, and I shivered, remembering the look in Remo's eyes when he'd slipped it on.

"I need to talk to Danilo," I said quietly.

Mom put the plates down, searching my face. She didn't ask why. Maybe she knew and could see it on my face. "Do that, sweetheart."

I nodded and turned to head for Dad's office. Samuel followed at my heel. "You're not going to marry him, are you?"

I stopped in the hallway and peered up at my twin. There was no judgment in his voice, but there was relief. "I can't."

He touched my shoulder. "I'm here for you."

"Won't you have to go to Chicago to work with Dante?"

He shook his head, mouth thinning. "We decided against sending me away. Dad needs me here. We need to protect our territory."

Me. They needed to protect me ... and Sofia.

"I want to talk to Danilo alone, Sam."

He frowned, protectiveness flashing in his eyes.

"Sam," I said firmly. "I can handle it."

I'd handled Remo for months. Nothing could scare me anymore. Maybe the same thought crossed Samuel's mind because he nodded with a grimace.

"I'll wait in the hallway," he said, leaning against the wall beside the wooden door.

I knocked twice then walked in, not waiting for a reply.

My breath caught in my throat at the mess. Someone had thrown two book cases over. Ripped books and broken glasses. Dad's beloved collection of whisky tumblers scattered the floor. The leather sofa was slashed, filling poking out everywhere.

Danilo had done this and nobody bothered to clean up afterward.

My eyes found my fiancé. He was controlled, so much like Dante that he probably couldn't stand being compared to him anymore. I couldn't imagine him doing this. His brown eyes latched onto mine, full of regret and anger.

"Dove?" Dad asked.

I cleared my throat, realizing he and Dante were staring at me as well.

"I'm sorry for disturbing you," I said. "But I need to have a word with Danilo."

Dad hesitated, his eyes flitting between my fiancé and me. Dante put a hand on his shoulder and eventually they both left. Danilo faced the window, his hands pressed into the wall on both sides.

The door closed with a soft click, and silence reigned in the room.

Danilo's shoulders heaved. He was tall and muscular, but not quite like Remo.

"I ..." I began but then didn't know how to go on, how to explain that I was lost to him.

Danilo turned around slowly, a haunted expression on his face. He smiled but it was strained, tired, and behind it lurked something dark and broken. "Serafina," he murmured. He took a step closer but stopped when I tensed. "I still want to marry you. If you want me."

I regarded Danilo's handsome face. He knew to hide his violence better than Remo. He was elegantly handsome, not brutally attractive like Remo. Remo. Always Remo. *I own you.*

"I'm not the girl you were promised anymore," I whispered. "I'm ... lost."

He shook his head and came closer, but still not close enough to touch. "He will pay. In these last two months, I've spent every waking moment thinking about you, going crazy with worry and rage. Your family and I ... we wanted to get you back ... We failed ..."

"It's okay," I said softly.

"And I don't care that he ... that you aren't ..." His face twisted with guilt and fury. "I still want to marry you, and you don't have to be scared, Serafina. I won't touch you until you've healed, until you want me to, I swear."

I moved toward Danilo. We could have been happy. He would have been kind to me, as good a husband as a Made Man could be. I didn't kid myself into thinking he wasn't a monster, but he was a restrained one. I touched my palms to his chest and looked into his eyes. Something in them had changed from our last encounter two months ago. They were harsher, darker. My captivity had left its mark on him too.

"I can't. I'm sorry," I whispered. "You deserve someone else. Please find someone who deserves you."

He regarded me, his jaw flexing. "From the moment I saw you the first time, I only wanted you."

I lowered my eyes because from the moment Remo had laid eyes upon me, I had been his.

"I'm sorry," I repeated.

He nodded slowly. I dropped my hands from his chest and stepped back. "Falcone got what he wanted, didn't he?" he said hoarsely. "But your family and I will bring him down. We will destroy him."

I shivered. I slid my engagement ring off my finger and handed it to Danilo. "Don't waste your time on revenge, Danilo. Move on. Find someone else. Be happy."

He shook his head, obviously fighting for control. "Revenge is all I want, and I won't stop until I get it. Remo will curse the day he took you from me."

Remo already did, but not for the reason Danilo wanted him to.

He left without another word. Swallowing hard, I leaned against the windowsill. This was it. I was no longer engaged ... I was nothing. I was ...

ruined. In our circles, I was ruined. If I'd married Danilo, things might have been different, but now ...

There was a soft knock and Mom entered, looking worried. I gave her a small smile, wanting to banish the hard line between her brows. "Danilo told me you don't want to marry him."

As if it was as easy as that. Wanting had little to do with it. I couldn't because deep down I knew I needed to loosen Remo's hold on my stupid heart before I could ever consider moving on.

I knew the rules of our world, even now they still bound me, bound my family. We had promised the Mancinis Dante's niece, and now they wouldn't get what they wanted, what they expected as the ruling family of Indianapolis. Maybe Danilo had accepted my decision but his father was still alive, sick and bedridden, but alive. He pulled the strings in the background. The Mancinis wouldn't settle for just anyone as my replacement.

"I can't," I said quietly. "I can't ever marry, Mom. Don't make me."

Mom rushed toward me and embraced me. "We won't. Not me, not your father, not Dante. We all failed you horribly. You don't ever have to marry, sweetheart, you can live with your father and me for as long as you wish."

"Thank you, Mom," I said, and even as I said it I knew it wasn't what I wanted.

She pulled back, frowning. "Your uncle would like a word with you. I told him it's still too soon, but he insists it's necessary. Still, if you aren't ready, I will stand up to him."

Dread filled me but I shook my head. "It's fine. I'll talk to him."

She gave a terse nod. "I'll get him. He needs to return to Chicago tomorrow morning. He's been gone for too long these last two months."

She kissed my cheek before she left.

Dante stepped in a moment later, tall and controlled as always. He closed the door then paused, his cool blue eyes flickering to my throat where Remo's marks had been—no longer visible, covered by layers of concealer, just like my traitorous feelings for him were covered up by stacks of lies. I flushed and touched my skin in shame.

"Don't," he said firmly.

I frowned. He moved toward me slowly, cautiously, as if he thought I might bolt. I lowered my hand from my throat when he came to a stop in front of me. "Don't be ashamed for something forced upon you," Dante said quietly, but his voice was off. It had a note to it I had never heard before. I searched my uncle's eyes, but it was difficult to read him. He exuded control and power. But there was a flicker of regret and sadness in his gaze. "I don't want to open up painful wounds, Serafina, but as the Boss of the Outfit, I need to know everything you know about the Camorra so I can bring them down and kill Remo Falcone."

I swallowed, looking away. This war would become so much bloodier and crueler soon. As if that would undo my kidnapping. As if Remo's death could change anything. But my family and Danilo needed to make amends for their guilt. Nothing I could say would change that.

"I don't think I know anything that will help you."

"Every small detail helps. Habits. The dynamic between the brothers. Remo's weaknesses. The layout of the mansion."

Remo's weakness. His brothers. Remo's biggest weakness may be his only one.

"Remo doesn't trust anyone but his brothers and Fabiano. He would die for them," I whispered.

For some reason I felt almost guilty for revealing that to my uncle, as if I owed Remo loyalty, as if I owed him anything at all. He had kidnapped me and then let me go. I wasn't sure what made me hate him more.

"Apart from the family, only Fabiano and Leona are allowed inside the mansion, and occasionally cleaners. Remo keeps a knife and a gun close at all times. He's a light sleeper ..." I froze, falling silent.

My skin burned at what I'd just revealed, but Dante only regarded me calmly. No judgment or anger. I still had to lower my gaze from his because his understanding made me feel even worse. He didn't know I'd come freely into Remo's bed, enjoyed not only the sex but also the tenderness afterwards. It was a side of Remo no one knew and that he had showed it to me meant more to me than it should.

Could I reclaim what was lost? I began shaking, overwhelmed with the situation, with my feelings.

"Serafina," Dante said firmly, touching my shoulder. I raised my eyes to his and shook even worse, overcome with the need to spill everything but not brave enough. I pressed myself against my uncle, and he touched the back of my head in comfort.

"What am I going to do? How will I belong again? Everyone will look at me with disgust."

Dante's body coiled tighter. "If anyone does, you'll let me know, and I'll deal with them."

I nodded.

"And you never stopped belonging. You are part of the Outfit, part of this family, nothing changed."

Everything did. Worst of all, I had.

When we finally emerged, Samuel took his place as my shadow again. We were on our way into the dining room when the front door opened. One of our bodyguards stepped in, and then Sofia shot inside. Her wide eyes landed on me, and she stormed off in my direction. She collided with me, and I would have fallen backward if Samuel hadn't steadied me.

"You're back!" Sofia hugged my middle tightly, and I rested my chin on top of her head, smiling. When I pulled back, her eyes were alight with happiness despite the tears in them. "I missed you so much."

"I missed you too, ladybug."

I wondered how much she knew, how much my parents and Samuel had divulged or had been unable to hide from her.

Valentina entered with her two kids, Anna and Leonas. Anna was around Sofia's age, and they loved each other dearly. They were not just cousins but best friends despite the distance between them. Leonas was almost eight and the spitting image of Dante, except for the eyes. Anna and Leonas gave their mother a questioning look, and she nodded before they came toward me as well. I hugged them, though it proved difficult because Sofia continued to cling to my arm. Anna and Sofia sometimes were mistaken for sisters because their hair color was similar.

Valentina was the last to greet me. Her embrace was gentle as if I was breakable but I gave her a firm smile.

"We can have dinner," Mom said with a brave smile of her own. With the kids around, she wouldn't burst into tears again nor would anyone else.

Conversation flowed easily at the dining table. Too easily. I could tell everyone was trying to create normalcy for my sake and their own. Danilo wasn't there. I assumed he wanted to be alone after I'd broken off our engagement, and he wasn't part of the family and now he'd never be.

It was strange being surrounded by my family again. I sat between my siblings, both of them eager to be close to me, but my thoughts kept straying to Las Vegas, to Remo.

"How was Las Vegas?" Leonas blurted when we were done with dessert, a decadent chocolate cake, my favorite.

"Leonas," Dante said sharply.

My cousin flushed, realizing his mistake.

I took a sip from my water then shrugged. "Not worth visiting if you ask me."

Leonas giggled, and my family relaxed again. Samuel squeezed my hand under the table. Maybe I could find my way back to them.

It felt strange being back in my own bed. I had trouble falling asleep. Too much had happened. This morning I'd woken in Las Vegas with Remo, and now I was here.

The door opened and Samuel slipped in. I made room for him in the bed.

"Awake?" he asked quietly.

"Yeah." I didn't elaborate. He lay down on the covers on his back. "What about you?"

Samuel was quiet for a couple of heartbeats. "I was in a late night meeting with Dante and Dad."

"Oh," I said. "About your plans to get revenge on the Camorra?"

Samuel swallowed audibly. "No. Not that. It was about Danilo. His father isn't happy about the state of things."

Worry overcame me. What if they married me off to him despite everything? What if his family insisted on being given Dante's niece?

"Sam," I whispered, and he reached for me in the dark, his hand covering mine.

"Dad promised Sofia to him."

I froze. "She's a child."

Samuel sighed. "They will marry the day after her eighteenth birthday."

"That's still six and a half years away."

I could feel Samuel nod. "They think Danilo is still young and busy taking control over Indianapolis and taking care of his father. He can wait." He paused. "And it's not like he can't keep himself busy with other women until then."

I closed my eyes. "What will Sofia say? It's my fault. I should just marry him."

"No," Samuel growled. "We won't let you. That's a point we all agree on, Fina. You won't be given in marriage to anyone. You've gone through enough. You'll stay here until you feel better."

"And then?"

"I don't know," he admitted. I couldn't live on my own. As a woman that wasn't an option. They'd have to marry me off or I'd have to stay with Mom and Dad forever.

"You come live with me eventually."

I laughed. "Yeah right. I'm sure your future wife will be ecstatic to have me under the same roof."

"She'll do as I say," he murmured.

I fell silent. "Once you marry, it's your duty to protect her, to be good to her, Sam. I won't be your responsibility anymore."

"I'm not going to marry anytime soon, not with the way things are developing with the Camorra."

"When will Sofia find out?"

"Dad will talk to her tomorrow first thing in the morning. Danilo insists on it. He also insists we up the number of guards."

"He doesn't want history to repeat itself, I suppose," I said softly.

Samuel stiffened. I pinched him lightly. "Stop it."

"Why did you do that?"

"Because you were feeling guilty again, and I want you to stop. I want things to go back to how they were before."

"I want that too," Samuel said. We both knew it wouldn't be that easy.

Samuel was already gone when I woke the next morning. He'd always been a late riser, but that, too, seemed to have changed. I slipped out of bed and dressed before I left my room. Instead of heading downstairs, I moved down the hallway to Sofia's room and knocked. My stomach tightened painfully.

"Come in!" she called.

Frowning at her chipper tone, I slipped in. Sofia lay on her stomach, her ankles crossed. She was drawing. When she spotted me, she flushed. I walked toward her and perched on the edge of the bed. Her arms covered her drawing, and I tilted my head.

"I wanted to talk to you about Danilo. I assume Dad already talked to you?"

She gave a tentative nod, biting her lip. "Are you mad at me?"

"Mad?" I echoed, confused.

"Because Danilo wants to marry me now and not you."

The tightness left my chest. That was what they told Sofia. Good. I regarded her closely. "No. I'm not. I want you to be happy. Are you okay?"

She bit her lip again and gave a small nod. With an embarrassed smile, she pulled her hand away from her drawing. It was her name and Danilo's over and over again.

Surprise washed over me. "You like him?"

Her cheeks blasted with heat. "I'm sorry. I liked him even when you were promised to him. He's cute and chivalrous."

I kissed the top of her head. Was I this innocent once? This hopeful and clueless?

I pulled back and gave her a stern look. "He's a grown man, Sofia. It'll be many years before you'll marry him. He won't come anywhere near you until then."

She nodded. "I know. Dad told me." She sounded disappointed. So beautifully innocent. I stroked her hair.

"So we're okay?" she asked.

"Better than okay," I said then stood and left my little sister to her daydreaming. I missed the days when I thought a knight in shining armor riding a white stallion would steal my first kiss.

Instead a monster had claimed me, body and soul.

My stomach led me downstairs, but I paused when I spotted Danilo in the foyer. I assumed he'd gone over the details of his engagement to my sister with my parents and Dante. For some reason, I was furious. Sofia might be happy, but she didn't know the extent of her promise. Of course she would have been promised to someone eventually but not as a consolation prize because the Mancinis wanted Dante's niece.

I walked straight toward him. His face flickered with regret and self-hatred as he looked at me. "Sofia is a girl. How could you agree to that bond, Danilo?"

His expression flashed with anger. "She is a child. Too young for me. She's my sister's age for God's sake. But you know what's expected. And we won't marry until she's of age. I never touched you and I won't touch her."

"You should have chosen someone else. Not Sofia."

Tension shot through his body. "I didn't choose her. I chose you. But you were taken from me, and now I have no choice but to marry your sister even though it's you I want!"

A sharp intake of breath made us both look up at Sofia, who was standing on the highest stair, watching us with wide hurt eyes. Her chin wobbled and she whirled around, storming off.

"Damn it," Danilo muttered. He made a move as if to follow, but I grabbed his arm.

"What are you doing?"

"I should talk to her."

"I don't think that's a good idea."

Danilo pulled back, his expression back to being controlled, calm, poised. "I should apologize."

"I'm not sure she'll talk to you. But we can try," I said quietly. I led him upstairs, trying to ignore the way his eyes lingered on my throat. I hadn't covered the marks this morning.

I pointed at Sofia's door, and Danilo knocked firmly.

"Go away!"

"Sofia," Danilo said calmly. "Can I talk to you?"

It was silent behind the door for a long time. Danilo's brows drew together.

"She's probably trying to clean up her face so you don't see her tears."

He gave a small nod and again glanced at my throat. I sighed and looked away.

"I will protect her. I won't fail her like I failed you," Danilo muttered.

My eyes shot up but the door opened in that moment. Sofia stood in the doorway, looking shy and embarrassed. Her eyes moved from Danilo to me, and I gave her a smile.

She flushed when she raised her eyes to Danilo.

"Can I talk to you for a moment?" he asked.

Sofia looked at me for permission.

"Sure," I said. I knew custom forbade girls from being alone with men, but Sofia was eleven and Danilo had always been a perfect gentleman with me.

Sofia walked back into her room and perched on her plush pink sofa. Danilo followed her inside, leaving the door open. His eyes took in her pink girly room, and I could see how uncomfortable he was. He sank down on the sofa with as much distance between them as the piece of furniture allowed. He looked out of place in the room, like a giant beside her. The contrast couldn't have been bigger: Sofia in her pink dress with her boisterous nature, and Danilo in his black pants and black dress shirt with his cool demeanor. He had already seemed so much older to me, but in comparison to Sofia?

Not that she seemed to mind. She was peering up at him with so much childish adoration that even my crushed heart sang with joy. I hoped she could hold on to it for a long time. I took a few steps back and gave them a moment of privacy. Two minutes later, Danilo stepped back out. He ran a hand through his dark hair. His eyes met mine, and again I saw the flash of longing and fury.

"And?"

He gave a terse nod. "I think I managed to convince her I said those things to make it easier for you."

"Good," I said.

Danilo shook his head, his brows drawing together. "Nothing is good about this situation, Serafina, and I'm surprised that from all of us you are the one who seems to be dealing with it the best."

I stiffened. "I just want things to return to normal. That's all."

He nodded tiredly. "They won't, but I understand. I need to go now." He left without another word. I waited until his tall form had disappeared before I stepped into Sofia's room. "Everything okay?"

She was still sitting on the sofa, staring down at her hands. "I think so," she said thoughtfully.

"You will be the most beautiful bride, I just know it."

Her eyes lit up. "You think?"

"I know it." My chest ached for what I'd lost, for what I could never have, especially not with the man who had my heart.

CHAPTER 22

REMO

Roger's Arena was packed for my fight as I strode in. Nino followed close behind as we walked toward the booth where Adamo, Savio, Kiara, Leona, and Fabiano were waiting. I was already in my fight shorts, and my body thrummed with barely contained bloodlust.

Roger helped behind the bar for once and gave me a nod in greeting, which I returned. The audience was throwing glances my way, eager, curious, terrified. My fights were always particularly popular—for those who could stomach them. Griffin looked fucking ecstatic as he noted the bets down.

"Who are the unlucky souls you'll fight?" Savio asked curiously.

"Ask Nino." I didn't care who they were. I'd rip them to shreds either way.

"Two ex-cons. Both on the run. Both in desperate need of money and new identities. Out of options," Nino said matter-of-factly. "One of them kicked his pregnant wife half to death and she lost the baby. Already served a sentence because of manslaughter. The other spent half of his life in jail for child molestation."

"Sounds like they deserve their death sentence," Fabiano said with a grin, his arm wrapped around Leona and she smiled up at him in adoration. The sight spiked my fury, and I focused on the cage. "They will wish for the death penalty when I'm done with them."

The ref called out my name, and I walked through the parting crowd toward the cage and the two dead men waiting for me inside.

The crowd roared and clapped, ecstatic. I swung myself into the cage and assessed my opponents. One of them was taller and broader than me. Maybe I could imagine it was Luca. It would add a nice thrill. The other was short but bull-like, and his stance suggested he was a boxer. Both looked like they knew how to pack a punch. Good.

The moment the fight began, they attacked together. I gripped the short one and rammed my knee into his side but was grabbed from behind by the giant. Short guy scrambled toward me and landed a punch in my stomach. I jerked my head forward and smashed it against his. He staggered and I kicked out against his chest, catapulting myself and the fucker who held me from behind. We crashed into the cage, and I jumped out of Big Guy's hold. Whirling around, I pushed off the ground and flying-kicked his fucking face, breaking nose, chin, and cheekbone. Blood splattered everywhere, and he fell backward, holding his face. That would keep him busy for a while.

I turned toward Short Guy and smiled. The audience roared. They knew that smile. The look in my opponent's eyes was familiar: panic and horrified realization. I stalked toward him, and he raised his fists. I feigned an attack, causing him to stumble back. I chuckled. This was going to be fun. I lunged at him, kicking and punching hard without mercy. The cries of the crowd and the fucking whimpers of my opponent spurred me on, but the fucking hollowness in my chest remained. I kicked him over and over again until everything was red. When he didn't even twitch anymore, I let up.

The other guy had his back turned to me and was shaking the cage door, wanting out.

"No one's going to open that door. If you want out of this cage, you'll have to kill me."

Big Guy turned, face swollen and bloody. He tried his best. Soon I had him in a choke hold, and then I smashed his face against the cage. Once. Twice, and then over and over again. I couldn't fucking stop. I needed to crush something.

"Remo."

Smash.

"Remo!"

Smash.

A hand gripped my shoulder and ripped me backward. I released the bloody pulp and stared at Nino. His face was splattered with small red dots. Blood.

I glanced down at myself then at the floor. It was silent in the arena and everyone was staring at me in open horror.

"I won," I muttered.

Nino shook his head. "Come."

I followed him out of the cage and toward the changing room. The crowd parted even wider. The stench of vomit hung heavy in the air. Griffin was pressing a fucking tissue over his mouth.

Inside the changing room, I stripped off my drenched fight shorts, leaving a red trail on the ground as I stepped inside the shower. The hot water remained red for a long while, and Nino watched me the entire time from his spot on the bench, his elbows propped up on his thighs.

"Like what you see?"

He didn't say anything, and it was starting to piss me off.

Grabbing a towel, I stepped out of the shower and dried myself off. "Say what you've got to say."

Nino regarded me with a small frown. "Is this because of Serafina? Do I have to worry?"

My lips pulled wide. "I don't have a heart that can be broken, Nino. Stop the fucking hovering."

"She won't come back to you, Remo. She'll try to find her way back into the Outfit where she thinks she belongs. If you wait for her to come to you freely, you'll be met with disappointment."

I bent low, meeting his eyes. "I don't care if she comes back or not. There are whores to fuck, Outfit bastards to kill, and the fucking Bratva to piss off."

I got dressed in the pants Nino handed me. Then we left. Part of the crowd had already left, the others were whispering quietly. Nino led me toward the booth, but only Savio was there, and he regarded me like I had risen straight from Hell. "Where is everyone?"

"Well," Savio muttered. "Kiara and Adamo are probably busy throwing up, and Fabiano and Leona went outside with them to keep watch."

Nino's frown deepened at the mentioning of Kiara. We headed outside and found them all in the parking lot beside our cars. Adamo sat on the hood of Nino's car, smoking. Kiara was bent over behind the trunk, heaving, and Fabiano had his arm wrapped around Leona's shoulder, who looked a little faint.

Nino went over to his wife and rubbed her back.

Fabiano shook his head. "What the hell, Remo?"

I rolled my eyes. "You've seen me do worse. We tortured together." And after what he'd done to his father, he really had no business being shocked by me losing control.

Savio snorted. "We've all seen you torture, but you never lost control like that. Take a look at the video footage and if your expression doesn't scare even you shitless then I don't know what to say." He went over to Adamo and took the cigarette from him, taking a deep pull.

"You don't smoke," Adamo grumbled.

"I need to get rid of the vomit taste in my mouth."

"Don't tell me you threw up as well," I said.

Savio cocked his eyebrow. "No. But when people around me started ejecting their food, I could practically taste it in my mouth."

I felt Fabiano's eyes on me and met his gaze, daring him to say something. He didn't. Adamo couldn't meet my eyes, and I didn't have the necessary patience tonight to deal with him. Maybe tomorrow. Nino finally managed to calm Kiara, who leaned into him, pale and sweaty. She locked eyes with me. It wasn't disgust or fear I saw in her gaze but compassion and understanding, and it sent a new wave of rage through me.

"Keys," I ordered, holding out my hands to Nino.

He shook his head. "You're not driving anywhere right now."

"Give me the fucking keys," I growled.

"No."

"I can drive you," Adamo quipped.

I slanted a look at him. Of course he'd come with his new car, and of course he wasn't sitting on its hood. Nino nodded, as if I needed his fucking permission to get into Adamo's car.

"Then let's go, kiddo," I muttered.

Adamo hopped off Nino's car, threw away his stub, and got into his Mustang. The moment I sank down into the passenger seat and closed the door, Adamo shot out of the parking lot. "Where do you want to go?"

I rubbed my temple. "I want to kill and maim but now that I have you to keep an eye on, that won't fucking happen."

"I think I'm meant to babysit you tonight. Nino's worried," Adamo said.

I shook my head. "Fucking nuisances, all of you."

"You scared the shit out of me tonight."

"I hope that wasn't the first time or I'm doing something wrong."

"I've been scared of you before. When you sent Fabiano after me because of the cocaine. But today I was kind of scared for you."

"Trust me, Adamo, you have absolutely no reason to be scared for me."

Adamo frowned. "Is it because of her?"

My brothers seemed intent to test the limit of my patience. "Shut up and drive."

"Where?"

"Home. Just take us home."

SERAFINA

Mom and I sat in the garden on a swing, enjoying a warm fall day. I'd been back for only two days, and it was the first time Mom and I were really alone. Our feet gently kicked the ground to keep the swing in motion. Mom held my hand, peering up at the sky.

I knew she had questions but couldn't ask them, and I wasn't sure if I could give her answers.

"Why did you give Sofia to Danilo?" I asked eventually to say something.

"It's not what we wanted, not what Danilo wanted, but we need to bind our families. It's what's expected," Mom said. "And he's a decent man."

"You said the same words to me on my wedding day."

Mom paled but managed a small nod. "I wanted to take away your fears."

"I know."

Her blue eyes held mine, filling with anguish. She touched my cheek. "I wanted only the best for you. I wanted happiness. I wanted a man who would carry you on his hands, who showed you kindness like your father did to me." She looked away briefly, gathering herself. "I can't imagine the horrors you lived, Fina, but I wish I could have suffered them in your stead."

"Mom," I whispered. "It's not like you all think. I didn't suffer the way you believe. Remo didn't force me."

"Your father didn't allow me to see the video where *he* cut you, but I saw the sheets. I see the marks on your throat. Don't make light of your suffering to make me feel better, love. Don't."

She cradled my face, her eyes fierce, determined. She, too, would never understand the extent of my betrayal. My family needed me to be the victim in this.

I wanted to belong, wanted to be part of the Outfit again, but every passing day, it became more obvious that part of me had stayed in Vegas with Remo. People were talking. They did it behind closed doors mostly, but I caught the pitying glances of the bodyguards and maids. All my life people had regarded me with admiration and respect, and now I was someone to pity. They didn't know I wasn't the victim, not in the sense they all thought.

And I had been shielded from attention so far. I hadn't left the house, hadn't attended any social gatherings, but eventually I'd have to make an appearance or the speculations would rise even higher. I needed to show them that I wasn't hiding, that I had no reason to hide.

More than three months since Remo had kidnapped me. More than four weeks since he'd set me free—body *not* soul. Sometimes I managed to forget him for a few minutes, only to be reminded with a crushing force, but it was getting better. Maybe Sam was right. Maybe Remo's brainwashing was ceasing. Maybe I could be free one day.

Today my family would return to the public, would show strength, would show that we weren't broken, that I wasn't. It was Dad's fiftieth birthday, and the party had been planned for almost a year, a splendid feast with family and friends, with Underbosses and Captains.

My parents had considered calling the party off, but I had convinced them to celebrate. Life had to go on.

Dante, Valentina, and the kids were staying with us as well, and I was excited to see them again. I busied myself helping Mom prepare for the party these last few weeks, needing to distract myself, trying to ignore the nagging fear at the back of my head that grew louder every day.

I stared up at the ceiling in my room. It was already late, and I needed to choose a dress, get ready, and help Mom, but I couldn't move. For the last two hours I lay motionless, except for my shallow breathing.

I'd got my period the last week of August. It was the end of October now. My fingers traced my belly, terrified, immobilized.

Slowly, I got out of bed and perched on its edge for a long time, letting a horrible realization fill my bones. Two months since my last period. Closing my eyes, I swallowed. I'd never taken the pill during my time with Remo, and he had never used protection, wanting to claim me without that barrier between us. I stared up at the ceiling, praying that it wasn't true. It would be the end of all my hopes, of everything.

I swallowed again. A knock sounded. "Fina, are you awake?"

Samuel. It was already late and what he was really asking was if I was okay. I wasn't. I should be getting ready, should play my part, be strong for appearance's sake.

"Come in," I said.

He opened the door and stepped in, already dressed in dark pants and a royal blue dress shirt. His eyes took in my rumpled state. He moved toward me and crouched down in front of me. "What's wrong?"

I considered keeping my suspicion to myself, but it was a truth I wouldn't be able to hide from them. If it really was true ...

I met his gaze. "I think I'm pregnant."

Samuel froze, eyes widening in shock. "You mean ..." He swallowed, staring at my flat stomach. His expression twisted with anger, sadness and worse ... disgust.

Disgust, because this was Remo's baby. He leaned his forehead against my thigh and released a shuddering breath.

"I will kill him. I swear it. One day I'm going to kill Remo Falcone in the cruelest way possible."

I touched his head. "Can you ... can you get Mom? I need a pregnancy test. I need to know for sure."

Samuel straightened and stood. With a last glance at me, he left. I couldn't move. If I was pregnant with Remo's child ... I couldn't even finish the thought. I didn't want to, not yet, not before I had certainty.

A few minutes later, Mom stepped in, her face pale. We looked at each other before she walked toward me and touched my cheek. "Whatever happens, we'll get through this, Fina. We will get through this."

"I know," I said. "Can you get a test for me?"

"I will ask Valentina. Maybe she's got a spare test. She and Dante are trying for another child."

Mom dropped her hand and left the room. I stood, taking a deep breath. Maybe there was another explanation, but deep down I knew the truth.

Mom returned with a test. I took it from her with shaking hands. "Can you leave me alone? I'll come downstairs once I'm ready."

Mom hesitated but then she kissed my cheek. I watched the closed door for a while before I forced myself to get up from the bed and move to the bathroom. My heart beat in my throat when I unpackaged the test.

Fifteen minutes later I stared down at the test in my hands, at the truth that shattered the last shred of hope I'd held. Hope that I could ever find my way back into the Outfit. Hope that I could forget Remo. As if there was a way I could have ever forgotten him. I stared at the two lines on the test.

Pregnant.

With Remo Falcone's child.

A man of unparalleled cruelty and mercilessness.

The man who'd robbed me of my innocence, of my future ... of my heart. Body and soul.

I own you.

Oh, Remo, if you knew what you gave away ...

I set the test down and touched my stomach. It seemed unreal, impossible. Pregnant.

My heart was a war-torn land: two conflicting emotions battling for dominance, leaving nothing but devastation in their wake. Unbridled happiness that a small human was growing inside of me. A small part of Remo that would always remain with me. And raw fear of the future, of my—of *our* future. Our world was cruel to women who got pregnant out of wedlock; it was even crueler to children born out of wedlock.

Damned to be called bastards. A child of Remo Falcone couldn't hope for a kinder name. I'd protect my child, but I wouldn't always be there to fend off the attacks. It would be strong enough to defend itself, no doubt, but the idea that my baby would have to grow strong out of necessity, because the world forced it into a corner, made me furious. I tried to calm my raging emotions. I was getting ahead of myself. I came from a good family, maybe things would be different for my child, no matter who their father was.

Taking a deep breath, I headed downstairs. My family was gathered in the dining room, and when I entered they all fell silent. Mom. Dad. Valentina. Dante. Samuel. Dante's kids. Anna, Leonas, my sister Sofia. The room was already decorated for the event, and in the garden a white tent had been set up, which held the dance floor. The caterer would arrive in about two hours, the guests in three. A day of celebration.

Mom motioned at Sofia, Anna, and Leonas. "Out. Go to your rooms for now." They did, no protests. In passing Sofia gave me a small smile.

I looked at Samuel. He got up, slowly, hesitantly, and our eyes met. His expression fell, turning desperate.

"I'm pregnant."

Mom covered her mouth with her hand, and Dad closed his eyes. Valentina regarded me with sympathy, and Dante gave a terse nod. No celebrations. No happiness.

Samuel slowly sank back down onto his chair. From hundreds of miles away and not knowing it, Remo had landed another hit.

"It's still early. We can call the doc and he will get rid of it," Dad said, face pale and worried when he finally met my gaze.

My stomach tightened and something angry and protective reared its head in my chest. *My child.*

Mom nodded slowly. "You don't have to keep it."

Samuel only looked at me. He knew me. Until recently better than anyone else, but Remo had seen parts of me nobody knew, my darkest parts. "You want to keep it," he said quietly, uncomprehending.

I touched my stomach. "I will keep this child. I will take care of it and love

271

it and protect it. It's mine." And the moment the words left my mouth, I knew it with certainty. This child would be born, and whoever tried to take it from me would see how strong I was.

Silence greeted me. Then Dante nodded once. "It's your decision."

"It is," I said firmly.

Mom got up. It was obvious that she was fighting with herself. I walked up to her because she couldn't move and touched her shoulders. "We will get through this, right? This baby is innocent. It's my baby."

Mom smiled shakily. "You are right, sweetheart."

Dad got up and touched my cheek. "We will stand by your side." I could see how much these words cost him. I wasn't sure if my family could get past the fact that my child was Remo's child. Would they love it because it was mine or hate it because it was his?

CHAPTER 23

SERAFINA

I sat in front of my vanity and brushed my hair, stroke after stroke, trying to find calm. I could hear the first guests downstairs, could hear laughter and music.

I needed to go down. Taking a deep breath, I stood. I'd chosen a floor-length form-fitting dark blue dress matching the color of Samuel's shirt. I touched my stomach, still flat, but I knew in a few months I couldn't wear dresses like this anymore.

Remo's baby. I closed my eyes. I was happy and sad, terrified and hopeful. What would Remo say if he knew? Would he care at all? I had been a means to an end, a queen in his chess game, and he'd won.

He had let me go as if I was nothing.

I'd heard the rumors of his cage fights. He was back to fighting, back to living his life. I wondered if he'd already moved on to one of the many whores at his disposal? Probably.

I had been stupid.

Sam was right. Remo had twisted my mind so he could control me, and I had let him.

A familiar knock sounded and Samuel stepped in. We hadn't talked since I'd revealed my pregnancy to my family. It had become obvious that they needed time to let it sink in, time to put on their public masks so our guests wouldn't find out the truth. Not yet.

He stopped near the door, watching me like I was breaking apart right before his eyes. I turned around myself, showing him my dress. "We match." I wanted to see his smile, anything but the soul-crushing darkness.

"You are beautiful," he said, but he didn't smile. I walked toward him, and as I did his eyes were drawn to my stomach. "Fina, get rid of it."

I froze. Sam stepped up to me and gripped my arms. "Please, get rid of it. I can't bear the idea that something belonging to him is growing inside of you."

"Sam," I whispered. "This is a baby. It's innocent. Whatever Remo did, this baby won't suffer for it."

Samuel ripped away from me. "But you will! What do you think people will say if you give birth to his spawn? And the thing will remind you of the asshole every fucking day. How will you ever forget if you see the result of Remo's fucking sins every day?"

I turned away and moved toward the window, clutching the windowsill in an iron grip, trying to hold on to my composure. If I wanted to show up at Dad's party, I couldn't lose it now.

Samuel came up behind me and touched my shoulders. "I shouldn't have said that."

"It's okay," I said. I put my hand over Samuel's. "I need you at my side, Sam. The baby and I . . . we both need you. Please."

Samuel put his chin down on my head and sighed. "I'll always be there for you."

We stood like that for a while until I turned and gave Samuel a firm smile. "Let's go down there and show people that we are strong together."

Samuel held out his hand, and I took it. We moved downstairs together, and Samuel's grip on me tightened when the attention shifted to me. People were trying to be discreet about it but failing miserably. Every Underboss was there, even Danilo. He stood off to the side, next to the bar, nursing an amber colored drink. Our eyes met briefly, but then I looked away.

Samuel remained glued to my side. My shadow, my protector, but even his harsh gaze couldn't stop the pitying looks or the whispers, and people didn't even know about my pregnancy yet. I could imagine how much worse the gossip would become then.

I'd been known as the Ice Princess, meant to become the Ice Queen at Danilo's side.

Now I was the woman whom Remo had defiled. The men could hardly look at me. Somehow I had become all of their failures.

Samuel's hand on my lower back twitched, and one look at his face told me he was close to losing control.

"Dance with me," I pleaded.

Samuel nodded with a small, tight smile and wrapped me in his embrace then stiffened when my still flat stomach pressed up to him. His eyes darted down and anguish flashed across his expression before he could mask it. As if he could already see my pregnancy when it was still safely hidden. I tightened my hold on him briefly, and finally he met my gaze. We began to dance. All eyes were on us.

Samuel held my gaze because he was on the verge of losing control. One look at the others and he'd snap. I smiled up at him and he relaxed. I, too, felt the glances. Could practically hear the whispers. A few women my age who'd always resented me for my status looked almost ... triumphant, happy to witness my fall from grace.

I lifted my chin higher, angry and then worried ... because how would all these people treat my child?

After three dances, Dad took over and Samuel moved over to the side to watch.

"You are beautiful, dove," he said quietly. His expression was controlled, calm. His public face. Mom, too, looked poised and elegant as she stood beside Sofia, Anna, and Valentina.

"Thanks, Dad," I said then added, "I'm sorry I don't have a present for you."

I hadn't left the house since my return, and to be honest, I'd completely forgotten to get a present. My mind had been occupied with too many others things.

"I got my present already," he said, and for a moment I thought he meant my child but then I realized he meant my freedom. He didn't mention my pregnancy.

Dante danced with me next.

I met his eyes, wondering what he thought of my pregnancy, wondering what kind of future lay ahead for my child, if it was a boy. Would he be allowed in the Outfit? Or would his father's identity close every door before it could ever be opened? I didn't dare ask my uncle. Not in public, not on my father's birthday party.

After the dance, I headed back to Samuel, who was talking to one of his oldest friends. He gave me a nod, but he, too, had trouble meeting my eyes. Samuel noticed and his jaw flexed. He excused himself, touched my back, and led me away.

Samuel and I walked into the entrance hall. I had a feeling Samuel needed to be away from the festivities for a couple of minutes. A few younger Made Men I didn't know had gathered there, and when we passed them, their words managed to reach us.

"I don't understand why they don't keep her hidden. It's a fucking disgrace to have her walk around as if Falcone hasn't defiled her."

My shock had barely registered when Samuel attacked. He broke the first guy's nose with a sickening crunch then shoved the second to the ground, pressing his knife against the man's throat.

"Sam," I said firmly, clutching his shoulder.

He leaned down, bringing his face close to the other man's. "I should cut your throat for insulting my sister. Apologize."

The man glanced at his friends. One was nursing his broken nose, the other obviously unsure if he should interfere, considering our Dad was their fathers' boss.

"Apologize!" Samuel snarled.

"I'm sorry," the guy blurted.

I tightened my hold on Sam's shoulder. He jerked back, took my hand, and dragged me outside, not into the garden but into the driveway where we were alone. He released me, turning his back to me. He sucked in a deep breath. I pressed my palms up to his shoulder blades then rested my forehead against his back. "Don't let their words get to you. I don't care about them and neither should you."

"How can you not care about them? You are a mafia princess. I should cut their tongues out for daring to whisper his name in one sentence with yours."

His name.

Remo Falcone. The father of my unborn child.

And worse, the man who filled my nights not with nightmares but with longing.

The next morning, Dad, Samuel, and Dante wanted to talk to me.

When I walked into Dad's office, I knew from their expressions that it wouldn't be an easy conversation and definitely not one I'd like. Dad sat behind his desk, Sam perched on its edge, and Dante stood with his hands in his slacks beside the window. I made a beeline for the sofa and sank down. My brain felt sluggish from lack of sleep. I'd spent all night trying to come to terms with the fact that I was carrying a baby, Remo's baby.

"What do you want to talk about?"

Three sets of eyes darted to my belly, and my hand automatically—*protectively*—pressed to the spot.

"If you keep this child," Dante began.

"I *will* keep the child."

Dad looked away and then at the picture frame on his desk. A photo of our family taken shortly before I'd been kidnapped.

"You will have to keep it hidden," Dad said.

I blinked at them. "What?"

"Once you start showing, we'll have to keep you out of the public eye, Serafina," Dante said, his voice resolute. "I doubt Remo Falcone has the slightest interest in his offspring, but he might use it against us. The Outfit needs to be strong. This child might cause tension within the Outfit, and we can't have that at the current time."

"Or we could arrange a quick marriage with someone who agrees to a fake marriage and pretend it's his child," Dad suggested gently.

I stared between them. Samuel looked at the floor, his brows snapped together.

"I'm not going to marry anyone, and I'm not going to lie about the baby's father. People wouldn't believe it anyway."

Now I was the woman pregnant with Remo's bastard child. Soon my protruding belly would carry the guilt and shame of the Outfit.

"Eventually people will realize I have a child. Once it grows older, it'll be difficult to keep it hidden. And what if he's a boy? Won't he be part of the Outfit?"

They exchanged a look.

"You haven't even given birth yet. It's still early," Dante said tersely. I searched their faces, and as I did it was difficult to hold on to my indignation and anger. My kidnapping had left its marks. They were still shaken up. Maybe over time things would get better. I'd give them the time they needed to accept the situation. I owed it to them. I owed them more than I owed Remo.

This baby and I belonged in the Outfit. This was my family, my home.

Still, part of me wondered if I was lying to myself, if it wasn't better to return to Las Vegas.

But Remo had sent me away. I'd served my purpose. How much did I really know about him? And how could I be sure if everything he'd done hadn't been part of a show, his masterful manipulation. It had worked, hadn't it? And how could I even be sure what I was feeling was real? Could feelings like that be born in captivity?

My pregnancy became the pink elephant in the room, an ever growing presence that everyone tried to ignore, and I did my best to make it easy for them. I wore loose-fitting clothes, glad for the cold winter days that allowed for thick sweaters and even thicker coats. I think my family often managed to forget I was even pregnant.

Only when I was alone in my room did I allow myself to admire my bump.

It wasn't big yet. I had even managed to take part in Dante and Val's Christmas party because in my seventeenth week, if my calculations were accurate, an A-line dress still hid everything it should. If people suspected something, they kept it to themselves. It was a possible shame the Outfit didn't want to voice aloud.

It was early January when Samuel and Mom accompanied me to my first doctor's appointment. So far I hadn't asked for one, but Mom had surprised me a few days ago by asking if we should check on the baby. It was her silent apology, her attempt to accept what was so very difficult for all of them to accept.

The doctor had been working with the Outfit for years. She treated most of the pregnant Outfit women and would keep the secret I carried.

Fear filled me as I stretched out on the examination couch. I wasn't even sure what exactly scared me. It wasn't as if I didn't know I was pregnant. It was unmistakable at this point.

The doctor was on one side of me with the ultrasound while Samuel and Mom stood on the other. I swallowed when I pushed up my sweater, revealing the bump for the first time in front of others.

Samuel's face became still, and Mom swallowed before she managed an encouraging smile and squeezed my hand.

"This will be cold for a moment," the doctor warned me.

I nodded distractedly, my eyes fixed on the ultrasound.

The doctor started frowning, moving the ultrasound around on my belly. The thud-thud of a heartbeat filled the room and my own heart sped up, swelling with love and wonder. But the thud-thud was off, as if it was off-beat, two out-of-sync rhythms.

Mom's eyes widened, but I wasn't sure why, and fear filled me. I stared at her, then the doctor, then Samuel, but he looked as confused as I felt.

"Oh God," Mom whispered.

"What? What's going on?"

Mom's eyes filled with tears. "Twins."

The doctor nodded, and my eyes jerked toward Samuel.

"Like us," I said in wonder.

He managed a small smile, but his eyes held worry.

The knowledge that I carried twins changed things for Mom. It was as if she could finally see the babies as mine, not as something alien.

Samuel seemed to be coming around as well. He painted the nursery and set up the furniture for me. And Sofia? She was ecstatic about the prospect of being an aunt. But Dad ... Dad had a harder time. He didn't mention the pregnancy and never looked anywhere below my chin. I understood him, couldn't possibly be angry because his eyes reflected his conflict.

I often managed to feel like I belonged once more, managed to pretend I wasn't forced to hide in our home so no one found out I was pregnant. What I didn't manage was to stop thinking about the man who was the reason for everything.

Every night I lay awake in bed. Every time I stroked my bump I saw him before my eyes. And every time I was torn between anger and longing. Sometimes I wondered if I should find a way to let him know, but then I thought of my family, of their slow healing process, of what my kidnapping had done to them, and I couldn't do it. What did you owe the man who kidnapped you? Who tried to destroy the people you cared about? The man who took your heart, only to push you away?

Nothing.

I owed Remo Falcone nothing.

These were my children, and they'd grow up as part of my family, as part of the Outfit. I'd hide the truth from them as long as I could. They would not find out who their father was until they had to. If I wanted them to have a chance in the Outfit, they couldn't be Falcones. They couldn't be associated with Remo at all.

In mid-May I gave birth to the most beautiful creations I could imagine and knew with absolute certainty that everything I'd wished for them would never become reality.

CHAPTER 24

SERAFINA

I loved my family with all my heart. And they loved me. But the moment I held my children in my arms, I knew I could not stay with them forever, knew it with soul-crushing certainty.

Nevio and Greta were Remo. Dark eyes, thick black hair.

For everyone in the Outfit they'd always be Falcones, always the result of something horrid, born out of something shameful, something dark. But for me they were the most beautiful creation I could imagine. They were utter perfection. Twins like Samuel and me. They would lift each other up, make each other stronger like Samuel and I had done when we were younger and still did. It would be us against the world. It couldn't be any other way.

Samuel stayed with me in the hospital after the birth while Mom went home for a few hours of sleep after twenty hours at my side during labor. Samuel's eyes were kind and loving as they looked down at me, but these tender emotions vanished as soon as he turned toward my children sleeping in their cradle. He wasn't doing it on purpose, but my children reminded him of something he and everyone else were desperate to forget.

And how could he not be reminded when my twins looked like Falcones?

My heart ached fiercely when I looked at them, throbbing with a longing I'd tried to bury with the memories of Remo, but Remo wasn't a man that could be forgotten.

Not easily, not quickly, not ever.

Two days after giving birth, Mom and Samuel carried my twins into the house because I still had trouble lifting anything heavier than a glass of water. The family had come together for the occasion, but I knew it wasn't to celebrate. Dad and Dante probably needed to discuss how to keep my children a secret. The Underbosses knew. They had to for the sake of the Outfit. Danilo did, but I hadn't talked to him since the day Sofia had been promised to him.

Samuel held my arm while his other carried the baby carrier. Walking the stairs was more than a little uncomfortable, and I was glad when I finally arrived inside our house.

Valentina came toward me and hugged me gently. She and Dante were still trying for child number three, but so far it wasn't working. She peered down at my babies with a soft smile. "They are beautiful, Serafina."

"They are," I agreed.

Sam and Dad exchanged a look, and it felt like a stab in the heart because when they looked at my children they saw the black hair and dark eyes and nothing more. They saw Falcones. They saw shame and guilt. Would they ever allow my babies to be more than the greatest failure in the history of the Outfit?

Sofia rushed down the staircase followed by Anna. Leonas showed less enthusiasm than the girls as he sauntered down the steps, rolling his eyes.

Sofia stopped beside me and Samuel, looking down at Greta sleeping soundly in the carrier. I'd noticed that Samuel had insisted on carrying Greta, not Nevio, but I tried not to put too much meaning into it. Sofia hadn't been allowed in the hospital because we didn't want to draw too much attention to us, and her eyes were wide in surprise.

"Wow," she breathed. "I've never seen hair that black."

She'd never seen Remo.

Anna nodded as she lightly brushed a finger over Nevio's head. His eyes peeled open and as always when they did, my breath lodged in my throat. Dark eyes. Remo's eyes. Even at two days old, my boy was his father.

Dad averted his eyes, brows pulling tight, and looked at Dante with an expression that tore me cleanly in half.

Valentina squeezed my shoulder and leaned in. "It takes time, Serafina. Give them time. One day they will see your babies as what they are: only yours."

I nodded, but deep down I knew Greta and Nevio would never only be mine because they were also Remo's, and nothing could change that. And I didn't want it to.

The next day, I was cradling Greta in my arm while Nevio rested on the sofa beside me, deep asleep when Dante came in. He strode toward us, his eyes flickering over my children. His expression didn't give anything away, and I wondered if it was because he didn't resent my twins like everyone else or if he was too good at hiding his true feelings.

He sank down in the armchair across from me, opening his jacket so it didn't wrinkle. He gave me a tense smile. "How are you?"

I stroked Greta's cheek before I looked up again. "Good."

He nodded. "I know things aren't easy for you, Serafina. It was never meant to be like this. I've wanted to talk to you for a while ..." He trailed off, his expression tightening. "But I'm not in the habit of justifying my actions, nor apologizing."

I frowned. "You are Capo."

"I am, but that doesn't make me infallible." He paused. "I think you should know that when Remo kidnapped you, your father would have handed over his territory to save you. I didn't allow it. And Samuel attacked the mansion without my permission because I wouldn't have allowed it. I'm not a man who answers to another's demands. I refuse to be blackmailed. I have to think of the Outfit."

"I know and I understand, Uncle." Then I paused. "But in the end you gave Scuderi to Remo."

Something dark and furious flashed in Dante's eyes. "I did. Because I'm not only Capo. I'm a father. I'm your uncle. This is my family, and I owe it protection. I owed you protection and I failed." He lowered his gaze to my children. "You'll have to live with the consequences of my decisions."

I shook my head. "Those decisions gave me my children, and that's not something I could ever regret."

Dante got up and touched my shoulder. Then he traced his index finger over Greta's head before he turned. Like Samuel and Dad, he had a harder time looking at Nevio than at my daughter. I peered down at my son and took his little hand in mine, and not for the first time I wondered what Remo would see when he saw them.

A high pitched wail sounded.

Samuel and I jerked up at the same time from where we'd fallen asleep on the sofa in the nursery. We didn't bother going into our beds most of the time because Nevio and Greta woke every two hours. He and Mom took turns helping me, and during the day Sofia changed diapers and helped feed them as well. I couldn't remember the last time I'd slept more than two hours in the last six months.

Samuel rubbed his face. I knew he didn't sleep much on the nights he wasn't helping either. The Outfit was planning something. He had only hinted to it, but it could only be an attack on the Camorra. It scared me, *terrified* me because I wasn't only scared for Samuel and Dad but also for the man I couldn't forget.

I stood and so did Samuel. He reached for Greta like usual and I took Nevio. This was our routine, one I didn't question anymore. I was glad for Samuel's support, even if he couldn't bear being near my son.

Thirty minutes later, Samuel and I sat shoulder to shoulder, Greta sound asleep in his arm and Nevio wide awake in mine. He snatched at my hair and yanked. I loosened his hold, wincing, and pushed the strand out of reach. Nevio let out a happy yowl, eyes zooming in on Samuel.

I followed his gaze. My brother sighed and put his head back. "Don't give me that look, Fina."

"What look?"

"Like I'm breaking your heart."

"Why do you have such a hard time looking at Nevio but have no trouble holding Greta?"

"Because with her I can overlook the similarities, but with Nevio …"

Samuel shook his head, lowering his gaze to my boy who was happily chewing on his own fingers. "With him all I can see is Remo fucking Falcone."

"Shh," I shushed him. I stroked Nevio's head but he was oblivious to what was being said. One day he would understand, though. One day he would realize what the looks he got meant.

"You'll never be free of him because of them, Fina. Maybe without those kids people would have eventually forgotten what happened and moved on, but they are living breathing reminders. Once people find out they are Falcone's kids, and trust me everyone will know they are his, things will get really ugly."

I rocked Nevio and his eyes began drooping. "If anyone tries to hurt my children by making them feel less than, they'll have to go through me."

Samuel smiled sadly. "I'll be at your side. I'll always protect you."

Me. Not my kids. Never them.

Falcone. Falcone.

One look.

Falcone.

The same cruel eyes.

Pitch black.

Falcones through and through.

Shame. Sin. Dishonor. Bastards.

Why did she ruin herself by having his children? Why didn't she get rid of them?

Falcones.

So far the words were only whispered in the Outfit, but soon they would be screamed because every day my children looked more like Remo, like

Falcones. In a week my twins would be seven months old, and I hadn't even left the house with them yet. The only fresh air they got was when I was in the garden with them. The midwife and doctors had made home visits. Despite these precautions word about them was spreading among our circles. Maybe the maids let something slip. Maybe it was one of the bodyguards or maybe one of the Underbosses trusted his gossipy wife too much.

I'd attended two events with Samuel, and the whispers had followed me everywhere. The pity and curiosity. The incomprehension and even anger that I had chosen these children and not disposed of them, as if that would erase the kidnapping.

When we arrived home after one of these social gatherings, the birthday party of Dad's second-in-command, I lost it right in the middle of the lobby.

"I can't stand it," I said harshly. "Can't stand how everyone whispers their names as if they are something sinful. I don't want them to grow up ashamed of who they are."

Mom who'd stayed with the kids because she didn't feel well enough to attend an event appeared on the landing, looking concerned at my outburst.

Dad sighed, his expression reflecting pain. "Everyone knows what happened. Everyone knows what they are and that won't ever change."

"*What* they are ..." I stared at my father.

Samuel touched my shoulder, but I shook him off.

"They are mine! They are your blood too. They are part of the Outfit! When will you accept that? Will it take Nevio taking the oath for you to come to terms with it?"

Dad and Samuel exchanged a look, and I took a step back. "He'll become part of the Outfit, right? He'll become Underboss of a city one day? It's his birthright."

His birthright is to become Capo of the Camorra.

Dad gave me a sad smile. "Dove," he murmured.

"No," I whispered. "Don't tell me you won't let Nevio amount to anything because of who his father is."

Samuel gave me a look as if I was being unreasonable. "Fina, he looks like a fucking Falcone. They are all fucking insane. Remo's twisted blood runs through his veins. And just look at him. He's already got an impossible temper at only seven months."

"Our soldiers will never accept him, not after what his father did. We've still barely recovered from the attack. Every wedding is heavily guarded, every woman protected by twice the number of guards. That shame lingers and your children are a constant reminder of it," Dad said quietly.

I turned around and left them standing there. Rushing past Mom without a word, I stormed into the nursery and closed the door, breathing harshly.

Nevio and Greta were asleep in the crib they shared, both sprawled out on their backs. Greta's hand rested on Nevio's chest. They always ended up touching when they slept.

My children weren't something shameful.

I wouldn't allow anyone to make them feel that way. Not even the family I loved.

REMO

Kiara was in full-blown Christmas mode. She'd decorated every area of the house she was allowed into. I knew she would have loved to wield her magic in my wing as well, but she wasn't that daring yet. Good for her, because I was in a fucking foul mood, had been for days, and today was the worst of all.

The scent of freshly baked cookies wafted through the house as I read the email from Rick, the organizer of our races. Everything had been set up for the biggest race we'd ever held. Nino wasn't happy I decided to end it in Kansas City after the last incident, but I wanted to make a fucking point. The Outfit had been surprisingly careful in their attacks. An ambush here and there, a few dismembered soldiers, but nothing major. Until three days ago when they killed my fucking Underboss in Kansas City. A warning not to get so close to their territory. Maybe the beginning of more. Ending the race anywhere else would have sent the wrong message.

Kiara came in carrying a plate with what looked like small half-moons dusted in sugar. She held it out to me. "Kipferl."

"I'm not in the mood for something sweet." I was in the mood to blast something to smithereens, for blood and death, and more than that … Dante's fucking demise.

She frowned. "They're delicious." Her eyes moved to the screen. "Kansas?"

I nodded then grabbed one of the cookies and took a bite. Sweet and soft. I put half of it back down on the plate. Kiara took it and ate the rest.

I didn't like the way she regarded me as if she *knew*.

"I've been thinking about your offer."

I had no clue what she was talking about.

"About training with you."

"I made that offer more than a year ago," I said.

She bit her lip. "I wasn't ready then."

I knew another reason why I hadn't been part of her defense training in the last few months. Nino was wary of my emotional state, but he was out visiting a few of our drug labs. He was interested in the chemical processes, but I only in the end result. The only times I visited our labs were when they needed reminding to work more efficiently.

"And you think today's a good time to fight me?" I asked in a low voice.

"Not fight. Train," she corrected.

I pushed off the sofa, towering over her. She didn't flinch. "Now?"

She put the plate down and indicated the boxing ring. I shook my head. "In real life you won't be in a boxing ring when you're being attacked. It'll be in a dark alley, when you're on your way home. Your attacker will have been following and watching you for a while. He'll be behind you."

We both knew that it would never come to that. Kiara was never alone anymore, and the stupid bastard daring to look at her the wrong way would lose his eyes.

"Run."

She blinked. "What?"

I leaned down, invading her personal space, trying to get her pulse up. "Run."

Understanding filled her eyes. She took a step back and then she turned and began running.

I took another cookie and bit half of it off before putting it back down on the plate. Then I chased her. Running after Kiara brought back memories I didn't fucking need today or ever. Anger surged through me. I took the steps two at a time and caught up with her in the connecting hallway to their wing. I gripped her hand and jerked her back. Kiara gasped but acted immediately, whirling on me before I could press her to the ground. She knew she couldn't allow me to press her onto her stomach. Once my weight rested on her back, she wouldn't have a chance to defend herself anymore. She was good, but I was angry and not in the mood to take it too easy on her.

The second I straddled her hips with her arms pressed above her head, the flickers of panic filled her eyes.

"Snap out of it," I ordered.

I saw the struggle in her eyes, the memories threatening to burst forth even after all this time.

"Snap the fuck out of it," I snarled. I wouldn't release her if she didn't.

Indignation flashed in her eyes, and she bucked her hips, but I was too heavy. She was small and lithe, and managed to jerk her leg up in a way that her knee smashed right into my balls.

Every fiber in my body, every muscle, every fucking blood cell, acted on instinct, wanting to lash out. I shoved off her and sank back against the wall, chest heaving, trying to calm the rage in my veins.

"Sorry," Kiara said, sitting up and watching me worriedly.

I smiled darkly. "No need. You did what Nino taught you."

"But you didn't pull back because I hurt you ... only to stop yourself from hurting me in response."

I raised my eyebrows. She was perceptive. I wasn't sure if I liked it. "It doesn't matter. The average man isn't as familiar with pain as I am. A kick to the balls would distract them."

She nodded then she surprised me by sitting beside me against the wall. "Today's Serafina's birthday, right?"

"Kiara," I said in warning.

She tilted her head. "She didn't marry, did she?"

"I don't have spies in the Outfit, so I wouldn't know."

"It would have been in the news."

I had stopped searching for news on Serafina a few days after I'd released her. She was a thing of the past.

"I thought she was falling for you ..."

I stood, glaring down at her. "You women always need to turn everything into a fairy tale, even a kidnapping. Serafina was my captive. The only falling she did was her fall from grace."

She pushed off the ground as well. "You can pretend all you want, but I saw the way you looked at her."

I backed her into the wall. "You didn't see anything because there wasn't anything. I fucked Serafina and enjoyed every moment of it. I wanted to possess her, wanted to rip her innocence from her, and I did. That's it."

"If that were all, you would have bathed in your triumph afterward. But you hardly even mentioned her since you let her go ... as if you can't bear saying her name."

"Kiara," I growled. "Don't push me too far. Not right now."

She pushed against my shoulder, and I stepped back. Without another word, she left, but her eyes had said more than enough.

When I came back down into the game room to kick the punching bag, Savio and Adamo were on the sofa, playing some fucking shooting game. As if we didn't have enough bloodshed in real life. The plate with the cookies was empty.

"Are there more cookies in the kitchen?" Savio asked without looking up.

"How would I know? Ask Kiara."

Savio slanted a curious glance my way. "What crawled up your ass?"

I sank down across from them. "Right this moment? You. In general? Kansas."

"That race is going to be spectacular," Adamo said.

"Don't sound so fucking excited. You don't really believe Remo will allow you to race again after last time, do you?" Savio muttered, throwing his feet up on the table.

"That wasn't my fault," Adamo snapped.

"Sure. When you crash a car it's never your fault."

"I won't crash this time. I'm much better. I'll win."

Savio didn't look convinced. "It's the longest race. Eight hours minimum. That gives you plenty of time to fuck up."

"I won't fuck up. And the long distance is the best part. It's a cool layout," Adamo said.

"You won't drive," I said finally. "The race ends in Kansas City. I don't want you that close to Outfit territory."

"Nobody has to know that I'm there. I'm in a car. I can use another name."

"No. And that's final."

Adamo frowned and sank deeper into the sofa. "You promised me I could race more often if I didn't skip school and did my Camorra duties."

"And that promise stands, Adamo, but not this race."

"But Luke will be there again with a new car. He rammed me last time. I want to kick his ass and make him crash his car."

I leaned forward. "You won't go anywhere near that race, Adamo."

"Fine," he mumbled. "But next race I'm allowed?"

I nodded. I'd thought Adamo's fascination with races would wane with time, but it hadn't. He still lived for the occasional race, and I had started rewarding him with them for tasks well done. He was still a reluctant Made Man, but he'd improved, not just his fighting skills but also his guilt over what we did. Sometimes I wondered if I should just let him become the organizer for our races and have him race cars instead of trying to force him into another role, but we needed him. Open war with the Outfit required every Made Man we had.

CHAPTER 25

SERAFINA

Dad was antsy. He kept checking his phone, which rested beside his plate. He usually didn't have his phone on display when we had dinner. It was our family time.

Mom brought a spoon with pureed sweet potato in an arch to Greta's waiting mouth; she smacked her lips happily around the food. I, on the other hand, tried to stop Nevio from throwing his food around. He didn't like being fed and preferred to shove food into his mouth by himself, but he was still too small for that and made too much of a mess. I held his small hands so he couldn't grab the spoon and brought it to his mouth. It took three attempts before he accepted the food.

"They are cute but watching them eat is a bit disgusting," Sofia said, her nose wrinkled. "And since they started eating normal food as well, their diapers stink."

Dad frowned, obviously unhappy about the topic. He could eat dinner while someone was tortured right in front of him but a stinky diaper bothered him. Men.

Nevio let out an indignant howl when I tried for another spoonful of puree. He jerked in his seat.

Dad's eyes held disapproval. Seven months, and he still couldn't bear Nevio's sight. At least he'd held Greta a few times, but I didn't think he could ever look past their DNA.

The front door banged open, and Samuel rushed into the dining room, looking ecstatic and a bit unhinged. Dad rose slowly and Samuel smiled. I shivered because there was something dark and awfully eager in my twin's expression. "We got him," he said. "We got the bastard."

"Where is he?" Dad asked, knowing exactly whom Samuel was referring to.

I set down the spoon. Mom and I exchanged a look.

"Danilo and I took him to our safety house as discussed." Danilo? A horrid suspicion overcame me.

Mom began cleaning Greta.

Dad's eyes moved to me, and finally Samuel turned to me as well. I approached them. "Who did you catch?"

Samuel touched my shoulders lightly, his eyes bright, but in their depths something was lurking that scared me. "We got our hands on Adamo Falcone. He was taking part in a street race close to our borders and we caught him."

My insides turned to stone. "Why did you catch him?" I had a feeling I knew exactly why.

"To torture the little pisser and send Remo a video of it like he sent us a video of you. And maybe we will send him each part of his brother that we'll cut off, wrapped in a white ribbon."

"Sam, Adamo is only fifteen. He is a boy. It's not right."

Samuel's face hardened. "He is a member of the Camorra, the fucking tattoo and all. And Remo Falcone didn't give a fuck about right and wrong when he kidnapped an innocent woman on her wedding day and tortured and raped her."

The color drained from my face. "It wasn't like that," I whispered.

I glanced over my shoulder at my children, but Mom was already picking up Greta. I took Nevio out of the seat and handed him to her as well. She left quickly. I turned back to Samuel, shaking because he'd said a name I hadn't heard in a while. I still felt incredibly guilty because my family didn't understand that Remo hadn't forced me, didn't understand that he had only taken what I had given.

Dad stepped up beside Samuel. He still had a hard time meeting my gaze when this topic was addressed, too ashamed for not having been able to protect me. "Your brother is right. The Falcones get what they deserve. We will destroy their crazy family like they destroyed ours."

I swallowed. That's what he thought? That our family was destroyed? I saw it every time he looked at my children and his expression flashed with guilt and disgust.

"Remo won't stand back and let you torture his brother. He won't care about the danger. He will walk into our city and tear everything down that's in his way."

Samuel dropped his hand, face twisting with self-hatred. "Like we should have marched into Vegas and saved you."

Dad ran a hand through his hair. "You know we couldn't. Remo would have killed Fina the second we got close. We were lucky he didn't do so when you went there on your own. We couldn't risk it after that."

Remo would have never killed me, but they didn't know that, couldn't possibly understand, and how could I ever explain to them when I didn't understand it myself?

"Instead we sat back and waited for him to make demands while he was busy forcing himself on her and getting her pregnant."

"I'm here! Stop talking about me like I'm not here."

"Sorry, dove," Dad said with a sigh. My heart fluttered. He seldom called me 'dove' anymore, not because he loved me less but because he felt responsible for my broken wings.

"I'm not blaming either of you," I said firmly, looking first at my father then at Samuel. "But I know Remo and he will do anything to save his brother. Anything."

"We will see. We're going to do a live recording for the fucker today. He can watch his brother getting tortured live on the Darknet." Samuel grinned.

I took a step back. "You're joking."

"No," Samuel said. "I only came to pick up Dad. Danilo is already preparing everything, and Dante is supposed to arrive any moment as well."

"You planned this?"

"Not Adamo, no," Samuel said. "We wanted to attack the race. It was pure luck that the little bastard enjoys racing cars."

Dad nodded. "We should leave now. Let's go."

I gripped Samuel's arm. "Let me go with you."

He exchanged a look with Dad who said, "No, dove. That's nothing you should see."

"Why not? I've been a captive of the Camorra for months. Do you really think torture or blood still bother me? Do you think anything can bring me to my knees anymore? I'm not the innocent girl of the past. I have a right to be there. I was the one they kidnapped. You owe it to me to let me go with you."

They both stared at me like I'd punched them, and I felt a flicker of guilt, but playing the guilt card was my only chance to convince them, and I needed to see Adamo.

Dad closed his eyes briefly then gave a small nod. "Come on."

He went ahead. Samuel wrapped his arm around my shoulder and squeezed. "We will make them pay for what they did to you. Remo will regret the day he laid a finger on you."

I averted my eyes and followed Samuel out of our house, a place that felt less like home every day. Every day that Nevio looked more like his father.

The house they took me to was a shabby three-story building close to the tracks, located in the industrial part of Minneapolis. When we stepped inside, my eyes registered Danilo first. He had his arms crossed and was staring at a screen on a table against one wall. Beside him stood my uncle Dante, as usual dressed in a suit, but his jacket was already slung over a chair that sat in front of the screen, and he had rolled up his sleeves.

My stomach turned. I'd never seen him with rolled up sleeves, and I knew why. I had never been around when he'd tortured someone. There was another man, one of Dad's soldiers, who was working at a laptop, probably establishing the Darknet connection. They turned when we entered, and all eyes zeroed in on me. I wasn't supposed to be here.

Dante frowned and came toward us. Danilo stayed where he was, but he, too, watched me. I wasn't his fiancé anymore. I was nothing to him. My sister was promised to him, and now she was as precious as I had been. And yet he would be part in the Outfit's revenge because Remo had insulted Danilo in the worst way possible: he had taken me from him.

Dante stopped before us, his cool eyes resting on me. "Serafina, this is Outfit business. You shouldn't be here."

"It is my business, Uncle. The Falcones held me captive." I met his gaze head-on. After months in Remo's company, I didn't feel the urge to lower my gaze despite my uncle's own scary vibe, especially today. There was something predator-like about him, about them all. Eager to tear into their victim, to hear its screams and taste its blood.

He inclined his head. "It will be brutal and bloody. You are free to watch on the screen."

He turned and walked back to Danilo, followed by Dad. Samuel squeezed my shoulder. "If it's too much, go sit there." He pointed at a sofa behind the table with the screen. "You shouldn't leave the building. I don't want you outside without me or Dad."

I nodded. Samuel released me and joined the other men. Slowly, I moved closer and when I reached the table, I caught sight of the screen. My breath caught in my throat. It showed Adamo in an empty room, bound to a chair, his head hanging down.

"Ready?" Dante asked. Danilo, Dad, and Samuel nodded. Dante turned to the man at the screen. "Are we live?"

"All set. The camera in the torture room is sending."

"Good," Dante said coldly. With a last glance at me, the men disappeared through a door. A few minutes later they appeared on the screen, entering the room. I sank down on the chair beside my father's soldier, who gave me a quick curious glance. I could imagine what he thought, what they all thought. Since I had been kidnapped, I was only known as the woman Remo Falcone sullied. The broken one.

Samuel held something under Adamo's nose so he jerked upright, eyes flying up in shock. He had changed since I'd last seen him. His face had become harder, older, and he had grown and become more muscular. He wasn't wearing a shirt, and a few scars littered his chest but not nearly as many as Remo had.

The distant resemblance to Remo sent a stab through my heart.

Adamo's gaze wandered over my dad, Samuel, Danilo, and Dante, and for a second fear flashed across his face. Then he controlled his features.

Dante stepped forward, and the look on his face sent a chill down my spine. "Adamo Falcone. Welcome to Outfit territory."

Adamo smiled bitterly. "I would have won the race if you hadn't shot out my tires."

My eyes grew wide. Provoking my family in a situation like that was madness.

Dante's expression became harder. Samuel had already taken his knife out, and Danilo looked ready to plunge his dagger into Adamo as well. Only Dad remained back. He was a restrained man but his stance was off.

"You share the same arrogant disposition as your brother Remo, I see," Dante said pleasantly. "It's only fair that he gets to watch you pay for his sins."

Adamo shook his head. "No matter what you do, Remo won't care. Remo is crueler than all of you combined."

Dante tilted his head. "We will see." He took a knife from a table to the side and moved back toward Adamo, who tensed and leaned back. Dante reached down and cut Adamo's right arm loose.

Confusion drew my brows together. Dante grabbed Adamo's arm and turned it over, displaying the Camorra tattoo. "How long have you been a Made Man?"

"One year and four months," Adamo muttered, glaring up at my uncle.

"You will be judged as a Made Man, not a boy, Adamo Falcone."

Adamo grimaced. "I don't give a shit about all this. Do what you have to do. It won't change a thing."

Dante stepped back and gestured at the other men. "Who wants to go first? You are the ones who are closer to Serafina."

Adamo winced and looked at Samuel, who took a step forward. "I want to go first."

Tears stung in my eyes. Please don't, Sam.

Samuel moved toward Adamo and punched him hard. Adamo's head fell back, blood spraying out of his nose as it broke. I rose slowly from my chair, ignoring the stare from the man beside me. Samuel brought his knife down on Adamo's stomach and left a long cut. Adamo cried and lashed out with his free hand, but Samuel grabbed it and twisted the hand back, breaking it. I took a step back, my hand covering my mouth. I had never seen Samuel like this. I knew what he was, what they all were. This wasn't right. I had to stop them somehow.

"See, Remo, your brother will bleed in your stead. We'll tear him apart piece by piece for what you did to my sister. He will suffer for you," Samuel snarled. In that moment, little of my twin was left. A Made Man, a monster. Just because I never saw his monstrous side didn't mean Samuel was less of a monster than any other of the men in our world.

Dad pushed away from the wall, gripped Adamo's free arm, and jerked it back with a sickening crunch. He had a look on his face I had never seen. Adamo's screams blared through the speakers, and I began running.

Adamo didn't deserve this. And with their actions, they would make everything worse because Remo would seek retribution. He would attack viciously, would maim and kill, would leave nothing in his wake, and whatever the outcome, I would lose someone I cared about. Either my family members or the father of my children.

I followed the screams to the last door and burst through it then froze as the smell of burning flesh filled my nose. Adamo was screaming as Danilo was holding a lighter to his forearm, burning away the Camorra tattoo.

"Enough!" I cried. I stormed forward and pushed him aside before either of them could grab me. Danilo's eyes flashed with fury, and all the men stared at me. "Enough!" I screamed. "Enough!"

Adamo groaned and I turned to him, kneeling before him. Only a small part of his tattoo had been burned away, and the skin was blistered and red. I touched his shoulder and he flinched. "Adamo," I whispered.

He raised his head a few inches, teary eyes meeting mine. A weak smile pulled at his lips. "Serafina." How he could still sound friendly after what had been done to him was a mystery to me.

A shadow fell over me and I looked up. Samuel. "Fina, you should leave. He gets what he deserves."

"He is a boy," I said. "And he always treated me with kindness."

"He is a Falcone," Danilo said, stepping forward with the lighter still in his hand. His eyes were hard and merciless. "You were punished for something Outfit soldiers did. Adamo will pay for something his brother did."

"I suffered for your sins," I spat at them. "And he suffers for Remo's. I'm sick of it. This ends here. Adamo won't suffer any more pain under your hands."

"That isn't your call to make," Dante said firmly.

I looked back at Adamo, who looked resigned and had begun shaking. A phone rang and Dante picked it up. "Remo."

I jerked, my eyes widening.

REMO

Kiara was asleep with her head in Nino's lap. It was early afternoon, so I didn't understand how she could be tired. Maybe Nino kept her awake all night. I frowned then drew my gaze back to the screen where the race was playing out.

The number of participants was staggering. They had to start from different spots, all the same distance from Kansas City, to divert the attention of the police. A few of them would be arrested like usual, but that was part of the game. Eventually the different routes would merge to one for the last 100 miles before the end.

Car racing brought in good money, but I didn't really care for it. I preferred cage fighting.

Savio ate another bite of the cake Kiara had baked. "Do you think Adamo has a crush on that whore?"

"C.J.," Nino said.

"Whatever. He's been in the Sugar Trap an awful lot. They're definitely fucking. And come on, he spent the night with her again. What is he doing with her? Cuddling? He can't fuck her for hours. I'm surprised he gets one up at all. If he had to pay for her, he'd be broke by now."

I shrugged. I didn't care if Adamo fucked a whore or not. I'd never seen him talk to any of the other whores, though. It worried me, not to mention that it wasn't the first night he'd spent with the whore at the Sugar Trap. Fucking her was okay, but spending so much time with her could definitely prove to be a problem.

"Trust Adamo to fall in love with a whore and be monogamous when she's got about a dozen dicks up her pussy every day," Savio said.

Nino made an impatient sound, obviously keen on watching the race in peace. One of the participants was currently being chased by three police cars. Bets if the fucker managed to escape or not were probably burying us already.

"You don't know what's going on. Maybe he only enjoys her skills."

Savio scoffed. "She's not bad but there are better whores out there."

"It's not like he has many to compare her to," I said, growing tired of the discussion.

"One of these days he's going to bring her over here and keep her," Savio said.

The perspective switched to another drone camera, and my brows drew together. It briefly showed a few burning cars, some of them black limousines. The others were race cars. Then it changed back to the police chase.

"What the fuck was that?"

The front door swung open with a bang, steps thundered toward us. Nino put an arm over Kiara and pulled his gun. I rose with my own gun raised. Fabiano stormed into the living room, panting. "The Outfit attacked our territory!"

I froze. Savio jerked to his feet.

"What?" I growled. If Dante had set a single foot on Vegas ground, I'd walk into Chicago tomorrow. Then another thought struck me. "The race."

Fabiano nodded. "The organizer from the Kansas race called a few minutes ago. There was an attack on the race. I think he called me because he thought it would stop you from killing him."

Tough luck. I'd deal with him once I was done with the Outfit. "How long ago did they attack?"

"About an hour ago. There's chaos over there. But the race is going on with the remaining cars."

"Why didn't they alert us sooner?"

"They didn't know what was going on at first. When they realized it was the Outfit, they tried to divert the other race cars first so they could keep the race going."

Kiara stirred. "What's wrong?"

I pulled my knife, shaking, furious that Dante had attacked again. Nino stood, pulling Kiara to her feet. "Go to our bedroom."

She looked at me, eyes widening, then nodded quickly and hurried away.

My phone rang. I picked it up and brought it to my ear. "Remo," said a man. The voice was distantly familiar, but I couldn't place it. The background noise suggested he was in a helicopter or small airplane. "This is Danilo Mancini. I'm calling to tell you we have your brother and we're going to enjoy his screams like you enjoyed Serafina's. Tell Nino to set up a Darknet connection for later so you can watch as we tear him apart. I will enjoy slicing him into tiny pieces." He hung up.

It took my brain a few moments to process the information. "Call the Sugar Trap and ask if Adamo's there," I ordered.

Fabiano frowned but did as he was told. "Is Adamo there?" he asked without a greeting. "Then ask her."

"Remo, what's going on?" Nino asked carefully.

My phone beeped with an incoming message with detailed instructions for the connection.

I held it out to Nino, who took it from me, frowning. His mouth tightened when he read what the message said.

"He's not there. Apparently he left last night. C.J. said he asked her to pretend she was with him because he wanted to join the race."

I nodded, trying to ignore the way my chest kept constricting.

Savio didn't say anything, only stared at me. Fabiano had fixed himself a drink and downed it in one gulp.

Eventually Nino looked up from the phone. "We won't be quick enough to save him."

"There won't be anything left of him to save when they're done with him," I got out, fury and a weaker emotion burning through my veins. Why couldn't the kid have listened for once? Fuck it.

"Call Grigory. Tell him he can have Kansas if he attacks the Outfit."

Nino nodded, and pressed the phone back to his ear as he walked back and forth in the room.

Savio ran a hand through his hair. "Fuck. We have to do something."

From the words I caught, Grigory had no intention of getting involved. I flung my knife at the heavy bag. "Fuck!" I snarled before Nino had uttered a single word.

"He says this isn't his fight."

"Bastard," Fabiano muttered.

"I will soon make it his fucking fight. For this, I will declare war on him and the fucking Bratva in Outfit territory."

"Do you want me to set up the connection?" Nino asked quietly.

"Of course," I growled. "If Adamo has to suffer, we will watch. We will suffer with him. Fuck it all!"

Nino didn't move for a moment. Then he nodded slowly.

"We need to figure out where they are taking him," I told Fabiano. He knew the Outfit better than any of us.

"I assume honor dictates that they take him to Minneapolis because that's where her family lives. She wasn't married to Danilo yet or they would have taken Adamo to his city to dish out punishment there," he said.

It would take us at least three hours to reach Minneapolis and probably several more hours to figure out where they kept Adamo. The Darknet connection would begin in fifty minutes. I took my phone again and dialed Dante's number. He rejected the call.

"Fuck him," I rasped. "Call our pilot. The plane better be ready in twenty minutes or I'll kill him."

Nino made the call and we set out toward the airport. Fabiano stayed with Kiara, whom he was taking to a safe house with Leona. I'd alerted every fucking soldier in Las Vegas to be vigilant.

The plane was ready on time, and we started almost immediately. I tried to call Dante again, but he didn't pick up.

"It's his game this time," Nino murmured after a while.

Savio had his face buried in his hands.

"It is," I agreed. "And he'll win."

Nino raised his eyebrows.

"I'll allow him to put me checkmate."

"Remo," he began, but I smiled grimly and indicated the laptop. "It's time to turn this on."

I pressed the blade against my palm when Adamo appeared on the screen. He was slumped forward on a chair.

When they started cutting him, Adamo's scream filled the airplane, blaring from the speakers mercilessly, and fuck, they were the first screams in forever that got under my skin. The first since *her* screams. I cut into my palm, deep, drawing blood. Savio gripped the armrest of the seat, his arms shaking. Nino was behind me, one hand digging into my shoulder.

Danilo was next and took out a lighter. I jumped to my feet, shaking with rage ... so much rage, it threatened to rip me apart. Adamo's eyes widened. Fuck, he was a kid. He wasn't like us. This was supposed to be me. I was supposed to burn for them.

Danilo touched the flame to Adamo's skin, and his screams got louder. I reached for my phone again, knowing that Dante would reject my call like before and hating this fucking sense of helplessness. I was supposed to burn for them, for him, and I would.

"Enough!" a female voice rang out, and my eyes snapped back to the screen as Serafina threw herself in front of my brother, protecting him. I froze, unable to trust my eyes, to believe that the woman who haunted my nights was really in front of me.

Nino and Savio stared at me, as if they waited for me to lose my shit completely.

"Fuck," Savio murmured, shaking his head.

She hadn't returned to me like I'd thought she would.

She hated me more than I'd expected, and yet she protected Adamo. Because he wasn't the one she wanted to see suffer. She wanted to see me bleed. She would get her wish.

"Remo?" Nino said in a cautious voice.

I raised the phone to my ear, waiting for the inevitable, but this time it didn't come. He finally answered my call. "Dante, I'll give you what you really want. Tomorrow morning I'll be in Minneapolis and exchange myself for Adamo." He didn't need to know we were already on our way, but maybe he did.

"Remo," he said coolly. His eyes focused on the camera for a moment before the screen turned black and Serafina and my brother disappeared from view.

"It's me you want to see burn, not my brother, and you will get your chance."

"Tomorrow morning, at eight. If you're late, your brother won't be recognizable as your brother anymore, understood?"

"Understood."

"I'll have someone send you the details, Remo. I'm looking forward to meeting you again," he said coldly.

I hung up.

"They will kill you, Remo," Savio said.

"They will cut me, skin me, burn me, cut off my dick, and then maybe they'll kill me," I said quietly. And all I could wonder was if Serafina would watch them do it.

CHAPTER 26

SERAFINA

They allowed me to stay with Adamo, and I crouched at his feet, feeling sick to my stomach from what I'd witnessed and even worse thinking about what was to come.

"Remo will exchange himself for you," I whispered. "Tomorrow, you will be back in Vegas, and Nino will treat your wounds."

Adamo tilted his head, dark eyes bleak. "Remo is Capo. He won't die because I've been stupid enough to get myself captured. I've been a disappointment to him since I was born. He will use this chance and kill Dante instead of handing himself over."

I lifted soaked fabric from his burn, and he groaned deeply. His wrist and nose were broken and his shoulder dislocated. He must have been in horrible pain, and there was nothing I could do to help him. Playing the guilt card forced my family give me this small freedom. It didn't convince them to call a doctor though. They would have probably kept torturing Adamo if I hadn't refused to move away from his side.

"You're wrong, Adamo. Remo will protect you. He doesn't fear death or pain. He will take your place because you are his brother and he cares for you. He'd do anything for you."

Adamo let out a choked laugh. "Why do you speak about him as if you don't hate him? He kidnapped you. He ruined your life."

I looked away. I wouldn't tell him about Nevio and Greta and certainly not about my twisted feelings for his brother either.

Adamo leaned forward, wincing, and brought our faces closer together, a risk because we were undoubtedly being watched, and my family was still eager to spill Falcone blood. His or Remo's, it didn't matter, as long as it was a Falcone. I met Adamo's gaze, and realization settled on his face.

"Fuck," he whispered hoarsely. He leaned even closer, despite the rope binding his unharmed arm to the chair. "You're giving me the same look Remo has whenever someone mentions you."

My chest constricted. "I need to go now." I stood and took a step back. Adamo Falcone. Falcone, the name my children were supposed to carry.

"Goodbye," I whispered, but deep down I wondered if this was really the last time I would see him.

I turned quickly and left the room. Samuel waited right in front of the door. He regarded me, incomprehension in his features. "Why do you take care of a fucking Falcone bastard?"

"He never hurt me. He's a boy."

Samuel shook his head. "He is a Made Man, Fina. You should let us handle him and Remo. We are capable of doing what needs to be done."

We walked into the main hall where Dad, Danilo, and Dante were talking in hushed tones. They turned to us the moment we entered.

I faced Samuel. "And what is that?"

"Bring Remo to his knees. Make him beg for mercy. Beg for death. I will cut his dick off myself. Danilo will take care of his balls, and then we will keep them in a nice bag with ice so he can see them while we tear him apart. Then we'll shove them down his throat."

Danilo smiled grimly, and even Dad looked like he could imagine nothing better than committing the most brutal murder he could think of.

I swallowed. "He is the father of my children."

Samuel grabbed my shoulders hard, desperately. "He broke you, Fina," he said softly. None of them had ever asked if I considered myself broken. They had declared me as such, and all four of them made me feel like I was.

"He is a monster," Samuel added.

"He is not the only one," I whispered, my eyes wandering over the gathered men.

Samuel dropped his hands, face twisting as if I'd stabbed him. "I'm doing this for you. To avenge you."

"Did any of you ever ask what I wanted? If I wanted more blood spilled? If I wanted to be avenged?" I shouted.

Dante came forward, expression tight. "Don't you want to see Remo Falcone on his knees? Don't you want to see him broken?"

I did, but not in the same way they wanted. "I want nothing more," I said quietly, because they could never, would never understand.

Samuel wrapped an arm around me and kissed my temple. "Fina, let's go home."

"Yes, let's go home," I said quietly. I peered up at Samuel, realizing that for the first time in my life, we didn't mean the same place.

REMO

Nino, Savio, and I linked arms, pressing over the tattoo of the other. "You will be a better Capo than me, Nino. You won't kill people who might be useful to us. Your logic will make the Camorra even stronger."

Nino didn't say anything, only stared at me.

Savio shook his head. "Remo, let's attack them. I'd rather die fighting than have you in their fucking hands."

I smiled darkly. "You will have to die another day. I will pay for my sins."

Nino made a low sound. "She didn't return, Remo. She stayed in Minneapolis. They won't let you anywhere near her. You will die for nothing."

"No, I will die so she gets what she wants."

Nino pulled away. "Damn it. Be reasonable for once."

"I made my decision and you will accept it."

Cars pulled up, and I moved away from my brothers who took shelter inside the car. Nino and Savio raised their guns through the open windows. I wasn't armed as I walked toward the parked cars, my arms raised over my head. I didn't think Dante would attack Nino or Savio. Once he'd dismembered me in the cruelest way possible, he'd send my brothers the recording and probably to Luca as well. He'd try to break my family like I had broken his, killing us all just wouldn't do. Not yet.

Dante got out, followed by Samuel, Pietro, and Danilo, and more men I didn't know and didn't give a fuck about. Samuel walked around to the back of the car and pulled Adamo out.

Adamo could hardly stand as Samuel dragged him behind himself toward me. Rage boiled under my skin. Samuel shoved Adamo to the ground in front of my feet, and Adamo looked up at me with his blood covered face, cradling his broken and burned arm against his chest.

"Don't," he whispered. "Don't do this. Don't let them kill you because of me. I'm a fucking failure."

I moved toward him and touched his head briefly. "You are the one from all of us who deserves death the least, Adamo." I removed my hand from his head, but before I could move on, he grasped my forearm, his fingers curling over my Camorra tattoo. "It's us against the world," he croaked.

"Us against the world," I said.

Samuel gripped my arm, and I shoved down the instinct to smash his face. I saw his fist coming toward my face and smiled. The first punch only blurred my vision. His kick to my balls brought me to my knees. And his gun to the back of my head finally pulled me into blackness.

SERAFINA

Samuel and Danilo dragged Remo into the safe house, his arms and legs bound, his nose busted and dripping blood, his hair sticking to the back of his head with more blood. I slowly rose from the sofa where I had been waiting for almost one hour with two bodyguards.

Dad moved toward me, trying to shield Remo from my view—or me from his. I wasn't sure and didn't care. "Dove, you shouldn't be here." His eyes narrowed on my bodyguards, harshly, cruelly. I touched his arm.

"I will stay," I said firmly, my voice resolute.

Dante was the last to enter.

The men exchanged a look. Their word was law, not mine, but their guilt gave me power over them, more power than they'd ever held over me. I hated using it against them, but they would never allow me to possess power for any other reason.

I walked past my father, toward Danilo and Samuel holding Remo between them. His head hung down, body was slack. I tried to hide the tremor that had taken hold of me the moment I'd spotted him.

Remo Falcone.

Danilo's expression twisted like it always did when he saw me. With guilt and a flicker of humiliation because something had been taken from him, because Remo had taken it from him. He was a strong, powerful man, and having lost me haunted him like it haunted every man in the room. I was their failure. Their pride a tattered sullied rag. Every time they had to peer into my eyes, and worse the eyes of my children, they were reminded.

They'd never let me be anything but the dove with broken wings. They couldn't. But I wanted to fly.

"Have you come to watch the bastard die, Fina?" Samuel asked, his face cruel, eager, brutal as his blue eyes settled on Remo, who still hadn't moved, but I noticed the almost imperceptible shift in his shoulders, his muscles twitching. He was waking up.

My heart beat faster, my palms becoming sweaty.

"I know you deserve your revenge, dove, but this is going to be more than you can stomach, trust me," Dad said, coming up behind me and putting a hand on my shoulder. His voice was soft, compelling, but his face held terrifying eagerness and cruelty as he regarded the father of my children.

"What are your plans for him?" I asked my uncle, because he was the man who would have the last word on the matter.

His cool blue eyes weren't as controlled as usual. He, too, wanted to tear into Remo. They had waited a long time for this moment. "We will prolong his torture as long as possible without risking an attack from the Camorra."

"He won't die today?"

"Oh, he won't die today," Samuel muttered. "But he might wish for it."

I gave a nod. It was what I had expected. Remo wouldn't experience any mercy at the hands of the Outfit, not that he'd ever ask for it.

"He'll *beg* for death," Dad said harshly.

"I don't beg for anything, Pietro."

I shivered at the familiar timbre, at the underlying threat, the undercurrent of power. How did he do it?

Remo lifted his head, and my brother and Danilo tightened their hold, but they blended into the background when Remo's eyes finally met mine. Fourteen months.

The force of his gaze hit me like a tidal wave. In the time since he'd released me, I'd often wondered if I could ever forget him, if I could move on and live a new life, but now as I looked at him, I realized I had been foolish to consider that an option.

The corners of his mouth lifted in a twisted smile. "Angel."

My brother punched Remo's face, but he only laughed darkly as blood spattered on the ground.

"This is your chance to ask for forgiveness," Dad said.

Remo looked from each of them until his eyes finally settled on me. "Do you want me to beg for forgiveness?"

His eyes dragged me down fiercely, mercilessly, irrevocably as they'd always done. As they always would. "I won't give you my forgiveness," I said quietly.

Something flickered in Remo's eyes, but Samuel and Danilo wrenched him away from my view, down the corridor into their torture chamber.

Dad kissed my temple. "We will avenge you, make him pay for what he did."

He walked away, leaving me with Dante, who regarded me with calm scrutiny. He touched my shoulder lightly, and I met his gaze. "He will ask for forgiveness in the end," he promised.

I briefly touched his hand. "I don't want him to because it would be false."

Remo did everything with unbridled passion, with ferocious rage, without an ounce of regret.

He consumed, obliterated, ruined.

He took everything and left nothing in his wake. He was an unrepentant sinner. He was a destroyer, a murderer, a torturer.

A monster.

The father of my children.

The man who held my heart in his cruel, brutal hand.

"You will castrate him?" It was an unnecessary question. I knew they would, and it was only one of the many atrocities they'd planned. All I needed to know was when.

Dante gave a terse nod. "Tomorrow. Not today. It would speed up his death too much. Danilo and Samuel will do it. I'm not sure you should watch any of this, but maybe you need to. Today will be easier to stomach than tomorrow, so stay if it's what you want."

"Thanks," I whispered. Slowly I made my way toward the screen on the table and turned it on.

My brother and Danilo were kicking Remo in the stomach, in the side, and Remo made no move to defend himself. When they finally let up, because Dante had entered, Remo rolled onto his back and looked directly into the camera, knowing I was watching.

He didn't look away when my father took out his knife and cut his chest. Not when it was Samuel's turn. Not when it was Danilo's turn. Not when it was Dante's turn.

I'd spent so many hours, day and night, wondering how it would feel to see Remo broken, to see him on his knees.

This wasn't how I imagined things to be, my heart clenching in my chest so tightly I could hardly breathe, the tears pressing against my eyelids so fiercely I had to bite the inside of my cheek to hold them back. And even through the torture, Remo didn't look broken because he couldn't be broken, not with violence and pain. Maybe not at all.

I turned away from the screen and walked away. My bodyguards followed close behind, their steps slow and measured. Shadows meant to protect and save me. But I was beyond saving. My family tried to mend me, but I didn't need it because I wasn't broken.

Slipping behind the steering wheel of the Mercedes limousine, I revved the engine the second my bodyguards were inside. My foot pressed down on the gas. They slanted looks my way but didn't comment. They were meant to protect not judge.

I was allowed this freedom because my family's guilt had paid for it. They couldn't bear keeping the dove with broken wings in a gilded cage.

The second I had the car parked in front of my family's home, I killed the engine and got out, not waiting for them. I stepped inside and hurried upstairs, didn't stop until I entered the nursery. Both Nevio and Greta were asleep in their shared crib, looking peaceful and painstakingly beautiful.

I stroked their heads, the thick black hair like their father's. When my fingers brushed Nevio's temple, his eyes peeled open with those dark brown, almost black eyes. I leaned down and pressed a kiss to his forehead then to Greta's, breathed in their scent, then sank down in a chair and watched them sleep.

I wasn't sure how long I stayed like that when the door opened. Familiar steps sounded behind me, steps that had accompanied me almost all my life. A warm hand came down on my shoulder, and I covered it with mine.

Samuel pressed a kiss to the crown of my head then rested his forehead against it for a couple of moments. So gentle and caring, so very different from the man I'd seen torturing Remo. He straightened and I tilted my head back, peering up at him. His gaze rested on Greta and Nevio, but for him there was nothing beautiful about them. As always, his eyes shone with guilt and aversion when he regarded them before he noticed my scrutiny and lowered his gaze to me.

Warmth filled his expression. I wished he could spare some of it for the children I loved more than life itself. Samuel was my blood. He would always be. He was part of me as I was part of him, and I didn't resent him for his feelings toward my children. I knew he hated their father, not them, but more than that he hated himself.

I stood, grabbed his neck, and pulled him down until his forehead rested against mine. "Please, Sam, stop blaming yourself. Please, I beg you. I'm not broken. You have no reason to feel guilty."

He returned my gaze but I realized his guilt ran too deep. Maybe tomorrow he'd finally be free. Maybe he could let go of his guilt when he had to let go of me. "I love you," I said, knowing it was the last time.

Samuel wrapped his arms around me. "And I love you, Fina."

CHAPTER 27

SERAFINA

Dad and Dante didn't come home that evening. They would spend the night in the safe house. Safe house. What a name for a house to torture enemies.

After Samuel had made sure I was okay, he drove back there as well. Maybe they were worried Remo might manage to escape or maybe they wanted to keep torturing him throughout the night. Probably the latter.

I grabbed a bag and packed a few things for Greta and Nevio. Then I walked down into the basement where we kept our weapons as well as other necessities in case of an attack. I perused the display of guns and knives. I strapped a gun holster to my chest over my T-shirt. It allowed me to strap a gun and a knife to my sides as well as another gun to my back. Just to be on the safe side, I added a knife holster to my calf. I had chosen loose linen pants for the occasion just for that purpose. After that I rummaged through the medical supplies. Samuel had explained everything to me so I was prepared if something happened, not so I could use it against them. I grabbed a syringe with adrenaline and one with a sedative. After I'd put on my thick cardigan, I stuffed the syringes into its pockets and returned upstairs.

It was quiet in the house. Sofia was probably reading in her room before bed, and Mom was most likely doing the same.

The bodyguards were in their quarters in the back of the house, and two were guarding the fence surrounding the garden. I put on comfortable sneakers then headed for the nursery.

I considered going to my mother, saying goodbye, apologizing for what I was about to do, but words would never be enough to explain my betrayal. Words were too insignificant. They would never understand. I'd try to call her later, once we were safe.

Lifting the bag over one shoulder, I grabbed Nevio and Greta before I made my way out of the nursery, moving quietly.

I froze when I spotted Sofia standing in her doorway in her pink nightgown, brown hair disheveled. Her eyes took in everything and a small frown drew her brows together. "Where are you going?"

I considered what to tell her, how to explain to a twelve-year-old what I had done and was about to do. "I'm leaving. I have to."

Sofia's eyes widened, and she padded toward me with bare feet. "Because of Greta and Nevio?"

I nodded. She was young but she wasn't as oblivious as we all wanted to believe. She stopped right in front of me. "You're leaving us."

I swallowed hard. "I have to, ladybug. For my babies. I want them to be safe and happy. I need to protect them from the whispers."

Sofia regarded my twins. She leaned forward and kissed each of them on the cheek, her eyes filling with tears as she peered up at me. My heart clenched tightly. "I know what people say about them, and I hate it. But I don't want you to go ..." Her voice broke.

"I know." I tried to hold back my emotions. "Give me a hug."

She wrapped her arms around me and the twins, and we remained like that for a moment. "Don't tell anyone, please."

She pulled back with a knowing look. "You're going to return to their father?"

I nodded, a half-truth, but Sofia didn't need to know that our family and her future husband were currently torturing the man she was referring to.

"Do you love him?"

"I don't know," I admitted. Sofia looked confused for a moment, but then she nodded, biting her lip, more tears gathering in her eyes. "Dad won't allow me to see you anymore, will he?"

I swallowed. "I hope one day he'll understand."

"I'll miss you."

"I'll miss you too. I'll try to contact you. Remember I love you."

She nodded, tears trailing down her cheeks. I quickly turned before I lost it. I could feel Sofia's eyes on me as I walked downstairs. The light from upstairs illuminated my path as I headed into the garage. I put Nevio and Greta into their car seats then slipped behind the steering wheel. The guns were digging uncomfortably into my back and side. The garage door slid up, and I pulled out and steered the car down the long driveway. I pressed the button for the gate and it opened.

A guard stepped in front of the gate, and I had to pull to a stop or run him over.

The windows were tinted, so he couldn't see the kids on the backseat. I let down the window a gap.

"Miss Mione, nobody informed us you'd be leaving."

"I'm informing you now," I said firmly.

He frowned. "I'll have to ask the boss."

I scowled. "Get out of my way. I'm driving over to the safe house to kill the man who raped and tortured me."

His eyes grew wide, and he lowered his gaze, the shame of all Outfit soldiers reflecting clearly on his face. "I'll have to make a quick call."

He lifted his phone to his ear, and I considered hitting the gas. He lowered the phone, touched the screen again then lifted it once more. "Samuel, I can't reach your father. Your sister is at the gate, trying to leave."

He held the phone out to me. I took it with a glare.

"Fina, what's going on?"

"Tell him to let me leave."

"Fina."

"I'm coming over. I need to ... I need to see what you're doing. You owe it to me, Sam."

Guilt sliced through me, but I shoved it back.

"You should take a bodyguard with you."

"Sam," I whispered harshly. "Let me leave. Do you want me to beg? I've done enough of that, trust me." A lie, one I'd never wanted to use on Samuel.

He sighed. "Okay. But right now we're not doing anything. Dad, Danilo, and Dante are catching some shut-eye. It's been a long day."

"I'll be there in fifteen minutes. Let them sleep for now. They don't need to know I'm coming over yet. You know how Dad can be."

I handed the phone back to the guard and after an order from my brother, he finally let me through.

Samuel was waiting for me outside the safe house when I pulled up. I programmed the heating so it would keep the car warm for my babies before I exited. Samuel regarded me with a deep frown. He was wearing a different shirt than last time I saw him, and as I got closer, I noticed the red under his fingernails. He wrapped an arm around my shoulders, and for a moment I tensed because I worried he could feel the holster, but his arm was too high up and my cardigan too thick. He led me inside. My eyes searched the main area.

"They're in the sleep area upstairs. Do you want me to wake them?"

"No," I said quickly. My eyes were drawn to the screen. It showed Remo lying on the floor, not moving. I tried to gauge the angle. Samuel followed my gaze. "We'll continue in about an hour."

I raised my eyes to his. Dark shadows spread under his eyes. "You look like you should get some sleep."

"Someone's got to keep watch."

"He doesn't look like he can do anything."

Samuel's lips curled. "He's a tough fucker." His expression softened. "But we'll get him to beg. At some point, even he will break."

I doubted it but we'd never find out. "Do you have something to drink for me?"

Samuel nodded and walked over to the table in the corner. I took out the syringe before I followed him. "Water okay?" he asked as I stopped close beside him.

I touched his chest. "I'm sorry, Sam." His brows snapped together in confusion, and I shoved the needle into his thigh.

Sam jerked. "Fina? What?" But he was already staggering, his eyelids drooping. I clung to him, trying to stop him from falling and injuring himself,

325

but he was too heavy. He sank to the ground. His eyes began to lose focus. I bent over him and kissed his forehead. "I hope you'll forgive me one day."

I stepped into the torture room, my eyes landing on Remo. He was sprawled out on the floor, lying in his own blood, naked except for black briefs, his arms and legs tied to hooks in the ground with rope. Bruises and cuts littered almost every inch of him. On the table to the right, I could see torture tools. The knives covered in blood, but some of the others were still pristine and untouched, waiting for their purpose.

Remo's eyes peeled open in his blood-covered face, and they knocked the breath out of me again.

A dark smile twisted his mouth, but there was an emotion in his eyes that tightened my stomach. "Angel, have you come to watch your family cut off my dick? I hear that's scheduled for today."

I crept closer to him, my sneakers trudging through his blood covering the rough floor. My steps didn't falter. Blood did nothing to me. Not anymore.

Remo regarded me quietly. His eyes slid down my arm to the tip of the knife peeking out from my long cardigan sleeve. "Or have you come to do it yourself?"

I stopped right above Remo. Even though he was on his back, cut and bruised, covered in his own blood, he appeared powerful. Remo couldn't be broken because he didn't fear pain or death.

Was this love? Or madness?

I sank down to my knees beside him, kneeling on the sticky floor, my white linen pants soaking up the blood greedily. My pants soon stuck to my skin with Remo's blood. "No," I whispered, finally answering him.

Remo's eyes traced my face. He looked almost at peace. "To kill me?"

I tilted my head, regarding him. Remo was Nevio. Nevio was Remo. As if they had been carved from the same template. My children were the spitting image of their father. Even if I didn't have feelings for the man before me, I could never kill him because the faces of Greta and Nevio would remind me of him every day of my life.

"I always thought it was meant to be that way. Your hand ending my life."

I shook my head. "I won't kill you." I leaned over Remo, my fingers spreading through his blood on the ground, my hair dipping in it. So much blood.

"You didn't marry Danilo," Remo murmured.

"How could I?" I whispered, bending low until Remo and I were almost touching. "How could I marry him when I was pregnant with your children?"

Remo stiffened. I'd wondered how he would react if I ever told him about Greta and Nevio, but nothing came close to the look on his face. Complete and utter shock, and more than that ... wonder.

"When you gave me up, I carried your babies in me, Remo. You gave us up."

"I thought you'd return to me," he rasped.

"You pushed me away."

"I set you free."

"I wasn't free," I hissed. How could I ever be free when his name was etched into my heart?

"You were pregnant," he said quietly.

"I was pregnant, a living breathing reminder of the greatest failure of the Outfit, a living breathing reminder of something dark and shameful. A reminder that you took something from the Outfit, took something from me. That's what everyone thought. My family and everyone else in the Outfit. I knew giving birth to a child of yours would ruin any chance I had to find my way back into the Outfit, back into my family. I knew I'd seal my fate if I had your child. I'd be damned to live a life of pity stares and disgusted expressions."

Something flickered in Remo's eyes. Dread, maybe even fear. "You got rid of the babies." And his voice wavered ever so slightly.

A cruel, unbreakable man.

My nemesis, my captor, the man who took everything from me and without knowing it gave me the greatest gift of all.

I'd always wondered what it would take to break Remo, and I realized I held the power to do it, to crush the cruelest, strongest man I knew in my hand, held it on the tip of my tongue. One word would shatter him. The knowledge filled me with unparalleled joy, not because I could break the man before me. *No,* because our children even without knowing them meant so much to him that their death would destroy him.

"Oh, Angel, have they sent you to deliver the ultimate blow? Tell Dante he wins."

I shook my head. "No," I said quietly, then fiercer, "No. I didn't get rid of the babies even though everyone wanted me to do it."

Remo held my gaze.

"How could I get rid of the most beautiful creation I can imagine? Greta and Nevio are pure perfection, Remo."

He exhaled, and the look in his eyes ... God, that look. This cruel man had stolen my heart, and I had let him.

"They look like you. Nevio is you. Everyone who sees him knows he's yours."

Remo smiled the darkest, saddest smile I have ever seen. "Have you come to tell me before my death that I'll never see them? Angel, I must say you are crueler than I could ever be."

I linked my fingers with his bloody ones, the blade cupped between our palms. "Our children are perfection but here, in the Outfit, they represent shame and dishonor. People whisper behind their backs, call them Falcones as if it is something sinful, something dirty. Our children are beautiful." My voice became fiercer with every word. "They are meant to hold their heads high, not be ashamed for who they are. They aren't meant to bow, aren't meant to live in the shadows. They are meant to *rule*. They are Falcones. They belong in Las Vegas where their names carry power and respect. They are meant to rule at the side of the cruelest, bravest man I know. Their father."

Remo didn't say anything but his expression set me aflame with emotion.

"How badly injured are you?" I whispered in his ear.

"Badly," he admitted.

I nodded, my throat tightening. I reached for the syringe in my pocket and pulled it out. "Adrenaline."

Remo's mouth pulled wider. I injected him with the liquid and he shuddered. His pupils were dilated when he met my gaze again.

My lips brushed his lightly. "How strong are you, Remo Falcone?"

"Strong enough to take you and our children home where you all belong, Angel."

I smiled. I wedged the blade under the rope. "Swear not to kill my family. Not my brother, not my father, not my uncle. Swear it on our children, Remo."

"I swear it," he murmured. I cut through the rope when I heard the creak of the door. I dropped the knife in Remo's now free hand.

"Serafina, get the fuck away from the asshole!" Danilo growled, gripping me by the shoulders and pulling me to my feet. I whirled around on him, getting in his face. "Don't tell me what to do. I have a right to be here."

Danilo was breathing harshly, his chest heaving. I took a step back, closer to Remo again. Dante and my father stepped in. I shielded Remo mostly from their view but that wouldn't last long.

"You shouldn't be here, dove. This isn't something for a woman," Dad said gently.

He still believed in my innocence, but Dante and Danilo regarded me more cautiously. "Where's Samuel?" Dante asked.

I wrapped my arms around my body and slid my hands beneath my cardigan, my fingers curling around the gun strapped to the holster there.

"I'm sorry," I whispered and pulled the gun on them.

Dante put his hand on his gun at his waist but didn't pull it. My father and Danilo were completely frozen.

"Samuel's going to be okay. He's knocked out behind the sofa."

"Fina," Dad said in a soothing voice. "You've been through a lot. Put down the gun."

I took another step back, releasing the safety catch. "I'm sorry," I said again, biting back tears, thinking of Samuel, of what he would think once he woke up. In my peripheral vision, Remo cut through the last rope around his ankle.

Dante pulled his gun and so did Danilo, but I barred their view of Remo. They wouldn't shoot me, not even now that I was holding them at gunpoint. I was a woman, someone to protect. I was their responsibility and their failure. Remo staggered to his feet behind me, and Danilo aimed. I shot at him, nicking the outside of his upper arm. He gasped, his eyes flashing at me.

"Not a single move," I warned. Remo pressed up behind me, as usual not heeding any safety measures, towering a head over me. "We only want to leave. No one has to get hurt," I whispered.

Remo reached for my gun but I shook my head. "My back," I told him. His hand slid under my cardigan and pulled the gun from there.

"Dove," Dad croaked. "You don't owe this man anything. He raped you. I know emotions can get confused in a situation like this, but we have people who can help you."

I smiled sadly at him and then Samuel stumbled inside, holding on to the doorframe. I hadn't dared use a higher dose on him than was absolutely necessary; obviously it wasn't enough. He stared at me uncomprehendingly, his arm with his gun hanging limply at his side. My twin, my confidante. For most of my life I had been sure my love for Samuel, for my twin, could never be challenged, and I still loved him, loved him so much the look of betrayal on his face splintered me in half, but now there were my children and the man behind me.

Remo's gaze moved from me to him, and he touched my hip. I swallowed the rising emotion.

"Please let us leave, Uncle," I addressed Dante. "This war is because of me, and I can tell you I don't want it. I don't want to be avenged. Don't rob my children of their father. I'll go to Las Vegas with Remo where I belong, where my kids belong. Please, if you feel guilty for what happened to me, if you want to save me, then do this. Let me return to Vegas with Remo. This doesn't have to be an endless spiral of bloodshed. It can end today. For your children, for mine. Let us leave."

Dante's cold eyes were on Remo, not me. "Is she speaking in the name of the Camorra?"

Remo's grip on my hip tightened. "She does. You breached my territory, and I breached yours. We're even."

"We're not!" Samuel roared, stepping forward, swaying. Remo lifted his gun a couple of inches. "You kidnapped my sister and broke her. You twisted her into your fucking marionette. We won't be done until I'm standing over your disemboweled corpse so my sister is finally free of you."

"Sam," I choked. "Don't do this. I know you don't understand, but I need to return to Vegas with Remo, for myself, but more importantly for my children."

"I knew you should have gotten rid of them," Samuel rasped, his eyes glassy. Remo's hand on my hip jerked and I knew without the promise he'd given me, he would have killed my brother for his words.

Dad came up behind Samuel and put his hand on his shoulder. "Send them with him to Las Vegas. They are Falcones, but you aren't Fina. Be free of them and him. You can start a new life."

"Where my children go, I will go," I said. "Don't you think I've suffered enough for all of your sins? Don't turn me into another pawn in your chess game. Set me free."

Realization settled in Sam's eyes, and it broke my heart. I ached, ached for my family who would never understand. I could only hope they'd come to hate me one day so they didn't miss me anymore. Remo's grip on my hip loosened. Even the adrenaline wouldn't keep him on his feet for an endless amount of time. He was too injured for that.

"Let us leave. You failed me once, and now I'm lost to you. But please allow me to bring my children to a family that will love them. Allow me to bring my children home. You owe it to me."

Danilo made a disbelieving sound, his hand around his gun tightening.

I hated myself for playing the guilt card, but I knew it was our only chance. For Remo to get out of here alive, I had to hurt the family I loved.

Dante's cold eyes met mine. "If I allow you to leave today, you are a traitor. You won't be part of the Outfit. You will be the enemy. You won't see your family again. There won't be peace with the Camorra. This war has only begun."

Samuel heaved a deep breath, his eyes begging me to reconsider. Could I live without him?

"When will this war ever end, Uncle?" I asked quietly. He looked at Remo, and I knew what he would say. "Never," I whispered the answer.

Dante inclined his head. Dad looked at me as if this was the final goodbye, a daughter lost for good.

"Leave," Dante said coldly.

Danilo shook his head incredulously. "You can't be serious, Dante. You can't let them go."

Dante glanced at my ex-fiancé, looking tired.

"Set me free," I said softly.

"Leave."

Relief and wistfulness slammed into me hearing that word. "Thank you."

Dante shook his head. "Don't thank me. Not for that."

Remo nudged me lightly, and I walked closer to the door, keeping my body between him and the others. I walked backward to keep an eye on my family. They didn't attack. They didn't stop us. Dad and Samuel looked broken. I had landed the ultimate hit, had broken them. I wondered how Mom would react when she found out. She'd be crushed. My heart was heavy as I led Remo to the parked car. He sank down on the passenger seat, passing out immediately. I closed the door and got behind the steering wheel. Greta and Nevio were still fast asleep in their seats.

I hit the gas and sent the car flying down the long gravel road. I quickly connected to Bluetooth and called the Sugar Trap. It was the only number I'd found on the Internet.

It took a while before the guy I talked to agreed to call Nino and to give him my number. I was starting to go crazy.

Remo wouldn't survive if I had to drive all the way to Vegas with him, and I couldn't take him to a hospital in Outfit territory. What if my family got over their initial shock and decided to get rid of us after all? I needed to reach Camorra territory.

My pulse spiked when my phone finally rang. I picked up after the second ring.

"Is he dead?" Nino asked at once.

I glanced at Remo who was slumped against the passenger door, breathing shallowly.

"Not yet," I got out.

Nino was quiet for a moment. "Did you call to gloat? To let me hear my brother's last screams?"

That's what he thought?

"I'm in a car with him. We got out. We're on our way."

"You got him out?" Nino asked sharply. "Where are you? We're taking a helicopter and meeting you halfway. We're in Kansas City. I'll calculate the best spot now."

I told him where I was heading, and we agreed on a meeting place eighty miles from where I was.

"He's badly injured," I said quietly.

"Remo is too strong to die," Nino said.

Tears stung in my eyes. "I'm driving as quickly as I can."

"Serafina," Nino began. "He thought you'd come back. He wanted you to come back on your own free will."

I swallowed. This wasn't about Remo and me. This was about my children, and yet my chest ached with emotions as I regarded the man beside me. His dark hair sticking to his bloody forehead. "I need to drive," I said and hung up.

About one hour later I steered the car toward a deserted parking lot where a helicopter was already waiting. Nino and Savio stood beside it. I'd hoped Fabiano would be there. I trusted him more than these two.

I came to a stop. They had their guns out, not trusting me. And I didn't trust them either, but Remo was barely breathing. I gripped my gun and pushed out of the car. Nino approached, as usual a blank expression on his face. I had my gun pointed at him like he had his pointed at me. Of course, with his skills I'd be dead before my finger as much as twitched on the trigger.

I lowered my gun and walked toward the passenger door, opening it. Nino still regarded me cautiously. Savio came up behind him, his gun at his side, not pointed at me. "Will you help me? Or do you want Remo to die?"

Nino moved forward and the second he saw his brother, he shoved the gun into his holster and rushed to my side. He quickly checked Remo then gripped him under the arms. Remo groaned. Savio took his legs and they were about to lift him out when Greta woke and let out an earsplitting cry upon seeing two men she didn't know. Nino and Savio both jerked their heads back then froze. Nevio had also awoken and his dark eyes stared back at them. My small Remo.

"Holy fuck," Savio gasped. His brown eyes flew up to me. "They are Remo's."

It wasn't a question because one look at Nevio and they knew he was their brother's. "They are and he passed out before he could see them." My throat constricted.

Nino held my gaze for a moment and I knew then that I wouldn't regret my decision because already now I could see that my kids would be Falcones.

"Quick," Nino muttered, and he and Savio carried Remo over to the helicopter.

My heart thundering in my chest, I walked to the back door and opened it to unbuckle Nevio and Greta. "Shh," I soothed my daughter. Nevio looked merely curious and a little sleepy.

"Do you need help?" Savio asked close behind me, surprising me.

I looked over my shoulder, hesitating, my protectiveness rearing its head.

"Don't give me that look. Your kids are safe. They will always be safe, and not just because Remo would kill me if something happened to them."

I nodded. "Can you take Nevio? Greta doesn't like to be held by anyone but me."

Savio moved to the other door, opened it, and bent over Nevio, who regarded him with big dark eyes. "I've never held a baby," Savio said reluctantly.

"Speak to him soothingly and lift him against your chest. He can support his head by himself."

"Hey, Nevio," Savio said as he slid his hands under Nevio's armpits and carefully lifted him. It looked as if was holding a bomb about to detonate, but I was glad he was being careful. I hadn't thought Savio could be like that.

I turned to Greta and quickly lifted her as well then straightened to keep an eye on Savio. He held Nevio against his chest, and my son seemed content to be held by the unknown man. Savio's eyes were curious and fascinated as he looked down at my boy. No resentment, no associated shame.

Together we walked toward the helicopter. Greta pressed herself against me from the noise of the rotor blades. Nino was bent over Remo inside the helicopter. Remo was already getting a blood transfusion and another IV with a clear liquid while Nino felt his body.

A man I didn't know was in the cockpit.

Nino turned to us when Savio held Nevio out to him. He grabbed my boy immediately, a strange look on his face as he regarded him. Savio climbed in and held out his hand for me. I awkwardly got in with Greta still clinging to me for dear life.

I sank down on the bench, and Savio helped me buckle up. Nino handed Nevio back to him and Savio sat beside me. Nino's eyes kept darting between Nevio and Greta, as if he couldn't comprehend what he was seeing. The moment the helicopter lifted off, Nino returned to Remo's side.

Nevio stared down at his father, then at me, and I swallowed the emotion. What if Remo died before he could see his kids? What if my children never met their father?

I'd never expected Remo to want his children, but now that I knew he did, guilt washed over me. I thought I protected them by keeping them from him, by staying in the Outfit, but I had been wrong. Las Vegas was their home because it was Remo's home.

CHAPTER 28

SERAFINA

After we landed in Las Vegas, Nino immediately rushed Remo off to a hospital the Camorra worked with, and Savio stayed with me. I was exhausted and emotionally drained. "What happens with us now?" I asked tiredly.

Savio gave me a surprised look. "I will take you to the mansion. Remo will want to have you and his kids around when he returns."

"You think he will survive?"

Savio nodded. "Remo won't die."

I followed Savio to a car and sank down on the backseat with my children.

When I jerked awake, we had arrived and Fabiano was staring through the window as if he was seeing a ghost. He opened the door. "What the fuck?"

"Remo's got kids," Savio explained.

"I see that," Fabiano said.

Savio took Nevio again, and I got out with Greta, who had her face buried in my neck. Fabiano couldn't stop staring at Nevio, then finally he met my gaze. "You saved Remo?"

I nodded. Fabiano searched my eyes, and I wasn't sure what he was looking for. "It's too cold for Nevio and Greta to stay outside. Can you get my bag from the trunk?"

Fabiano nodded and walked to the back of the car. I followed Savio inside the house, a strange sense of familiarity washing over me. This place didn't feel like home. I'd only experienced it as a captive, and I wondered how things would be now that I had come here freely.

Could this become a home for me and my children?

Savio had said Remo would want me to live here with them, but I wasn't sure. It felt surreal being here, but there was no going back now.

The realization sank in slowly, and for a moment I felt immobilized by the weight of it. Holding Greta seemed to ground me. "You can give Nevio to me," I managed, offering my free arm.

Savio's brows drew together, but he gave me my son without hesitation, and I hugged him to me. Savio and Fabiano watched me for a moment, as if they weren't sure what to do with me.

"How is he?" Kiara asked, hurrying into the entrance hall. She jerked to a stop when she spotted me with the kids. Her eyes widened.

"Nino took him to hospital," Savio said.

Kiara only stared at me. Her eyes darted down to Nevio and Greta, and she shook her head in disbelief. A girl with freckles and brown hair followed Kiara and also stopped in her tracks.

Kiara was the first to move. She came toward me, her eyes alight with warmth. "How did Remo react?"

Tears sprang into my eyes, and her smile fell.

"He passed out before he saw them," I whispered.

"Nothing kills Remo," Fabiano said firmly.

I nodded.

Greta began crying, and Nevio, too, was becoming increasingly cranky. "I need to feed them and change their diapers. Then they need a place to sleep."

Savio glanced at Fabiano, who shrugged.

Kiara rolled her eyes. "Would it be okay if I took you to the bedroom you were in . . . last time? I don't want to open the other rooms in Remo's wing. Or would you prefer to stay in my and Nino's wing?"

I choked out a laugh. "I'll stay in Remo's wing."

The other girl smiled hesitantly.

"I'm Serafina. And this is Nevio and Greta."

"Leona," she said. "Nice to meet you." Fabiano stepped up to her and put his hand on her waist in a possessive gesture. So she was his girl.

Kiara took my bag from Fabiano and led me upstairs into Remo's wing. I knew the way by heart, but her company felt good. When we stepped into my old room, my breath caught in my throat at the rush of memories that overwhelmed me, but another loud wail from Greta snapped me out of it. I moved over to the bed and carefully lowered them down on it.

Kiara kept throwing glances at my twins, longing in her gaze. "How can I help you?"

I opened the bag and held out the baby formula. In the evening, they always needed the bottle to calm down. "Could you prepare two bottles?"

Kiara returned fifteen minutes later with the bottles and settled beside me on the bed. "Why don't you feed Nevio while I take care of Greta," I suggested.

Her eyes lit up. "Thank you."

I laughed. "You're helping me. I should thank you."

She grinned as she took Nevio and settled him on her lap.

"I should warn you. He's a bit of a wrestler."

Kiara brought the bottle to Nevio's mouth, and as expected his little hands reached for the bottle, trying to snatch it out of her hand. She laughed.

I blinked back tears as I focused on Greta, who was happily drinking, her big dark eyes peering up at me sleepily. Emotions painfully tightened in my chest.

Remo had to survive. I couldn't believe fate would be so cruel to rip him from me before he could see his children. Maybe Remo deserved death, but I didn't care. He needed to live for Greta and Nevio.

"He'll love and protect them," Kiara murmured.

Remo would protect them. Was he capable of love? I wasn't sure.

After Kiara left, I lay down beside my babies, who were already asleep after their feeding. I didn't have beds for them or anything else except for the few things I'd stuffed into the backpack.

I closed my eyes. The image of Remo in his blood flashed into my mind, and I shuddered.

I must have fallen asleep because Greta's wail woke me shortly after. It was the first night without the help of Samuel or my mother, and a heavy weight settled in the pit of my stomach thinking about my family. I wasn't sure how my future nights would be. Would I handle everything on my own?

I was up early the next morning and blinked against the soft light streaming in through the window. I had barely slept, and not just because of my twin's erratic schedule. Worry for Remo had haunted my sleep. I got myself and my babies ready before I headed downstairs, carrying them on my hips.

Following the scent of coffee and bacon, I made my way into the kitchen but stopped in the doorway. Adamo, Savio, and Nino were sitting around the kitchen table while Kiara was stirring something in a big pot. All eyes turned to me, and I swayed on my feet. I'd always been the enemy, the captive, and now I was what? A guest? An intruder?

"Good morning," I said then turned to Nino, fear clogging my throat. "How is he?"

"Stable. A few broken bones, bruises, rupture of the spleen. He's upstairs, knocked out with pain meds."

"He won't like that one bit," Savio said grinning. "You know he prefers pain to being helpless."

I still hadn't moved from the doorway.

"I'm preparing a pumpkin puree for the babies. I hope that's okay?" Kiara chimed in.

I nodded. Nino grabbed a chair and pulled it back for me. With a small smile, I approached the table and sank down. Nevio knocked Nino's glass over, spilling water over him.

"Sorry," I said, leaning back so Nevio's sneaky arms wouldn't get into more trouble. He still made grabby motions.

Nino regarded him intently as he dried himself with a dishtowel that Kiara had handed him.

Adamo shook his head. His arm was bandaged and his face was swollen. "I can't believe Remo's got kids."

"I bet the Outfit hated seeing them. I mean, there's no way they couldn't be Falcones," Savio said with a grin.

I stiffened, pain slicing through me. I looked away, swallowing.

"Is that why you're here?" Nino asked mildly. "To give them a chance?"

"I want them to be proud of who they are," I said. I didn't want to explain everything.

"They will be. They are Falcones," Nino said.

I looked into his emotionless gray eyes. "Just like that? My family tortured Adamo and nearly killed Remo and I'm technically the enemy."

"Just like that. You are Remo's and they are his too. You are family."

I frowned. "I'm not Remo's."

Nino gave me a twisted smile. "You are."

Kiara put a plate piled with eggs and bacon and toast in front of me.

"Do you have a blanket?"

She hurried off and returned with one a few minutes later, spreading it on the ground. I put Greta and Nevio down on their backs so I could eat. I smiled when Nevio rolled onto his stomach and raised his head curiously.

"This is too weird," Adamo said. I gave him a smile.

Savio shook his head. "I'm not going to change diapers. I don't give a fuck if Remo gives the order or not. I'm not going anywhere near someone else's shit, baby or not."

I huffed. "I'm pretty sure you come into contact with more disgusting things on a daily basis."

Adamo laughed. "He's full of shit anyway."

Savio punched Adamo's unharmed arm.

Some of the weight I'd felt since yesterday lifted from my shoulders.

REMO

I felt like shit, cotton mouth and a full-body ache. Peeling my eyes open, I found Nino staring at me. "You asshole. You gave me pain meds and some kind of fucking sedative."

"Your body needed it."

I tried to sit up but my body was very averse to the idea. I struggled and shot Nino a death glare when he tried to help me. Eventually, I managed to sit against the headboard, every fucking inch of my body throbbing fiercely. Most of my upper body and arms were covered with bandages.

Nino sat on the edge of my bed. "You looked like shit when Serafina brought you to us."

Serafina had saved my life. The woman I'd kidnapped, she'd saved my fucking life. "For a second I thought I dreamed up the whole shit, but the way my body screams with agony tells me it's true," I got out.

"They almost killed you, and they would have if Serafina hadn't gotten you out."

"Where is she?" I asked, ignoring the way my chest hollowed at the thought that she wasn't in Las Vegas after all.

"Downstairs," Nino said slowly, his eyes searching mine. "With your children."

"My children," I repeated, trying to make sense of the words, trying to fucking understand that I was a father. Greta and Nevio. "Fuck," I breathed.

"It's like looking at a baby version of you," Nino said with a disbelieving look.

"Make sure they have everything they need. No matter what Serafina says she needs, you get it for her."

Nino nodded. "She's here to protect her children because the Outfit didn't accept them. Not because of you."

I narrowed my eyes at him. "I don't care why she's here. All that matters is that she is. I told you before, I don't have a fucking heart that can be broken, or have you forgotten?"

Nino touched my shoulder lightly. "I know you better than anyone else, Remo. Or have *you* forgotten?"

"That's why you're so good at pissing me off."

"Do you want me to get her?"

I nodded. I didn't think I'd ever wanted anything more. I would have gone through days of torture, through weeks of it, to see Serafina. That she saved me? Fuck, I'd never considered it an option.

After she'd told me she wouldn't give me her forgiveness, I'd resigned myself to the fact that she wanted me dead, that she wanted to see me suffer. I deserved it. There was no fucking question about it. I knew what I was.

There wasn't anything white about me, very little gray, and a ton of black. And yet she was here.

She was here with our children.

I tried to imagine them, but I couldn't. I'd never wanted kids, because I was certain I'd never find a woman who wouldn't prove to be the same fucking failure my mother had been. I'd been certain that I'd break any woman, but Serafina was strong. She'd proven me wrong, had twisted my game until I felt like the loser, like the one who'd been checkmated.

SERAFINA

Nino walked into the living room where Kiara and I were sitting on a blanket with Nevio and Greta. Kiara was a natural with kids, and it was obvious how much she loved them. She held Nevio in her lap as she showed him a picture book. Greta sat in my lap, her tiny hand wrapped around my thumb and looking down at the book in my free hand.

I looked up at Nino but his eyes were on Kiara, who was smiling down at my son, practically glowing with happiness.

Slowly, he dragged his gaze up. "Remo just woke up."

Without thinking, I got up with Greta clinging to me. I didn't want my kids there when I first talked to Remo after he'd woken. I felt like we needed a moment before I could allow that.

I untangled Greta gently and laid her down on the blanket, then hesitated. Kiara looked up with a smile. "Nino and I can watch them while you talk to Remo."

Nino moved closer but I stayed where I was. I couldn't help it. This would be the first time I let them out of sight since our arrival. "Each of us would lay our life down for these kids," Nino said. "You brought them here. They are Falcones. They are Remo's kids. He burned for us. We will burn for them."

I gave a small nod and took a step back. Greta's eyes followed me. "Kiara, can you take Greta. She's very shy around people she doesn't know, especially men."

Nino lowered himself beside Kiara and took Nevio from her. I tensed when Kiara reached for my daughter, expecting a crying fit, but Greta's face scrunched up only briefly then smoothed when Kiara sang softly. I took another step back. Kiara beamed at Nino as he put Nevio down on his lap and pointed at the picture book. Nino oozed calmness, which was perfect for my kids.

Nevio ignored the picture book that Nino held up and stared at the colorful tattoos on Nino's arm, touching them with his small hands as if he thought they'd come alive under his fingertips. My heart swelled once more, and I turned quickly before I got too emotional.

I took a deep breath before I slipped into Remo's bedroom. He was sitting back against the headboard, elevated by pillows. His upper body was naked, except for the many bandages covering his skin—the cuts my family had inflicted to avenge me.

He looked up from his iPad, and I took a hesitant step closer as I let the door shut.

His face pulled into a strange smile. "I'd never have thought that you would be the one to save me."

I moved closer, half terrified, half excited, and stopped beside him. Remo's dark eyes burned with emotions that set my heart aflame, but I shoved the sensations back. "I saved the father of my children so they would be safe."

"My brothers would have protected them even if your family had killed me."

I put a hand down beside him on the headboard, hovering over him. "Nobody will protect them like you will. You'll go through fire for them."

I didn't ask. I *knew* it.

He raised his hand stiffly, most of his arm bandaged, and cupped the back of my head. I let him pull me down. "For them. For you," he murmured, fiercely, harshly, angrily. His lips brushed mine, and my entire being melted. I fell as I had the first time he kissed. Shuddering, I drew back and straightened. This was too soon. I needed to figure things out between us.

He watched me with a bitter smile. For some reason, the sight tore at me. I leaned down and briefly brushed his lips with mine to show him that my withdrawal didn't mean "never" only "later."

I quickly stepped back and turned.

"Will you show them to me?" he asked quietly.

I looked over my shoulder. "Of course."

I held Greta and Nevio tightly against my body as I nudged the door open. Then I stepped in. I was inexplicably nervous. My family had never looked at my children the way I regarded them, like they were something precious, a gift I wanted to cherish every single day. Remo's eyes zeroed in on our babies as I moved closer, and he didn't look away again, appearing almost stunned. I sat down beside him and carefully put Nevio down on his back next to Remo. Greta still clung to me tightly.

Remo's expression held wonder, and when he raised his eyes to mine, they were softer than I'd ever seen them. He stretched out his bandaged arm and stroked his fingertip over Nevio's chest reverently. Nevio being Nevio snatched up Remo's finger and brought it to his mouth to chew on it with a toothless grin. Remo's lips twitched. Then he raised his gaze to Greta, who'd turned her head to watch him curiously.

"She's shy around most people," I said. She'd always been like that, even when she was a tiny newborn.

I took his hand so she saw me doing it then brought it toward her. When she didn't protest, I released Remo's hand, and he caressed her back with his fingertips. He was so gentle and careful with her, I could feel a mix of happiness and wistfulness rise up in my throat. Greta watched him silently. Did she know he was her dad?

Tears ran down my cheeks. Remo stroking Greta's back and having his finger chewed off by Nevio was the most beautiful sight I could imagine. "I don't think I've ever been this happy," I admitted, not caring that I was being emotional in front of Remo. This was no longer a battle of wills, a twisted game of chess. These stakes were too high.

Remo locked his gaze with mine. "I *know* I've never been happier."

CHAPTER 29

SERAFINA

As far as patients went, Remo was a nightmare. He was a nightmare in many other regards as well, but giving his body time to heal wasn't on his agenda.

Nino wasn't happy about it. "You need to rest, Remo. It's been only three days and you're already running around."

"I've had worse. Now stop the fucking fussing. I'm not a child."

"Maybe not. But I'm obviously the only one of the two of us capable of sane decisions."

"Neither of you is sane. Now help me with this fucking crib," Savio muttered.

I leaned in the doorway of the future nursery. Nino and Kiara had gone shopping this morning, and now the four Falcone brothers were trying to put together the furniture. Though Nino and Savio were doing all the work because Adamo's arm was in a cast and most of Remo's body was bandaged, not to mention the many broken bones in his body.

Adamo sat on a plush baby blue armchair, which sat close to the window. Sometimes when he thought no one was looking, his eyes twisted with something dark, something haunted. Some wounds would take a long time to heal. Remo leaned against the windowsill, wearing only low cut sweatpants, barking orders.

A smile tugged at my lips.

"The instructions are quite clear, Remo," Nino drawled. "I don't need your orders on top of that."

Savio scoffed. "As if that'll stop him."

It was still difficult to grasp what had happened these last three days. I'd left my family, *Samuel*, to live in Las Vegas with the man who kidnapped me and his family who helped him do it. But with every passing hour, I realized it had been the right decision for my children and maybe even for me. The moment Remo saw his babies, a knot in my chest loosened, a knot that had strangled me since he released me, only to be pulled tighter when Greta and Nevio were born. They belonged here.

I had tried to keep my distance from Remo so far, only visited him twice so our twins could get used to his presence, and I knew he wasn't happy with it.

Remo spotted me in the doorway, his eyes becoming more eager and intent. My pulse picked up, and I turned around to return to Nevio and Greta who were waiting downstairs with Kiara.

Remo cornered me in the hallway. For someone with his injuries, he was annoyingly fast. "Are you running from me, Angel?" He backed me into the wall, his palms on either side of me.

"I've learned that doesn't work. You always catch me," I said, leaning back because with him so close I was having trouble focusing.

"I often imagined how it would be to see you again," he said in a low voice.

"But this wasn't one of the scenarios I came up with."

I regarded him. "When you sent me off like a thing easy to dispose of, it didn't seem like you wanted to see me again."

He shook his head, anger flashing on his face. "I gave you a choice, one you didn't have before ... and you chose to stay with the Outfit."

I huffed. "That's ridiculous. You traded me like a piece of cattle. Why would I return to you? I'm not in the habit of thrusting myself upon someone who obviously couldn't wait to get rid of me."

Remo leaned even closer. "Did you really believe that I didn't want you? Or did you tell yourself that because you didn't want to leave your family?"

I frowned. "You could have ..."

"What?" he growled. "I could have what? Kidnapped you again? Asked Dante to send you back?"

He had a point and it annoyed me.

"When were you planning on telling me about our babies? Would you have told me at all if Adamo hadn't gotten himself captured?"

"You sent me away, back to my fiancé. I didn't think you'd care what happened with me, much less wanted kids," I muttered, but something in his eyes made me continue. "I wanted to tell you. The moment I saw them, I knew I needed to tell you, but I didn't know how. I was ... a coward."

His hand came up, cupping my cheek, his dark eyes impossibly possessive. "I was sure you'd return to me." His lips brushed mine. "You aren't a coward. You saved me. You went against your family to protect our children. You gave up everything for them ... and for me."

I deepened the kiss, couldn't keep the distance I so desperately wanted to keep. Remo's lips, his tongue, the feel of his rough palm against my cheek awakened a deep longing, a desperate need I'd kept buried since he'd set me free.

My core tightened as his familiar manly scent flooded my nose, and memories of how Remo's hands, his mouth, his cock had felt came to the surface ...

I drew back, coming to my senses, and slipped out from under Remo's arm. He gave me a knowing smile before I hurried away. But I had seen the proof of his body's reaction to me in the bulge of his sweatpants.

Only one week until Christmas. The mansion was decorated beautifully with red baubles, golden tinsel, and sprigs of mistletoe. Luckily Greta and Nevio weren't mobile yet or the greenery would have had to go. I'd sent Samuel a few messages, telling him I was safe and asking if he was okay. He hadn't replied yet but I knew he'd read the messages. Maybe his hurt was still too fresh. Five days weren't enough to come to terms with the fact that your sister betrayed you for a man you hated more than anything in the world. My messages to Mom and Sofia hadn't even been received. I suspected Dad had gotten new phones for them so I couldn't contact them.

I approached Kiara as she stirred a new batch of baby food, a sweet potato puree. "Do you get Christmas presents for each other?"

Nino had given me a credit card from one of the Falcone bank accounts yesterday, and while I'd wanted to decline at first, I took the card. Remo seemed determined to make sure I had everything I needed. Still, it felt a bit odd to use their own money to buy them presents, but it wasn't as if I could access my family's accounts anymore.

"Well, last year was still a bit of a Christmas trial. Nino and his brothers still need to get used to a female touch in their life, but I got them gifts, and a few days after Christmas I got gifts from them as well." She laughed. "I think this year they might have gifts on time."

"I don't know what to get any of them. I don't know them well enough, and I don't really feel like part of this family yet ..."

She touched my shoulder. "But you are, Serafina. It's a strange situation for all of us, but it's the best thing that could have happened, especially for Remo."

"You think?" I whispered.

"I know it," she said firmly. "How are things between you?"

"I'm trying to keep my distance. I'm scared of allowing too much closeness too fast."

"But you want to be with him?"

I laughed. "I don't think I have a choice."

"He won't force you."

"That's not what I mean," I said quietly. "I don't think my heart or my body will leave me a choice."

She nodded, understanding filling her face. "I'm so happy for the both of you, the four of you."

"Do you think Remo's capable of ... love?"

Kiara looked thoughtful. "He and Nino went through horrible things as children. It formed them into the men they are today. It still affects them. I'm not sure what it did to Remo. If parts of him were irrevocably destroyed ..."

I didn't ask what kind of horrors lay in Remo's past. Kiara would have told me if she thought it was her place to share. If I wanted to find out, I'd have to ask him.

"If you want to go Christmas shopping, we can go together tomorrow. Fabiano could guard us."

"That would be nice," I said.

Despite Nino's words of protest, Remo came down for dinner that evening, and we all settled around the dining room table. Greta and Nevio were in their new high chairs between Kiara and me. I had taken over the job of trying to wrangle food into Nevio's mouth since Greta seemed to do well around Kiara. I could feel Remo's eyes on us the entire time with an expression I could only describe as longing. My food was getting cold anyway, so I decided to give him a chance to be a real dad.

"Why don't you give this a try?" I asked Remo. I wasn't sure if he was interested in feeding or if he was like some fathers whose interest in their children ended when it required them to do something.

Everyone paused what they were doing for a moment. Remo put down his fork and stood. His movements were still stiff, not just because of the bandages; it would take some time for his broken bones and bruises to heal. I gave him my chair, took my plate, and settled into the place he'd vacated. Nevio was making grabby motions, but the spoon and bowl were out of his reach. I could tell that he was getting frustrated with the situation and a hissy fit was fast approaching.

Remo took the spoon and lifted it toward Nevio's face, but he didn't restrain his arms. Before I could warn him, Nevio snatched at the spoon and catapulted sweet potato puree through the room. Most of it landed square on Remo's shirt. The rest in Nino's face.

I bit the inside of my cheek to stop laughter.

Kiara didn't show the same restraint. She burst out laughing. Nino wiped his face with a napkin, his eyes on his laughing wife—and softer than I'd ever seen them.

Nevio rocked excitedly in his chair, a toothless grin on his face. Remo glanced down at himself, then at his son, and his lips twitched. This time he took Nevio's hands in his big one before he brought the spoon toward his mouth. Nevio pressed his lips together, obviously unhappy about the situation.

"This reminds me of you, Adamo," Remo said.

Adamo grimaced.

Nino nodded. "You always made a mess during feeding as well."

"If we start exchanging baby stories, I'm out," Savio muttered.

Remo turned back to Nevio and nudged his lips with the spoon. "Come on, Nevio."

I stood and got on my haunches beside Nevio's high chair. "Come on, Nevio, show your dad how well you can eat."

Remo looked down at me, his expression stilling when I called him 'dad.' After a moment of hesitation, Nevio finally allowed Remo to put the spoon in his mouth.

I smiled, straightened to my feet, and pressed a kiss on Nevio's head. Then I leaned over Greta and did the same. She smiled at me with the spoon in her mouth, and my heart just exploded with gratefulness. I caught Remo's eyes but quickly glanced away because the look in his threatened to crush my resolve to keep my distance.

After bringing the twins to bed, I grabbed my phone and headed for Remo's bedroom. Nino had practically dragged him there so he could lie down and rest.

I knocked.

"Come in, Angel."

Frowning, I entered. "How did you know?"

He regarded me with an expression that sent a little shiver down my spine. "Because my brothers don't knock, they barge in, and Kiara usually stays away from my bedroom."

I nodded, my hand still on the door, debating if I should leave it open just to be safe.

Remo smiled knowingly. "I'm practically bedridden. No reason to be worried. I won't attack you."

Bedridden. As if. That man couldn't be broken easily. I closed the door. I wasn't worried about Remo making a move. I was worried I'd throw caution in the wind and do what I'd been dreaming of forever. "As if that would stop you."

Remo didn't say anything.

I held up my phone. "I thought you'd like to see photos of Nevio and Greta."

"I'd like that," Remo said, moving to the side so there was room beside him on the bed. I eyed the spot then Remo leaning against the headrest with his naked upper body. Even the bandages didn't make Remo any less attractive.

Trying to hide my thoughts, I strolled over to him casually and sank down beside him, legs stretched out before me. Remo's eyes lingered on them. I was wearing a dress and no tights because it was surprisingly warm in the house. Goose bumps rippled across my skin. I cleared my throat and clicked on the first photo, which Mom had taken shortly after I'd given birth to the twins. I held them in my arms and looked down at them with an exhausted yet adoring expression.

Remo leaned in and his arm brushed mine. Despite the material of my dress between us, a tingle shot through me at the brief contact.

"You look pale in the photo," he said quietly.

"After twenty-two hours of labor everyone does."

Remo's dark eyes flickered with a hint of wistfulness.

"I wish you could have been there...if I'd known what I know today, I would have come to Vegas sooner. I'm sorry I took that away from you."

Remo cupped my chin and I tensed because he looked like he was going to kiss me. "Regret over the past is wasted energy. We can't change the past, no matter how much we want to do it."

"What would you want to change?" I asked, trying to ignore the feel of

Remo's touch.

He shook his head with a dark smile. "Not your kidnapping. I don't feel an ounce of regret about stealing you."

"You don't?" I frowned, pulling back slightly but Remo leaned in, fingers still on my chin.

"Not one fucking bit. I'd kidnap you again to be the one you gift yourself to. You could have never been mine if I hadn't stolen you."

I didn't argue, neither about me being his, nor about the fact that without the kidnapping we would have never found together.

"What about you?" Remo murmured. "Do you regret becoming mine?"

"No," I admitted, and finally drew back from his touch. "Not that. I just wish it wouldn't have cost my family so much."

Remo nodded and settled back against the headrest. "Hardly anything worth having can be gained without loss and pain and sacrifice."

My eyes trailed over his wounds and bruises. He'd sacrificed himself for his brother. But I had a feeling it wasn't the only reason why he'd allowed my family to capture and torture him. He'd accepted pain, maybe even losing his life, for a chance to see me again.

I cleared my throat and clicked on the next photo. The first photo of Nevio and Greta lying in a crib beside each other.

I showed him photo after photo, neither of us saying anything. It was difficult to focus on anything but Remo's warmth, his scent, the strength and power he oozed.

When I finally shut off my phone, my body was humming with need. I met his gaze, which rested unabashedly on me. Remo regarded me with an expression I knew too well. Hunger and dominance. He touched my bare knee.

I exhaled.

His hand slipped slowly up between my legs. "Remo," I warned, but he held my gaze, his lips pulling wider.

"Have you let anyone touch what's mine?"

I glared, but my body screamed for more. For Remo's touch, for his lips.

He knew the answer, could see it on my face. "No," he said quietly. "All of you is only mine."

"You set me free, remember? I belong to myself."

We both knew it was a lie. I'd never been free of his hold on me, but he, too, had lost his freedom. His hand slipped higher until finally he brushed over the fabric of my panties. They were drenched, just from being in his presence.

Remo groaned, low and dark, and my resolve crumpled. His thumb drew small circles on my crotch, and I could feel myself growing even more aroused. Remo's dark eyes held mine, and as usual I couldn't look away. His thumb pushed under my panties and between my folds, spreading my wetness. I whimpered from the contact, skin on skin. So good, so desperately needed. He drew small circles on my clit, round and round and round. I parted my legs a bit more and gripped the sheets, needing something to hold on to as I stared at Remo. His gaze possessed me like it always did.

"Are you going to come, Angel?"

I gave a small nod. It had been too long. I was falling apart so quickly. He didn't speed up the pace as his other hand pushed up my dress so he could see his finger working me. Round and round. "Part your legs more," he growled, and I did.

He slipped between my folds again, spreading my wetness some more. "I want to fuck you so badly."

"You're still healing," I rasped. His broken bones needed to mend. One of us needed to be the voice of reason, even if my body hated me for it.

He sat up stiffly. "Straddle me with your ass facing me."

"What?"

"Do it," he ordered.

I didn't question him, could barely think straight from the throbbing between my legs. I pushed up and climbed over Remo, careful not to ram my knees into his ribs. My palms rested beside his knees as I knelt over him, my ass pushing out. Remo lifted up my dress until I was exposed and my core tightened in anticipation. "Fuck," Remo murmured, causing me to shiver again.

I gasped when he pushed two fingers into me, my back arching at the delicious sensation of my walls gripping him. Remo let out a low groan, and I almost came hearing it. I could see the proof of his own need straining against his sweatpants.

"The sight of your pussy taking my fingers is the fucking best."

I whimpered in response and began to meet his thrusts, needing his fingers deeper, faster, harder.

"Yes, Angel, take them," he rasped.

More wetness pooled between my legs. I threw a glance over my shoulder. Remo was focused on his fingers as they fucked me, his dark eyes burning with so much desire it stole my breath. I shuddered with pleasure. He glanced up, his lips curling in a pleased smile.

"Come on, Angel. Fuck my fingers." Remo added a third finger and my eyes rolled back in my head at the sensation.

I ground myself against Remo's hand, driving his fingers deeper into me. He watched me intently and his other hand began massaging my butt. I wanted to grasp his erection, but I could hardly support myself with two arms, already spinning out of control. He gathered my wetness with the fingers of his other hand, and then I felt one finger against my back entrance. I tensed but didn't stop riding Remo's fingers.

"Relax," Remo ordered, his eyes compelling. "It'll be good."

Anxious and excited, I gave a small nod. Slowly he pushed a finger into me. "Oh God," I gasped as I felt his fingers in both my openings. There was a slight discomfort, but it didn't stand a chance against the pleasure Remo's fingers in my center caused.

Remo established a gentle rhythm with his finger while I kept grinding myself against his other hand. He didn't take his eyes off me as he worked my body, and I could feel the first traitorous spasm of my orgasm. My pussy clenched around his fingers. I moaned, the sensations overwhelming. I felt a second finger at my back entrance and tensed again. Remo stroked my butt cheek, and as I drove his fingers deep into me he curled them and hit my g-spot. I came hard, crying out desperately, and he pushed the second finger into my back entrance. I gasped from the pain and my orgasm heightened in force. I shuddered, caught between intense pleasure and dull pain. My arms gave way, and I braced myself on my forearms. Remo kept thrusting.

"Yes, Angel, I told you I'd show you pain and pleasure."

Half lowered onto him, I could feel his erection digging into my belly. He groaned again, almost in agony. I was completely overwhelmed, stunned, and a little embarrassed. I'd never considered allowing someone to go anywhere near my ass. Of course Remo wanted that part of me as well.

Remo pulled out of me slowly, and I gasped. His hands came down on my ass cheeks, and he massaged me gently. "If I died now, it would be worth it."

I huffed. "You won't die today. I won't explain that to Nino. No thank you."

Remo chuckled and the sound sent a different kind of shiver through my body. I loved the sound of Remo laughing, especially if it was earnest.

I pushed myself up then knelt beside Remo. He curled his hand over my neck and pulled me toward him for a slow kiss. When he drew back, his eyes searched my face. I knew my cheeks were flushed, not just from my orgasm but also from embarrassment.

"There's so much pleasure I still want to show you," Remo murmured, tracing his lips over my jaw and cheek.

He dropped his head back against the headboard, sighing as he reached for a glass filled with dark liquid on his nightstand.

I recognized the scent immediately. "Scotch, really?"

"It'll help with the healing, trust me. I've done a lot of research in the past."

I shook my head.

"And," he added, with a challenging smile, "it seems to be the only pleasure I'm allowed today." He took a sip.

My eyes darted down to the impressive bulge in his pants. I knew what I wanted to do. I wanted to render him into a helpless mess of desire as he did with me.

"Trying to decide if you're brave enough?"

I glowered. "I've given you a blowjob before."

His mouth twitched. "You tried, but you didn't finish, so it doesn't count."

I knew he was trying to goad me. Unfortunately, it was working.

I moved down until I knelt beside his groin. Remo reached for his pants and pulled them down, wincing as he did so.

"Quite eager, aren't you?" I teased.

He smiled but it was dark and hungry, and his body was tense. I lowered my head and took his tip into my mouth. Remo moaned, his fingers tangling in my hair. I swirled my tongue around him, and my own core tightened with renewed need. Remo's breathing deepened, his muscles tensing as he watched me.

"Take more of me," Remo ordered quietly, and I did. I let him claim my mouth until he hit the back of my throat. He thrust into me slowly, his hand in my hair keeping me in place. He held my gaze as I let him claim my mouth. His other hand cupped my cheek. Remo. Brutality and tenderness. I still didn't understand him or us.

Remo's body coiled tighter, his hips jerking up with less control, lips parting in a low moan.

"I'm going to come," he rasped. I saw the question in his expression, and my heart swelled with affection … and God help me … love.

I gave a small nod around his head before he drove deeper into my mouth again, and his grip on my neck became firmer. His face twisted with passion, his eyes almost harsh with lust as he tensed and came with a sharp exhale. I had trouble swallowing around his length, and Remo loosened his hold on my neck so I could pull back slightly. He kept rocking his hips, his breathing harsh.

Remo's gaze laid claim to another part of me, possessive and warm, as he stroked my cheek. I slowly released his cock from my lips and swallowed, frowning at the taste. Remo drew me toward him, brushed my lips with his, and handed me his glass with scotch. I took a sip and coughed. That tasted even worse.

"You'll get used to the taste," he said with a small laugh.

"The scotch or your …?"

He gripped my arms and wrenched me against him so I was cradled against his chest. I caught the wince but then it was gone. "My cum," he murmured as he licked my lips then dove into my mouth. Our kiss was slow, almost teasing, until it wasn't. It became needy and eager.

He positioned me so one of my legs was thrown over his groin, my head against his shoulder. His hand parted me then his fingers slid over my drenched panties. He pushed the fabric aside and slowly pushed two fingers into me. His other hand began pinching and twirling my nipple. He played me masterfully with his fingers as I lay draped over him. We kissed softly, our eyes locked the entire time, until a new wave of pleasure shot through me.

I'd barely caught my breath when Greta's cry rang out.

I sighed with a small smile.

"Perfect timing," he murmured, giving me another lingering kiss. I quickly slid out of bed and rushed into the bathroom to wash my hands before I returned to the bedroom. Remo stood beside the door, waiting for me.

"You should stay in bed and rest," I said.

"I should help you with our children."

His voice didn't allow any objections, and I had to stifle a pleased smile. By the time we arrived in the nursery, Nevio had started crying as well. I took Greta because she didn't know Remo well enough. Remo lifted Nevio out of the crib without hesitation and pressed him to his chest. It was obvious that he'd held a baby before, that he knew how to handle them. I took a whiff. "New diapers."

Remo carried Nevio over to the changing table and began his work. I watched him for a moment longer, my body flooding with so many hormones, I could feel the waterworks beginning. I blinked and looked away. "I'll go into the kitchen and prepare their bottles."

Remo glanced up, his gaze lingering on my eyes, then nodded.

When I returned ten minutes later, Nevio was already dressed and resting in Remo's arm. I handed him a bottle, and he sank down in the armchair, wincing again. He was moving more stiffly than before, probably from overexertion.

I changed Greta's diaper before I settled on the armrest beside Remo and started feeding her. "This is strange," I whispered after a moment.

Remo frowned. "It's not what I imagined when I kidnapped you."

I searched his face, trying to figure out what this meant to him, what I really meant to him, but I didn't dare ask. I knew it was futile to stay away from Remo, not only because my body was already calling for his touch again but also because my heart yearned for his closeness.

After they had fallen back asleep, I was on my way toward my room when Remo gripped my wrist, stopping me. "Stay with me."

I nodded and allowed Remo to pull me back to his bedroom, where I put one of his shirts on before slipping under the covers. Remo pulled me against him, wincing as I touched his bruises. "You're in pain," I protested, trying to put distance between us, but Remo tightened his hold on me.

"Fuck the pain. I want you in my arms."

I stilled and finally relaxed against him, my cheek pressed up to his strong chest. This felt too good to be true.

CHAPTER 30

SERAFINA

Christmas rolled around. The first Christmas for Nevio and Greta. The first Christmas as a part of the Falcone clan. After wishing Samuel a merry Christmas and not hearing anything in return, I went downstairs with Nevio and Greta. Remo was already in the living room with his brothers, discussing their plans for future races. After the Outfit attack, safety measures would have to be doubled. I was supposed to help Kiara in the kitchen but still needed to figure out what to do with the kids.

Remo looked up when I entered. As usual, his expression stilled when he saw me with our twins, almost as if he still had a hard time trusting his eyes. "Can you watch them?" I asked as I headed toward them.

Nino sat beside Remo. Adamo and Savio were on the couch across from them. "Will you take Nevio?" I asked Nino who rose at once and took my son from me. Nevio didn't mind, too fascinated by the tattoos on Nino's arms.

I moved closer to Remo. Greta was clinging to me, still shy around others. Remo gave me a questioning look. He hadn't held his daughter yet. The only person except for me who didn't make Greta wail was Kiara.

He gently stroked her black tuft of hair then ran his hand down her back. His voice was low and soft as he spoke to her. "Greta, mia cara."

My heart seemed to skip a beat. It was the first time I heard Remo speak Italian. My family and I had only ever spoken Italian when we were surrounded by outsiders, and I knew many families handled it the same way. I carefully untangled her from my neck and gave her to Remo. Her big dark eyes blinked up at him, and her face began to twist. Remo rocked her gently in the crook of his arm then lowered his face and kissed the top of her head. She let out a hesitant cry, as if she wasn't sure if she wanted to wail or not. I handed him her favorite rattle, and he showed it to her.

She reached for it, eyes already brightening, and he helped her shake it. I took a step back then another as Remo rocked her. Remo sank down, still rattling and whispering words of consolation. Greta's expression made it clear that she wasn't convinced yet but that she wasn't wailing was a good sign.

Savio and Adamo looked as if they were having a stroke. I got it. Remo was one of the most feared men of the country, and here he cradled his baby girl in his arms, patient and careful. Nino was rocking Nevio on his thigh, and my son let out delighted screeches.

"I suppose that's the end of my whoring days in the house," Savio muttered.

Remo looked up from Greta, his eyes narrowing. "I don't want a fucking whore anywhere near my children."

Greta cried at the harshness in his voice, and Remo's lips tightened. He shook her gently then murmured something I didn't catch. The moment she stopped crying, I turned and left. My babies were cared for.

I finally went to help Kiara in the kitchen. Kiara was taking care of the vegetarian appetizers and the vegetarian main course, while I tried my hand at a roast beef and a chocolate cake. I didn't have much experience preparing any kind of food except for the occasional baby puree, so this proved to be a challenge.

Later we all settled around the table with a well-done roast beef, not medium rare as intended, and a slightly burnt chocolate cake, but nobody minded. During my captivity I'd only caught glimpses of the brotherly bond Remo and his brothers shared, but now as I became a part of their family, I realized just how strongly they cared for each other. Remo had traded himself for Adamo, had signed his death sentence so Adamo could live. There was no greater sign of love than that. It gave me hope that Remo was capable of that kind of emotion.

When Remo and I returned to our bedroom that night, I risked another glance at my phone, and my shoulders slumped. No messages.

Remo came up behind me, his hands on my waist, his lips hot on my throat. "Do you regret leaving the Outfit?"

I leaned back against him. His chest was bare and he'd removed most of the bandages despite Nino's protests. "No. Greta and Nevio will be happier here."

He bit down on my throat gently. "And you?"

I turned in his hold and kissed him. "I think I'll be happy too."

Remo pulled my dress over my head before he backed me up toward the bed, and we both fell down. We kissed for a long time until I was desperate and hot. Remo moved down my body and removed my panties then stretched out between my legs. His lips and tongue pushed me over the edge within a couple of minutes, then he climbed back up, his body covering mine, his weight braced on his forearms. His eyes held mine when he slammed into me, claiming me fully for the first time in fourteen months. "Remo," I gasped out.

Despite the flashes of pain on his face, Remo's thrusts didn't falter. He hit deep and hard, his eyes owning me. When he reached between us and stroked my clit, I cried out, clenching around him and gripping his shoulders tightly. Remo growled in pain and pleasure but kept thrusting as I rode out my orgasm. He kissed me fiercely, possessively, then pulled out.

He turned me on my stomach before he kissed my ear as he settled between my thighs. I felt a firm presence at my ass and stiffened in surprise and fear. Remo stroked my back, massaged my butt.

"I want to own every part of you," he murmured, kissing my shoulder. He turned my head so I met his gaze and kissed me slowly. Remo had put his fingers into me a couple of times, but his erection was so much bigger.

"Say something," he urged.

I swallowed, nervous. "I'm yours. All of me."

Remo's eyes softened. "Relax, Angel. I'll be careful."

For a moment his weight lifted, and I heard him take something from the drawer. Over my shoulder I saw him covering his cock with lube then he was back over me. He bit down on my shoulder blade lightly as he pushed forward, and I arched up when the stretching got too bad. Remo stopped, kissed my shoulder, my cheek. His hands slid under my body, found my nipple and my clit. He tugged at my nipple while his fingers stroked my clit and opening. Soon, I loosened around him as pain and pleasure mixed. He pushed two fingers into me and groaned roughly, the sound so primal and erotic my core clenched with arousal. "I feel my cock inside you. It's perfect."

I moaned as he moved his fingers slowly while his other hand kept twisting my nipple. Despite the pain, I felt a release approaching. My lips parted and my muscles tightened as pleasure overcame me. Remo pushed his cock into me all the way, and I moaned and whimpered, caught up between pain and pleasure. I'd never felt more stretched, teetering on the edge of overwhelming pain and yet happy that Remo had claimed this part of me as well.

I shivered, overcome with sensations.

Remo kissed my cheek. "Can I?"

I gave a nod and he pulled almost all the way out. I trembled as he pushed back in. He kept working my pussy as he thrust into me slowly.

"It'll get better, Angel," he murmured.

His movements became faster, and I bit down on my lip. Pain and pleasure mingled, almost becoming one. Remo's body pressed me into the mattress as his cock and fingers claimed me.

With a guttural groan, Remo slammed into me one more time, and I felt his release. I shuddered desperately under him. Remo stayed inside of me for a couple of heartbeats, his breath hot on my shoulder, his fingers gentle, almost soothing on my clit.

He pulled out of me carefully then turned me on my side and pressed up behind me, kissing my shoulder. I couldn't move, overwhelmed, stunned. Every time I thought Remo had taken everything, he took another part of me.

"Angel?" he asked in a low voice.

I turned around in his embrace and nestled close to him, my nose buried in the crook of his neck. Remo tensed and gripped my chin, nudging my face up. I could see a hint of hesitation on his face as he evaluated my expression.

"You will never surrender to my will because you think I want you to. Was it too painful?"

I glanced up, swallowing hard. Remo was concerned for me. Cruel, merciless, brutal to the very core, and yet *concerned for me*. "I wanted to surrender to you, to give myself to you like that. You already own every other part of me."

His brows pulled together even further. He traced my face with his finger. "I don't enjoy hurting you unless it heightens your pleasure."

I tilted my head. "You sound surprised."

"I enjoy hurting people, but not you, never you."

I fell silent, wondering what it meant. Remo pushed up and reached over me and into the drawer of his nightstand. He pulled out a small parcel then set it down between us. "For you," he said.

My eyebrows rose. He hadn't given me a present earlier, but I had assumed the gifts for Greta and Nevio had been meant for me as well. It had been difficult enough to get something for Remo. Eventually I'd opted for a guide of running trails of the region as well as a quickly assembled photo book from our twin's first seven months.

"What is it?"

"Open it," Remo demanded, fingertips tracing my side and hip.

I lifted the lid and my breath stilled as my eyes registered the necklace with the pendant in the shape of wings. It was a beautiful piece of finely worked gold-smithing. Intricately gorgeous. I took it out carefully.

"Where did you get it? You didn't leave the house."

"I had it handcrafted by a local goldsmith shortly after I released you."

My lips fell open in surprise. Remo helped me put the necklace on, and the cool gold settled in the valley between my breasts. "Ruinously gorgeous," Remo murmured as he traced my skin.

I gave him a curious look.

"You ruined me for all other women."

A wave of possessiveness overcame me. Remo was mine.

REMO

I watched Serafina as she stroked the heads of our children, patient, loving, even though they both had been crying on and off for hours. She sang to them, whispered words of sweet nothings to them. She had left her family for them so they would be safe, so they would get the life they deserved, the life they were destined for. I had seen the look in her eyes when she'd said goodbye to her twin. Serafina had given up so much for our children.

Her body was weaker than mine. She wasn't as harsh or cruel or fearless.

But God she was strong.

When Nevio and Greta had finally fallen asleep, she straightened from where she'd been bent over their crib and when she noticed me, she tensed slightly but came toward me. She'd been oddly quiet today, and I knew something was bothering her, but I didn't talk emotions if I could help it.

Serafina stopped in the hallway. "I've been here for three weeks, but I still don't know what we are."

I braced myself beside her shoulders, peering down at her. "You are an angel, and I'm your ruin." My lips pulled into a wry smile.

She shook her head almost angrily. "What am I to you? Your lover? Your girlfriend? A nice change from your usual whores?"

My own anger spiked. "What do you want me to say?"

"Nothing," she said quietly. "I want the truth. I need to know what to expect from you."

"I love death. I love spilling blood and causing pain. I love to see terror in people's eyes, and that won't ever change," I whispered harshly because it was true.

She looked up at me. "You are the cruelest man I know. You took everything from me."

I nodded because that was true as well. "Few women can bear the darkness. I can't ... I won't force you to be with me. You are free."

"Free to do as I please," she murmured, warm and soft against me. Tantalizing. "Even take another man into my bed?"

A burst of rage filled me. I wanted her for myself, wanted to remain the only man who'd ever tasted those perfect lips, who'd ever claimed her, but more than that I wanted her to want it too. I swallowed my fury. "Even that," I said then continued in a harsh whisper, "I won't stop you. I won't punish you for it."

She smiled a knowing smile. "But you will kill anyone who touches me."

I brought our lips close. "Not just kill them, *obliterate them* in the cruelest way possible for touching something they are unworthy of."

Challenge flickered in her eyes. "Are you worthy?"

I claimed her mouth, hard and desperate, before pulling back. "Oh no, Angel. From the day I saw you, I knew I was the least worthy of them all." I should have never laid a hand on her, but I was a fucking bastard and had taken everything she was willing to give.

She tilted her head up, regarding me. She opened my shirt slowly, one button after the other, and it gave way under those elegant fingers. She rested her palm against my chest, over my heart. "Is there something in there capable of love?"

My fucking chest constricted. "Whatever's in there, it's yours. Whatever love I'm capable of, it's yours too."

She cupped my face, her eyes fierce, almost brutal in their intensity. "You are beyond redemption, Remo," she whispered, and I smiled bitterly because I knew it.

She shook her head. "But so am I because even free to do as I please, I choose you. I'm no angel. An angel wouldn't love a man like you, but I do. I love you." And she kissed me harshly, brutally, all rage and love, and I kissed her back with the same love, the same rage.

This woman had stolen my black heart. From the first moment I saw her, I wanted to own her. At first to destroy the Outfit and Dante then later because it became an irresistible need, a voracious longing. And in the end, Serafina was the one who owned me, black heart, condemned soul, scarred body.

Every fucking part of me was hers, and if she'd let me, I'd be hers till my last day.

SERAFINA

My heart burned with emotions. Fiercely. Remo had declared his love for me. Something I'd never considered a possibility.

This cruel man owned my heart, and I didn't want it any other way.

Remo's kiss was violent, harsh. Then he pulled back. "Marry me."

I froze. It had been an order. Remo wasn't a man who asked for anything. I leaned back against the wall slowly, searching his eyes.

He didn't let me retreat. He kissed me again but gentler. "Marry me, *Angel.*"

It still wasn't a question, but his voice wasn't dominant anymore. It was soft, compelling, raw. "Become a Falcone?" I murmured against his lips.

"Become a Falcone. Become mine."

I smiled. "I have been yours for a long time."

"Is that a yes?" he asked, his hand sliding over my outer thigh, stroking, distracting me.

"Yes," I whispered.

"Serafina Falcone," he murmured. "I like the sound of it."

I smiled because this name sounded right, more right than Mancini ever had.

Was this love? Was this madness? I didn't care. It was perfection either way.

CHAPTER 31

SERAFINA

I was inexplicably nervous when Remo told me he wanted to announce our wedding to his brothers and Kiara the next day. We'd all gathered in the kitchen for breakfast, Nevio on Kiara's lap and Greta on mine.

"You have a new wedding to look forward to," Remo said without warning.

Every pair of eyes darted from him then to me. My cheeks flushed. I wasn't sure what Savio and Nino thought of the situation. Adamo and Kiara liked me, but the other two ...

"Will we be allowed to kidnap someone? Or at least spill some blood? Since you sampled the goods before, bloody sheets won't happen after all," Savio drawled, grinning.

Remo reached over the table and hit him over the head. Savio only chuckled.

"Be careful I don't spill your blood."

Adamo smiled at me then rolled his eyes at Savio.

Kiara got up, handing Nevio to Remo so she could hug me. "I'm so happy."

Savio and Nino definitely didn't look unhappy, but their reaction wasn't as enthusiastic as Kiara's or Adamo's, not that I had expected it to be.

When Savio got up to take a call, I followed after him but waited until he was done before I approached him. He eyed me curiously when he noticed me. He didn't look like a teenager anymore, especially now that he was sporting stubble.

"Are we good?" I asked.

"If you're talking about the soup incident, that's forgotten. Trust me, most people want to do worse to me, especially women, so I've learned not to hold grudges." He shrugged. "And we were the ones who held you captive, so you have more reason to be pissed."

"True. But my family kidnapped your younger brother and almost killed your oldest, so I guess we're even?"

Savio's expression tightened briefly at the mention of my family and my own stomach churned painfully. "You are part of our family now. I don't give a fuck about the past. Just make sure you don't break Remo's fucking heart."

"Do you think that's a possibility?" I teased.

His dark brows drew together. "Before you, I'd have bet my balls against it. To be honest, I wasn't sure if Remo had something resembling a heart."

"He loves you."

Savio looked away, obviously uncomfortable. "We are brothers. We'll die for each other."

I smiled.

"We should return," Savio muttered. "I don't want Remo to think we're getting it on behind his back."

I snorted. "Sorry, Savio, nothing against you, but you don't stand a chance."

Savio gave me an arrogant smile. "You like what you see, admit it." He sauntered back into the kitchen before I could shoot something back. But for some reason his insufferable ego was almost endearing. It reminded me a bit of Samuel, which was consoling and painful at the same time.

After my conversation with Savio, I felt better. Now I only needed to straighten out things with Nino. He and I had never really warmed up to each other, and I wasn't sure if it was because Nino didn't like me or if it was because of his nature.

Remo leaned in when I sat down beside him. "Did he behave?"

Savio rolled his eyes at his brother.

"He tried," I said.

"That's all I can hope for. Maybe they'll try your patience as they do mine."

"Raising twins will teach you the patience of a saint. I doubt your brothers can test me."

"We'll see," Savio said with a chuckle. "And don't hold your breath. Remo won't reach sainthood anytime soon."

"I don't want him to be a saint," I said, looking at Nevio and Remo, both watching me with those impossibly dark eyes.

After breakfast, I asked Nino if we could talk. We headed into the garden despite Remo's suspicious expression.

"Do you disapprove of our wedding?"

Nino assessed me without a flicker of emotion. "No. I never considered marriage an option for Remo, but that doesn't mean I don't think it's a good thing. It was for me despite my own reluctance in regards to marriage."

I nodded. "You never seemed to like me much."

"It was never a matter of dislike, Serafina. You were our captive, the enemy, and I didn't want Remo to lose himself in his game. I thought it wouldn't work. But I was wrong. You saved him."

"I couldn't let my family kill him."

Nino shook his head. "That's not what I mean."

I waited, watching Nino's profile as he stared off into the distance.

"Remo and I, we are messed up in ways that can't be fixed, not really. For someone to accept us despite what we are, it takes a lot of forgiveness and love. Our past ... it broke certain parts of us."

"Remo never talks about the past."

Nino nodded. "He'll tell you eventually. Give him time."

"We have all our lives."

REMO

I held Serafina in my arms after sex, my chest pressed up to her back, my nose buried in her soft hair, relishing in her sweet scent. She traced the scars on my palm. She did it often. In the beginning it had bothered me because it was a part of me I didn't share with anyone except for Nino.

"I was nine," I began then stopped because even with Nino I'd never discussed what had happened. Words had always seemed lacking to convey our shared horrors. The smell of blood filled my nose as it always did when I remembered that day. Soon the stench of burning fabric and skin joined the metallic tang.

Serafina's fingers on my palm had stilled. "I love you no matter what. I've heard of every horror you committed, and I'm still here."

She was. I could imagine what kinds of stories were whispered in the Outfit and they were all true. And Serafina had experienced a small part of our nature when I'd captured her, when I'd cut her. Looking at the faded white scar, I still felt a fucking twinge in my chest. I brushed aside her hair and kissed the nape of her neck. That she found it in her heart to love me despite it all, that she trusted me with our children, it seemed impossible.

"I know what I am. But my father, he was monstrous in a different way. He enjoyed torturing the people he was meant to protect, just as much as he did his enemies, maybe even more. My mother loved and feared him equally, and she allowed him to humiliate and torture her because of it. Allowed him to do the same to us. Love made her weak."

Serafina gave a small shake of her head. "Real love doesn't make you weak. Love how it's meant to be makes you stronger. But there's no room for fear where there's love."

I tightened my hold around her. "Don't you fear me?"

"I used to, but not anymore and never again."

I rested my forehead against her hair. Very few people didn't fear me. My brothers and maybe Kiara, and that was what I wanted, what I worked for. "Eventually she hated my father more than she loved him, and she decided to punish him in the only way she thought she could."

I closed my eyes, remembering that day.

Mother came into my bedroom in her long nightgown, which was straining over her belly. She never brought us to bed or said goodnight, so I tensed when I saw her in the doorway. I'd gotten me and my brothers ready for bed while she lay on the sofa, staring at nothing.

"Remo, my boy, can you come with me?"

I narrowed my eyes. She sounded too caring, too loving. My boy? She sounded like a mother. She smiled and I took a hesitant step forward, more hopeful than suspicious.

"Nino and Savio are already in my room."

That convinced me. I followed her toward her bedroom. For a second I considered slipping my hand in hers, but she had never held my hand like that and I was too old now. The moment

I stepped inside the bedroom, she threw the door shut and closed us in. My eyes registered Nino kneeling on the floor, cradling his arm. Everything was red. Rivulets of red trailed down his arms, his wrists gaping open. His eyes locked on mine. He wasn't making a sound, only crying as he bled. Blood. Everywhere. It clogged my nose.

I frantically looked for Savio and found him motionless on the bed. A cry wedged itself into my throat until I noticed the rise and fall of his chest. Not gone.

Mother stepped in front of me and grabbed my arm. Silver flashed before my eyes and I jerked. My hands and face burned as the blade cut me. I hit and clawed and roared, fighting her off. And then she stopped and the smell of smoke filled the room. The curtains were burning. We'd burn. We'd all burn. Nino began to hum, rocking back and forth, pale and sweaty.

I rushed toward the window. Outside I heard the shouts of my father's men. I ripped at the curtains and flames licked at my palms and neck and arms, snatching hungrily at my skin. I screamed as I broke the window. I helped Nino out then grabbed Savio and jumped out of the window with him in my arms. Bones broke and I burned all over. Agony, pure and overwhelming. Staring up at the window, I saw our mother's crying desperate face amidst the smoke and flame. Crying because I'd taken her revenge from her, because I hadn't died with my brothers as we were supposed to. I wanted her to burn, wanted her gone from our life. I wanted her dead.

Serafina was quiet when I finished. She swallowed. "How can a mother do that to their children? I'd die for Greta and Nevio. I'd never hurt them. And if you ever hurt them, Remo, I'll kill you. That's a promise."

"I hope you will because if I hurt them, I deserve nothing less than a knife to the fucking heart."

Serafina turned around in my arms, her blue eyes fierce and trusting. "But you won't ever hurt them. I know you won't and you protect the people you love."

I nodded. "I won't and nobody else will either." I'd fucking destroy anyone who tried.

She traced the scar over my eyebrow. "I know it's wrong but I wish I could have killed your mother for what she did to you."

My chest tightened. I didn't tell her that my mother was still very much alive. I brought Serafina's hand up to my face and kissed her palm then the scar I had created. "I won't allow you to be dragged down into my darkness."

I was going to kill my mother one day.

One day, Nino and I would be strong enough to do it.

"That's not your choice alone."

"I rule over hundreds of men. I can be very convincing if I try."

She smiled a slow, fierce smile. "Believe me, I know. You convinced me to fall in love with my captor. But I can be very stubborn."

I pulled her closer. "That's true. You almost brought me to my knees."

She raised one perfect blond eyebrow. "Almost?"

"You had me lying in my own blood at your feet, isn't that enough?" I asked in a low voice.

"Don't do that ever again."

"I won't. The next blood I'll bathe in won't be my own."

Realization flickered in her eyes. She sighed then kissed me. "You swore not to kill my family."

"Angel, I swore not to kill them that day. The men in your family are high-ranking Outfit members. Your uncle is Dante fucking Cavallaro. If I want to win this war, I'll have to kill him, and I *will* win this fucking war. Because if I don't, Cavallaro will and that means Nevio and Greta, you, my brothers... won't be safe. And I don't care how many I'll have to kill to guarantee your fucking safety. I will kill everyone who threatens the people under my protection." I touched her throat, stroking the soft skin there. "You can't have it all. You have to make a choice."

She shook her head. "I made my choice, Remo. I chose you and I'll choose you over and over again."

Fuck. I didn't deserve this woman.

SERAFINA

We'd been living in Las Vegas for two months now. I was starting to feel at home, more at home than I'd felt in Minneapolis since I'd given birth to my twins. I kept sending Samuel messages, but they became less frequent because of his lack of reaction. Every week I'd send him a short note telling him I was well and a photo of the twins and me. He hadn't replied so far, but I knew he'd read them and even that was a small victory. He hadn't blocked me. He still wanted to know how I was doing even though I was practically the enemy now. The war between the Camorra and the Outfit wouldn't end anytime soon, even if things had calmed down for the moment. Dante was probably planning something, and I was fairly certain Nino and Remo wouldn't ease down on the Outfit either.

Remo's birthday was tomorrow and even if he didn't celebrate it, I wanted to give him something special. It was difficult to come up with a present for someone who ruled over the West Coast and could buy anything he wanted because money wasn't an issue.

It had taken me a long time to come up with something that held meaning and showed Remo what he meant to me. Early in the morning, after another sleepless night with the twins, I approached Nino who was swimming his usual laps in the pool. Kiara was keeping watch over the babies since they were both rather needy at the moment due to their teething.

Nino noticed me standing beside the pool and swam toward the edge. "Is something the matter?"

"I have a favor to ask of you."

Nino hoisted himself out of the water. My eyes scanned the myriad of tattoos on his upper body and thighs. Nino regarded me curiously, and I realized I'd been staring. "Sorry. I didn't mean to gawk, but I was wondering where you've had your tattoos done."

Nino walked over to the lounge chair and picked up his towel. "Some of them I did myself. The ones in places I can't reach I had done in a tattoo studio not too far away."

"You do tattoos?"

"I can do them, yes," he said. "Why?"

I hesitated. "Because I want to get a tattoo. Can you do it for me?"

"That depends what exactly you want."

"I want angel wings on the back of my neck," I said, a flush spreading on my cheeks under Nino's scrutiny. I wasn't sure if he knew Remo's nickname for me, but it felt like something personal I was sharing.

"Wings, I can do ... if you have a design in mind. Can you show me where exactly you want the tattoo?"

He came up to me and I pushed my hair to the side, baring the nape of my neck and touching the spot. "Here."

"It will be painful," Nino warned.

I sent him a look. "I gave birth to twins. I think I can handle a needle."

Nino inclined his head. "That is true. While I can't assess the force of labor pain since I've never experienced it, I assume it's excruciating."

"It is," I said. "So you will do it?"

"If it's your wish, then yes. When?"

"As soon as possible. The tattoo is Remo's birthday present."

Again Nino gave me a mildly curious look. "We can do it later in the afternoon. I can set up everything in one of the guestrooms."

"Thank you," I said.

"Thank me once it's done and you're happy with the outcome." He paused. "I assume you don't want Remo to find out for now."

I nodded. "If possible."

"It's a secret I don't mind keeping from my brother."

As promised, Nino had set up everything in a guest bedroom in his wing. I was nervous despite my best intentions not to be.

Nino oozed calm as I stretched out on my stomach on the bed. He disinfected my neck before he touched the tattoo needle to the skin, and I winced at the first sting. I soon got used to the burning sensation. Nino moved quickly, meticulously, and I didn't speak as he worked, not wanting to distract him. When he was finally done, I sat up and accepted the mirror Nino held out to me. He held a second mirror behind my neck.

The outcome was more stunning than I could have ever imagined. I didn't know it was possible to paint such intricate artwork with a needle. The feathers of the wings looked so real I expected them to flutter in the wind.

"It's beautiful," I admitted.

Nino nodded. "Remo will appreciate the message."

"You know that he calls me Angel?"

"I overheard him saying it, yes, and you are the counterpart to his fallen angel on his back."

"Did you tattoo it as well?"

"I did," Nino murmured.

"Why the broken, singed wings? The fallen angel is kneeling, and the tips of the feathers are crooked and burning."

Nino regarded me closely. "What did Remo tell you about our past?"

"He told me your mother tried to kill you and that you almost burned to death."

Nino's face tightened and he nodded. "Remo burned to save us. I never asked Remo about the details why he wanted to get the tattoo, but I think it has something to do with that day."

"Thank you, Nino."

Nino gave a small shake of his head. "No, thank you."

Hiding my tattoo from Remo proved difficult. I had it covered with my hair, but when I moved my head, I often had to stop myself from wincing.

That evening, after bringing the twins to bed, Remo pulled me against him in our bedroom, his hands squeezing my butt before they moved higher. He kissed me and touched my neck. I drew back with a wince before I could stop myself. His eyes narrowed.

"What's wrong?"

I considered making up something, but Remo was too good at detecting lies, and his birthday was only two more hours away. "This was supposed to be your birthday present," I said softly as I lifted my hair and turned so he could see my neck.

Remo was quiet and I risked a look at him over my shoulder.

Slowly he raised his eyes from my wings with a strange smile. "Wings."

I smiled. "Because you gave me wings."

He shook his head, his dark eyes softening. "Angel," he said quietly, brushing his fingers over my tender skin. "You had wings all along. You only needed a little push to spread them and fly."

I turned back to face him. "Maybe, but I wouldn't have done it on my own."

We kissed slowly at first, but Remo quickly deepened our kiss, and suddenly we were on the bed tugging at our clothes and stroking every inch of naked skin we could reach. I pushed Remo onto his back, smiling, and his answering smile, all desire and dominance, sent a stab of arousal through me. Leaning forward to claim his mouth for a kiss, I lowered myself on his erection, groaning at the feeling of fullness. Remo pushed up into a sitting position, bringing us chest to chest, racing heartbeat to racing heartbeat. I gasped at the shift of him inside of me, at the feel of his strength as his arms slung around my back. I rolled my hips, driving him deeply into me as we kissed.

We held each other's gaze as we always did, and those dark eyes captivated me as they'd done from the very start. So often cruel and merciless but passionate and reverent when they rested on me, tender and caring when they regarded our twins.

When we'd both found our release, we stayed wrapped up in each other like that, our breathing ragged, bodies slick with sweat. I ran my fingertips over Remo's back, tracing the spot where the wings of his fallen angel spread out. He trailed his own fingertips upwards, along my spine until he reached my new tattoo. I winced slightly and Remo's touch turned even softer. My heart was ready to burst out of my ribcage from the look in his eyes.

Remo scanned my expression, his brows drawing together.

I sighed. "Sorry. Since my pregnancy I'm more emotional. I hope it'll go away soon." I cleared my throat then rested my palm over his shoulder blade. "What's the meaning of your tattoo? You know why I got mine, but I wonder why you got yours."

A hint of wariness flashed in Remo's eyes, the walls he was used to keeping up wanting to lock back in place. "Nino did it. About seven years ago."

I nodded to show him I was listening.

"It's a fallen angel, like you said. It represents the fall Nino and I took on the day our mother tried to kill us."

My brows snapped together. "Fall? You saved your brothers. How's that falling?"

Remo's expression was dark and twisted, his eyes far away, haunted, angry. "Until that day Nino and I were innocent. After that we weren't. We'd already experienced our fair share of violence from our father, but it never affected us like that day did. The flames of that day they singed our wings and our fall into darkness began. We became who we are today. That's why the fallen angel is kneeling in pools of blood."

I'd noticed that the fallen angel knelt in pools of some kind of liquid, that a few of its singed feathered dipped into it, but I hadn't realized it was blood. For a moment I wasn't sure what to say, how to console Remo. Could words ever be enough to make the horrors of his past better?

"I'm sorry," I said quietly.

Remo's gaze focused on me, tore away from the images of the past. "You aren't the one who should be sorry. And I won't forgive her no matter how often she'd apologize. Not that she ever did."

I froze. "Your mother didn't die that day?"

"No. Even though I wanted her dead, I'm glad she survived that day or Adamo wouldn't be here. She was heavily pregnant with him."

I shook my head, completely at a loss over what Remo's mother had done. "Where is she?"

"In a mental facility." Remo's voice dipped and turned vicious. "We are paying for it so she can live and breathe and exist, when she shouldn't be doing either."

"Why haven't you killed her?" With anyone else I would have never asked something like that, but this was Remo. Killing was in his nature, and his words made it clear that he hated his mother.

Remo pressed his mouth to the crook of my neck. "Because," he growled. "For some fucking messed up reason Nino and I are too weak to kill her. We haven't seen her in over five years ..."

"Do Savio and Adamo know what happened?"

"Savio has known for a while. And we talked to Adamo a few months after he got initiated."

I stroked Remo's neck. "Have you thought about visiting her again to try and find closure?"

Remo looked up, his expression harsh. "There won't be any closure until she's dead. I don't want to waste another second of my life on her. She's already fucking dead to me. You and Greta and Nevio are what matters now. My brothers are what matters. That's it."

I kissed him to show him I understood. I didn't think it was as easy as that. Their mother still dominated part of their existence, but I respected that Remo wasn't ready to seek a solution now. It wasn't my place to meddle. He and his brothers would have to face their mother one day, and maybe then they could move past their demons.

All I could do was show Remo a better future. A future with a family that loved him. He'd always only had his brothers, but now he had us as well.

CHAPTER 32

REMO

Serafina, Leona, and Kiara were busy in the kitchen, baking birthday cakes for the twins whose first birthday was today. It was already close to noon. I doubted they'd get the cake ready in time for the afternoon, but I didn't say anything.

"It seems like a waste of effort to create elaborate cakes in the shape of a unicorn and a car when their only purpose is to be eaten," Nino commented as we left the kitchen to give the women their space. They'd found images of complicated cakes on the Internet, and were determined to recreate them for Greta and Nevio.

"I don't give a fuck, but Serafina is so damn excited about the cakes, so I guess it's worth the work. I doubt the kids will care much. They'll only smash their hands into the cake and stuff their faces," I said, peering down at Greta whom I cradled in the crook of my arm. She felt completely comfortable in my presence now, and it felt like one of the biggest triumphs in my life to have her big dark eyes look up at me with trust. And by my fucking honor and everything else that mattered, I'd never do anything to betray that trust. When she'd been wary of me in the beginning, it had felt like a knife to the heart. I'd always relished the fear in the eyes of others, with the exception of my brothers, but with my children and Serafina I never wanted to see it again.

"I never considered marriage an option for the two of us," Nino said thoughtfully as we stopped beside the pool.

"I never thought I'd find a woman I wouldn't want to kill after a few hours."

Greta gave me a toothy grin, and I stroked her hair back. It had grown quite long and curled slightly like Adamo's hair did.

"Hmm, *mia cara*, ready for your first swim?"

Nevio was nestled in Nino's arm and as usual making grabby hands at the colorful tattoos. I could already guess what he wanted to get once he was older.

Fabiano was already lounging on the pink flamingo float Savio had used before I'd banned any kind of whoring in the mansion. I rolled my eyes at him. "That's a disturbing sight."

Fabiano shrugged. "It's comfortable."

Savio and Adamo were playing water ball close to the waterfall in the pool and bickering as usual.

It was the first swim for the babies since we didn't have a heated pool before and only had it installed now that the babies were part of our household. Nino slowly stepped into the pool with Nevio.

Nevio let out a screech, smiling at me. My fucking heart swelled with pride. That boy didn't fear anything. Sometimes it almost worried me how similar to me he was. He'd get himself in trouble as soon as he could walk better.

Nino moved over to Fabiano on the float, and Nevio made his grabby hands, wanting to ride on the flamingo with Fabiano. Fabiano raised his eyes to mine, asking for permission. I nodded, twisting my forearm with the tattoo. Between us it meant more than just an oath to the Camorra, more than being a Made Man. The day Fabiano had sworn himself to me, to the Camorra, he'd become family, and I trusted him with my kids. I'd never told him, but I got why he'd acted the way he did when I tried to drive a wedge between Leona and him. He wanted to protect her, wanted to protect someone who could see past the fucking darkness, who loved him despite it all.

Serafina had changed my view on things, and if it was in my nature I might have apologized to Fabiano for how I'd acted.

Fabiano held out his arms, and Nino handed him Nevio, who kicked happily with his legs until he sat in the front of the float, holding on to the neck of the flamingo.

"I hope you gave that thing a good scrub," I called over to Savio who gave me the finger.

I went down the steps into the pool. The moment Greta's feet touched the water her face twisted, but I made a low soothing sound and she relaxed. Shifting her so her head was level with mine, I lowered us further into the warm water. Greta held on to me, eying the water critically. After a while she smiled and hit the water with her palm. I went over to the flamingo float, but Greta tightened her hold on me when I tried to put her on it.

Nevio babbled, his tiny legs wiggling as Fabiano held him by the waist. Both Greta and Nevio were big on the babbling, but they both hadn't said any word except for 'Mom,' and while Nevio was already making his first steps, Greta only crawled. She was a cautious kid and reminded me a lot of Nino.

Nevio grinned at me, squeezing the neck of the flamingo before he extended his arms with his grabby hands. "Dad. Daaad."

For a moment, I froze, my expression stilling. Fabiano grinned and Nino squeezed my shoulder. I wrapped my arm around Nevio and pressed him to my chest. Greta pressed her wet palm against Nevio's cheek, giggling. I waded through the water with the two, dipping lower, causing them to scream with joy.

Serafina headed toward us in a heart-stoppingly sexy white bikini, Kiara and Leona close behind her.

She lowered herself to the edge of the pool.

"Mom!" Greta called, and I handed our daughter over to Serafina. I stayed close and touched Serafina's thigh. She raised her eyebrows. "Something the matter? You have a strange expression."

"Nevio said Dad," I told her.

She leaned down and kissed me, her expression so full of happiness it filled even my cruel heart with warmth.

"Dad," Nevio confirmed, hitting the surface with his palm again and sending water everywhere.

Serafina shook her head with a soft smile as she slid into the water with Greta pressed to her chest.

"This is close to perfection," I said, indicating the people gathered around us. "Everyone who matters is here."

And I'd fucking protect them all with my life.

A shadow passed over Serafina's face, and she averted her gaze, blinking. I curled my hand over her neck, bringing our faces closer together. She locked gazes with mine. "I know you miss them, especially your brother."

She nodded. "I do, and I wish you could meet Sofia and my mom. I wish they could see you as I see you."

Serafina saw me in a way most people never would because I'd never allow them to do so. "I can't promise you peace. It's not only my call to make, and there's a lot of bad blood between the Camorra and the Outfit. I won't back down, not when Cavallaro was the first to breach my territory."

I still wanted to bathe in Cavallaro's blood and I knew he shared the sentiment. Peace would never happen.

"I know, and I can deal with it. This is my new family now, and I'm happy that the babies and I are here where we belong." She paused, sighing. "I can't help missing my family, especially Samuel. We've always been so close, and now I haven't heard from him in so long. It's hard."

I was used to handling things, used to things going my way, but this was one thing I couldn't change for her. I wasn't going to make a peace offering toward Cavallaro, even when the attack on Roger's Arena was orchestrated by Scuderi, but the attack on our race in Kansas definitely wasn't. He'd tortured my brother. That was another thing I couldn't easily forget. I wanted them to bleed. At least Dante fucking Cavallaro.

Greta giggled again and Nevio fell in. Serafina's expression brightened, and she smiled at me. Fuck. That smile got me every time.

SERAFINA

Nevio was a small whirlwind, and it had only gotten worse since he started to walk. It was the day before our wedding and only four days since the twin's birthday, and Kiara was busy with last minutes preparation, even though it was going to be a small affair. Adamo had babysitter duty for Nevio, which mainly consisted in running after him and making sure he didn't break his neck or got his hands on anything breakable.

Every time Adamo lifted Nevio into his arms, he began wailing in protest. I gave Adamo an understanding smile when he let out a sigh. "I can take over if you want?"

Adamo smiled sheepishly. "I need a break."

Chuckling, I took Nevio from him and hoisted him up on my hip despite his loud protest. "Mom, no. No. No. No!"

"I was so looking forward to them speaking," Remo said from his spot on a blanket where he played with Greta while trying to get work done on his iPad simultaneously. "But Nevio enjoys the word 'no' a bit too much for my taste."

"No," "Mom," and "Dad" were the only words that Nevio had mastered so far.

"No!" Nevio bellowed.

I laughed.

Remo shook his head. "Nevio, that's enough."

Nevio frowned, his lips turning into a pout. "No?"

Remo's mouth twitched.

"If you're being quiet, I'll set you back down," I said. Nevio regarded me, then Remo, obviously unsure if our offer was worth it.

Greta crawled closer to Remo, and he looked back down to her. She pressed her hands to his legs and slowly pushed up, her butt raised, then she stumbled to her feet. Remo reached out, and she curled her tiny hand around his index finger and Remo's other fingers covered hers, steadying her, and my eyes began to water.

"Good," Remo encouraged.

She looked at him, surprised, and still a bit unsure.

She took a hesitant step, and he smiled. "Very good, *mia cara*." Her smile widened and she took a few uncoordinated, shaky steps and stumbled into him. He became still as she clung to his shirt and finger, peering up at him with absolute trust.

I set Nevio down because I could tell he wanted to join them. The second his tiny feet hit the ground, he wobbled toward Greta and his dad. Remo wrapped an arm around him as well.

Greta released Remo's shirt and made the grabby motion when she wanted to be picked up. She still preferred to be carried. Remo put one hand under her backside while the other steadied her back and pressed her to his chest. He held out his hand to Nevio. "Arm?"

Nevio nodded for once, and Remo bent down to lift him up as well. He straightened with a kid on each hip and pressed a kiss to the top of their heads. His eyes found mine, and I didn't care that he saw my tears. Today I gladly gave them to him.

Remo was beyond redemption in the eyes of so many.

He was the cruelest man I knew.

But with every atom in my body, I knew that he would never hurt our children. He would protect them. They were Falcones. They were his. *Ours.*

We would both die for them, for each other.

Tomorrow I'd officially become a Falcone, and so would my kids. I knew we'd all carry the name with pride.

CHAPTER 33

SERAFINA

The wedding was scheduled for late afternoon. I chose a Boho-style dress without pearls or a bodice. The top was knitted with a V-neckline, and the skirt flowed freely around my body, touching the ground in soft waves. My hair was down and fell in untamed curls around my shoulders.

I allowed myself another moment to regard my reflection. This day felt so very different to my last wedding day. Back then I'd been scared of the unknown but determined to do what was expected of me, content to marry a man I hardly knew and definitely wasn't in love with. Today I was absolutely certain of my love for my future husband. Remo held my heart in an iron grip, and I wouldn't have wanted it any other way.

Love can bloom in the darkest place, and ours did wildly, freely, untamable.

I hadn't thought it possible to feel that way for someone; occasionally I'd dreamed of it or foolishly hoped for it, but I knew it to be a rare gift in our circles.

I left our bedroom and walked through the silent hallways of the mansion, a place that had become my home and a safe haven for Greta and Nevio. Falcone. A name we all would carry with pride. A name that our kids would always be able to speak with their heads held high.

Adamo waited for me in the game room and smiled when he spotted me. The French windows were open and a gentle breeze carried in, warm and soothing. Adamo was dressed in slacks and a white shirt and had gotten a haircut to tame his wild curls for the occasion. Tears sprang into my eyes, and my chest constricted painfully. This was supposed to be Samuel. I wanted him at my side in one of the most important moments of my life. He was meant to walk me down the aisle. It had always been meant to be him, but he wasn't here.

Adamo extended his hand and I put mine in it. He squeezed. "One day your family will understand. One day there will be peace."

I peered up at him, at his kind smile and warm eyes, then lowered my gaze to the burn mark on his forearm, on the healed cuts. Occasionally, I still saw the haunted look in his eyes and I wondered if he hid the worst of his struggle from us. He was barely home anymore. So much pain and suffering in the name of revenge and honor. "You want peace after what my family did to you?"

"You're going to marry the man who kidnapped you."

I laughed. He had me there. If someone had told me on the day of my almost wedding to Danilo that I'd ever consider becoming a Falcone, I would have laughed in their face. So much had changed since then. I hardly knew the girl from back then anymore. She had been replaced by someone stronger.

Adamo lightly tugged at my hand and indicated toward the gardens. "Come. They're all waiting, and you know how Remo is. Patience isn't his strength."

No, it wasn't, but he'd waited for me more than once.

Adamo led me out of the mansion and past the pool toward the small congregation down the lawn.

My bare feet touched the warm grass, and then I spotted Remo at the end of the aisle below a white wood arc, and a sense of rightness filled me. Blood-red roses trailed around the arc, contrasting beautifully with the white. Kiara had arranged everything with Leona's help.

It wasn't a big feast with hundreds of guests, most of whom neither of us would have cared about. It was just us, Remo's brothers, Fabiano, Kiara, Leona, and the twins, and it felt perfect that way. By not inviting every Underboss of the Camorra, Remo had risked insulting a lot of people, but knowing him he didn't give a damn and his soldiers probably knew better than to voice their displeasure should they feel it.

In his dark slacks, black dress shirt, and blood-red vest, Remo was a sight to behold. Tall and dark and brutally handsome. His eyes scorched me even from afar, and one corner of his mouth pulled up in that twisted smile, always on the verge of darkness, that I'd come to love.

"Ready?" Adamo asked when we arrived at the starting point of the long aisle of white petals. I didn't even want to know how long Kiara and Leona had spent arranging them neatly in a pathway, but they had insisted on doing it.

"Yes," I could say it without doubt, without hesitation.

Everyone had gathered to both sides of the arc. Kiara held Greta in her arms and Nino held Nevio. I couldn't wait for them to be parents as well. And then I caught sight of a blond head off to the side, away from the rest, at the very fringes, and my throat tightened up. My gaze locked with Samuel's. He stood with his hands shoved inside his pockets, his expression unreadable. For a moment I was completely immobilized by my emotions. Pure joy and a flicker of worry, because there definitely wasn't peace between the Camorra and the Outfit. I pushed the last sentiment aside, focusing on the fact that my twin, my Samuel was here on one of the most important days of my life.

Adamo and I started walking down the aisle. I still wished Sam was the one walking beside me, but I understood why he couldn't, why his pride didn't allow him to hand me over to Remo.

My gaze drew away from Samuel toward the man who had captured my heart with wild abandon. Remo's dark eyes held mine as I headed toward him. When we arrived in the front, Greta spotted me and gave me a huge grin. A single petal stuck to the corner of her mouth. That was why Kiara had only bought edible flowers. She was just perfect with kids.

My heart overflowed with love for all of them. Nevio stood beside Nino, or rather held onto his leg, but I could tell that he was growing tired of standing still. He'd soon roam the gardens on unsteady legs.

I let go of Adamo and took Remo's outstretched hand. Smiling up at Remo, I whispered. "How? How did you get Samuel to come?" My eyes darted to my twin for a moment, disbelieving, incredulous, and so impossibly happy.

I looked back up to Remo, trying to hold back my emotions.

Remo ran his thumb over the back of my hand, his dark eyes filled with warmth he didn't bestow on many.

"I swore he'd be safe if he came. I used your phone to call him. It was a difficult process."

I swallowed. I could imagine how much time and effort it had cost to convince Samuel to come here, to risk so much. And I knew that Remo would have to let go of some of his pride to make a step toward my brother, the enemy. He'd done it for me. "He tortured you, almost killed you..."

Remo squeezed my hand. "I did worse. I took you from him. If I was him, I wouldn't forgive me either."

"Thank you for bringing him here, Remo." I touched his chest, hoping he could see just how fiercely I loved him.

"Whatever's in there, it's yours," he said with a dark smile.

"And I love every part of it, *of you*, the good, the bad, the light, the dark, even your blackest corners."

Remo's eyes flashed with fierce affection.

Nino did the ceremony since we didn't want any outsiders around for our special day. He'd gotten the license to do so only recently, which didn't pose a big problem in Las Vegas.

We kept the ceremony short, foregoing a long-winded traditional speech before we spoke our vows. We each had chosen rings for the other that we hadn't seen yet.

I took Remo's hand and slipped the ring on. It was a black tungsten carbide ring with an ebony wood inlay. Remo raised his eyebrows in surprise. "Carbide is twice as strong as steel," I whispered. "Because you are the strongest man I know." I smiled at the flicker of adoration in his eyes. "And ebony because wood is enduring and because you gave not only me roots but also our children and your brothers."

The look on Remo's face made it clear that I had made the right choice and relief filled me. He took my hand and slipped on a ring in the shape of two entwining wings, one dotted with white diamonds, the other with black gemstones.

"The white wing represents you," Remo said in a low voice, leaning closer so only I could hear him. "Because you are pure perfection, my *angel*. And the black wing with the black sapphires represents me, my darkness, that you manage to accept."

Remo kissed me, his fingers touching the tattoo on my neck.

"You set me free," I said, my voice thick with emotion.

He shook his head and our lips brushed, his eyes dark and intent. "I was the one who needed to be freed."

I kissed him fiercely. Free of the shackles of his past. When we pulled away, I realized everyone had taken a few steps back to give us privacy. My eyes were drawn to Samuel whose expression was like stone.

I needed to talk to him, to embrace him. Remo squeezed my hand to show me it was okay.

I headed for Samuel and Remo released my hand, but my fingers clung to him, pulling him along.

"Angel, you had one ruined wedding. Do you want to add a bloody one to your list?"

I glanced at him. "You won't attack my brother."

His eyes went past me. "*I* won't."

"And Samuel won't attack you either," I said firmly.

Samuel stood tall, expression harsh as it settled on Remo. I finally let go of Remo's hand, and he stayed a few steps back as I bridged the remaining distance between Sam and me. I stopped right in front of my twin. I peered up at Samuel, and he lowered his gaze to mine, and despite everything I had done, everything he knew, his expression softened with love and tenderness.

I started crying because I hadn't realized how much I'd missed him, how much I longed for his forgiveness. "You came."

I wrapped my arms around his middle, and he hugged me back. "I'd do anything for you Fina, even stare into the eyes of the man I want to kill more than anything in this world." We stayed in each other's embrace for a few moments, trying to make every second last a lifetime because we knew there would be few chances like this in the future.

I pulled back, searching his blue eyes. "They don't know you're here."

"Nobody knows. If they did … it would be considered betrayal. We're at war."

"You're risking too much for me," I whispered.

"I didn't risk enough. That's why we're standing here today." He sighed. "I got all of your messages. I read them and I considered replying so often, but I was an idiot. I was angry and hurt."

I touched his cheek. "Forgive me."

"Fina, I'd forgive you of anything. But him..." Samuel indicated Remo "...him I won't ever forgive for taking you from us, from me. Not in one million years."

I swallowed. "I love him. He's the father of my children."

Samuel kissed my forehead. "That's why I won't put a bullet in his head today, even if I considered doing it on the way here."

Samuel's love for me stopped him from killing Remo, and Remo's love for me stopped him from killing my twin. I wished their love could also make them see past the feud, past the old hatred. "Will you be safe?"

"Don't worry about me, Fina." He raised his gaze to the man behind me. "I don't have to ask if you'll be safe because his eyes tell me all I need to know. He's a fucking murderous bastard, but a bastard who will kill anyone daring to look at you the wrong way."

I glanced over my shoulder at Remo, who was regarding us with intent. He looked relaxed to someone who didn't know him very well, but I caught the subtle tension in his muscles, the vigilance in his eyes. He didn't trust Samuel. Further down beside the arc, Nino kept throwing evaluating looks our way as well. "Remo will go through fire for me and our children," I whispered.

Samuel nodded. I could tell that he needed to go. He was surrounded by his enemies, and even if I knew he was safe because Remo had declared him as such, he felt uncomfortable.

"Will I see you again? I can't lose you, Sam."

Samuel rested his forehead against mine. "You won't lose me. I don't know how, but I'll try to talk to you on the phone and reply to your messages. But I can't come here again. And you can't come to Outfit territory."

"Thank you for being here."

He kissed my forehead again. Then with another hard look toward Remo, he walked away, sideways, never fully turning his back because he didn't trust Remo's promise. When he finally disappeared from view, I released a sharp breath. A bittersweet happiness filled me.

Remo came up behind me, his arms wrapping around my chest, pulling me against him. "You'll see him again. He won't give you up. He's as stubborn as you."

I gave him an indignant look. "I'm not stubborn."

"Of course not." He kissed my shoulder blade then lightly bit down on the crook of my neck, making me shiver with desire. I couldn't wait to be alone with him.

REMO

Serafina was practically shaking with arousal as I led her to our bedroom after the wedding feast. She was a beautiful bride, free and untamed and glowing with happiness. She was everything she was meant to be.

When we arrived in our bedroom, she pushed me against the door, shutting it in the process. Standing on her tiptoes, she pressed her body against mine, her fingers raking through my hair as her mouth tasted mine. Fuck. I met her tongue with hunger and need as my hands cupped her ass through her dress, squeezing hard. She moaned into my mouth, rubbing her breasts against my chest. One of her hands slid down my chest and closed over my cock, which was already painfully hard.

I rocked my hips, driving myself against her palm.

Snatching up Serafina's hand, I turned us around, trapping her between the door and my body, her arm raised above her head, pressed into the wood. "So dominant," she teased, and I silenced her with a harsher kiss, thrusting against her to show her what awaited her. I gathered her long skirt. "Hold it up, Angel," I ordered.

She bit her lip, stifling a smile. Her fingers curled over the fabric, and she held it up, revealing a flimsy lace thong.

I got down on one knee, smiling darkly as I slid the thin piece of clothing down her legs, laying her pussy bare to me. "Remember the first time I tasted your pussy?"

She widened her stance slightly, making a small impatient rocking motion with her pelvis. "How could I ever forget? It was the best thing I'd ever felt." Her voice was heavy with arousal.

"I'm going to make today even better," I promised.

"Please, Remo, just taste me already."

I hooked my palm under her knee and opened her up as I pressed her leg up against the door. Finally, I leaned forward and took a long lick. Pulling back, I rasped. "Oh, Angel, you're already so fucking ready for my cock."

Her eyes narrowed. "I don't care. I want your tongue first. Now stop talking."

I chuckled, ridiculously turned on by her desire and bossiness. Thrusting two fingers into her, I began sucking her clit. She cried out, one of her hands clutching my head as I alternated between sucking her nub and her soft lips while my fingers worked her deeply. Her wetness and the heady scent of her arousal drove me insane with desire, my cock close to combusting. I just wanted to fuck her, but she'd get what she wanted first. Her moans and whimpers turned more desperate as I drove her close to the brink only to release her clit and suckle the inside of her thigh, my fingers stilling.

"Remo," she said, half angry, half desperate.

I closed my mouth over her clit as I slammed my fingers into her, and Serafina arched up, crying out my name as her release shook her body. I kept thrusting and suckling until she began jerking, overwhelmed by the sensation. Sliding my fingers out of her channel, I dipped my tongue in, causing her to let out another low moan. I pushed to my feet, shoving down my pants and crashing my lips down against hers so she could taste herself. "Ready to be fucked now?" I growled.

"Oh yes," she groaned, her marble cheeks flushed with desire.

I hoisted her up against the door, her dress bunched between our bodies as Serafina wrapped her legs around my hips. Locking gazes, I drove into her in one hard thrust. Her walls clamped down around my cock, and she tilted her head back with a gasp, baring that perfect throat. I marked her unblemished skin, my fingers digging into her soft thighs as I slammed into her again and again. She clung to my shoulders, her lips parted, lids hooded with pleasure. Her grip turned painful as she got closer, her heels digging into my ass. I groaned, my balls tightening, but I kept thrusting into her, pushing her up against the wall, and then she froze with a beautiful cry. It took all my fucking self-control not to be swept away with her. Grunting, I kept rocking my hips until she softened, and her head fell forward for an uncoordinated kiss.

"Don't get too comfortable. I'm not done with you," I said roughly.

She smiled against my mouth, her blond hair sticking to her and my forehead as I carried her over to our bed. I dropped her down on the mattress, and she let out an indignant huff, her legs already parting in invitation.

I shook my head with a dark smile. "On your knees."

She rolled over, presenting her round ass cheeks then knelt on the bed. The sight of her waiting for me like that made my cock twitch. I leaned over her and bit her ass cheek before I pulled her toward my waiting cock. I caught the slight tensing of her muscles, the way she braced herself but she loosened, turned soft when I slid into her pussy not her ass.

We'd tried it a few times. It had always been my favorite before her, but I could tell Serafina only did it for me. She didn't enjoy it and in turn it had lost its appeal to me. I wanted Serafina crazy with lust not tense with discomfort.

I established a hard, fast rhythm, my balls slapping against her pussy. Serafina reached under her body and began stroking her clit, brushing my dick with her nails in the process, driving me completely crazy. Leaning forward, I brushed her hair aside so I could see her inked wings. I had already been close, and as I slammed into Serafina deeper than before, I finally let loose. Serafina got caught by my climax as well and bucked up, her arms giving out as her own release hit her. I kept pumping into her until I was completely spent. I gave her ass a clap before I pulled out and dropped down beside her. She snuggled against me, our breathing ragged, bodies slick with sweat. We shared a slow, lingering kiss.

I wrapped an arm around her shoulder, and Serafina linked our hands, holding them up. The winged ring with the diamonds and black sapphires looked perfect on her long finger. I had it made for her, and it had taken the jeweler several tries to get it exactly how I wanted it. His forehead was always slick with perspiration the moment I'd paid him a visit.

Serafina had caught me by surprise with her choice for me, but she couldn't have chosen better. The black carbide with the ebony center didn't feel foreign on my hand like I'd feared it would. I'd never worn any kind of jewelry, and I had thought I never would. Marriage had been out of the question. I'd never understood its appeal. I had companionship with my brothers, and I had enough women at my disposal for sex.

I'd never cared for any woman, except for Kiara maybe, but that was a different kind of caring. And then came Serafina, my angel, the woman meant to be my greatest triumph, and she was—only not in the way I'd thought she'd be.

"What are you thinking?" Serafina murmured, her voice slow and relaxed.

"That you are my greatest triumph."

She peered up at me. "I'm the queen. You are the king. And you used me to put the Outfit in checkmate."

Her voice was soft and teasing because she knew I didn't mean it like that, not anymore.

"If anyone's been checkmated, then it's me," I murmured. "You knocked me over, wiped away my resolve, captured my cruel black heart."

She raised her head. "Neither of us has been checkmated. We both won the game. We got each other. We got Nevio and Greta."

"You had to lose something to win."

She nodded but her eyes weren't sad. "I did. But losing something makes you appreciate the things you have so much more. I don't regret a thing because it brought me here. I love you with every fiber of my being."

I pulled her in for a kiss, still stunned that she could ever love me after what I'd done. I lightly traced the almost invisible scar on her forearm. "And I love you," I murmured harshly. I never thought I'd utter those words to anyone, even though I'd admitted my feelings to Serafina before. "Because you brave my darkness every day, because you should run but you don't, because you gave me the greatest gift of all, our children and yourself."

"I brave your darkness gladly because your light shines all the brighter against it," she said. I kissed her fiercely.

This woman had my cruel heart. She'd always have it.

I was cruel.

I was beyond redemption, but I didn't care as long as Serafina . . . as long as Nevio and Greta saw something redeeming when they looked at me. I'd make sure I'd never betray their love and trust. And if anyone ever dared to take them away from me, I'd show those unfortunate bastards what I was to those I didn't give a fuck about: the cruelest man of the west.

Read more about the Falcone brothers in

TWISTED BONDS

Nino and Kiara's novella, coming later this year!

ACKNOWLEDGEMENTS

To Sejla and Selma for their encouragement and excitement. You were my (and Remo's) cheerleaders from the very first chapter. Writing this book would have been so much harder without you.

To Caro and Ratula for helping me make this book better, and for sharing my Remo obsession. But he's mine.

To Emily for being my lifesaver/assistant. Without your organization of my online life, my real life would be even more of a chaotic mess.

To Cora's Turf. I didn't even know authors having groups was a thing when Emily encouraged me to get one a few months ago. Now I can't imagine being without you guys. Your obsession with my ruthless mobsters equals my own and for that I'm impossibly grateful.

To my Street Team. I'm so glad to have you at my side. Thank you for helping me spread the word about my dark mafia world.

To my readers. You are the reason why I want to do this. I feel incredibly blessed to have the most enthusiastic and adorably obsessive fans. I want to thank you for spreading your love of my books. Without your enthusiasm my books and I would be nothing.

BOOKS BY CORA REILLY

BORN IN BLOOD MAFIA CHRONICLES

Bound By Honor

Bound By Duty

Bound By Hatred

Bound By Temptation

Bound By Vengeance

Bound By Love

CAMORRA CHRONICLES

Twisted Loyalties

Twisted Emotions

Twisted Pride

ABOUT THE AUTHOR

Cora Reilly is the author of the Born in Blood Mafia Series, the Camorra Chronicles and many other books, most of them featuring dangerously sexy bad boys. Before she found her passion in romance books, she was a traditionally published author of young adult literature.

Cora lives in Germany with a cute but crazy Bearded Collie, as well as the cute but crazy man at her side. When she doesn't spend her days dreaming up sexy books, she plans her next travel adventure or cooks too spicy dishes from all over the world.

Despite her law degree, Cora prefers to talk books to laws any day.

Made in the USA
Las Vegas, NV
30 October 2023